"Where is Ahsylla?" Syren asked in a soft, somnolent voice, tucked under her pink blanket with pirouetting ballerinas embroidered into the fabric.

"It's nowhere and everywhere. It could be right in front of you but you wouldn't know unless you have the key to enter."

Syren smiled but it never reached her sapphire eyes and as Isabeli gazed at her dispirited seven-year-old offspring, noting her sadness but ignoring it, she continued with her story.

"It wasn't always so. Once upon a time, anyone could enter Ahsylla. Those who entered would bring back to their home stories of a place like heaven, where everyone roamed carefree and happy. There was no hunger, no pain, no sadness, no death."

"What happened? Why did they hide?"

Isabeli took another slow, soft breath then reached out and touched Syren's cheek with her frail fingers. One stroke was all she could manage.

"Are you alright, mom?" Syren asked.

For much of her life, she'd known her mother as the decrepit woman who sat in front of her. Beautiful, and so frail that even at her tender age Syren realized her mother's worsening condition.

"Tired," Isabeli whispered with a sigh. Her cadence was accented with french, the language from her home country. "Ahsylla enjoyed eons of prosperity. They believed they were unmatched in strength and intelligence and that was their first mistake."

Isabeli leaned against the pillow and laid beside Syren on her bed. She no longer had the strength to hold herself up. In response, Syren scooted further to the middle of the bed that was much too large for her tiny body, making space for her mother.

Her bedroom in High Palace was fit for a princess, though she wasn't one. Her room walls were painted a beautiful petal pink and in the walls of her room was every form of unnecessary luxury a seven-year-old would ask for.

"It began with the arrival of 'other beings' as they were called by Ahsyllans. The Ahsyllans had technology that could tell them everything that could possibly happen on earth but the technology couldn't prepare them for things not from Earth. That was their second mistake." Isabeli took a raspy breath and continued. Her sound resembled a withered nonagenarian, contrasting her forty-year-old frame.

"When the other beings arrived, they were friendly, at first. Friendly because the Ahsyllans were beautiful, charming, and opulent. Friendly because their general Majikai was infatuated with the queen."

"Did the queen love him back?"

"No. She didn't much like him either. Her rejection began a war." Isabeli took a moment to catch her breath before she continued. "The Ahysllans gathered their forces. They had dragons as large as football fields. Tigers with saber teeth that were longer than cars and Elephant mammoths so strong they crushed stone under

THE QUEEN AND THE VESSEL

Asia Gouldbourne

Chapter 1: I want to die

"Imagine beauty. Imagine breathtaking, awe-inspiring beauty. Imagine it surrounding you like a blanket on a cold winter night. The air surrounding you was beautiful, the land around you, the life. That was Ahsylla."

Isabeli paused, weakened by the softly spoken sentence. Her form was drawing to its end. She only had days left.

their feet. Their swords glistened and they had gilded armor that could blind their enemies in the sun."

"What happened?" Syren asked, excited now, to hear the outcome.

"For every one of Majiaki's soldiers that fell, fifty Ahyllans fell with them. We were decimated and it took half the Ahsyllan population to rid the planet of Majikai."

Syren scrunched her eyes, confused. "If he left then how did they lose?"

"He left to gather more men. It took twenty of his men to kill half of the Ahsyllans but he had countless more on his home planet."

"What did the Ahsyllans do? Did he come back?"

"He's on his way back at this very moment," Isabeli responded softly.

"How will the Ahsyllans win?"

"By being just as ruthless as their enemies." Isabeli took another labored breath. "What was the lesson of that story?"

Syren pursed her lips and thought for a silent moment before answering. "Never underestimate your enemies...or your friends."

"No."

"Um...never let your guard down?" Syren asked hesitantly.

"No."

"I don't know," Syren admitted.

Isabeli drew in a hoarse breath. "Think."

Syren was quiet as she sat up and gazed at her mother, trying to wrap her brain around her mother's hidden lesson. Moments passed and she finally tried again.

"You have to be the most powerful always then it won't matter if you let your guard down or if you underestimate anyone."

Isabeli nodded slowly in approval. "There is power in all of us Syren. Maybe there's a little more in you than there is anyone else. One day, very soon you'll have to access that power. You'll have to need it, more than you need air to breathe. You'll have to crave it, more than you crave love and friendship and revenge. When the time comes, rip it from yourself like the parasite because that's what power is- a parasite."

Syren reflected on her last memory of her mother as she stared out from the clear glass wall of her fourth-floor office. "Power is a parasite. Power is a parasite," she repeated inwardly. It was all she could do to stop herself from flying her jet to Marcus' prison and killing him herself. She had the power to do it but it was wrong. Years after her mother's death, she pulled the opposite meaning from her last lesson and lived by the reverse lesson religiously.

In a moment, she shook the soured memory from her mind and returned to the present. "I want to die."

"You don't mean that," Athena, her assistant, responded absently.

"I do. I want to go up to my balcony and fling myself off," she insisted.

"Don't let Teddy hear you say that," Athena said. She was too focused on the device in her hand to engage Syren and her whining.

"But Marcus almost got out. You have to make sure you strengthen the security at the prison. I can't worry about this every day, it's too stressful."

Syren sauntered to her desk and plopped down on the white leather chair. She threw her head back and stared at the smooth white ceiling scattered with LED spotlights. After a moment it began to hurt her eyes and she looked away.

"Is it?" Athena questioned.

"I don't know- I'm just talking." Syren looked to Athena and admitted.

"It's not. It's nowhere close. You are older and smarter and better protected. What happened before will never happen again."

"Maybe you're right," Syren mumbled.

"I am."

"Your interviewer is ready," Athena said, "Let's head to the press room."

~~~

"You run the most profitable company in the world while being the youngest CEO in the world," the male journalist began. He flipped a blue pen on the edge of his knee, against his black cotton pants as he spoke.

He had a sloppy appearance. His shirt was wrinkled almost to distortion and his hair was moistened with nervous sweat. Flaps of adipose flesh hung from the edge of his pants and peaked from under his shirt. He was still stunned at her beauty which puzzled him as he'd interviewed Syren several times before.

"Well, I take issue with the framing of that question?" Syren said politely with a smile to ease her interviewer's visible anxiety. It was a thing she did often, as everyone seemed to be nervous in her company.

"Oh- " he began but she cut him off.

"-It presupposes that I've somehow earned the title when I did no such thing," she said with a shake of her head. "We can be candid. I inherited the most profitable company in the world," she said, very matter of factly. "It has been for centuries."

Syren looked across the room to the tall, expresso-skinned brunette, Athena, then returned her attention to her interviewer.

Athena stood in observance of Syren's show of charisma that she performed for the camera.

"You are right, Ms. Excellci," her red-haired interviewer agreed. "It's been almost a year now in which you've helmed as CEO. Excellci Corp is one of the world's oldest companies and is the world's first technology company. It's credited for some of the most important advances in history and has funded many of the world's greatest scientists, inventors, and doctors for centuries. Do you intend to continue on this path or do you see a new direction for your company?"

Syren took a thoughtful- rehearsed breath.

"There have always been three arms of Excellci Corp; the sword, the shield, and the advance. I think my ancestors set a great precedent for the way they intended our company to be run and I don't plan on deviating one bit. In a few days, we will have our annual conference showcasing all our new products and I think everyone will be very impressed with what we've been working on," she said with a smile.

"Gosh, I-I...think I speak for everyone when I say we are all very anxious to see the unveiling. It's been trending on social media periodically. I must ask though...um..will we see lower prices for certain products at this unveiling. There have been complaints from consumers that your prices have been excessive. Do you have a response?"

The polite smile never left Syren's lips. She knew any unplanned movement on her features would be dissected endlessly by the world press.

"No one in the world can reproduce the quality and the technological superiority we've achieved in our products and services. Perennially, we have the highest salaries for even our starting jobs, comparable to the rest of the jobs market. Paying your employees a luxurious salary has certain costs. That cost is covered in the price of our products. This is a business after all so no, the prices will not be reduced at our upcoming unveiling."

"Do you have any plans to take your company public?"

"Not unless I want to be haunted by my mother's ghost perpetually," she joked.

"Wow-" her interview exclaimed, flustered again and turned to the camera, knowing his time of two minutes had ended. "I-it's been incredible chatting with the insanely brilliant Syren Prinsloo Excellci. I'm Josh Hunter, for Tech New Now."

"You're too kind, Josh," she flattered. "Insanely brilliant- no. I think I'll just settle for insane."

He blushed and ran his hands through his sweaty, scarlet curls.

She was accustomed to her last names being used interchangeably. Prinsloo was her father's name. It was Dutch in origin but passed to her father's African ancestors through American slavery. Now it was hers, hyphenated before Excellci, her mother's name, the name that she couldn't escape, which had a much more complex history.

It began in Florence, Italy, just before the renaissance. Her ancestors settled there from a small - now none existent island called Ahsylla. Her mother taught her about their amusing culture, technology, and art. She'd told her about dragons as large as football fields created by their scientists. They were fun stories but they stopped when her only source to those stories, her mother Isabeli Excellci, died.

As far back as her ancestry was tracked there had been no men born in her family. It was then tradition in her family that daughters took their mother's name and so the name Excellci had been in her family for almost a millennium. Her ancestor Astrid de' Excellci was pivotal in the Italian renaissance. She was passionate about art and science and funded much of the advances of the renaissance through profits from weapons and technology she created and sold to countries at war. Her family enjoyed prominence and influence in Italy that rivaled it's monarchs until the late

1400's when a soured courtship with the King of Italy sent her ancestors to France where they lived for centuries in a plot of independent territory just outside of Paris. She was the last living heir of the Excellcis. The most powerful name in the world.

"Thank you- and we will be at the Excellci unveiling in a few days. I hope to chat with you again."

The heavyset man reached out to shake her hand but she gently rebuffed.

"God, it's always so awkward when I do this but I'm a germaphobe, Josh, you know that," she said with a smile. "How about a crisp air high five?"

He nodded shyly and they quickly shared a non-contact high five. The black leather of her skinny pants squeaked as she stood from the metal chair and walked over to Athena. She paired her pants with a white long-sleeved cotton shirt and black patent leather four-inch stilettos.

"You stuck to the script," Athena, her assistant, remarked, "very good."

Syren nodded and took her phone. She scrolled through social media as they both walked across the carpeted press room to the glass door exit.

"Anything else on the docket today?" Syren asked as she stared at the screen of her phone.

They walked quickly down the hall to Syren's office.

"Our day is drawing to a close, we just have to touch base with Lisa about her trip to Texas to finalize the deal with Governor Reese for the new plant and then we'll have taken care of all our business today," Athena responded. "After you've met your new intern Alexander West."

"Is that the one Calabar sent up from MIT?" Syren asked as she walked into her office.

"Yes."

"Great-" she said with a sigh, "get Lisa up here, we'll touch base and then you can send him in."

Her office was located on the fourth floor of her seventy floor, glass facade high rise in the middle of Manhattan. It was built by her mother almost two decades earlier and consumed an entire New York City block known as Excellci Plaza. The lower fifty floors functioned as the headquarters of her company while the top twenty floors contained residences. The penthouse where she lived, with her father and two adopted sisters, was among the residences.

Her office was extravagantly large with clear glass walls. The outer wall faced the view of Central Park and the inner wall faced the long hallway filled with executive offices. The floor of her office was tiled with grey marble which was stark against her all-white furniture. There were large bouquets of pink peonies scattered all over the room. Other than her proclivity for floral arrangements in her office space, there were cleverly placed accents and frames to enhance the decor.

"She's a minute away," Athena answered.

"Good- let's get this over with. I want to pick Ruby up from school on her first day back."

After she met with Lisa she left her chair and walked to the clear glass wall. She liked to gaze at the strangers roaming Excellci Plaza below. Four floors above was as close as she could get without a barrage of strangers demanding photographs of her.

Moments later, Athena opened the clear glass doors and walked inside, followed by Alex.

"Hello, I'm Alexander West," he said, "it's quite an honor to meet you."

Alex had an accent she couldn't place. It wasn't British nor was it American, it was in between as if he'd spent equal amounts of his life in both countries. Still, he was indubitably a sight to behold.

He had wavy, jet black hair that was neatly pulled from his face. One lock of curled hair fell away from the rest and rested lightly on his forehead. He had sharp features and the slightest dimple in his chin that made him look like an archetypical fictional prince and the navy blue tieless suit he wore complimented his polished features perfectly.

He stretched his hand for a shake and then pulled back."I forgot, you're not a hand shaker are you?" he said in a velvety, baritone voice.

"Did Calabar tell you that?" Syren asked.

"-Yes," he answered with a smile so charming that it was only her resolve that prevented her legs from buckling underneath her.

"Have a seat," she said as she gestured to the white leather sofa across the room.

"I'll be right back," Athena said as she closed the glass door.

Syren followed and sat on the sofa opposite Alex. Her leather pants squeaked when she crossed her legs. She took the flat Excellci tablet from the glass coffee table between them and retrieved the digital profile Athena created on Alexander.

Alexander stole a glance every so often as he waited. It wasn't often that women looked at him and had no reaction at all. He, on the other hand, had taken her in, even if it was just in small glances. He'd been preparing himself to meet her for quite some time. He knew she was beautiful but he was still awestruck on their second encounter.

"Of course she was beautiful," he thought, "she'd had infinite lifetimes to become that perfect. Infinite mutations and with each cycle her features improved to something more devastatingly beautiful."

But even with her beauty, it wasn't what he saw that stunned him, it was the way it tortured him inside

He was awed as if he beheld some spectacular natural scenery. Nostalgic, as if he had heard the most beautiful composition in the world. Warm, as if the sun shone on him from both sides. It all seemed to happen at once, continuously.

She had skin a shade of brown. Her eyes were mysterious and feline, when she walked in moments ago they were a clear blue but as the moments passed they seemed to be shifting every second, now as she sat down, they darkened to a cobalt blue. She had the type of full lips that left a permanent pout on her face, with her bottom lip just slightly fuller than the top.

They were so many things no one understood about Syren. Her long, golden luminescent hair that had a light metallic shine in any direct light. Her changing irises. The fact that she seemed to be brilliant beyond normal human capabilities and most notably that she seemed to be a carbon copy of every ancestor as far as there was visual proof.

It was almost a running joke.

No one understood why she was the way she was but she always seemed to have a semi-plausible explanation for any question that may arise as did her mother and grandmother. For her shiny hair, she'd said the proteins in her hair arranged in such a way to reflect light, similar to the cremello Akhal-Teke horse breed found in parts of Asia. For her changing eyes, she'd simply said a genetic disorder allowed the melanin in her iris to fluctuate in ways that were out of her control. For why she looked exactly like every ancestor going back centuries, she simply said, "the genes are strong."

She was lying of course, although whether wittingly or unwittingly, he wasn't certain. He'd studied her for years. He also knew of her kind. Most of his information was secondhand but so far it seemed accurate.

When her eyes changed, there almost always seemed to be an emotion attached to it. So far, he'd gathered that blue was the ground state, it was also the most frequent color her eyes displayed. He surmised that when she was doing nothing particularly interesting or feeling nothing particularly rousing her eyes were blue. He'd seen her angry and in those cases, her eyes were black as obsidian but he knew they could get red. A slight blue-lavender, the prettiest color of all, when she was surrounded by her family; her father, grandmother, and sisters. The other colors he couldn't figure out what they meant. Rarely, there was green and once there was a dull amber. It was all in pictures, of course, he'd never seen it at such proximity until now.

He realized, to his chagrin, that he'd severely underestimated the effect she would have on him. As he sat with an elevated heart rate and hormones creating turmoil for his emotions, he realized now the effect he had on others. It was nowhere near this strong, as he was only a knockoff version of her kind. He wasn't as strong or fast or beautiful nor was he as powerful and though he had more abilities than others of his kind, he could never challenge a true Ahsyllan. Syren wasn't just a true Ahsyllan, she was their Queen and she was their Prime, the first and the most perfect version of their form and the oldest living being on the planet.

With all the stories he'd heard, passed on from Hhera and her futura, about the vast evolutionary importance of this form of the Ahsyllan Prime, about the war that was to come, he was aghast that she was living an outwardly normal life instead of preparing.

He didn't know futuras well. There was only one that he'd ever come across but over the thousands of years, he knew the probabilities she calculated were as unreliable as they were reliable. She saw too many paths into the future, too much information, too many choices that then changed the path. It was sometimes better not to know at all except for the times it was necessary to do so and for him, this time, it was necessary to do so.

He watched her for what seemed to be a long time but might have only been a few minutes and then she placed the tablet back on the table.

"So, Calabar says you're really good. At what age did graduate high school?"

"I was fourteen, Ms. Excellci."

"Oh god no- please- just Syren," she responded without any readable change in her expression.

He tried not to look directly at her and Syren found herself doing the same.

"How old are you now? She asked.

"Twenty."

"Before MIT?" She asked though she knew the answers as she'd just read it in his profile.

"Harvard?"

"What program?" she questioned.

"Pre-med, neuroscience."

"Why did you transition from a pre-medical program to engineering?"

"As I studied neuroscience I became very interested in the ways we could interface technology and our brains to make our technology smarter and more suited to us individually. I wanted to pursue neurosurgery, my whole life actually, but the more I studied, the further I ventured away from the medical field. After completing my degrees at Harvard, I enrolled at MIT to pursue bio-engineering," he said. Alexander wiped his sweaty palm against the fabric of his pants and hoped his anxiety wasn't obvious.

"And you're on track to complete your Ph.D.? Is that correct because you completed the bachelor's and master's in simultaneously? At Twenty years old, that's quite an achievement."

"Thank you," he responded with a nod and a smile which Syren did not return.

"Do you have a residence in the city?" Syren asked.

"No, my home is just outside the city, a forty-minute drive from here."

"Okay, well when Calabar sends someone, I can't refuse them, he's brilliant and I trust his judgment," Syren began. "You can start in a few days. Stop by human resources on the eleventh floor to complete all the necessary paperwork and discuss how you will receive your weekly stipend of $2,000."

"I was under the impression that this was an unpaid internship, those were the guidelines set by MIT."

"I don't believe in unpaid labor. If you'll be working here as an intern then you won't receive a salary but you'll receive a stipend. Calabar knows that."

"I'm sorry but I don't think I can accept the stipend," Alexander said. "I can't risk it."

"Okay, if you think that's what best. As long as you have adequate housing and your basic needs fulfilled then I won't harp on this. If you change your mind you can talk to Athena."

"I think it was a very generous offer and I truly appreciate it."

Athena walked into the office and handed him a small flat box.

"You'll have an Excellci Laptop, phone, tablet for work purposes," Athena began as she led him from the room. "You'll begin your usual day at 9am and the work-day ends at 5pm although Syren does have unpredictable hours at times. Do you have an issue staying later or beginning earlier?"

"No, not at all."

"Sometimes you'll have to travel and work on weekends? Do you have a passport?"

"Yes," he responded.

"You must sign a non-disclosure agreement-"

Once they were outside Syren took a deep, soothing breath, glad to have escaped his presence.

At the end of her day, she drove to her younger sister Ruby's school and picked her up before she headed home. When she walked through the door of her high rise condo with Ruby in tow, she saw her father walking about in a silk floral kimono and matching bed slippers. He was the same shade as Ruby's hazelnut tone. His hair was short and finely twisted into what looked like dreadlocks but wasn't and he wore small gold ornaments along the strands. On his arm were many small tattoos, most of them tributes to Isabeli, and others were a tribute to Syren.

"Daddy, I thought you were going to be at the studio creating a new masterpiece?" She walked over and leaned down to kiss her father's cheek and gave him a hearty bear hug.

"I was but I don't know, my energy isn't there today," he said with a shrug as he kissed his daughter back and then broke the hug. "How was your day?"

"Not very interesting," she lied, "I'll have an intern hovering around the next few months alright?"

"He or she?" Teddy asked.

"He."

"Interesting," Teddy said with a smile.

"No, not particularly," Syren responded as she plopped herself down on the large black leather sofa placed at the center of the ridiculously large, high ceilinged living room.

"How old is he?" Teddy asked.

"Twenty- I think."

"Gosh, that's a little older. I was hoping it would be someone your age."

"Daddy, it doesn't matter. It's one intern, I've had other interns, calm down."

"Never your age, you could use a friend" Teddy responded with a smile then he turned to Ruby, lifted Ruby in the air and kissed her chin. "How was your first day of 5th grade?" he asked.

"Good, I like all my teachers and I'm with my friends."

He smiled at her warmly.

"Okay, go wash up and then I want more details. Fleur is in your bedroom, she wants to see you."

Ruby ran off to her room.

"Bye Sy," she yelled as she ran.

"Goodbye Rubes," Syren called back.

"So what are your plans for the evening?" he asked Syren.

"Working, why?"

"Katherine has a senior class meet up at Central park, I think you should go," Teddy suggested.

"You do realize that I never went to high school or college because I'm above that, right? What interest do I have attending a class meet up for a class that I'm not a part of?"

"I know 'Miss genius of our time'," he mocked slightly. His speaking voice and singing voice were exactly alike, both beautiful and child-like. "But this could be a great opportunity. Since you were little, I feel like you skipped the naive, exploratory, fun stuff that every kid should experience. You were born and then suddenly, you know all these things that were impossible for you to know and since then you've just been so-"

"-Adult?"

"No, I was gonna say mature and responsible. An old soul."

"I don't see how that's a bad thing daddy…and I'm not so sure I'm that mature, Athena is quite tired of my whining, you know."

"It's not and you are but..it's just that I wish you would make a mistake now and then and learn from it, I wish sometimes you'd take a night off and just go out with your friends or date some idiotic high school boy and then dump him when you realize you're too good for him," he said his piece and then sighed. "But you don't have friends and you don't date. You don't do anything Syren except work, meet with world leaders and attend charity balls and visit your factories…"

"Dad, it's my life-"

"I know but I just think you'll enjoy other experiences too," he said with an expression of hope. "Detach yourself from all the serious grown-up stuff, focus on the last few months you'll have as a child. You'll be eighteen in December, there's no going back after that. This is the final thing I'm asking you to do before you enter adulthood, as your father-" he stopped as if he just realized he had one more convincing argument, "by the way, Katherine seems to love the balances she's struck. All I'm asking for is balance."

She rolled her eyes and smiled as if she surrendered. "Katherine doesn't have balance. She goes to school for a social life."

Katherine walked down the large floating staircase across the room. Her unnaturally brown waist length hair swung across her back as she moved. Her beauty straddled the line between spectacular and plain. Syren called it 'pageant beauty', something Katherine considered the highest compliment.

"-Because everything else is so boring," she said in response. "There's a senior class party later, you're coming," Katherine said as if Syren had no say in the matter.

"Dad already said that. I'm not going. Not today, I'm busy. The unveiling is days away. Another day would be fine."

"Don't care. You're coming," Katherine said as she walked to the kitchen, not waiting for a response.

Teddy smiled winningly, "you heard her, you're going."

~~~

Syren walked into the open lot space in Central Park with her best friend and adopted sister Katherine in tow. Her bodyguards were a few feet behind and a few feet ahead. There were several more of them than usual now that they were outside.

Katherine attended Locke school, a pretentious and ridiculously expensive private school for years. Every year in the afternoon of the first day of the semester, the senior students would gather in Central Park for a first-day get together.

When Syren entered the space everyone stared shamelessly with wide eyes and open mouths. It became blisteringly uncomfortable very quickly.

"Hey Kat, what's up?" a teenage boy yelled from across the park to Katherine, though his eyes were fixed on Syren.

Katherine waved back with a wide smile as she pulled Syren closer. "Come on, let's have some fun, you boring blob of blonde hair."

Syren returned the smile and ignored the stares, "alright fine, I'm a bit hungry."

Katherine pulled her over to the snack tent where they grabbed food and ate as Katherine walked around and introduced Syren to her longtime friends. As they mingled, Katherine saw Henry, a blonde haired boy from the senior class, and tugged at Syren's arm.

"Look at him, I was saving him for you, he's gorgeous, isn't he?"

"Not particularly," Syren responded, uninterested.

Her eyes met with Henry's for the briefest of moments before she rolled them and turned around. He seemed hopeful as if Katherine had promised him something; a date or an introduction...

"You don't like him?" Katherine asked. The disappointment was evident in her voice as her lip turned down into a frown.

"No, he seems...tedious."

Katherine shook her head and rolled her eyes, "you don't like anyone."

"You know I have to be careful Katherine."

"Okay, one guy recorded you kissing. It was just a peck," Katherine sighed.
"Look, you always have to be careful but I also think that you shouldn't overthink it, just have fun, he's cute and I've known him for like a year now. He's one of the only guys here that I can stand. Don't let your paranoia get the best of you."

"Yeah, fine," she said to end the conversation although she hadn't changed her mind. She couldn't focus on Henry when she hadn't yet scrubbed the image of the beautiful, dark-haired intern from it.

They continued walking around until they needed to walk no more because a group of twenty students had permanently gathered around them. They were Katherine's friends and acquaintances. All seemed intimidated by Syren's presence, she realized, which was good because it meant fewer questions and the fewer questions that were asked, the faster the evening would draw to an end and she could escape.

Chapter 2 - Unveiling

When Syren walked into her bedroom, she dropped her purse on the floor and made a beeline to her bathroom.

"Athena set a hot bath for me and sprinkle a little vanilla-lavender essential oil mix in there."

"Sure," the voice responded from a ball of light that appeared at the center of the bathroom.

She walked over to her white marble bathroom vanity and stood in front of the mirror for a moment, gazing at her ethereal reflection. She leaned closer into the mirror and checked the color of her eyes. They were pure blue. The fact that they changed color was not something she could control or was even aware of when it occurred. After, she felt the lump on the back of her neck. On some days it hurt more than others. In the morning it was quite sensitive but now the sensitivity had waned. Once the tub was filled with warm water, she stripped her clothes and stepped in.

~~~

Syren plopped down in her neatly made bed and took a deep breath, inhaling the sweetened lavender that still lingered on her skin. She gazed at the ceiling through the white sheer covered canopy of her bed.

"Athena?"

"I'm here," the voice responded.

"I need you to complete a background check on Alexander West."

"We already have one, as we do on all employees."

"No, not the standard, take your time- I would like it to be very thorough."

"Seems excessive," Athena remarked to herself, "Will that be all?"

"For now. Thank you."

The next morning when Syren arrived at her office, her day was busy with preparations for the Excellci unveiling. At the beginning of her workday, she visited the Lincoln Center at the edge of the city by the Hudson River to watch as the final preparations were made. There were people camped outside on the banks of the sidewalk, waiting to enter the center for the unveiling and it came as quite a surprise to them when she arrived earlier than expected to view the center. When she left the center she made her way to news broadcast locations to perform press interviews in anticipation of the unveiling. Late in the night, she traveled to the late show, to perform her final press appearance on the tour.

"You have two minutes," Athena said. "We should head to the stage."

"Okay," Syren responded as her personal stylist Sadie checked her red lips in the mirror.

"You're good," she responded.

A stagehand knocked on the door of the green room."Syren, we're ready for you," he said.

"A moment," she called as she stood and made a beeline to the door.

They walked to the stage from the green room and waited for Syren's introduction.

"I want to welcome tonight, our special guest, Syren Prinsloo Excellci," the host announced enthusiastically. The crowd of guests applauded.

Syren walked out to the stage in her cream silk de chine wide-legged pants and matching long sleeve blouse. Her white-gold hair curled into long waves that stopped down her lumbar.

She smiled and waved as she walked to the couch beside the host's chair and sat.

"Wow-" the host, Carter Falwell began, "you are very striking to look at."

"Striking? That's new," she responded with a smile, staring into his eyes. Something she did to intentionally fluster her company. It always seemed to work. "How are you, Carter?"

"G-good- I'm fine," he stuttered then took a breath. "You have a very intense stare, gosh, no wonder you rule the world, who can look you in the eye and tell you no," he said.

"No man. That's for certain," Syren responded.

He chuckled uncomfortably and slicked his strawberry blonde hair back with his sweaty palms.

"Very mature for seventeen," he mumbled.

"Thanks...I suppose."

"Urm..so the Excellci showcase... can you reveal anything before it's showcased at the event."

"No," she began, "but I can tell you that you should tune in online, it will be live-streamed or you can stop by the Lincoln Center.." She began the same spiel she'd done at every interview earlier in the day.

~~~

She arrived home a little after 1am. She was exhausted and hungry. After her routine hot, scented bath and a snack from the pantry, she brushed her teeth and crawled into bed.

"Athena, what do you have for me?" Syren asked as laid buried in a mountain of silk pillows.

She stared at the wall of her bedroom. She could see the tactile light illustrations projected on the white background. She could touch, or move the program at will even from her bed if she needed to. It responded to her every thought.

"Regarding your inquiry on Mr. West?" Athena asked as if she hadn't been connected to Syren's mind and knew the question before asking.

"Yes," Syren responded through a yawn.

"After a conclusive search, there was nothing that linked Mr. West to you, not through associates or any known contacts. In fact, he hasn't many associates at all, most are in attendance at MIT or are alumni of MIT and Harvard School. Mr. West resides 40 minutes from the city in a suburb called Park Hills."

"For how long?"

"As far as I can tell, it's been for the past 9 months according to his global position system data. He resided at university residence for some time as well."

"Educational history?"

"Various schools across Great Britain before attending university in the United States. Would you like me to list them?"

"No. Nothing stinky Athena, at all?"

"Well…" the program responded, "there is the issue of family. There seem to be no parents in the picture, both deceased."

"He's Twenty right? Who was his guardian before?"

"An older brother and two sisters, named Seth, Cleopatra, and Isis West. Isis retained guardianship and had for at least two years before he reached legal adulthood."

"What about texts? Emails? Has he said anything for concern?"

"In the past year no but I can search further if you'd like?"

"No, I think I've gone far enough, thanks, Athena."

"Would you like me to surveil him to let you know if any untoward behavior surfaces."

"Light surveillance - actually no I think maybe I'm going a little crazy digging into his life like this- no surveillance- just keep an eye out okay." Syren paused for a thoughtful moment before she began again. "My instincts aren't usually wrong but maybe I am this time. We'll see."

"As you wish. Anything else?" Athena asked.

"Yes. Update on Marcus since his attempted escape?"

"Still confined."

"No attempts since the last?"

"No."

Syren breathed a sigh of relief every time she heard this.

"What about the rest?"

"They still evade us, Osiris is looking for any sign of their presence on the surface. We'll be ready."

"Okay," Syren said through another yawn.

"Would you like me to put you to sleep?" Athena asked.

"No, I'm quite tired. I shouldn't have any trouble sleeping tonight..."

~~~

Alex arrived on the fourth floor of Excellci headquarter a half-hour before he was to begin. To his surprise, Athena was already in.

"I'll show you to your office," she said with her nose buried into the screen of a tablet.

Alex stood, grabbed his briefcase from the floor of the private lobby, and followed Athena to his office. He was surprised. It was rather spacious for the lowly intern he was.

"You can personalize it to your liking. Syren will arrive soon but in the meantime, you can go up to the employee cafeteria on the 28th floor. There is a complimentary breakfast spread for all employees from 8 am to 11 am."

"Thanks, I'll be sure to give it a visit."

Athena nodded and headed out.

He watched Athena as she walked out and surmised it was unlikely she was human. He'd never seen a cy-vessel before but he couldn't imagine that she wasn't one of them based on what he'd heard of them. He quickly scrubbed thoughts of Athena's origins from his mind and ventured to the employee cafe. It was quite a luxurious breakfast spread but then again it was quite a luxurious cafe, fit for a five-star hotel. There were many amenities for employees at the headquarters. During his tour two days earlier, he's seen a nursery for children of employees and after school care. There was a basketball court, a tennis court, swimming pool, game room and gym in the basement of the large building. He hadn't visited the residences but on the rooftop of the building was a heliport and rooftop deck where employees could venture for their lunch or breaks.

Alexander took breakfast down to his office and ate. When he was finished, Syren had arrived. Almost an hour later, he was called into a meeting in the conference room opposite her office.

"This is Alex," Syren said. He was the last to arrive at the meeting because he was the last to be called. "He's my new apprentice and he will be with us for four months, I believe, is that right Alex?"

"Yes," he responded.

Syren noticed the reaction of the women in the room. Some of them more than twice his age, blushing and gawking at him. She ignored them and continued with her meeting.

"Do you have the final count for all in attendance at the unveiling?"

"Close to 40,000," Nikole responded, "11% increase from last year's numbers although most are attending to see you."

"It's better than them not attending at all," Syren responded graciously.

The meeting lasted almost fifty minutes.

"Alexander, I'd like to see you in my office," Syren said as the other employees left the conference room in groups.

In her office, Syren sat at her desk. Built into the clear glass, were computer displays and a keypad. The software program could be lifted from the glass into three dimensional light illustrations in a tactile form but she mostly just worked on the screen in the two-dimensional form in her clear glass screen.

Alex entered moments after she'd taken her seat. He observed the framed black and white portraits above the shelf behind Syren's desk. He didn't see them when last he was in her office. There was Angela Davis. Fannie Lou Hamer, Mamie Till-Mobley, Earth Kitt, Astra Excellci, and May Prinsloo.

"You can have a seat here, Alex," Syren gestured to the chair in front of her desk.

Alex took a seat and placed his white flat tablet on his lap in case he needed to take notes.

Syren leaned back in her leather and crossed her legs and sighed. "A little about me," Syren began. "I take a siesta every day right after lunch. My favorite shows are 'Curb your enthusiasm' and 'The Office', which I have watched continuously. I rarely listen to music past the year 2000. My favorite food is orange chicken. Now tell me something about yourself, Alexander."

"Please, just Alex," he said with a light chuckle.

"Alright, just Alex..."

He smiled. "I um..I do agree with you on the music bit. I quite like your father actually."

"I hate his music," Syren said.

"Oh. That's...odd."

"Not to me but we mustn't digress, continue."

Alex wasn't sure where to continue. It took him a moment to begin again. "I like to compose original works on my guitar. Whenever I get the chance I find myself on the coast of some island surfing or on somewhere in a mountain hiking-"

Syren barely gazed at him as he spoke but she listened intently.

"I'm not a very interesting person so I'm afraid that's as much as I can share. With my academic studies, I don't have much time for anything else."

Syren nodded and stood. She walked to the front of her desk and leaned against the edge just over a foot away from Alex.

"At the end of the week, we'll travel to France for a charity event I have to attend. Are you available to accompany me on the trip?" she asked.

"I am."

"We'll have a few other senior members of the team as well. After the event in Paris, we'll travel to Kenya to visit the Nairobi manufacturing plant, then we'll return on Monday evening."

Alex nodded.

"I've got my hands quite full with the unveiling for right now so I want you to spend the day at product development on floors 29-35. David will introduce you to all the products we'll be unveiling tomorrow at the event so that you'll be some-what familiar with them for tomorrow."

"Okay, sounds good."

"Alright, thank you, Alex," Syren said.

"-A moment- um, might I ask you a question?"

"Sure," Syren responded.

"Those portraits. I didn't see those when last I was here..."

"They were being cleaned. I like to keep them in perfect condition."

"Why do you have them there?"

"This would've been a very different country for me, if not for them. When my maternal grandmother Astra Excellci came here from France, she was the wealthiest person in the world, far outpacing anyone else. Even then, her wealth and beauty didn't save her from torment, harassment, and racism because she had skin a shade of brown like mine. Still, she was far luckier than my paternal grandmother May, who had to suffer through it without wealth, celebrity, or education for what was a few decades too long in my opinion."

Alex smiled softly, "I think you've chosen extraordinary women to admire."

Syren nodded and her expression softened but didn't return the smile, "thank you."

He left the room. Once Alex was out of sight, Syren took on a deep breath and relaxed. She had goosebumps, inexplicably and that annoyed her but still, she went about her day, quickly scrubbing the encounter from her mind.

~~~

In the morning of the unveiling, Syren began her day early at almost 5 am. It was the first unveiling since she had taken control of her family's company and she knew any failures would be endlessly dissected in the press as a reflection of her.

That could not happen..

The event needed to be perfect. It began at 9 am, with remarks from the more well-known executives from her company. There were videos on the history of the company and videos detailing the most important advancements made by the company in the technological field.

It was quite tedious, she thought, but it had been done every year since her grand-mother Astra Excellci inaugurated the annual unveiling.

At noon, she graced the stage, wearing a white. She performed her keynote speech and unveiled the newest 'Ex' car line, the newest laptops, phones, desktops com-puters, and the rest. The unveiling lasted three days. The first day was the advance, the most popular component with many typical consumers and fans in attendance. On the second day, was the shield and in the audience were many ministers of de-fense and security ministries and firms from the globe around. She showcased de-fensive weapons, aircraft, and protective software. On the third day, the sword, she showcased offensive weapons, military technology, software, and aircraft.

At the end of the third night and last night of the unveiling, Athena brought Syren to her office under the guise of important business needing her attention. As she walked past the clear glass wall she saw Katherine, Ruby, and Teddy as well as her senior management team and Alex. when she entered, she was immediately greet-ed with a crystal tulip of champagne.

"Congratulations," the group cheered with raised glasses.

"Thank you," Syren said with a smile, shaking her head, "I shouldn't take all the credit but I will anyway." There were scattered chuckles across the room in response.

"Can you stop," Katherine scolded with an eye roll. "You deserve all the credit."

Ruby ran to her and hugged her tightly. "Good job," she said.

"Thanks, Rue," Syren kissed her cheek and hugged her little sibling. Teddy also offered his congratulations and a hearty hug.

"I'm proud of you. Very proud."

"Thanks, daddy."

Katherine walked over and pulled Syren away from Teddy. She bit her knuckles dramatically and closed her eyes. "Who the hell is that?" she asked as she gestured surreptitiously to Alexander with her eyes.

"He's my new intern or...apprentice. I haven't decided which term is less condescending."

"Syren- he's a dream, why didn't you tell me he looked like this. How can you stand to be so close to him and not attack him."

"Because that's illegal," she said matter-of-factly.

"I hate you so much- you don't even know," Katherine replied with snark.

"Katherine," she said with a chuckle as she took a sip of her champagne.

"-Not too much champagne Syren, just one glass, you're only seventeen!" Teddy called from across the room.

"Alright, daddy!" Syren called back.

"Syren you better hold onto me because I think I'm going to go kiss him."

"You're not going to kiss him," Syren responded.

"No, I think I am. Help me, get him away from me. He's too beautiful."

"Katherine stop," Syren whined, annoyed.

"Ugh...even torturing you is boring."

Syren smiled hesitantly, "torturing me?"

"You obviously like him and that makes you uncomfortable."

"How did you figure that? You met him tonight."

"I know these things Sy, just one look at you when you came in here and I could tell."

"I don't have any affection for him, Katherine. He's beautiful, I'll admit that but that doesn't mean I'm going to jump on him. I don't have time to chase after interns."

"Gosh, if only fifty-year-old men felt the same way about banging interns as you do we wouldn't have so many workplace harassment cases."

"True," Syren said with a chuckle.

"I'm gonna go talk to him. Bye," Katherine said then stepped off before Syren could stop her.

"Hey, you're Alex right?" Katherine said with a smile as she stopped in front of him after a short jog.

"Yes. you're Katherine Prinsloo. How are you?" he stretched his hand for a shake.

"God, you have an accent too," she gushed as she shook his hand, "Holy shit!"

"What?" Alex asked with a raised eyebrow, amused.

"Nothing," Katherine said, blushing. "Ugh, it's just...your eyes are so blue…"

Syren pulled Katherine away from Alex, "excuse her. She might have had too much to drink," she said quickly and walked Katherine across the room.

When she felt the champagne tulip pulled from her hands she looked over and saw Teddy. "That's enough sweetie, I said half, I toss the rest," he said and took Katherine's champagne glass as well. Syren inwardly complained that she'd only taken a few sips but she wasn't keen on alcohol so she didn't bother vocalizing her thought.

"Athena, I'm ready to leave," Syren commanded her assistant telepathically.

"Gosh, look at the time, I think we should call it a night," Athena announced to the room. "Syren has a flight to catch and so do a few of you."

"Remember, I'm coming with you," Katherine said, "I have the meeting in Paris."

"I am well aware Katherine but if you can't control yourself…"

"I was kidding about that stuff- well not really but I wasn't actually gonna do it- I actually would have, you know what, I'll stop talking," Katherine rambled and then shook her head.

"Yes, please do," Syren responded.

Teddy and Ruby left for the residence after saying their goodbyes. Katherine, Syren, Alex, and three of Syren's employees went to the rooftop to the helipad where an Excellci Corp Helicopter waited to ferry them to John F. Kennedy airport. At the airport, they boarded a private Excellci Corp aircraft bound for Paris.

Chapter 3 - High Palais

In the morning, Syren woke in France at High Palais. The home of her mother and grandmother and every ancestor of her mother's lineage going back a half a millennia.

High Palais, most times called High Palace; named so because it sat atop high hills on the outskirts of Paris purchased under a treaty with the French King Marc Paul. Amabella Excellci paid a handsome sum of francs to the king under the agreement the land would be separate territory not under the jurisdiction of France. The treaty still stands.

The land occupied seven square miles, which included the hills around the gates of the palace. It was one of the largest in the world, along with her family's ancient Italian castle in Florence.

High Palais comprised over seven hundred rooms and almost one million square feet of floor space within the palace. The palace was mostly gilded and had all the superficial embellishments of 15th-century French opulence.

Syren never understood why the property was built so largely. Her family, even in that age, had been notoriously small. The palace was fit for hundreds of guests, it made no sense to her it's purpose, other than the extreme gesture of wealth that it seemed built to be.

Underneath the property was a lab. Built many years prior by her grandmother Astra, it was a state of the art weapons and technology lab with a medical facility attached. She wasn't as interested in engineering as her ancestors had been. Of course, she excelled at it, she seemed to excel at everything, even she had to admit that, but she was more comfortable planting cy-vessels in the lab to do the creating for her, instead of being stuck there all hours of the day as she remembered her mother had been during her temporary stretches of good health.

Cy-vessels were grandmother's greatest creations, so she was told. They were vessels of consciousness, "vessels of your will", she remembered her mother calling them but really they were just bio-genetic robots. You could imprint them with a pale shadow of your consciousness which meant they could think they way you did, shared your intelligence, and made the same decisions you did. You could also create them with no consciousness at all so they could only follow codes programmed into their nuclei.

The Cy-vessels still functioned with her mother's brain signature even so many years after her death. It wasn't a difficult task to imprint her brain signature into the vessels but Syren never changed them. So many years later, they functioned as her guards, housekeepers, butlers, her inventors at Excellci Corp, her engineers, doctor, and her assistants. She was surrounded by them. Athena's physical form, which worked as her assistant at her company, was a cy-vessel and the only cy-vessel Syren created who had been imprinted with her consciousness. The cy-vessel retained the ability to communicate telepathically once paired with a brain signature. It was how Syren communicated with Athena.

Only her immediate family knew of the cy-vessels but even so none of them understood them.

Syren bathed and ate breakfast in the principal kitchen then made her way to the main courtyard of the palace. She was greeted by her cremello akhal-teke horse who she'd named Peony, after her favorite flower.

"Bonjour Peony, tu m'as tellement manqué," she uttered in her first language of french, "it's so good to see you," she added as she ran her fingers through her shiny, champagne gold coat.

Syren took a moment to examine her mare, petting, and massaging her coat as she went. This did not go unnoticed by Peony. She whinnied and galloped excitedly at her master's attention.

Syren mounted her steed and strolled easily down the concrete road to Sapphire Lake almost a mile from the main court. The royal blue lake was half a mile wide with ultramarine waters so clear you could see the large smooth stones at the bottom of the lake bed and aquamarine life scattered throughout. Across the water was an arched, cobblestone bridge supported by several pillars that delved deep beneath the waters. Viridescent willow trees lined where the banks met the water.

Syren walked Peony across the bridge to High Garden. Through the entrance of the garden was a hundred-foot white marble path in between rows of cherry blossom trees. Down the end of the path was a circular labyrinth of perfectly manicured lavender flower plants. Outside the labyrinth were banks of flowering pink peonies and stalks of orange and red dahlias. All colors of roses and camellias, bunches of white gyps, Himalayan blue poppies, purple statice, red snapdragons, and green poms were lined in rows. The edges of the garden were bordered by boxwood ball topiary hedges.

It was a feast for the eyes.

She walked further down the marble path to her family memorial. The strong edge of lavender aroma carried in the air, overpowering the softer scents emanating from the soft pink roses and peonies.

The memorial ground was the very center of the garden. On the other side, laid the same arrangement of flowers, trees, and shrubbery as the entrance until you reached the greenscape.

Large pillars of white marble statues erected from the ground, forming circles around the main statue, a figure of Astrid de Excellci, her first known ancestor. Each statue looked exactly like the other and all of them were the exact image of Syren.

She dismounted her horse at the edge of the memorial and removed her tool kit from her saddle. She began at the center of the circle with Astrid, using a small soft brush to clean the crevices of the marble.

Hours passed, she wasn't sure how many when Athena spoke to her.

"Remember your meeting begins at 3 pm, you have almost an hour. You should be getting back. Katherine is also trying to reach you, I'll put her through."

"Sy, where are you?" Katherine asked.

"In the garden," Syren answered aloud though the voices were only in her head.

"Oh god, don't tell me you're in the garden crying again."

"I'm not crying Katherine, what do you want?" Syren snapped.

"Come with me to Paris, we'll have lunch before I meet with Chanel."

"I just got done with Khione, I have four more left then I have a meeting- by the way, Katherine I can feel the eye roll from here- quit it okay."

"Whatever," Katherine said dismissively, "I just wanted to tell you I'm leaving for my meeting. If I don't see you later then I'll see you in New York.."

"Good luck," Syren wished.

"I don't need luck," Katherine retorted, "my last name isn't Tran anymore, it's Prinsloo now, remember?"

Syren chuckled and responded, "yes and we're both the better for it."

"Don't get mushy on me, I love you, bye."

"I love you too sister," Syren returned.

Katherine ended the call.

Syren scrubbed the last bit of dirt from the sculpture of Khione Excellci and lightly kissed her lips then she moved to the next sculpture. It was a sorrowful experience to know where she would lay after she died. Her spot at the memorial was inevitable so she resolved to acquaint herself to the place before she was to spend an eternity there.

"Your guests have entered the High Road," Athena said an hour later.

"Have them wait for me by the Impasse Gate or better yet, have them wait at Isabeli fountain. I'll make my way over now."

Syren packed away her tools and mounted Peony and rode to Isabeli fountain.

~

Alex spent the better part of the day in his suite at the Four Seasons George V. The charity event was set to commence at 8 pm in the grand ballroom of the hotel but before then he was to meet Syren at her palace along with the other executives who'd made the trip. There was Ama Abara, the VP of the African Division; Sarai Temple, VP of Environmental Impact; Felix Felton, VP of Human Resources; Emma Lang, President of the Excellci Foundation and John Stern, VP of Global Operations. Ama and John hadn't traveled with them from New York but met them in Paris. They each had an assistant accompany them which brought the total number of occupants in the black Mercedes sprinter to almost a dozen as they drove to High Palace.

At the foot of the hills was a security checkpoint. They were all asked to disembark the vehicle by armed guards.

"Do you understand you are entering territory independent of France and that the laws and all protections offered by the French government are invalid beyond this entrance and within the confines of this gate?" an older gentleman asked loudly. He spoke English but every word was accented with french.

The group nodded.

One at a time, a guard brought a small Excellci tablet to each individual and they were made to sign with the scan of their thumb. At the end of what appeared to be a brief security check but one Alex suspected was much more in-depth, they were allowed to board the vehicle and enter through the checkpoint. After a four-minute ride, they arrived at a second gate. This gate had large golden bars with gold leaf details fashioned in a frivolous pattern. It stood almost thirty feet high and the walls attached to the hinges stood just as high as the gate.

Through the gate was High Palace. It was picturesque, with fervent green lawns and manicured topiary shrubbery. The main palace stood almost five floors high and was gargantuan in size.

Alex watched awed faces as they drove through the gate to the main courtyard. A marble fountain in the middle of a concrete roundabout driveway was where the van stopped in front of the palace.

The statute in the fountain had the name 'Isabelli' carved under it but still, the visage of the marble was a copy of Syren's.

"Wait here," Athena said as she walked to the group from the entrance of the palace, "Syren will be here momentarily."

Alex's suspicions about Athena were confirmed when she arrived since he knew Syren had left her in New York City. He realized then Syren had to have multiple copies of Athena in her cy-vessel form. They waited by the Isabelle fountain for almost five minutes when the sound of galloping hooves striking the pavement turned their attention to Syren.

Her white-gold hair dancing in the wind as she rode and she seemed oblivious to all the eyes that watched her when she parked her horse by the fountain and dismounted the saddle as gracefully as a ballerina. She kissed her horse Peony, who's cremello colored hair was just as striking as Syren's, then she waved goodbye to the horse. A uniformed worker appeared from the palace and led the horse down the western outer corridor.

"Bonjour tout le monde." Syren greeted the group as she walked quickly towards the palace. She made it a point of duty to not look at Alex, she wasn't in the mood to be flustered by him.

The group returned greetings, though Syren was already ahead of the group and seemed to be in a rush.

"We've moved the meeting from the blossom room to the Lily pool," Athena said.

"Great," Syren said.

Inside the palace teemed with uniformed workers. Everyone was in sync with not a beat out of step, like a hive of bees working together. They walked down the gilded hall. It was quite a walk for the halls of a residence. When they exited the other side of the palace, at the top of the grand staircase, they were greeted with a view of Paris.

"Wow," Ama mused.

"Follow me, come on," Syren said as she walked down the black and white harlequin tiled terrace. The group of eleven followed. They passed along the shallow pool, filled with all colors of lotus and water lilies floating on the surface. There were small gentle fountains of water lining the center of the pool. On the other side of the terrace were garden tables and chairs filled with china of finger sandwiches, pastries, and tea. Petals of pink peony flowers garnished the tables.

It was opulence to an obscene degree.

At the table, stood six women uniformed in light lavender knee-length dresses with white frilly aprons. One held a sizable metal bowl filled with water and soap.

Syren stopped and washed her hands in the bowl quickly then took the white towel that hung on the woman's arm and dried her wet hands.

"Merci Constance," she said, then quickly stuffed a feta and spinach sandwich in her mouth.

When she finished, she finally smiled and took a breath. "God, I am starving," she chuckled then ate another.

"Find your name and help yourselves," Athena said to the group, "we'll begin shortly."

Another woman walked over and poured Syren a cup of steaming jasmine green tea from a china pot as she ate. "Merci Cateline," Syren said through sips of hot tea.

The group split and Alex and Ama took their seats at Syren's table while the others went to their places at three tables and the meeting on their upcoming trip to Kenya commenced.

～

Alex arrived at his hotel suite shortly before 6 pm. He began preparing for the ball shortly after and made his way down exactly as the event commenced. He was one of the first guests to arrive and was quickly escorted to the company table. There, he waited as each member of their team arrived. Syren was the last to appear and it seemed fitting that she would make him wait.

She was truly a vision in a white silk de chine fitted gown and short fur stole. Her lips were red as rubies and she was shroud in white diamonds, so large they could be mistaken as fake if not for their unfalsifiable beauty and glare.

Syren was accompanied by a squad of guards, six of them, as she usually was whenever she was outside the comforts of her high rise or palace. Three stood at the exits of the room while the others accompanied Syren as she sauntered over to the table to greet the group with Athena in tow.

"How has it been so far? Boring?" she asked.

"Not too bad," Emma responded as she ran her fingers through her silky black hair and then checked her face in the mirror. A thing most women did in the presence of Syren.

"It's usually tedious," Syren said, "but not tonight, I feel like dancing. Dance with me Emma, before these old men seek me out."

Emma stood immediately at the request and placed her clutched purse on her gold-lacquered chair.

A bulky, white-haired man walked over the moment Syren spoke the words. He was older and had an expression on his face that managed to be both stern and charming.

"M-may I have a dance?" he asked with heavily accented french elocution.

He outstretched his hand to Syren and waited for a response.

"How old am I?" She asked as she took a sip of her water, not particularly looking at the man.

"Dix-sept ans?" he responded.

"Bien. How old are you?"

He chuckled nervously, "oh, I get it."

Syren turned and stared into his eyes.

"No. I asked, now you answer. How old are you?"

He was flustered and red now. "Cinquante sept," he responded.

"At least you have the good sense to be embarrassed now. Thank god for the little things." Syren turned to Emma.

"Emma?"

"I'm ready," she responded with a smile.

"Ama and Sarai, you're welcome to join us," Syren said.

The older man had trudged whence he came.

Syren blew raspberries from her lips and sighed."When will the bidding start Athena?"

"Soon."

"Ugh."

Alex watched her with a slight smile on his lips. He'd never seen her so petulant in the confines of her office.

"Patience," Athena cautioned.

"Alex, you're amused?" Syren asked when she caught the handsome smile on his lips from a wary glance. It was the first time she'd allowed herself to look at him, truly look at him all day but now that she did he was striking. She stared into his eyes, mischievously testing the limits of her charms. 'Would he be flustered' she wondered inwardly.

"No," he said plainly without a stutter as he stared back, "not at all. You just seem very bored."

"I am!" she said with a chuckle then reluctantly broke the stare and turned to Emma, Sarai, and Ama. "Allons-y, Allons-y," she sang.

She was intrigued by Alex. it wasn't often anyone could return her gaze with equal intensity. A gaze that made her hot inside.

The sound of soft french jazz played by the live band emanated from all corners of the room and the front by the stage."Athena, I can't listen to this, I'd like some Earth Kitt or Jane Birkin, not this," Syren complained.

"I'll try," Athena said.

Syren stood waiting as Athena set out to complete the task but at the moment she was available, the guests began to flock to Syren's side, conversing about what she felt were unimportant matters but she indulged them all the same. Her plans of dance and foolishness for the night had been dashed and shattered. Soon after, the bidding began with speeches from several guests in attendance about the import of the cause. She spent a quarter of a million dollars on several offerings of the night.

At the end of the event, Alex and the team that accompanied her returned to their suites on the upper floors of the Four Seasons George V while Syren returned to High Palace. It was only to gather their belongings and rendezvous at the Charles De Gaulle airport where they boarded a large private aircraft to the Jomo Kenyatta airport in Nairobi, Kenya.

In the flight, Syren was cloistered from the group in her cabin of the aircraft. As she laid in bed, Athena's cy-vessel form announced to her that Ruby was calling from across the room. Syren answered immediately.

"Rue?" she said.

She had the habit of speaking aloud though the voices were only in her head.

"Hi Sy, I miss you," she greeted.

"I miss you too. What are you doing?"

"I'm watching tv, Fleur says I have to go to bed and it's not even that late."

"That sucks," Syren said with a smile.

"Um..when you come back can we do something together?" Ruby asked.

"Absolument!" Syren said, "what do you want to do?"

"Anything, I just want to hang with you?"

Syren thought for a moment, "well, when I get back it will be fashion week and I have to see a few shows, we can go together to one of them, get all dolled up and spend the day together."

"Oh my god, that's perfect. You're the best. I'm gonna call my friends. Bye."

Ruby hung up without waiting for a response.

"Athena-"

"I'll arrange the plans," Athena responded.

"Thank you," Syren said through a yawn.

"Would you like me to-"

"Yes."

Syren felt a low pulse emanating from the lump behind her neck and instantaneously she slipped into the blackness of sleep.

Chapter 4 - Hotel Serena

At the Jomo Kenyatta, seemingly the entire Kenyan government awaited them at the runways of the airport. When Syren descended her aircraft, she was immediately greeted by the president of Kenya, Reth Sironka, a tall, lanky man, who appeared younger in person than he did in the pictures Syren had seen of him.

The heat of the sun was in stark contrast to the coolness she'd left behind in her cabin of the plane and for a moment it made her dizzy. There were flashes of pictures taken from the Kenyan press and a few American journalists who had traveled independently to cover Syren's trip to Kenya.

Ama stood by her side, as she was responsible for the entire process of coordinating with the government and local authorities in opening the plant. The rest of the group stood back with Athena by the aircraft.

"Syren, this is President Reth Sironka," Ama said, "President Sironka, this is Syren Prinsloo Excellci, the owner and CEO of Excellci Corp."

"Wow, w-" he stopped to clear his throat, "welcome to Kenya," the president greeted with a smile.

"Thank you for having me, President Sironka," Syren said with a smile and a wave.

She walked beside the president, dressed in a cream button-down silk shirt and matching pants of a cotton blend fabric. She thought her fashion choice would aid with the heat but so far, it had done nothing of the sort.

"I just would like to personally tell you how much the Kenyan people appreciate what you've done here. Oftentimes when foreigners come to Kenya, they come under the guise of conducting charity or giving aid but that's not what the Kenyan people want. They want good-paying jobs that provide shelter and help them to take care of their children, in this case, you offer much more than a good-paying job, you offer a lifestyle change for all of the workers hired at your plant. You pay the rates on par with U.S. workers and I tell you, it's more than appreciated, there are no words to summarize our gratitude for choosing Kenya."

Syren smiled warmly, "thank you so much and I agree with your sentiments exactly but I'd just like to add that I think I'm getting as much from this partnership as my workers are. The people of Kenya are very hardworking and I think that fact is well known so it's about time they got paid commensurate with their dedication. I'm excited to be in a beautiful country but I'll tell you, I'm even more excited to see my factory," Syren said with a smile.

The president chuckled and nodded, "very well said Ms. Excellci, we'll head there right away."

"Oh stop with that nonsense, call me Syren," she said with a smile. "I expect we'll be good friends in the future as long as this partnership stands."

"I expect the same," the president returned with a shy smile. "We have a few key members of the senate and some of my officials that I'd really appreciate if you would meet. They were instrumental in bringing the plant to fruition."

"Oh, of course, I would love to," Syren responded.

After working her way through a large greeting party, Syren's group along with the Kenyan delegation headed off to the Excellci shield manufacturing plant. Syren toured the facilities, consulted with workers about conditions and complaints so far in the past month the plant had been operational. She reviewed inventory and asset management and then they had a brief ribbon-cutting ceremony.

In the night, they returned to Nairobi and resigned at Hotel Serena. It was beautiful and in the night as she sat outside the banks of the pool, she could finally experience the enchanting beauty that is Kenya in the night time. At night the heat was more bearable.

She was wet from her swim and the only reason she'd left the pool was to further indulge in the mandazi treats she had requested from the hotel kitchen. She first tried them earlier at the greeting party at the hotel and loved them so much she requested them again. The hotel's version of the treat was even more delectable than the original.

A guard stood in each corner of the large, empty pool deck as none of the hotel guests were allowed to venture to the deck during her stay. She rented the entire area along with a floor for her guests.

"Someone is coming," Athena said.

"Who?"

"Alexander," Athena responded.

"Interesting," Syren said then she allowed herself to fall into the glowing blue water of the pool. When she reached up for air moments later, Alex stood on the banks of the pool.

"I didn't know you were out here," he began, "I can leave if you want to be alone," he said.

"That's not necessary," she said as she stared at him with esoteric, indigo eyes.

Alex nodded and took in a deep breath he felt as if he hadn't been able to grasp before. He stepped down the stairs of the pool until he was waist-deep in the water.

He wore a t-shirt and shorts that seemed inappropriate for swimming.

"Don't stare at my horrible choice of clothing," Alex said, as if he'd read Syren's mind, "I didn't expect to be swimming so I didn't bring swimwear." He said the words then dove into the water. He was to the other end of the very large pool quicker than she thought possible. Syren climbed back unto the banks and ate another mandazi.

Alex came up for air only to see Syren sitting and a bathing suit the same tone as her skin. She almost looked nude, a sight he couldn't stand, so he quickly went back underwater. No air was preferable to having to gawk uncomfortably at Syren.

After coming up for air several times he realized he'd taken a rather ridiculous approach. His solution was to leave, it seemed to be the only resolution to his plight. As soon as he made the decision he thought better than to tarry. He quickly exited the pool.

"I'll see you tomorrow," he said.

"You won't," she said, "you'll head to New York with the team and I'll be staying here for just a while longer."

"Why?" he asked but then decided to retract, "nevermind, It's not my business. I should go."

"Why the rush," Syren asked, curiously.

Alex sighed, "no particular reason."

"If there's no reason then there's no rush," She countered.

Alex shook his head, "fine. I hope you'll appreciate my honesty when I tell you that I'm just not comfortable being here with you."

"Why?" she asked, flatly.

"Do I need to give a reason?" he said.

Alex found it difficult to converse with her while he stared everywhere except at her and he would have managed just fine if she didn't find his eyes everywhere they roamed and stared directly back at him, holding him accountable. She noticed he wouldn't let her in and that was never a good sign. Someone who couldn't look her in the eye was someone who had something to hide.

The things that she did to his heart rate, to his thoughts, to his senses, were more than unfair, they were cruel and it never felt more so than when she was peering into him.

"I can't resolve the issue if you don't tell me."

"There's nothing you can do to correct it and you shouldn't have to."

"What is it?" she asked again, impatiently.

"Excuse me," Alex said then turned and headed back to the main villa of the hotel.

Syren had the urge to press on but decided against it. If he said he was uncomfortable then she'd respect his feelings, though she suspected it might only have been because of her rather skimpy swim attire. Still, she thought he had more nerve than to duck away like a frightened boy.

She spent a while longer by the pool but her mood had soured. She returned to her suite before she had originally intended and retired for the night.

The following day, Alex and the team returned to New York, while Syren flew to Botswana, for a short visit to an elephant sanctuary of which she was the sole benefactor. After touring the grounds she was quick to make her way back to the airfield and even quicker to return to New York. She was back in the city by Tuesday night and in the office on Wednesday morning.

Chapter 5 - The 40th floor

She met Alex on the 40th floor in her personal lab space. With the unveiling behind them and initial pre-sale numbers quite a bit higher than expected, it was time to decide what new ideas, created by her team she wanted to bring into production. There was also another large project she'd been working on but she wasn't ready to reveal it to the world as yet.

The lab at High Palace had much more advanced technology than what was produced at Excellci Corp but her mother had always warned her that the world wasn't ready for the kind of technology they were capable of producing. They took a safer approach, releasing products advanced enough to stay miles above their competition but not advanced enough to maximize their capability. It was a preferable business model and it had worked for over half a millennia.

Athena had asked Alex to wear casual clothing of his choice since they would be spending the day in the lab and not the office and would continue to do so for weeks. Casual for Alex, Syren realized, meant a white t-shirt, blank chinos, and an old blue jean jacket with black old skools. It was the first time he looked younger than the twenty years he claimed to be. Casual for Syren, meant black leather mini skirt, black sheer tights, oversized black sweater, and old black converse sneakers. Much of the same.

"Good morning Alexander," she greeted.

"Good morning," he returned.

"How was your day off?" Syren asked.

"Useful, I caught up on some research work I'd been ignoring," he said.

"Oh, good for you, procrastination has been the doom of many," she said, peering into his eyes, though it was more difficult now than just a few days earlier and for no particular reason since he stood just as handsome in a suit as he did in chinos and a t-shirt. Syren turned to the door. "And finally, to the part you came for," Syren said as she accessed the lab security system with a scan of her palm then retina.

"These past few days haven't been so bad," Alex said softly.

Syren smiled as the door opened. Syren had such a sweet friendly smile that it warmed him inside every time he saw it. She reminded him of the women from the early 20th century. She had the same edge of performative daintiness and charisma.

He quickly pushed his comparisons to the side and focused on the task at hand.

When he stepped inside the lab he wasn't surprised. It was state of the art. More advanced than any lab he'd ever had the pleasure of working in and in the past few years he'd found himself in some of the best university research labs in the country and still Syren had them beat.

"Wow," he said, feigning shock.

"You don't seem that shocked?" she remarked.

"I just expected the best and you lived up to that so I guess maybe I'm not shocked."

Syren nodded, "I love being steeped in praise," she mused with a bright closed mouth smile, "and so we're going to work through some code today and I have to approve product samples."

Alex nodded with a smile, "sounds fun."

"I must ask though, are you comfortable working here alone with me? After the Hotel Serena, I'm not so sure."

"I'm quite comfortable today actually."

"Oh, what's changed between today and a few nights ago."

Alex shook his head, "you're going to make me say it, aren't you?"

"Whatever 'it' is, yes."

"Very well," he began, "I didn't want to look at you in a swimsuit. You're my boss and your seventeen."

She tilted her head side as she weighed his argument.

"Boss, I guess I understand but I'm seventeen and your twenty, not much of a difference in regards to age."

"It's quite a lot actually, to me, maybe not to you but it's a difference nonetheless and also there were no good choices. I either gawked at you or avoided you completely, so with that in mind I decided to remove myself from the situation altogether."

"Wise choice," Syren said. "Although, I don't know why the simple fact that I existed while wearing a bikini at a pool was enough to cause you such discomfort. All the same, I thank you for your honesty," she said mischievously.

"Of course you wouldn't understand, I don't suspect anyone has the gall to have ever made you uncomfortable," Alex countered.

"No one can make you uncomfortable Alex. Being uncomfortable is a choice you make."

"Well said but some of us are only human, after all."

"I'm human."

Alex shrugged which confused Syren but she decided not to press on.

When they weren't in the lab working on code, approving software updates, and products, they were on business trips. They'd gone to Nigeria and then to Burkina Faso, to tour another of Syren's manufacturing plants. In Zambia and Rwanda and Benin, they visited the opening of three more plants. There was another trip to Paris, to the old Excellci headquarters and to China.

After weeks of being close to Alex, Syren had grown fond of him. He seemed to be the opposite of everything she'd assumed of boys his age. Most surprisingly, he's managed to never seem interested in her beyond a professional relationship. It was a new thing for her; to have a man, younger or older, not manifest any hint of attraction to her. She would have been insulted if she didn't find it amusing. Nevertheless, it was moot, he was her intern and while she found respite in fantasizing about the possibilities, there were no actual possibilities because they would never be anything more. She'd told herself this multiple times but still, she struggled to believe it.

It was another of their lab days, now in mid-October.

"What would you like for lunch?" Syren asked.

They'd worked into a comfortable routine.

"I'm not sure. I'll just go and get something later."

"Nonsense," Syren said, "my chef prepared orange chicken for me. It's my favorite."

"Yes, I know," he said, "you have it every other day we're here."

"Good, so you must know how spectacular the chicken is. Would you like some?"

"Does anyone refuse you?" Alex asked with a smile.

Syren smiled a warm smile at him, "tell Gus to serve for two," she said though Athena wasn't in the room.

"What?" Alex asked. "Oh- Athena, right?"

"Yep," Syren responded.

Syren had already told Alex the lie about the ear chip she had in her ear that kept her in contact with Athena.

Syren was quiet for a moment before she began. She'd been trying not to delve into his personal life or to talk about anything personally really but then she found herself wondering if that rule was really necessary. She questioned it until she decided it was arbitrary and convinced herself to break it.

"What are your plans after you leave MIT?" she asked. "You'll be Dr. West, though I'll admit the Ph.D. is much too pretentious for my tastes. I would have preferred you as an M.D. "

"Would you now?"

"Very much. At least an M.D. is useful."

"Ouch," he responded as he pressed his palm against his heart, feigning hurt with a dazzling smile.

"Is that mean? I don't mean to be mean," she said, with a tone of regret.

"No, it's not," he said with a sideways smile, "It's true and I did consider that before I changed programs. To be forthright, I haven't quite figured out what happens after."

"Why not?"

"Because I don't know what I want. I have one very specific goal that I need to accomplish, after that, I'm quite alright with anything."

"So you're an academic, that's it. You just want the degree and the title."

"I never said that. You don't even know what the goal is."

"Fine, maybe I assumed…" she said with an airy laugh.

"Your life seems to have been planned from the moment you were born. Not all of us have a path laid out for us, we have to choose, and more often than not the choice isn't easy."

"I suppose but neither is it easy to have your path chosen for you. I have had my life planned for me that's true but it's not what I wanted," she said. "For you, you could change your mind, you could decide. I can't."

"But of course you can," he countered. "You could appoint someone else as CEO and have them run your company while you pursue whatever venture you'd like." he smiled, "will it be modeling like your sister?"

"God no," she said with an insulted scowl. "I can't disappoint my mother. This is what she wanted. This is what every ancestor I've ever known has done. It's bigger than me."

"Maybe...but I still think you could," was all Alex responded.

"Gus says to make your way up," Athena said to her telepathically.

"We'll be right there," Syren said lightly.

"That was Athena?" Alex asked.

Syren stood and spoke. "Yes. Let's go, he's almost done."

When Alex entered Syren's apartment there wasn't much time to absorb the decor before he was whisked to the kitchen by a well-dressed butler who introduced himself as Tumas. Syren washed her hands at a small marble sink just outside the kitchen and Alex did the same before they sat at the kitchen island and were served by Gus. Syren watched as Alex tasted the small bit of chicken.

"Tell me?" she said as he chewed, "isn't it the most delicious orange chicken you've ever had."

"It is," he said after he'd swallowed the bit of food.

She smiled and clapped excitedly then spoke with uncontained excitement, "did you hear Gus. You've made the best orange chicken he's ever tasted."

Alex smiled then bit another piece.

After lunch, as they made their way back to the lab Katherine met them at the door of Syren's condo. There were three girls with her.

They seemed dazed as they stared between Syren and Alex, dumbfounded at their collective beauty.

"Sy, I'm glad your here," Katherine began.

"Hello girls, how are you?" Syren said. "This is Alex."

"I'm Lizzy," the first girl said as she stretched her hand out for a shake.

She had wavy brown hair and dorky glasses. She had the appearance of a preteen though she was eighteen years old.

"Nice to meet you, Lizzy," Alexander said with a dazzling smile.

Lizzy seemed too dazed to respond.

"I'm Josie," another girl said. She was almost as tall as Syren with coiled hair pulled high into a ponytail. Her skin was beautiful ebony and her eyes were the same shade.

"Nice to meet you Josie, such a pretty name," Alex said with a smile.

"Oh Jesus," Josie mumbled.

"I'm Skylar," the last girl said.

"Nice to meet you as well Skylar"

Skylar blushed in response and tucked an imaginary loose strand of her strawberry blonde hair behind her ear. She had multicolored braces that distracted from her plain features with a nose that was round as a maraschino cherry.

"So uh...wow you're like really smart it must suck to miss high school huh?" the girl named Lizzy asked Alex. She'd heard Katherine gush about his beauty on several occasions.

Alex shook his head, "no, not particularly."

"He's as boring as Syren," Katherine said.

"No, he's not," Lizzy said in defense of Alex, though she'd only known him for minutes. "You're kind of beautiful...like bad," she said it as if she would explode if she'd kept it inside.

"You're one to talk," Alex responded kindly.

Lizzy blushed heavily at the compliment and finally stopped talking to give herself a moment to recover. Syren found herself growing annoyed at the exchange.

"We should be going now, I'll see you later Katherine," Syren said. Before she could walk Katherine handed her a small papyrus card.

"What's this?" Syren asked.

"It's an invite to Ben's birthday party later," Katherine said."It'll be at Press, you know where everyone goes to eat every weekend- well you don't know because you don't go anywhere - but his dad rented out the location for the night. You're going."Katherine looked to Syren then to Alex. "You too Alex. You're coming."

"I don't think so, Katherine. I probably won't be able to make it-"

"-Yes you are. We're all going tonight, that's why my friends are here. They'll be sleeping over and for once in your life, you'll get to experience a fun, age-appropriate night Syren."

"Yeah, Ben's dad is loaded, so I know this party will be fun," Lizzy said.

"We'll talk about this later, Kat."

"He's my boyfriend and he invited you. You're coming," Katherine said.

"Please," Lizzy begged.

Syren relented. "Fine, fine, fine."

Lizzy smiled and nodded. They had become good friends over the past month and she was glad because friendship with someone like Syren was not something she ever thought possible for her. Though she went to a high tuition private school, it was through a scholarship from the state, which was how most of the lower-income students were able to attend the school. It was either through a scholarship from the state or Locke school, or they were scouted for sports. Her mother was a professor and her father was a lawyer and still, their income was on the lower end of what most parent's made in the school.

"Alex?" Katherine called.

"I'm not a fan of parties and I live 40 minutes outside of the city anyways, to drive forty minutes home and then forty minutes back and then do it all again at probably two in the morning doesn't sound fun."

"You should come. I've never really been to many birthday parties with kids my age before and I'm guessing you haven't either. It might be fun..." Syren said.

"I'll try," he said with a nod, trying not to give in to Syren's request right away.

"And if you want I can have one of my drivers take you home...if you can't drive yourself."

"I don't drink so I think I'll be fine to drive."

"Sure but you might be exhausted..."

He nodded "okay."

"And," Katherine began, "we were thinking that after the party we could go to Coney Island and hang out."

"Won't that be too late?" Syren asked.

"Maybe to you, granny."

Syren cackled, "gosh. Okay."

"We could leave early. If the park isn't open, we'll sneak onto the beach," Katherine suggested.

Lizzy nodded in agreement.

"Whatever you say, Kat," Syren responded.

"I'm glad you're coming, Alex," Before he could respond Katherine smiled and cut him off, "I'll see you tonight."

"You don't take no for an answer, do you?" he asked Katherine.

"People tell me no about as much as they tell Syren no," Katherine said with a smile.

Outside of her apartment, once she was allowed to leave she stopped Alex.

"You don't have to come - I only said the things I said because I knew Katherine wouldn't let you leave if we didn't placate her."

"I already told them I would attend, I won't go back on my word."

"Honor. I've heard of it but I don't actually have any myself."

Alex chuckled, "I keep a bit just for credibility."

Syren smiled at him and handed him the invitation. "You should take the rest of the day. The invite says 8 pm but why don't you meet us there at 9 or 9:30?"

"I'll see you later then," he said with a nod as he took the invite and headed for the elevators. "The chicken was delicious."

"I know," Syren said with a smile.

He arrived home after a forty-minute drive. The suburbs of Park Hills were where wealthy New Yorkers found sanctuary outside of the city. The homes were large and secluded. His was the largest on the terrace, much too large for the three people who resided there.

It was in the french architectural style with a grey brick exterior that stood three stories high. The windows were so large that you could see clearly inside the rooms of the house on each level.

When he let himself in he saw his brother, Seth, standing in the foyer underneath the large crystal chandelier, waiting for him.

Seth was older than Alex and handsome too, just not as handsome. A cocky grin was never far from his thin lips. He resembled his father that way. His hair was dirty blonde and the length brushed past his shoulders.

"What?" Alex asked.

"Anything?" he asked.

"No."

"You have to try harder," Seth said, "we need her back."

They were all frustrated. Isis had been gone for years now and there was no telling what was being done to her but with history as a guide, it was nothing good. She was the glue that brought them together, the oldest of the quartet and with her gone, they were falling apart.

Alex took his phone from his pocket and turned it off before he spoke.

"There's nothing else I can do, she's smart, if I try too hard then it won't work."

"We've been preparing for this for a very long Alex," his brother stepped closer, "you just need a second to do it."

"It's not that easy and you know it," he said, the tone of frustration was thick on his voice.

"I never said it was - you've had weeks now," his brother retorted, "have you checked for shields? What about her guards-"

"You know we can't talk about this," Alex barked.

He pushed past his brother and walked up the white concrete bifurcated staircase that led up to the second-floor hallway. He dropped his gym bag in his bedroom then turned his cellphone back on. After checking to make sure there were no messages, he headed to the bathroom for a hot shower, there was a lot he needed to contemplate.

Chapter 6 - Ben's Party

"Are you guys hungry?" Katherine asked the group.

"Yeah, I'm starving," Lizzy responded.

"I'm pretty hungry too," Josie said.

Skylar nodded in agreement.

"What do you guys want?"

"Anything," Lizzy said.

The group seemed to agree.

"Okay, I'll be right back," Katherine said.

Tumas appeared from the hallway. "Can I take your bags ladies?" he asked.

All three girls looked at the short, plump man with blonde hair slicked back.

"No, we're good," Skylar said.

"Are you sure?"

They began to second guess themselves and then agreed. He took their bags and placed each one in a separate guest room that had the girls' names placed on the door on white placards.

Syren walked through the front doors.

"I thought you were going to your office," Lizzy asked.

"I've decided to abandon my responsibilities for the day. I'm going to be a teenager." Syren said.

Skylar and Josie nodded in agreement, "good."

"Gus is on it, he's making us sandwiches…" Katherine said as she walked from the direction of the kitchen."Oh- Sy, you're back."

Syren nodded.

"Are you staying?" Katherine asked.

"Yes," Lizzy answered excitedly.

"Um..why don't we go up to my closet," Syren suggested.

The girls followed Syren and Katherine to Syren quarters. It consisted of her bedroom, private bathroom, office, and a very large closet.

"What time do you want us to head to the party, it starts at 8," Katherine said as she sat on the tufted pink velvet sofa.

"Like 9:30 at least," Lizzy suggested.

"Yeah, we can't get there too early, it'll be lame," Josie added.

"Okay, 9:30 then, that's what I told Alex." Syren agreed.

"Look at your closet?" Lizzy said, awestruck.

There were too many shoes and clothes and purses to count.

Syren walked to the rack of dresses and began flipping through them. All her clothes were arranged by color and she already knew she wanted to wear black. There were some clothes assorted on a rack on the other side of the room. Clothes her stylists had set aside for work events.

"Wear something short," Katherine said.

Syren shrugged.

"For Alex," she added knowing it would annoy her.

"That's enough!" Syren grunted and jumped on her without pause and they both fell to the floor from the couch. Lizzy, Josie, and Sklyar jumped back as they rolled and wrestled and laughed on the floor. When Syren got up she kicked Katherine playfully on the leg then walked back to the dresses.

"Katherine said it so I have to ask. Are you and Alex thing because everyone thinks so," Lizzy said, finally feeling brave enough to ask. "It's all the gossip blogs talk about because he's always with you on trips and stuff."

"He's my intern," Syren said flatly.

"He's really handsome and he's so sweet, and hot, he is so hot," Skylar added.

"So?" Syren shot back.

They pulled back. Katherine finally stood from the floor.

"I'm going to my bathroom, I'll be back," she said as she walked out, fixing her tousled hair.

"Something pink would look pretty on you," Lizzy suggested.

"I do love pink but if I wear it, I just feel like I'll stand out too much," Syren said. "Did Katherine tell you if she hired hair and makeup?"

"Yes," They responded.

"I'm so excited, we're gonna look so hot," Josie exclaimed.

Katherine returned. "What are you gonna wear?" she asked.

"Black," Syren answered.

"I knew you were gonna say that, but it should be pink or blue," Katherine responded.

"That's what I told her," Skylar added.

"Okay, maybe I can do pink," Syren conceded.

"Why don't you own your freaking beauty," Katherine said, sounding frustrated.

"Kat it's not about owning my beauty. My self-esteem is fine. I'd just rather not attract any extra attention."

"Why not?"

"Because it's unnecessary," Syren responded.

"If I looked like you Syren, I would walk around like I knew it," Katherine said. "And even if you wrapped yourself in a blanket everyone is gonna be staring at you anyways so you should just wear what you want."

Syren hated when she spoke that way, it made her uncomfortable. Katherine was beautiful.

"I have skin a shade of brown, golden-white hair, my eyes change color and on top of that I'm two inches shy of six feet. I don't need any more attention, Katherine."

"Can I change your name in my phone from 'sister' to 'the worst'?"

"I'll wear the pink dress," she paused for dramatic effect, "happy?"

"Ecstatic," Katherine responded with a smile.

Ruby walked in."Sy, why didn't you tell me you were home," she said as she walked over and hugged Syren then Katherine.

"Where's dad?" Syren asked. "Did he pick you up from school?"

"No. He's at the studio downstairs, I guess he was missing your mom Syren and he said his soul craved musical energy or something..."

Katherine looked to Syren.

"You should go talk to him," she said.

"I know how this ends, it only upsets him and then he cries and it makes me sad," she said with a shrug and a sigh, still intending to try. "I'll be right back."

Syren left the downstairs studio, a gift she'd made for her father a few years ago. She found him sitting by his custom black Steinway piano, singing to himself.

"Why do birds suddenly appear

Every time you are near?

Just like me, they long to be...

Close to you..."

Her father had the most beautiful voice she'd ever heard, besides her mother. He'd been famous for most of his life for his mellifluous voice. First, he was in a musical group with his siblings and then eventually he branched off into a solo career. Now, he was one of the best selling musicians in the world.

"Daddy?" she called.

He turned around. A heartbreaking sadness clouded his features to distortion. With one look at her, he turned back to the piano and continued playing. Syren walked to the piano bench and sat beside him.

"Do you need a minute? I can leave..."

He turned to her. The sadness hadn't moved an inch. He took her hands and kissed it softly.

"Oh sweetie, I never want you to leave..it's just that sometimes I miss her too much and it's hard because every time I look at you, I see her." Tears suddenly weld up in his eyes, as if an emotional damn broke when he said the words. Syren wiped them away and hugged him but said nothing. After a few silent moments, he seemed to gain the strength to sit up from her shoulder.

"Did I tell you the story of your birth?" he asked, with a small smile now. He told her the story every few weeks. Without waiting for a response he continued."How the second I looked at you I was enchanted."

Syren's lips curved into a small, shy smile, "I know daddy."

He was such a gentle soul. It made her heartache.

"I should've named you Enchanted, that's a beautiful name."

"That's the worst name ever, daddy. It's not even a name, it's a feeling."

"Well, it would have been accurate. You enchant everyone around you, just like your mother."

He pinched her high cheekbones and smiled even wider.

"Aren't you going to a party tonight?" he asked.

"Yeah," she answered. "How do you know?"

"Katherine told me yesterday."

"Of course she did."

"What are you doing down here? Go, go get ready, and have fun." He practically shoved her off the bench.

"I'm going, I'm going," she said as she quickly left the room.

Teddy sat for a moment until he closed the key lid and broke down in tears, once again overcome from the grief of his lost wife.

Upstairs, Syren found Katherine, her three friends, and Ruby eating lobster rolls on the floor of her closet with an assortment of pink dresses pulled from the rack of multicolored dresses.

Ruby jumped up and grabbed one of the dresses.

"This one," Ruby said as she held the dress in the air, displaying it.

It was short, tight, and pink and it had a matching long boxy blazer the exact same shade of bubblegum pink.

"Fine," Syren said, "the blazer sold me. Where's my roll?"

"Gus said you just ate," Ruby said.

"Athena?" she called.

The program appeared in the center of the room. In the form of a violet light sphere. It looked like a brain, with some area of violet more concentrated than others and some areas blinking as if she was thinking.

"Can you ask Gus if he can make another?"

"Sure."

The violet light disappeared.

"What the hell was that?" Lizzy asked.

All three girls were now sporting ashen, shocked faces.

"That's my virtual assistant, she's a program named Athena. I also have an actual assistant named Athen but it's just a coincidence," she lied.

Syren turned around and walked to her wall of shoes. She picked a pair of nude ankle-strap stilettos and dropped them on the floor. They were four inches high.

Gus appeared a few minutes later, clearing his throat to announce himself.

"Thanks so much, Gus," Syren said as she took the small tray with a lobster roll and glass of sparkling water with lemon. She guessed that Gus, who was well familiar with her appetite had set a roll aside for her.

"No problem, anything else I can get for you girls?" he said as he stroked with his silver goatee. His look was always stern until he smiled and his english was accented with french. Most of the house staff at Syren's condo were imported from High palace and had served her mother and grandmother.

Syren shook her head. "No thank you, and this looks delicious. I can't wait to eat it."

He smiled, nodded, and left.

Hours later hair and makeup had arrived. They were all showered and sporting white robes. Syren's closet was where Katherine had a hairstylist and make-up artist set up. Skylar went first. She usually wore her hair in a wild, curly but tonight she asked the stylist to straighten it. It reached her mid-back when it was finished. Her make up was soft and pretty. Lizzy was next, she asked for the same hair as Skylar with a smoky eye look. Josie didn't want her face done and asked her usually coily hair to be pulled into a high ponytail. Katherine asked for a ponytail as well, only with half her hair up and the rest curled down her back.

"What would you like, Sy?" James asked he was their go-to stylist.

"I don't know, curly maybe?" she responded.

"Finger waves, side part," James said matter-of-factly.

His partner Sadie nodded in agreement beside him.

"Sure, yea," Syren responded.

"And I know just what look to give you," Sadie added.

Syren hair usually reached the small of her back. With the finger waves, it was a few inches higher up.

"I love it," Ruby said excitedly.

Ruby, her doting younger sister was never far from her, especially if she felt something exciting was afoot.

"Thanks, Rue."

It was almost 9 pm when they each went to get dressed. They arrived at the event an hour later. When the black SUV parked on the curb, immediately a flock of paparazzi swarmed the car. Syren was the last to exit the car. She was surrounded by six bodyguards in a phalanx blocking the photographers from her with their bodies. She felt eyes on her, that was usual. She was about one hundred feet from the entrance of the party, not a long walk.

There was a line of students with invitations waiting to get in. As she walked down the curb with the girls she could hear paparazzi screaming her name. She blocked them out and scanned the line as she walked, wondering if she would see Alex. She was almost at the entrance when the familiar jet black curls drew her eyes.

There was no need to see his face to know it was him. She wasn't sure if he saw her but as she walked past she stuck out her arm and grabbed him and smoothly pulled him into their group. Without missing a moment, her guards welcomed him into the square and kept walking. At the entrance, her group was allowed in without pause. It took a few seconds for her to register the fact that it was her first time touching him in the almost two months she'd known him. His fingers were long and tense which instinctively made her grab then tighter.

Once inside, her guards broke the square and allowed them to wander. She let go of his hand and Alex finally had the chance to see her.

"Woah," the word escaped before he could contain it. He was flustered and he hated to be flustered. He worked very hard not to be flustered because of Syren and her appearance but still, he was flustered.

"What?" she asked.

The music still hadn't reached full volume as they were still separated by another door from the event space.

"Wh-uh-no-nothing," he said, tongue-tied and growing more embarrassed by his display as the seconds passed.

She wasn't just beautiful, she was otherworldly. He simultaneously couldn't look at her nor could he keep his eyes off her. The choices left him at an unfortunate impasse once again.

His reaction sent her cheeks flushing. She knew when she got dressed up the way she did, for a party that she otherwise would have no interest in attending if not for his presence, she was searching for some reaction from him. The one he gave was exactly perfect.

"Um..you came?" she said, searching for anything to distract them from the uncomfortable moment.

"Yes, I said I would."

"Ah, there's that honor again," she teased.

"Sy?" Lizzy called from down the hall.

She hadn't realized they kept walking without her.

"Let's go," she said with a small unreadable smile.

He wasn't sure what the smile meant but he returned it. He walked slightly ahead of her because he didn't want to stare, which allowed Syren to do just that. She started at the bottom with the black old skool vans sneakers. His black chino pants seemed tailored perfectly to his toned legs. He stuffed his hands into his pockets as he walked down the hall. Syren kept examining him. The way he walked, relaxed but alert enough that he seemed prepared for anything. He wore a long-sleeve, loosely hung white t-shirt. He was perfect.

Suddenly he turned and looked back at her as if he left her eyes dissecting him. Their eyes met for the briefest moment still not at eye level. She wore four-inch heels but he had an inch over her.

He turned around, they were at the second entrance.

Alex opened the door and immediately, they were swallowed by loud cacophonic music and chatter.

The girls walked in, then Syren and finally Alex, who let the door close behind him.

Ben greeted Syren immediately then he hugged Katherine and kissed her lips, "you guys look amazing." He screamed over the music. "My table's over there," he said even louder. He cupped his hands around his mouth as if that amplified his voice. He was wearing another version of the same stupid Connecticut casual outfit he wore every time Syren had seen him. Khaki pants, a colored shirt, and a distracting tie pattern with a blazer.

He turned to Alex.

"Hey man."

Alex nodded but said nothing. Ben seemed annoyed that Alex was there.

"Hey you guys wanna follow me to the section?" he asked again.

Katherine nodded and the group followed him to the empty section her guards had set aside for them. At the roped-off section of the venue, they ordered virgin drinks that her guards were attentive to make sure nothing was slipped in from the staff or anyone else. Guests at the party snuck pictures of Syren as they sat waiting.

After the first round of drinks, Katherine pulled Syren from the sofa.

"We're dancing," she yelled. "Are coming, Alex?"

He shook his head and mouthed, "no."

The group of them left him and headed to the center of the room where everyone danced. Katherine danced circles around Syren until Syren was forced to join in. She began to enjoy the music much quicker than she expected. They played what she liked and she wondered if Katherine had something to do with it.

"You are the dancing queen

Young and sweet

Only seventeen

Dancing queen

Feel the beat from the tambourine

You can dance

You can jive

Having the time of your life

See that girl

Watch that scene

Dig in the dancing queen."

She sang the words to Katherine and Katherine sang them back to her as they danced. Alex smiled as he watched her. He'd never seen her so careless as she was when she danced with Katherine. She somehow still seemed dainty compared to everyone else but that might have been why he was so amused as he watched her.

After an hour of being bombarded by loud music and occasionally stealing glimpses at Alex, Syren was ready to leave.

"Hey," she said, leaning into Katherine's ear, "are you ready to leave?"

"Not really, are you?" she said close to Syren's ear.

Syren nodded.

"Okay..um..let me ask the girls…"

She asked Josie, who was ready to go. Skylar agreed but Lizzy wanted to stay or at least spend another half hour. After a few more ear whispers, Syren agreed to stay another half an hour.

Katherine went to tell Ben that she was leaving and Syren could see him pleading for more time but Katherine wasn't moved.

"We're leaving now, are you still coming with us?' she leaned and whispered in his ear. His scent filled her nose so sweetly that she almost tasted the musk on her tongue. She'd never been close enough to him to catch his light scent.

She stepped back after saying the words and waited for his response. He pulled her close to him by the arm and whispered, "yes."

Chapter 7 - Coney Island Queen

As she walked in front of him, this time he was the one staring. Her legs seemed unending and were made even longer by her heels. They were toned and thin. He stopped himself at her legs when he felt his pulse racing at the thought of roaming higher. Syren stopped at the door before the last exit.

"There's no space in the car for Alex," she wondered aloud.

"I drove," he said matter-of-factly, glad his mind was now elsewhere.

"I know but you shouldn't drive alone. Do you want me to drive with you?"

Without thinking he nodded.

Katherine wiggled her eyebrows suggestively and smiled but never faced Syren. She didn't want to do anything that would break the streak that they seemed to be on.

Syren looked to her guards.

"We'll follow behind," Enguerrand said. His voice was so smooth it sounded fake.

"Do you know where my car is?" Alex asked.

The man nodded.

Onfroi, another guard opened the door and again they were enveloped in a phalanx. Once again, paparazzi swarmed them. This time it broke in two as they approached the black SUV that had ferried them to the event. A two guards led the four girls to the van while another quad continued with Syren and Alex further down to the parking garage where he parked his car. They knew the exact spot where he parked his car on the second floor and when they arrived on foot, there was already a van with one guard beside Alex's silver Mercedes SLS AMG. The guards broke apart around them and headed to their SUV.

Alex opened the gullwing door on the passenger's side for Syren. She slowly stepped in and strapped the seatbelt across her torso. In a flash Alex was on the other side, strapping himself in the driver's seat and adjusting the car for a trip. When he ignited the engine, his radio emanated through all speakers of the car. He lowered the volume down to a whisper.

Syren looked around the car. It wasn't the car he usually drove to work, that was a less flashy car, a black Mercedes sedan. She wondered how he could afford such a car. It cost two hundred thousand at least and she knew that because she was gifted one for her sixteenth birthday.

"Do you want me to look into it?" Athena asked as the thought crossed her mind.

"No," Syren answered.

"What?" Alex asked her.

"Nothing," She responded.

At the entrance of the parking garage, Katherine's SUV waited for them. He pulled out in the street behind them with blinding camera flashes in his eyes for a few seconds before they disappeared behind him. She realized how much their presence together would be dissected in the media but she'd pushed those worries to another day.

Once they were a few blocks from the chaos, Syren relaxed in her seat. He kept his eyes on the road, not interested in that added stress the response of looking at her legs would cause to his senses.

They'd been driving for all of five minutes before Athena spoke in her ear.

"Katherine is attempting to call you, I'll put her through to your cell device," she said.

Syren's cell phone chimed in the large square pocket of her jacket moments later. She accepted the call and placed the phone by her ear.

"Kat?"

"We're gonna stop and get liquor, do you want anything?"

"No, I don't need any alcohol Kat," Syren answered blankly. "Who's getting it for you anyway?"

"Guiscard- umm...Ask Alex," Katherine requested.

"Alex do you want-"

"No," he said before she could finish.

"He doesn't want any."

Syren hung up.

"Do you drink alcohol?" she asked, "at all."

"Not really."

"Why not?" she pressed.

"It just doesn't do anything for me. Do you?" he queried.

"I've had a sip here and there but no, not really- it tastes bad," she said with a scowl. "Also I'm underage and if the press found me drinking alcohol, I'd be forever known as a drunk."

He was silent for a moment when he spoke just before the silence became awkward.

"You look really beautiful tonight," he said, his eyes were still staring straight ahead, "well...you always do."

"Thanks. I should say you too, right?" she said with red flushed upon her cheek.

He chuckled amusingly."You don't have to."

"You too."

His lips curved into a half-smile.

"You should say thank you," she scolded playfully.

"Thank you," he began, "for my afterthought compliment."

Syren laughed lightly, "hey, at least I returned it."

Moses Sumney's doomed' began on the radio. He reached instinctively and raised the volume.

"You like this song?" she asked.

"I love it."

"I do too but I prefer to listen to it when I want to be reflective and sad."

"Me too..well...I don't intend to be reflective and sad right now but I just can't change it. It's too good."

She smiled, "How did you find out about him? He's sort of new."

"It played in the end credits of a show and I couldn't get it out of my head after hearing it so I searched online until I found it. How did you?"

"He records at my dad's studio, we met once and he asked me to listen to a single of his and I've been in love with his art since then."

"You win," he conceded.

"I'm not trying to," she said with a shy smile, "it's the truth."

Katherine's SUV turned off and stopped across the street from a liquor store.

"Just keep going? Do you know the way?"

He nodded.

"Can I ask you something?" he said after they'd hit the expressway.

"Um..sure," she answered, slightly hesitant because whenever someone preceded a question with that question, anything that came after was personal or uncomfortable.

"You know what the colors mean- when your eyes change color? Don't you?"

He's already heard her say no to others but he decided to press again.

"Some of them yes, sometimes it'll be a random color that I can't connect to a feeling or a certain hormone increase."

"So each color means a different feeling or emotion?" he asked this but he already knew the answer.

"Yeah, I guess so. When I'm not feeling any overwhelming emotion they're blue. It ranges from light blue to dark. When I'm sad it's navy blue, grey or black. Black though means I have to be devastatingly sad. The first time they were that color was after my mom died or I guess the first time I noticed it was when my mom died."

"Really?" he said, his voice was disquieted.

"Yeah, red is when I'm angry. I have to be very angry..seething angry for it to be red though. There was gold a few times but I don't know what that means."

"Doesn't it change when you're happy?"

"I mean, if I'm feeling happy it's still blue, I don't know why it doesn't change with happiness. Although if I'm feeling any sort of affection for someone in a moment they'll turn lavender like my mom's. Her eyes were lavender and blue-lavender a lot with my father so I guess it's that way when you're in love too." She paused for a moment, wondering if it had been a wise decision to reveal the connection between her eyes and her emotion, it was something only a few people knew. "I never usually tell anyone this. It's kind of personal," she added.

"Yeah, and you don't want anyone to read into your emotions while you're experiencing them, right?"

"Would you want someone doing that to you?"

"No, not at all."

"Precisely," she said while fighting the smile that tugged on her lips. "Don't use it to psychoanalyze me."

He turned and looked at her eyes briefly. There was enough light from the street reflecting in the car for him to see them.

"Blue, that means you're not feeling anything? Did I get that right?" he asked with a smile before turning back to the road.

"Stop it," she whined. "And I didn't say it means I feel nothing, it just means there's a balance. Did you forget that part?"

"No, I didn't," he said with a chuckle, "what about your hair…"

"Don't get me started on that, it's extremely irritating," she mumbled.

"It's beautiful."

"No. Annoying. I have a special relationship with my hair. Is it more special than what anyone else has with their hair, I can't say."

"Why don't you dye it then?" he asked, curiously.

"My hair can't be dyed, I've tried. I thought about wearing a wig but I hated it."

"What do you mean it can't be dyed?"

"I mean, I've tried to dye it black or brown and it doesn't take, it washes right out instantly as if it was never there and so instead of having it dyed, I'm just smothered in dye all over. It's a very messy affair and you only make that mistake once. In my case, it's been four times."

"That's…something," he was genuinely surprised at this.

"Yeah, I can't cut my hair either, it hurts like I'm cutting a limb or something. The most a can cut from it is maybe an inch or two off the bottom and it only stings but anything more and it's painful. Even when I cut the inch off it grows back after a few nights."

"So that's why it's so long…"

"Yes, I'd give anything for a short cut or a bob or anything different," she complained.

"So your hair is kind of alive," he joked, glimpsing at her before he turned his eyes back to the road.

"I don't know. It certainly has a mind of its own," she said with a smile. "I can curl it though and straighten it, the heat doesn't affect it. Thank god because otherwise, it'd be a mess."

"Can I call you Rapunzel?" Alex asked with a boyish grin.

"Not if you want to keep your tongue," Syren mumbled.

Alex chuckled lightly and shook his head, " Can I call you 'Not Rapunzel'?

"No," she yowled.

"Fine," he said with a chuckle.

When they arrived at the beach, Katherine and the girls met them on Surf Avenue where all the beach shops and restaurants were. Luckily, they were still open even though it was after midnight and Katherine swore they would be closed because the website said so.

"What should we do? Should we eat or should we get on a ride or something-"

"Eat?" Syren said before Kat could finish.

"Of course you wanna eat," Katherine commented with an eye roll.

"I can't be the only hungry one here?" Syren asked.

"No, I'm starving too," Lizzy agreed.

"Yeah, I think I want a hamburger and we need to hurry because I think the shops will close soon, Josie said.

"I want cheese fries," Syren said as she looked at the white Nathan's sign, above the entrance of the restaurant.

Katherine looked around and noticed inquisitive eyes watching them and she knew it would only moments before a crowd gathered.

"If you go in there everyone's gonna know you're here and it's gonna get crazy. Why don't you and Alex go to the beach and wait for us and we'll get food. What do you want?"

Syren thought for a moment.

"I want cheese fries with bacon, a double cheeseburger with bacon and mozzarella cheese or swiss, not american and um..ginger ale and if you can find a funnel cake with strawberries and whipped cream then get it and oh please don't forget cotton candy."

Alex's mouth fell open and then curved into a smile.

"You are insane? I don't care if people see you, just order your own food," Katherine said.

Syren smiled cheekily, "perfect," she said with a wiggle of her eyebrows.

They stopped at a beach shack on the boardwalk and ordered food. Syren's guards never strayed far from them but now a small crowd was scarcely gathering and capturing pictures of the group on their phones.

After ordering food, they stood at the high tables waiting for it to be prepared. "You can't walk straight to the beach," Athena said in her ear, "you will be followed."

"What do you suggest," she asked in a voiceless response.

"Walk up to Mermaid Avenue, go across four blocks, and then walk back down to Surf Avenue. Continue to Poseidon playground and from there you can enter the beach. I'm not sensing any heat signatures for hundreds of meters from there. It is empty -someone is approaching," Athena said.

Syren turned around and saw a little girl. She looked to be no more than ten years old and reminded her of Ruby with her mocha skin and short curly hair pulled into two pigtails.

"Um…" she began in a soft, small voice, "can I take a picture with you?"

In her hand was a sleek silver Excellci Corp Ex-phone, the latest one, made from clear glass.

Syren smiled at her warmly. "Sure," she responded.

She stooped down in her heels beside the little girl.

"What's your name?" Syren asked.

"Chanel," the girl responded, awestruck.

"Such a pretty name," she said with a smile, "come on, let's take the picture."

The little girl didn't move, she just stared.

"What's wrong?" Syren asked.

"You're so pretty," she mused.

Syren shook her head and pulled her closer to take the picture.

"As are you," she said. "A beautiful girl with a beautiful name."

With a blushing smile, the girl opened her phone and took a self-portrait of them both.

"Thanks," she said before running back to her mother who stood in the spectating crowd.

"Food's ready," Katherine said quickly as she took Syren by the arm and pulled her out of the restaurant, "we don't need fifty other people asking you for pictures."

After collecting food, the four guards led them up Mermaid Avenue while two stayed behind to make sure no one was following. They walked for almost fifteen minutes before they reached Poseidon playground. Through the playground, they made it onto the boardwalk before the sandy beach shore. As Athena foretold, there was no one on the closed beach as far as they could see.

Syren attempted to bend and unstrap her heel but Alex stopped her.

"I can do that for you," he said as he kneeled on the boardwalk.

"Thank you," she responded with a smile.

He unbuckled the straps of her heels. His hands felt soft on her skin this time. When Syren looked over to Katherine her mouth hung as wide and as long as Ghostface from 'Scream'.

"Shut it," she mouthed to Katherine.

A moment later Alex stood with both her heels in his hands.

"Thanks," she said as she took the heels and held them against her chest. They walked closer to the beach. It was 69 degrees, warm for an October night. A little chillier by the beach but bearable.

They sat on the sand and ate. Alex tasted a piece of his chicken and chewed then gagged and spat it back on his plate. Alex became distracted by Syren staring at him, she seemed amused.

"What?" he asked.

"What's wrong with it?"

"It tastes old and refried. It's terrible."

"It can't imagine why it's called junk food," she said with a smile.

"I had hope. You seem to be enjoying yours well enough."

"It's delicious and always has been. Every time I come here I order the same thing and every time, it's been perfect."

"Every time you come here? How often do you come here?" Alex queried.

"As often as I can. I am the Coney Island Queen- although I usually hide behind a scarf or hat or way too much clothing to be noticed." She said in response and ate another one of her cheese fries. He was surprised she ate as much food as she did. After eating her fries and burger, she started with her funnel cake purchased by a guard.

Katherine had a small bag with liquor, cups, and ice. She went with Izzy, Josie, and Skylar closer to the water to drink leaving Syren and Alex alone.

Chapter 8 - We're Just Talking, Katherine!

"I was nice of you to do that for that little girl," he said as he watched her eat.

She smiled and shook her head, "I always take pictures with children because they're the only people I can stand."

He laughed, "so if an adult asks you…"

"I'd say no. It's weird, why do you want to take pictures with a seventeen-year-old.

Frankly, it's kind of a mystery anyone wants to take pictures with me at all. I don't sing, I don't act. I don't do anything particularly interesting or entertaining."

"You're Teddy Prinsloo's daughter and you're an Excellci. You've been named the world's most beautiful woman and before that the world's most beautiful child. Truthfully, they've named you the world's most beautiful everything. Every time I pass a magazine or newspaper stand, I see your face."

"That's all bullshit to me," she said with a chuckle.

"Why?" he asked, curious to hear her response.

"The idea of beauty and that I'm the most beautiful woman in the world- it's all bullshit. Beauty is so subjective, who decides that my features are most beautiful? A bunch of guys who make these lists. They've decided my skin color isn't dark enough to offend them and my ass isn't fat enough to disgust them so I'm the world's most beautiful woman? It's bullshit."

"That's valid but Syren," he paused, "people have found you beautiful for centuries…" he said only to realize his mistake after.

"What?"

"I just meant that for centuries people have found you and your ancestors beautiful," he said.

"That's another thing. Isn't beauty supposed to be rare, literally every one of my ancestors looks exactly like me."

"That's not a bad thing, Syren," Alex responded.

"Beauty is supposed to challenge you. Excite you. It should take all the things you think are horrid and make them beautiful. It's not just about what you see, it's about how you feel when you see it."

"Are you trying to convince me you aren't beautiful?" he asked, confused. She'd just described herself perfectly but she seemed to have the opposite intent.

"I'm not sure honestly," she said with a chuckle.

She broke another piece of her funnel cake with her fork and dipped it in whipped cream before eating it.

"Your hair shimmers in the light. Your eyes change color-"

Syren shrugged and countered, "it's a light luminescence. Let's not get crazy."

"It bothers you that people think you're beautiful?" he asked.

"I don't know...I guess it doesn't matter what they think if it meant they wouldn't gawk at me and objectify me."

He sighed lightly."But come on..you know why people do it."

"No, I don't," she insisted, "I really don't get it."

Alex decided to push her on it. "Why are you pretending you don't know how devastatingly beautiful you are - which even those words seem insufficient to describe you..."

"To you. Not to everyone."

"I would say that was a fair assessment- if it were true."

Syren smiled and conceded her point with a shrug.

Just the thought of her thinking of herself that way made him smile because it was so ridiculous. What was even more ridiculous was how their months together had changed his thinking. He was beginning to feel like a traitor.

"Why'd your parents name you Syren?" he asked with a smile, figuring it was a good opportunity to change the subject.

The sound of the waves roared in the silence of the empty beach but it seemed to fade into the background when he spoke. All she could hear was his voice.

She playfully pushed him."Don't laugh at my name," she scolded, with her mouth still full of fried dough.

"I'm not laughing at your name," he said, fighting the even wider smile on his lips, "I don't know, I saw your dad immediately I could see why he'd give you the name he did. He's exceptionally eccentric."

She smiled and rolled her eyes.

"Please. Syren is tame compared to the other things he wanted to name me and I say things because they were like adjectives and verbs, not nouns."

He smiled slightly though he was thoroughly entertained."You have to tell me now?" he said.

"Enchanted-" she began.

"What?"

"Chocolate. Vibe. Luck. Serendipity. Earth. Energy. Spirit. Kaa. Goldie. Gaia."

With each name, he laughed harder until she listed Gaia. "Gaia isn't that bad though."

"Yeah, if I were some ancient Roman nobleman's wife or a brand of yoga workout clothes then fine, but not a person born in the 21st century."

"Why'd he decided on Syren."

"He said that when he met my mom, he was wholeheartedly enchanted by her and it reminded him of this story he read about Sirens, you know, the ancient man-eating mermaids that would lure men to them with their beauty and song."

"Yeah."

"He said he was enchanted by my mom and then by me when I was born. He said we were his Sirens, minus the man-eating part, I guess."

"That's actually kind of great."

"I'm just grateful he stopped at Siren and not something else. Occasionally, a random asshole will make a siren sound at me but I can handle that," she said with a smile.

"Your dad seems like a character, that must be fun."

"It is. He's the best. He loves me fiercely and I feel that every day so I'm lucky that way... even though my mom is gone I have my dad."

When she said the words she remembered that Athena told her Alex had no parents and immediately she left like a jerk for waxing poetic about her father. She also remembered that she wasn't supposed to know that but she couldn't help it.

"I'm sorry, I don't want it to seem like I'm bragging or anything."

"Why would you think that?"

She paused for a moment before continuing."I know your parents are gone…"

"How do you know that?"

"Truly," she said with a hesitant pause, "I had you looked into."

She said the words quickly and waited for his reaction. It was unreadable. Alex had expected that. He'd been preparing to meet her for years so he had ample time to make sure there was no untoward detail out in the world to be found that could give her a reason to push him away or doubt him.

"Did you think I was gonna rob you or sabotage your companies or something?"

"I guess it's honesty night tonight…" she said with a dry chuckle, "when I first met you I was a little unsure of you."

"How so?" he questioned.

"Not anymore but back then I couldn't read you and that terrified me," she chuckled at how utterly ridiculous she sounded. "I sound insane, I know, but usually I can look into someone's eyes and get them, their story, their intentions, and most importantly- what they want from me but I couldn't with you," she admitted. "I have a similar suspicion about everyone whose intentions I can't immediately interpret so even if it weren't you, if it was anyone else that I was unsure of, I would've done the same."

Alex was stunned but took a deep breath and calmed. The feeling of committing great treachery overcame him again. "Why would you think that?" he asked.

"Do you see how many guards follow me around? I haven't had the best experience with people. Most people see me and they see a target. After a while, you think everyone is after you. It's unfair to those who aren't but it's how you protect yourself."

"That must be hard," he said, ignoring the knot in his stomach from her words.

"Not hard, just exhausting," she said with a small, humorless smile.

She ran her hands through her hair, ruining her perfect curls then crossed her legs in the sand. She shoved her toes deep into the cool sand and wiggled them until they were so deep she couldn't shove them any further.

"Enough about me," she said, changing the subject before she could go down a rabbit hole of hurtful memories. "What about you?"

"Don't you know it all already?"

"I guess I deserved that," she said, feigning hurt with her hands pressed against her chest. "If it makes you feel better my assistant has a crush on you."

"Which assistant? Is she nice?" he teased.

Syren pulled out her cellphone and held it faced up in her palm.

"Athena?"

Her phone lit up and a red ball of tactile light projections appeared above the screen.

"Yes?"

She looked over at Alex who seemed impressed then confused.

"Athena, I just told Alex about your little crush and I think he might be open to some man on program action."

Athena chuckled in her smooth unreal voice. She sounded more robotic than her counterpart cy-vessel form.

"That fact that I have a crush on Mr. West very clearly explains why you inquired about whether or not he had a girlfriend. How very inappropriate of me. My apologies Mr. West." Athena said sarcastically.

"Mute," Syren said quickly.

Alex laughed hysterically, "so you have two assistants named Athena."

Syren wasn't ready to reveal the origins of Athena to Alex. "Yup," she fibbed. She put her phone away and sat with tightly pressed lips while Alex enjoyed a laugh at her expense.

"What the fuck is so funny between you and your boyfriend?" Katherine yelled from down the beach, slightly buzzed from her liquor.

"Mind your business. We're just talking, Katherine!" Syren yelled back.

"Are you done?" she asked Alex, annoyed.

He took a deep breath."Athena is tired of you."

She rolled her eyes."Please, it's not what you think." she lied.

"Mhmm," he said. "I think it's amazing that you're able to create things like her though. It's brilliant."

"Thanks," she said, the compliment sent her blushing, she wanted to change the subject, "tell me about your family... Athena said you have three siblings."

He took a moment before he answered."Seth, Cleopatra, and Isis," Alex said softly. "I don't get along with Seth. Cleopatra is kind of staying to herself right now, she lost someone really important to her a while ago and she's still recovering. I'm closest to Isis. I mean she raised me, she's the best sister I could've asked for and I'm lucky to have her, she's funny and fun, she's kind and she's selfless. She didn't have to care for me but she did."

"What about your parents?" she asked.

"I didn't know my mom, she died giving birth to me and my father, I don't like talking about it but according to my older siblings he was pretty horrible so I guess it worked out for me."

"I'm sorry."

Alex shrugged but didn't respond and she got the sense that he wanted to change the subject.

"I hope Ruby talks about me the way you talk about your sister," Syren said softly.

"Ruby, the few times I've seen her, she looks at you as if you're her entire world and nothing else matters. I think you're doing a great job at being her elder sister."

Syren blushed slightly."I love her dearly, she's like a little daughter to me which I know sounds odd because I'm only seventeen but it's true."

"That isn't weird, look at me and my sister, she wasn't that much older than me but she took care of me like her own child."

"And it works out for me because I can't have children of my own- well won't." She said it with a chuckle that confused him.

"You won't do your part to further the Excellci bloodline," he mocked.

"Every ancestor, going back as far as we can track has died shortly after having a child, somehow they keep reproducing because of this slavish idea of bloodlines and the family name and wealth, it's horrid."

"I agree but you're here because of everything they did, don't you feel some sort of gratitude?"

"I'm here because my mother decided she'd die so I could live. I don't feel gratitude, I feel a burden, as my life has some great purpose I need to fulfill to repay her sacrifice. With the idea of having a child- I sort of wonder: do I have to do the same thing she did so that her sacrifice paid off? It's very frustrating."

"I don't think she did that so you could repay her, I don't think any parent would," he said softly. "My mom died giving birth to me, it's easy to feel guilty but you have to remind yourself that it wasn't your decision to come into this world."

Syren nodded."It'll be a lot easier if my dad wasn't crying every other week about how much he missed my mom. At times I wonder if he'd make the same decision again, knowing how he'd feel after."

"The man loves you unconditionally, you said so yourself, that's very clear to anyone, don't doubt that," Alex scolded gently.

"You're right -"

"Hey- lovebirds come join us!" Katherine screamed from the beachfront.

Syren rolled her eyes.

"We're fine, Katherine," she yelled back with a chuckle.

"She's definitely something-" Alex observed.

"She definitely is," Syren agreed.

"What about your other family- your dad has a lot of family, you never talk about them?"

"I love my grandma to a degree bordering on unhealthy. She's the sweetest, wisest, smartest, funniest person I've ever met and my grandpa is great too. I see them as often as I can, especially my grandma but they live in California so it's a bit difficult to travel there as often as I'd like. She's coming to visit me the week before thanksgiving. Um..my cousins and aunts and uncles are all in California too. We only see each other on holidays, mostly thanksgivings but we don't get along that well."

"Why not?"

"It's a long story."

"We have time."

"Well...when I was born my dad's family didn't think I was his child. 'I didn't look anything like him,' they said. They fell out and my dad never really forgave them for that. But I mean I guess I can sort of see where they're coming from. I don't look anything like my father but no woman in my family has ever looked anything other than the way I look. I don't know if there's anyone on earth my mom could have procreated with that would make me look different."

"Isn't that weird though, that you look exactly like them?" he asked, curious of her answer.

"Yeah. I still don't know why but I've added that to the long list of questions about myself that I can't answer," she looked up at him through her lashes, their eyes met for a moment, and then she turned away.

"What?" he asked.

Syren shook her head, "nothing...you're just very handsome, it's a bit vexing. I don't want to look at you but I always end up forced to look at you. I'm good at ignoring guys but it's hard to ignore you. Is that an inappropriate thing to say?"

"God! Isn't this the behavior you just moments ago detested," he teased lightly.

"I am if dichotomy were a person," she said sardonically. "I should've kept my mouth shut about that."

And that she was, Alex thought. Somehow both coy and brazen, delicately feminine and ruggedly unfeminine, vulnerable and protected, shallow but still retained an unfathomable depth about her.

She existed always in two states, never one without the other, like a coin.

Alex gave her a charming sideways smile, "you say this now but when we first met you ignored me as if I were air."

"It wasn't easy."

"The distinction," he mocked.

"There is a distinction though, you little goodie two shoes."

"What?" he said with a scoff.

"You heard me."

Syren stood slowly from the sand and stretched her legs.

"What are you doing?" he asked.

"I'm going for a walk. I need to throw the trash from all this food out."

She gathered the remains of the food from the sand. Alex helped as well and then they walked for the beach, away from Katherine and the girls. Four guards followed behind and two stayed back with Katherine.

"Where are you going?" Katherine yelled at them.

"I have to throw the trash away Kat, we'll be right back."

Katherine waved her off and then went back to her tipsy foolishness with Josie, Lizzy, and Skylar at the edge of the water.

"I wonder what that goodie two shoe comment was about," he wondered aloud.

"Nothing, you just seem disciplined. Do you ever let loose?" she teased.

"Why does everyone keep saying that?" he wondered again. "Am I such horrible company?"

"Oh-no, no, no, you've been lovely- actually Kat tells me I'm sucky company all the time so if it's anyone it might be me."

He chuckled, "she tells you that?"

"Yep but she says it's not my fault. I'm beautiful and so I've never really had to hold a conversation."

He laughed even louder now. "That is something she would say."

Syren dropped the ball of trash in the can and then turned to him.

"What should we do now?"

"You should answer my question?" he said.

"What question?" Syren responded with a raised eyebrow.

"Why did you ask Athena if I had a girlfriend?"

She thought about the question for a moment.

"Why do you want to know why I want to know why you have a girlfriend?"

"Charming."

"Fine- I don't really know," she said, "I just- I guess I was trying to form this pic-ture of you in my head; who you are and what you could want from me and I thought that bit of information would help me figure it out."

"Did it help you figure anything out?" he asked, curious.

Her hair blew about wildly in the wind but without a hair tie there was nothing she could do but ignore it and face his question. "No. As I said, you're very hard to figure out Alex. Every man I've ever met seems unable to reign in their affection for me. I can almost see what they think of me when I look in their eyes. I see the dirty thoughts, I see the fantasies, sometimes it's sex or money or fame. I didn't see that in you. You look at me differently..it's a bit endearing, it's not the disgust-ing fetishizing, lusty way that the other guys look. You're kind of the antithesis of the guys I pictured and prepared myself for."

"Prepared for?"

"Yeah, the one Katherine complains about after she dates and inevitably breaks up with them. The one you see on television and read about it in books. I don't know if you know this but I've never been to any sort of standard schooling before, there was MIT when I was younger but that is it. Everything I know about men and boys, I've learned superficially or from Katherine vicariously or from my grandmother."

He chuckled softly. "You've never been around guys your age?"

"Not in any meaningful way."

"How do you date, it can't be younger and it can't be older because that's illegal, both ways I think."

"Oh, I don't date. Why does everyone assume I do?" she wondered. "I'm busy!"

"Why did you assume I do?" Alex responded.

"Come on," she said with an eye roll, "look at you?"

"Look at you?" he returned.

"Yes but-"

"But nothing," he finished.

He gazed into her eyes, they were still blue. "Let's go back to Kat," he said, "it's getting late."

"Oh no-I was having fun," she complained.

As she said the words she felt a spasm of excruciating pain emanating from the bump of the back of her neck. She dropped in the sand, gritting her teeth with her fist balled tightly. The pain left her stiff.

"-Athena- help me," she choked out softly.

"I'm working on it - the guards are coming for you," Athena whispered telepathically.

Syren began to feel the pulsing all over but it only worsened the pain."Athena, it's not working-" she screamed in sweaty agony.

"Sy?" Alex said as he dropped beside her, trying to comfort her. "What's going on?" he asked nervously.

After saying the words, three guards were beside him.

Katherine came running over moments later.

The pain rose higher and higher. Each moment she thought she couldn't bear anymore it grew worse. She was still now, no longer gritting her teeth or gripping fistfuls of sand. From the lump on the back of her neck, she felt a pulse of numbness wash over, it was more powerful than the first, and this time it worked. A few seconds later, she was unconscious.

"Shit," Katherine cursed, inebriated."I was having fun! Take her to the car. I'll be right behind you."

Engeurrand lifted Syren's limp body easily in his arms and walked her back to the car. Jealousy and terror overcame him. He should be the one carrying her and caring for her. He'd never felt more inadequate than in that moment of helplessness.

Josie, Skylar, and Lizzy came running over as well.

"What happened?" Katherine asked but she didn't seem particularly interested in the answer.

"She just dropped in the sand and got stiff-" he found himself distraught that she'd left, "why did that happen?"

"Sometimes she gets sick, don't worry she'll be fine."

Katherine seemed so indifferent that he found himself increasingly annoyed. She kneeled and grabbed Syren's heels from the sand.

"Night's over I guess, let's go."

The look on Josie, Skylar, and Lizzy's face expressed to him that they shared his confusion. Katherine walked first and the rest followed.

"Did you want a driver to take you home or not?" Katherine asked him.

"No, I'm fine," he said dismissively. "Will Syren be okay?"

"She's gonna be fine, don't worry, she's just gonna sleep it off and she'll be good as new tomorrow."

Kat gave him a sympathetic pat on the shoulder which told him that the look on his face must've been pathetic enough to earn it. She left with the girls and guards and he was stuck in Mermaid Ave contemplating everything he'd done up until that point.

Chapter 9 - Strictly Professional

Alex arrived at the office earlier than usual. He remained hopeful about seeing her until about halfway through the day he realized she wasn't coming, she'd never been that late before. That continued for three days until she returned on Thursday. When he walked into the morning meeting, she was there, fresh-faced and beautiful the way she always was. There was no sign of the incident on her face.

"I was worried about you?" he said in place of a greeting when the other fifteen attendees of the meeting had left.

She chuckled lightly."Good morning."

"I'm serious," he said, not returning the smile.

Her smile faded, "I'm fine. It wasn't a big deal, just a headache."

"A headache slipped you into unconsciousness and kept you out for three days after the weekend."

"I flew to Paris to take care of some business."

"Sure."

"I govern a very large company, you know that right?"

He nodded, "yes... well... as long as you're alright."

He seemed to not believe her but that was as much information as she was willing to give so she left it alone."How was the consultation of the project with Mr.

Broady?" she questioned.

"It went well. He wasn't thrilled you were absent."

"Yeah, there seems to be a lot of that going around today."

Alex stared at her a moment. He was annoyed.

"What?" she asked. "Have I upset you?"

He took a deep breath before he spoke. "I enjoyed Friday night but I think in the future it's best we not do that again. I've had paparazzi and online stalkers harassing me constantly since."

Syren swallowed hard before she spoke. She realized it was for the best but all she could feel was the sting of his rejection. "Oh, I'm truly sorry about that. I knew it was a mistake but alas, I wanted to be a stupid teenager for the night. I'll see if I can get them off you and if you're worried about your safety I'll assign a dyad of guards to you."

"I don't need any guards but thank you," Alex responded, staring into her eyes that had shifted from a light sky blue to a dark navy blue.

Syren nodded then regained her composure and smiled brightly."Oh good, but if anything changes, let me know," she said as she sauntered out of the room. "Remember we're heading to Mt. Sinai children's hospital at noon for the opening of that wing I donated," she called over her shoulder.

Alex nodded though Syren had long passed the threshold of the glass door of the conference room. It was as if she was running from him.

~~~

The moment she opened the door of her condo she was overwhelmed by the scent of burning sage.

"Sy?" her father called.

Syren quietly snuck across the length of the living room. She knew exactly what he wanted but wasn't in the mood.

"Sy?" he caught her at the bottom of the stairs. "Come Sy, I made you some sage tea, we need to renew our energy. It's been a month since we've done it."

"Daddy, I can't renew my energy right now, I'm really quite busy," she said softly.

"Where's Kat?"

"She went to Skylar's house."

"Come on sweetie, it'll only be one cup. I already have it burning."

"I can't right now, daddy." She disappeared up the stairs to escape and fulfill her most pressing need; solitude.

After her shower, she laid in bed, simultaneously tired and hungry but unsure of what to eat. She fell asleep trying to decide.

Syren woke, remembering being peppered with kisses on her neck and feeling his body against hers. No matter how hard she tried, no amount of contact was close enough. She remembered insatiably craving more and then there was nothing. Since their night at the beach, it seemed like every night he laid a sweet assault on her body...in her dreams. It was becoming a nightmare and so it continued for weeks as she watched him avoid her.

He was exasperatingly professional. There were no lingering stares anymore, no witty banter as they traveled between countries. There was no hysterical laughing at silly things as they'd done countless times before. Occasionally he would smile but only if it were awkward not to do so.

It was the Monday before Thanksgiving and as Syren sat in her office she could barely focus while the sales executives presented third-quarter sales figures and discussed projections for the holiday season. With black Friday nigh, there was much preparation in anticipation of the largest single sale day of the year.

Alex sat in on the meeting, as he usually did. Syren was unusually excited because her grandmother would be spending the week for thanksgiving and she welcomed the distraction like a desert nomad welcomed cool water.

Syren had warned Athena not to foretell her of her grandmother's arrival. She wanted to be surprised.

She checked her watch seemingly every five minutes until there was a knock on her clear glass door and her grandmother walked inside the room. She was stylishly dressed in a black waterfall wool coat with black leather gloves up to her elbows and black boots. Her grey and black hair was wrapped neatly with a jeweled clip and were stark against her toffee skin.

"Where is my sweet granddaughter?" May announced to the room. The loud, commanding voice that emanated from her cords betrayed her septuagenarian frame.

Syren jumped up and ran to her. "Grandma," she screamed as she hugged her and swallowed her grandmother's small 5'2 frame.

When Syren released May from the hearty hug she took Syren's hands into her and gazed into her eyes."Let me see them," she said as she stared. "Oh sweetie, tell me all about it," she began.

"Oh grandma, I just missed you, that's all," Syren said.

May kissed her hands and smiled, "I missed you too sweet girl. You've grown," she said.

"Grandma, I've been 5'10 since I was fourteen years old."

"I don't mean physically and you get more beautiful every time I see you, eventually we'll all go blind staring at you."

"Grandma…" Syren whined with flushed cheeks.

"Why don't we adjourn the meeting until tomorrow," Athena said to the group.

"Yes, I'm stealing my granddaughter for the day," May said as she pinched Syren's cheeks.

The group of executives and Alex began to gather their notes and papers filled with numbers.

May reached into her black Hermes Birkin purse as they waited to have the office to themselves.

"I made your favorite cookies, just like you like them."May handed Syren a pink pastry box filled with chewy, salted caramel cookies that read 'May's Cakes'. Syren opened them immediately and bit into one.

"Hmmm, it's so good," she mused.

Alex was the last to leave. The entire exchange had warmed him. It was nice to see her so happy.

Athena closed the door behind him but stayed in the room.

Syren was on her second cookie when they were finally alone.

"I know those eyes," May began, "you haven't been telling me everything that's going on have you?"

Syren shrugged, "I'm okay grandma, I really am."

"No, you're not? What is it? Is it too much...all of this?" she asked.

"Sometimes," Syren responded.

"You should be in high school with kids your age. Not here. Not this."

"I know grandma," she answered softly.

"I told your father you should but he doesn't insist on anything with you. He doesn't put his foot down. I would but I'm your grandmother, it's not my job to parent you. I'm just here to spoil you rotten."

Syren smiled brightly only to smear it with a sad frown.

Athena tinted her glass wall facing the hallway so no passers-by could see inside of her office.

Syren relented, "I think I have a crush on my intern."

"That's exciting but how old is he?"

"Twenty."

"You're seventeen, that's not too bad but for the sake of avoiding any controversy, you should wait until your eighteen. The truth is I first fell in love when I was seventeen."

"With grandpa?"

"God, no!" May said with a chuckle, "my first love, Henry."

"You've never shared that. What happened to him?"

"Nothing. We weren't the same color. Back then, in the south, that was considered wrong and his family never stopped until they'd driven us apart. One of my biggest regrets was that I didn't fight for him, that I didn't persist because he was worth it."

"Oh grandma, I'm sorry, that's terrible."

"Don't be. I met your grandfather years later and look at us now. Old and grey together, still in love, and from that love we've raised a gorgeous family." May sighed sadly as she reflected on some memory Syren was not privy to. "You're a beautiful girl, cheer up, if it doesn't work with him, there will be many more like him to drive you mad."

Syren shook her head   and sighed. "Maybe saying it was a crush was a tad underwhelming. I think maybe I love him because I can't stop thinking about him. I'm only seventeen and I'm not used to being around boys. This is the first one that hasn't repelled me so maybe it could just be infatuation. I don't know. It doesn't matter if I am or not. I'm his boss and he's already told me that he just wants to keep it all professional so I should leave him alone right?" Syren asked, hoping May would give her the permission she craved to pursue him.

"What do you mean you don't know if you love him?" May asked.

"My eyes should be purple or lavender if I love him but they aren't."

"Being in love isn't worth a damn unless you allow yourself to feel that love. If you're busy denying it, of course, you won't feel it, of course, you won't see it. Love is too complicated to be just right or wrong. There are always arbitrary rules but as long as you're not hurting anyone, ignore them. I wish I had."

"I'm not as brave as you are grandma."

"Shush, you're the bravest soul I know," May said as she pinched the peak of Syren's cheek. "And as for you being seventeen, I know when I was seventeen my love was real. It was young and foolish love but it was real."

"Grandma," she whined with wet eyes.

"Hush away that crying," May scolded, "you've been around you father too much."

Syren wiped her eyes and smiled."Alright, no crying. I don't even know why I'm so emotional, it's probably just because you're here. I was fine before."

May took Syren's hand and pulled her towards the door.

"Some man he must be, to resist you," May wondered.

"Maybe he's not a man," Syren joked.

"Alright, enough about him. You'll be eighteen in a month. What are your plans?" May asked as they walked down the hall.

"Nothing. I'm not celebrating-"

"-Oh no, that will not do," May responded with a smile.

May's stay at the condo for the week of thanksgiving presented a wonderful distraction. She'd refused to allow Syren to her office during her stay and instead opted to venture throughout the city with her granddaughter. For May, that meant, sojourning the high restaurants of Manhattan at brunch and lunch. It also meant daily trips to Tiffany's and Barney's and Hermes for purses, shoes, and jewelry. Syren didn't mind. She craved the normalcy of shopping trips and daily brunches with her grandmother. Normalcy was a luxury to her. Even more so, the fact that no one dared approach her while her grandmother was close.

After thanksgiving, Syren begged May to stay in New York as she always did but the answer was the same. Grandpa wouldn't move so neither could she, besides, she had her pastry shop to run.

With May's absence, things were much the same again but still, Syren was grateful for the distraction.

~~~

"Alex?" Katherine called. She'd made her way down to the offices when she knew Syren had left to attend Ruby's ballet recital and wouldn't be back for some time.

"Hey Kat," he said in what Katherine thought was a ridiculously formal tone.

"I need your help?" she said with a mischievous smile.

"What do you need?" he hesitantly said.

"Syren's 18th birthday is almost upon us and I need your help planning everything and of course you have to come."

He shook his head."I'm not a party planner."

"Think of it as..hosting."

"I'm not a host either," he said, standing his ground.

"You're coming to this party," she said matter-of-factly.

"I don't think that's a good idea."

"Why not?" she asked, ready to rebuff whatever excuse he gave.

"It's just not."

"That doesn't sound like a proper response from someone who is completing a doctorate at MIT?" she teased.

"What do you want from me Katherine?" he asked, annoyed now.

"I want you to say yes to the party or I will strap you to the top of our private jet and fly you to the party myself. I can do that you know, I can make that happen. Besides, your internship will be over by then, won't it."

"Wait -fly?" he asked, confused.

"Oh, it's in Paris at her palace. It's a surprise party."

"I'm definitely not going then."

"You definitely are."

"Why is it so important that I go, I can't imagine it's a task finding willing partici-pants."

She walked closer and threw her hand around his shoulder, almost patronizing him.

"Because I think my sister would like it if all her employees were there…" she paused and smirked, "and besides what kind of party would it be if the hottest guy in the building was absent."

He rolled his eyes."Not that again."

She scolded him with a wave of her hand."It's true, now let me hear you say yes."

"I'm sorry Katherine, I really can't."

She snatched her arm from his shoulder, irritated.

"Why not?"

"I don't want to go, Katherine." He opened the door of his office and before Katherine could respond. He slid out smoothly while Katherine stared, disappointedly.

He was home in thirty-five minutes instead of the usual forty despite the evening traffic. Both Seth and Cleo were home now. With their ability to travel in and out of space, it was hard to stay in one place long when there were so many possibilities. He, however, had to stay put. Tensions hadn't eased between them; it got worse. Now it wasn't just Seth that was angry with him, it was Cleo as well.

When he walked in, he could hear Cleopatra, his brown-haired, older sister in the kitchen. Seth was in the kitchen with her as well. He didn't go to them, opting instead to go to his bedroom after dropping his briefcase in the foyer.

After he showered, he returned downstairs in search of what Rosa, his housekeeper, prepared for dinner. It was then that he heard the rev of an engine outside. When he looked through the window, Katherine stood in front of his door with a black Excellci E3-Ash convertible behind her.

He opened the door quickly. Her presence in his space made him anxious."Katherine?" he asked puzzled with a hint of annoyance riding under the surface of his tone.

"Hey," she said blithely as if it was no big deal that she showed up unannounced and uninvited. Katherine looked him over now. He was wearing heather grey joggers and a white t-shirt. She stopped at his bulge and tilted her head as she stared for a moment then she met his eye.

"Alright Alex-," she began to tease.

The rage that filled his eyes stopped her before she went any further.

"-Fine," she conceded, accepting that was too far. "Are you coming to the party or not?"

He closed the door behind him and walked outside barefoot. It must have been around a low 50-degree night but the cold didn't bother him. What he was worried about were his siblings overhearing the conversation.

"This is not alright Katherine, you can't just show up here. I'm not going."

"I know it's because you like her. I might act like an airhead but I'm not stupid. I just can't understand why liking her equals you not wanting to go to the party? You're being really weird and distant, it's kind of annoying?" she asked, confused. "Is it depression or something?"

"I'll go to the party Katherine," he said flatly. His lips barely moved from the hard-pressed line. His siblings could hear everything, he was sure so there was no sense fighting it anymore.

She seemed to accept her victory but it was soured by his reaction.

"You used to be nicer, now you're kind of being a dick."

"Goodbye."

He turned and walked back to the large white large french door and let himself inside his house then shut its doors behind him. From his kitchen, he could hear her drive off. That was when Seth came.

"You know this is over right?"

"I don't know what you're talking about?" Alex responded, not looking at him but looking in his general direction as he ate cold food.

"You have to do this," he said. "If you don't do this I'll never forgive you. Cleo won't forgive and if Isis survives she'll never forgive, not after she raised you herself when our father was ready to murder you in your crib!"

"I don't care if you forgive me and I'll get Isis back assuming he plans on giving her back at all," Alex fired back.

"Will you?" he asked rhetorically, "because you've had months now where you could've gotten her back and you've done nothing."

Alex offered no response as he stuffed another fork full of seared lamb in his mouth and chewed.

"Have you tested her home yet for a shield?"

"Yep," he said as he ate another fork full of food.

"And?"

"There was none."

"I don't understand you, Alex, I really don't-"

"Why don't you try? Go on, give it a try, since it's so easy," he fumed. "Travel into her building and take her out and then drop her in front of Set and then bring Isis back!" he barked. "Let's assume that the thousands of camera's don't get you and then your plaster your face over every television for a century. Let's assume her guards, who are vessels, I realized that a while ago, aren't as strong or faster than you and why don't we also assume that she isn't hiding her abilities and that when you touch her against her will she won't turn you to ash right then and there."

Cleo was now in the kitchen, ready to get involved.

"Let's assume all of these things don't happen and you get her in front of Set, what's to stop him from taking you next or Cleo or not giving a fuck about anything and keeping both of you there and Syren too, while he does whatever fucked up thing he's planning to get her powers. Nothing is stopping him because it's just a game to him and we've been playing this game for over two thousand years, I'm exhausted."

"So that's it?" Cleopatra asked, bewildered, "we're just gonna leave her there?"

"I didn't say that."

It was true. After everything, he'd said the thought of leaving his sister in that place or even considering it as an option had taken him to the darkest depths of self-loathing. Of course, Set had to take the sister that nursed him from birth to childhood and raised him to adulthood. The sister he was closest to and loved the most. The sister- he would do anything to get back...or so he thought until he realized that switching Syren in her place was just as impossible as leaving her there. It was clear to him that Set knew that; which is why he'd made her release contingent upon Alex bringing Syren back. It must have also been that he was the only one that the futura saw could be successful.

Almost three millennia with his sister for what was only a few months with Syren. It shouldn't have been an impossible, agonizing choice but it was. He'd been wavering for weeks but the night at Coney Island undoubtedly changed everything.

Distancing himself from her gave him fewer opportunities to do it but when he inevitably did, at least he'd have some time away from her, he hoped then that it would hurt less and feel less like the betrayal that it was.

Somehow the opposite happened.

Being around her all day but never really able to see her, not having their little talks or head butting banter sessions, trying to purposefully drown out his thoughts so she wouldn't fill them and drive him insane was actually driving him insane. To leave the internship was to admit that Syren won. That it was her over his sister and he couldn't do that.

"Are you going then. I'll come with you, I'll help you," Cleopatra offered.

Alex nodded and responded. "I'm going."

Chapter 10- Teddy's gift

"Daddy, no-" Syren stood aghast, not sure what words should come next. She took a deep breath knowing her father was too sensitive to survive a tantrum of hers with his mental state intact. She took another breath and another. "What did you do?"

He smiled, trying to hide the panic he felt from her reaction.

"Sweetheart, you'll be eighteen in a few days and I just think that it would be good for you to have your own space."

"My own space?" The words tasted like bile in her mouth as she repeated them.

She looked around the apartment and it was furnished with mostly new decor. All evidence of her father; his platinum records, his awards, even the portrait of him and her mother on their wedding day that was kept on display in the living room had vanished.

"Yeah, I umm...think you're old enough to live on your own now, I'll be in the apartment uptown with Ruby. She wants to stay but she's too young and it's not your responsibility to take care of her, it's mine. Katherine said she wasn't leaving but Kat's eighteen, I can't force her to do anything. Do you like the decor? I had Tabitha work on it. I'm amazed she was able to get this all down while you were away."

She was speechless again and without response, she robotically walked to her room and shut the door once she was inside. All while Teddy chased behind her begging her to discuss her reason for being so upset with him.

"Athena?" she said once she kicked off her shoes and dropped her purse.

"No contact, I understand," Athena responded as she silenced Syren's phone and locked the doors. She drew herself over to the neatly made bed and dropped herself face down.

"Athena?" she called softly.

"Yes?" Athena responded.

"Let me sleep."

The floor to ceiling glass wall on the side of her room with a view of the city tinted black to block the late afternoon light. After the windows closed and the room was in complete darkness except for the gentle violet light glowing from Athena's program form.

Immediately, Syren felt a pulse of calm wash over her from the lump on her neck, and seconds later she was asleep.

When she woke in the morning, her stomach was knotted from hunger. She showered and dressed first. Once she emerged from her bedroom and walked downstairs, she saw her father waiting for her in the foyer.

"Syren, we need to talk honey, I didn't know you'd be this upset."

'Yes, you did," was all she said as she walked to the kitchen.

He followed behind her.

She grabbed a pomegranate, coconut oat bowl pre-made for her in the walk-in refrigerator pantry.

"Let's talk about this?" Teddy said when he caught up to her. "I'll only be 15 minutes away. You can come over anytime."

When she walked out of the fridge and closed the door behind her, Teddy was right in front of her but she still tried to pass him and continued walking.

"Syren, I'm speaking to you. Stop right now." It could have been considered yelling if Teddy was capable of that, instead, it was so soft it sounded like he was singing.

She stopped and turned around, waiting to hear what he needed to say.

"Why are you so upset about this? I thought you would like this."

"No daddy, this is what you wanted. Don't posture as if you haven't been counting down the days until you can get away from me."

"Why would you say that," he said, with a look of bewilderment frozen on his face.

"Because it's true," she half-yelled back, "ever since I hit puberty you can barely look at me because I look like her. I've known that all along and I suppose I knew this was coming too, it's my fault I wasn't better prepared for it." She turned and headed out the door too fast for him to be able to respond.

~~~

When he saw her something was amiss, even as quick as the glance was he knew she was upset. Her eyes were so bright that it was usually the first place someone's eyes were drawn to on her. For the past few weeks they'd been consistently dark blue, today they were pitch black. Her usual stoic expression was replaced by utter sadness. One look was all he needed, he couldn't bring himself to look again.

She stood at her usual spot in the front of the large rectangular table in the conference room as she conducted their morning meeting. Though her visage appeared tortured, she looked exquisite in a winter white belted wool blazer and matching pants.

There were scores of executives connected through video and teleconference. Now that Syren had announced her plans to launch a medical subsect under the Excellci Advance arm of her company, she wanted everyone to be on the same page and voice their questions in one sitting. That idea was bearable before her fight with Teddy, now it was tedious.

"Questions?" she asked after she made her address.

Rupert, the VP of sales raised his hands and spoke, "I'm just concerned because if our goal isn't to increase profits then this will be a major liability. The Excellci brand is set apart from other brands because everything we do returns a profit to us. I understand the goodwill here but I just don't think this is a very good move for our brand. Our focus should be where we can return a profit and also, the three arms of Excellci have been so for centuries, I think it should stay that way."

Syren was quiet for a moment. Livid, but quiet as she tried to take a few slow breaths and calm herself. Her eyes were still black. The fury hadn't broken through the sadness to turn them red.

"That's not what I asked though, it is?" she began.

Rupert chuckled nervously, "I didn't mean-"

"Don't ever presume to lecture me on what's best for my company. You're the head of sales, your job is to meet and exceed sales goals, which I set. If I tell you to figure out a way to return a profit on this new subsect, then that is what you will do and if you're not up to the task, tender your resignation and I'll find someone who will."

"I'm sorry, I just-"

"-any other question?" Syren asked the room, cutting off Rupert.

Natalia Brown, the VP of manufacturing, raised her hand and spoke, "would you want to open up new manufacturing plants for production or would you create new space in current plants?"

"Good question," Syren said before responding. She took a few other questions and then the meeting branched off to questions about other topics.

As she spoke in response to another question, Katherine walked into the room without notice.

"I've been calling you," she said to Syren, "since last night?"

Syren didn't respond.

"Katherine right now is not the appropriate time," Athena said. Her vessel form stood only feet away from Syren.

Katherine waved her off and walked quickly towards Syren. She glanced at Alex. She noticed that both their faces looked miserable and immediately she became overwhelmingly frustrated. "Why the hell was everyone so miserable," she yelled inwardly.

"What the hell happened this morning," she spoke loud enough, not particularly concerned about who could hear.

Syren didn't respond to Katherine directly but continued to speak. "-as I was saying, beginning next year we're rolling out the new phase of development of the E3-Ash convertible with mach one capabilities-"

"Silent treatment?" Katherine asked incredulously, "really mature. You know Teddy was a mess this morning when I came downstairs."

"I don't want to talk about it Kat, just drop it," she said softly.

"Look," Katherine said with a sigh, "I told him not to do that, I told him you didn't want that."

"Doesn't matter," was all she responded before she returned to the subject at hand. "I've decided that we'll have a limited offering of twenty pieces."

"The public won't be happy about this. We could sell a few thousand easily, everyone with a little money wants to get their hand on an E3-Ash," Sheeba, retail VP, commented. "The first complaint will be that it isn't available to the general public."

"It will, through a draw, not that the general public has any interest in a million dollar car-"

"-Syren," Katherine called, flat and low, "why are you ignoring me!"

Syren sighed and closed her eyes, "we'll reconvene tomorrow." She marched to the clear glass door. Katherine followed.

In her office, the clear glass tinted dark when Katherine stepped in behind Syren and closed the door.

"Don't you have school, Katherine?"

"Stop being a bitch and listen to me," Katherine barked, "being mad at doesn't mean you have a right to be mad at me. I didn't leave, in case you haven't noticed, I'm still here."

"I know," Syren responded.

"Then why are you so mad at me?"

"I'm not angry at you Katherine, I'm just angry and I want to talk about it."

Katherine sighed and nodded. "Fine, I guess but at least answer the phone when I call."

"I will."

"I told him you'd be mad about this but no one listens to me," Katherine said mostly to herself as she opened the office door and left.

Athena walked at the moment Katherine walked out. She had a stack of folders clutched under her arms. Without a word, Syren walked to her chair and took a seat then lifted a fountain pen from the pen stand, prepared to sign.

Athena placed the first folder on her desk. "First, write a letter of Alex's performance evaluation for MIT," she said." and sign."

Syren nodded and took the blank cardstock paper She glanced over the sheet and began to write:

Darling Calabar,

Alexander West has been exemplary in conduct, wit, and ingenuity. He displays superlative attributes that have forged him into an essential member of our team. It will be a task returning to regular order with the absence of Mr. West in our executive offices and our labs but alas, we realize that we must let him go. I am pleased to know that MIT continues to foster exceptional scholars and I look forward to future additions to our team here at Exellci Corp.

Best,

Syren Prinsloo Excellci

Syren Prinsloo-Excellci,

CEO and Sole Proprietor

Excellci Corp

"A handwritten note from you carries a lot of weight, I'm sure MIT will be pleased," Athena said as she took the sheet from Syren.

"He deserves it, he's been great," Syren said with a sigh,

"Really?" Athena responded.

"Please," Syren said, "I don't think my character is so low that I would jeopardize his future because of unrequited affection that was inappropriate to have initiated in the first place."

"It's his last week, it's now or never. You should try."

"I will not," Syren said sharply.

Athena nodded and continued handing Syren sheets of paper to sign or approve, most were checks allotted to family members and friends as gifts for Christmas. She was finished just before 11am; in time for her scheduled trip to Javits High school where she would speak at the annual STEM convention for young girls.

Syren left through the front entrance of the building because it was quicker to do so. Alex, Emma; the chair of the Excellci foundation, Athena, Samar, the head of talent, and Andre, the head of the outreach program accompanied her along with a team of guards.

Across the pavilion, they walked to a line of vehicles waiting to transport them to the event. There was a large crowd of spectators, there usually was whenever they had a public event to attend. They gathered in hope of glimpsing Syren.

Today, there was a group of men wearing identical shirts with Syren's face printed on the chest, chanting at her as she walked. It was easy to block them out as they screamed.

"Syren's future husbands," the shirts read.

The group crossed the great cascading fountain in the middle of the pavilion.

"They just arrived," her Athena program told her telepathically. "They are a group of supporters, four dozen and one to be exact - from an online club for men who claim to carry affection for you. They are unarmed."

"Fine," Syren said inwardly to Athena and continued walking.

"I don't like this," Athena said. "I'll order Onfroi to turn back."

"No. I'm not running. We are not running," Syren barked aloud this time.

They were a ways from the edge of the curb. The closer Syren got, the crowd of many men grew more restlessly from behind the confines of the barricade then chaos ensued.

As she reached near to her vehicle, the men broke out from under the barrier and rushed towards the city police who were permanently at the plaza.

"They are coming for you," Athena said. "Stay calm."

~

Syren woke in the hospital to a dozen eyes staring at her. She tried to move but she felt heavy.

"Careful, love," May said softly as she caressed her cheek.

There was Teddy and Ruby and Katherine. Grandpa Thomas, uncle Leo, uncle Marvin, aunt Lyla, and aunt Diana were there as well. She could also see Athena and her cousins Jade and Cierra.

Suddenly she was dizzy again as she tried to replay the event that transpired outside Excellci Plaza. Drowsiness overcame her and once again, she was lost in the blackness of sleep

Chapter 11: Happy Birthday

She woke in her room but not the room she was expecting. She wasn't in New York at the hospital, she was in High palace. It was a stark difference. Where her bedroom in New York was modern. Her room in Paris was straight from the 1500s, the era in which the palace was erected. The walls were twenty feet high and painted the lightest shade of lavender they could find before it became the color white. There were baroque gold leaf carvings to complement the lavender. Her large double king-sized bed had a large canopy streaming down from the ceiling. The cloth of the canopy was white and sheer.

The furniture was cream with gold detail, as was her bed. She had deep purple velvet sofas adjacent from her bed with a glass coffee table with a gold base. The shades that hung from the large windows were white velvet. The floor was marble with hand-painted gold details that matched the walls and the chandelier above was a magnificent array of crystals and light.

When she sat up, Ruby was sleeping on her bed beside her, though it looked like she was taking a nap based on the clothes she was wearing. She didn't remember an injury to her head but she remembered being in the hospital. The gaps in her memory, she blamed on sleep.

"Good morning, Syren, Happy birthday," Athena said in her ear.

"Thanks, Athena," Syren responded. "What happened?" she asked Athena only to be cut off by Katherine who walked in with a wide smile.

"God, you look even prettier than usual which is good because it is your birthday and we have big plans for you."

"Hey Kat," Syren said with a smile.

Teddy walked moments later.

"Hi, sweetie, how are you feeling?" his voice was full over concern as usual.

"I'm fine- when did you guys bring me to Paris?"

"Last night," Katherine said excitedly.

Ruby heard the voices and sat up. When she saw Syren was awake she leaped over the bed and hugged her.

"Happy birthday Sy," she said with her sweet little voice.

"Thanks, Rue."

"Are you up now for good?" Ruby asked.

"No-no-no, you need rest, in fact, you should be in bed all day or at least your room, that's what the doctor said." It was a lie but Katherine needed her in bed all day while they made preparations for her party in the grand ballroom.

"I feel fine."

"Yes, exactly why you need to be in bed because as soon as you get out of bed you'll feel sick again."

"Are you making that up?" Syren asked.

"No."

"Okay, what happened? I just remember sleeping a lot. Where's grandma?"

"She went to Paris. She'll be back soon and that's as specific as I'd like to be," Katherine responded.

"I'll have breakfast brought to you," Teddy said.

"I can do it," Katherine said. She walked out after eyeing Teddy, hoping he didn't ruin her surprise party. Teddy walked over to Syren's bed oblivious to Katherine's glare.

"Are you sure you feel better?" he asked.

"Yes."

He sighed, "you scared me, there was a lot of blood- you know- coming from your nose but you heal quickly, just like your mom, I don't know how but I'm glad." As much as Teddy knew about her maternal side of the family, he was never curious to know why they were the way they were.

"I feel fine. What happened?"

"You had a headache, a bad one when they attacked you. Your mother never had these Syren, I think you should see a specialist. Dr. Marcus did such good work it was such a shame what he got himself into."

Syren gazed at Teddy for a moment, curious how he could divorce himself reality in such a way that left him clueless as a child.

"Why are you here Teddy?"

He could still hear malice in her voice. It was curt which was unusual for Syren when she spoke to him.

"Ruby can you give us a minute please sweetheart," he asked gently.

"Okay," she responded before she hugged Syren and held her tightly for a moment longer before she left.

"I know you're still upset with me," he began.

"I'm not upset with you, not anymore."

"You should be because what you said was true and I'm sorry that it is. I wish it wasn't."

Syren didn't respond because it seemed like he wasn't finished.

"When your mom died, I wanted to die. Literally, die. All I could think about for days after was offing myself. A piece of me did die. I don't know how I found the strength to overcome the place I was in mentally- well I know how I was able to- it was because of you. You were our little girl and I know I couldn't just leave you.

"This past decade, I've watched you grow and before that, I guess I always knew there was a possibility you'd look like her but once it started happening- it was so much worse than I thought it would be. It's like you are exactly her, a replica, and I tried so hard to differentiate you two. I kept saying to myself; Isabeli is my wife, Syren is my daughter but you're too alike. It's hard.

"It's like every day, every time I look at you, I'm reminded that she's gone. It's not just that you look-alike, you act alike, you make the same faces, the same gestures, you dress alike. It's been a decade and I still can't even look at another woman because I'm so in love with your mom. Now that you're old enough to take care of yourself, I think I need some time to process the fact that she's gone." He sighed heavily. "I wish I could tell you that I'm gonna move back in, I wish I could but I can't."

"I'm eighteen now, if this is what you have to do then you can do it," she responded softly.

She wished she could understand, that she could sympathize but she still didn't want him to leave. It wasn't her fault she looked like her mother, Syren thought, but she felt like she was being punished for it all the same.

"I don't plan on not being your father anymore. I'll be there so much you'll probably be tired of me. I'll call you every day but I have to do this."

She nodded.

Teddy hugged her and kissed her forehead. He knew she didn't accept his explanation, the blackness in her eyes told him as much. They were still hard, Isabeli had the same look whenever she was upset with him.

"I'm gonna make sure Rue is okay. Get some rest, okay?" Teddy said before standing. "I really hope you enjoy your birthday today. I got you presents but Katherine won't let you open any gifts until later."

"Thanks."

When Teddy left, she went to her bathroom to bathe then dressed in her closet. Food was waiting on her coffee table when she returned to her bedroom.

As she sat eating she realized she didn't know what time it was. The shades blocked all light from the windows.

"Athena, what time is it?"

"4:23 pm." Athena responded.

"God," she said with furrowed brows, "it's late."

"I hope that means you slept well? Your vitals look okay. Great actually."

"I feel fine," she responded. "Where's my horse?"

"Peony is resting by the lake."

"Let me see her," she said, her voice muffled by the croissant in her mouth.

The violet light appeared in front of her on the coffee table then she saw video images of her mare by Sapphire lake.

She smiled.

"I'm going to see her, can you call her back to the courtyard?"

"I did overhear Katherine ask specifically that you remain in your room," the voice from the program said.

"Didn't you hear, Athena, I'm eighteen now, I don't have to listen to anyone," Syren said snarkily.

She swallowed her croissant then took a few sips of rose tea.

"I simply think it would be more prudent to stay inside."

Syren realized why.

"Oh god, what are they planning? If grandma's here that means they're planning something big."

"Katherine was very clear I shouldn't tell you. Of course, you could override that order but I wouldn't recommend it."

"Is it a party? I don't want a party."

"I'm not at liberty to say."

"Aren't you though?"

"If you wish."

Katherine walked in.

"Stop bothering Athena," she commanded.

"What are you doing?"

"We're making plans for your birthday of course," she said cheerfully.

"Why are you so happy?" Syren asked puzzled.

"It's your birthday and since you're being a sour puss, I'm hoping my happiness will rub off on you and you'll cheer up. Also, you did go all out for my birthday earlier this year so I'd like to return the favor."

Syren shrugged at her reasoning. "I don't want to celebrate. I'm not in the mood this year, I told you that."

"You don't even know what I'm planning. It could be a nice dinner, it could be a party or it could just be us watching a movie in the theatre room."

"Katerine, the first thing my father did on my birthday was to get himself as far from me as he could. Who would want to celebrate that?"

"Lots of kids and by the way, I think you're forgetting you still have me and I'm plenty."

Syren was quiet for a reflective moment then she responded. "You're right, I'm lucky to have you because you did stay. Thanks for doing all this for my birthday, whatever it is you're doing even though I don't want it-thanks for doing it anyway."

"See, that's all you had to say," Katherine responded with a winning smile. "Now take a few hours. Clear up those eyes, they should be blue and maybe later they'll be purple, we'll see."

"What are you talking about?" Syren asked, intrigued but puzzled.

Katherine didn't want to alarm her. "Because you'll be so filled with love-" She headed towards the door, "and maybe something else. We'll see."

"Kat..."

Syren's mind flashed to Alexander. Her handsome intern who seemed to grow more repulsed by her with each day. She wondered if Teddy's decision to leave hurt so much more because it was just another rejection on top of Alex's months-long crusade but quickly discarded the thought because she was afraid of the truth in it.

"Wait- what happened Katherine, can you at least tell me that? Teddy said I had a headache. I remember being in the hospital but barely…"

"Yeah, those perverted losers tried to assault you outside the plaza. Once they attacked the guards the rest of the crowd felt embolden and joined in. They bum-rushed you, in the chaos, I guess you panicked and had a headache. Your nose started to bleed and you passed out. It looked pretty bad so we just took you to the hospital since everyone saw you fall.

"Samar and Emma were a little bruised up but no one on our side was hurt badly. Oh and Alex, you should have seen him, he was great, he punched the one guy in the face and knocked him out cold. The guy is still in the hospital, I think he has brain damage."

"Alex?" was all Syren responded, shocked.

"Yeah, I used to think he was so sweet but now I think I probably don't want to mess with him," Katherine teased. "but obviously the police aren't pressing charges, they attacked you. By the way, he stayed at the hospital with you all night. He only left when May kicked everyone one out."

"Why are you telling me this?"

"Because…" Katherine began, "I think he likes you." She opened the door and walked out right then.

Syren stuffed more bacon in her mouth.

"Athena, what did the doctor say when I was brought in?"

"Well, you were healed when you arrived at the hospital but I kept you asleep because the public saw you fall. I felt it safer to have the doctors observe for a while, for the optics. They concluded a concussion."

"Oh, how are Samar and Emma?"

"Good. I've given them some time from work and their bills are all taken care of with insurance."

"I can't help but feeling like this is all my fault," Syren mumbled.

"It is," Athena responded.

Syren sighed. "Fine. Just let me sleep, the dreamless kind," she said after thoughts of Alex kept resurfacing.

"I don't think that's wise. You've been sleeping a lot lately."

"And you said my vitals were great."

Athena sighed.

"Very well, once you're finished eating, I'll put you to sleep," Athena responded.

∾

When Katherine looked around the ballroom, she felt pleased with the decor. It looked less like a room fit for a coronation and more like a room fit for a birthday party.

She had a bar in the far corner. To the far side of the room, she had an elegant buffet with multiple suited servers behind each table. An assortment of tables were in the back and the middle of the room was space for the dance floor. There was a stage at the front. White lanterns lined the ceiling and white fire lights and columns of large black, gold, and white balloons lined the walls. There were champagne towers and sparkling dancers hung from rings in the ceilings.

Each table was covered with a white cloth and surrounded by gold chairs. A bouquet of varied ranges of pink peonies, Syren's favorite flower, centered every table accented with a feather arrangement. Some dancers roamed the room dressed like flappers in vivid colored sequin and feathered dresses. The theme was the roaring 20's and it was May's idea. She was very detailed in her approach.

Katherine had help from event coordinators and May but she still credited herself for all the work.

"I think she's going to love it," May remarked.

"She better," Katherine said excitedly. "We should probably start getting ready now since people should be showing up soon. I'll go wake her up. Do you remember where your rooms are?"

'This place is insanely huge, of course not," Lizzy responded.

The rest of the trio, which consisted of Skylar and Josie agreed.

"Constance," she called.

Constance was one of the palace managers, in charge of ensuring the palace was properly taken care of and had adequate staff. She was also a vessel and had been working at the palace for centuries.

"Mademoiselle Katherine?" she answered.

"Can you take my friends to their rooms please and have the sound guys start the music and play it throughout the palace. I need something to get ready to.'

"Absolument," she responded, "this way."

The girls followed her, leaving just Teddy, Ruby, May, and Katherine.

"Okay, let me go get ready," Katherine said.

"I'm coming with you Kat," Ruby said.

"Sure, you can get ready with me and Sy."

Ruby nodded excitedly and followed beside Katherine, May went as well. In her mid-seventies, such a walk to the residence was too far. She took a golf cart instead.

Back in Syren's bedroom, Katherine tore the sheets from Syren with a cheshire grin on her lips.

Syren opened her eyes, slightly disoriented from a deep sleep.

"Get up loser, let's have some fun."

She could hear music. "Oh god."

Katherine smiled even wider, so did Ruby who was standing by her side. May walked closer and kissed Syren's cheek and hugged her tightly.

"Happy birthday sweetheart, how are you feeling?"

"Thanks grandma," she said with a smile, "I feel better. Much better."

"Good," May said as she pinched Syren's cheeks.

"Let's get ready." Katherine took Syren by the hands and pulled her from the bed.

"What did you decide to do?" she asked even though she heard music and was almost sure she knew what it would be.

"A party," Ruby did a small dance as she said with words.

"I need to shower and wash this sleep off then," she said the words with a slight frown.

"That's the spirit-" Katherine said sarcastically, "we already showered so we'll wait for you and um...hair and makeup are set up in your closet."

Syren nodded.

"Fix your eyes," May warned.

She nodded again, "I'll try."

In the bathroom, she starred in the vanity mirror at her pitched black irises."Athena set the bath please, with lavender and vanilla," she said aloud.

"Sure thing," Athena responded.

She closed her eyes and breathed in deeply and held her breath as she counted to ten then she opened her eyes and looked at the color. Still black. She filled her mind with images of Ruby hoping that would help then closed her eyes and breathed in again. When she looked they were still black which made her realize Ruby might not have been a good choice since her leaving the house was one of the sources of her sadness.

Syren gave up and showered, brushed her teeth then slipped into her robe, and went to her wardrobe room. Katherine, Ruby, Lizzy, Skylar, and Josie were there.

"Happy birthday!" they all screamed together.

Syren smiled and it finally reached her eyes. They lightened to gray. "Thank you."

"How does it feel to not be the only one under eighteen anymore?" Skylar asked.

"Hey," Ruby interjected. "I'm still under eighteen."

"Ruby," Syren said with a smile, "by the way thanks for coming." She said to Lizzy, Josie, and Sklyar.

"It's my first time in Paris," Lizzy said.

"Me too," Josie agreed.

"Do you like it? When did you guys get here?" Syren asked.

"Friday," Josie answered. "How are you feeling? Kat said you felt better?"

"Yeah, loads better."

"This place, by the way, is huge. It's insane," Sklyar added. "How do you walk around in here, isn't everything too far."

"The way it was designed, it has clusters of everything within a certain vicinity. There's a bathroom in every room and there's a kitchen in every wing, not just one kitchen for the entire place so you don't have to walk far for anything. There are a lot of exits and so on. We kind of do have to walk far for the ballroom though so we'll probably take a golf cart," she finished with a chuckle.

"How do you clean it?"

"A lot of housekeepers, it's kind of like a hotel and even though a lot of wings are closed, well most wings of the palace are closed we still have to clean them so it's a lot.."

"Enough about that, let's get ready," Katherine said, "one of you guys should go next."

Ruby already had her hair curled. Lizzy and Skylar went next. Katherine brought four stylists this time so they could go two at a time.

"What am I wearing?" Syren asked.

Katherine smiled hesitantly.

"It's not new but…" she took a garment bag from the hook on the wall. "You know how I loved the dress your mom wore to the Met Gala back in the '90s?"

She opened the bag and removed a white satin strapless mini dress that had off the shoulder silver beaded exaggerated puffs attached to glove sleeves. It has a pearly and jeweled headpiece and a light lavender mink fur stole which Syren knew was added to the original costume.

"Daddy is gonna die if he sees this, you know that right?" Syren said.

"I picked this out before I knew all of that and in any case, it's your freaking birthday. It's not about Teddy...as much as I love him."

Syren was the last to finish her hair and makeup. Lizzy, Jose, and Skylar left to get dressed. She planned to meet them at the party.

Katherine dressed first in the room after they sent the stylists away. Ruby dressed next and Syren was last. After slipping on her dress and matching satin heels with ribbons that tied into a bow around her ankle, Katherine brought over a blindfold.

"Isn't that a little much, Katherine?" she asked hesitantly.

"No, it's just enough."

"Can we do it in the hall?"

"Sure."

Once they were in the hallway Syren turned to Katherine, speaking low enough that Ruby who had hopped into the golf cart couldn't hear.

"Is he gonna be there?"

"Yep and he's no longer your intern so it'll be a fun night."

It was impossible to fight the smile that crept on her lips.

"Okay, blindfold time."

"Oh, look who's excited now," Katherine mocked.

As Katherine stood closer and lifted the blindfold to cover her eyes she noticed the hue, a lavender-blue mix. The prettiest she'd ever seen them. She decided not to tell her and finished tying the silk blindfold around her eyes then helped her in the golf cart.

Katherine texted instructions to various workers and Athena during the drive so everything and everyone could be where they needed to be before Syren arrived.

Outside the ballroom, Katherine helped Syren out of the cart. When Teddy saw her, his heart sank and for a few moments, he fought the urge to leave but realized he couldn't do it.

As Katherine was ready to take Syren into the party, Teddy was heading away from the party.

"Teddy, where are you going?" Katherine called.

Syren slipped off her blindfold and looked to Katherine then realized Teddy was behind her and turned around.

"Daddy?" She called, confused.

"I'm sorry- I can't do it anymore...I can't do this- I love you but I can't sweetie," his voice broke as he turned quickly and walked.

She shook her head and smiled sadly. Her throat burned as she felt the tears swelling in her eyes.

"He's mourning Sy, you just have to let him."

She shook her head angrily. "I lost her too. I look in the mirror and I see her too. I'm not acting like that."

"I know it sucks but are you gonna stay out here and cry or are you gonna go enjoy the party I made Teddy pay for," Katherine said with a teasing smile on her face.

"I don't wanna go anymore." She wiped her wet eyes and cheek, smudging her makeup terribly.

She felt small hands patting her back. "It's okay Sy, don't cry," Ruby said.

"Can someone get her a tissue," Katherine said aloud.

Several workers were buzzing around in the hallway outside the large gilded doors of the grand ballroom. A few moments later a vessel named Julienne brought a tissue. Katherine took the tissue and wiped Syren's eyes and cheeks. They were black again.

"You are going to this party. If you had any idea how much work it takes to get this many assholes in one room you'd be in there already.

Katherine tapped her face until she felt her makeup was mostly intact.

"You wanna put the blindfold back on? That was a part of this whole thing."

She shook her head.

Katherine rolled her eyes and sighed. "Fine."

A vessel opened the door and the trio walked inside the party.

Chapter 12: The Decision

"HAPPY BIRTHDAY!"

There had to be at least three hundred people in the room. She couldn't wrap her head around the logistics of getting that many people in Paris. The very large ballroom had been transformed into a beautiful party space that reminded her of the roaring 20s. The thought of all the work Katherine and May did forced a smile on her face.

"Wow! Kat, you planned this?"

"Yep. All by myself."

Syren grabbed her and hugged her tightly. "It's perfect, I love it...even the peonies on the tables, it's...perfect."

"Happy birthday, I'm not buying you anything, this is your gift."

Syren smiled in response, "I don't need anything." She turned back to the crowd and smiled.

"Thank you so much for coming," she said as loudly as she could over the music that had been lowered for the moment.

When she said the words the music shot back up. Then she was surrounded by a crowd of people wishing her happy birthday and inquiring about her health after the incident in the street. As she moved through the crowd she kept her eyes fixed for one person, who she didn't see.

When he saw her, she was an absolute vision in white. He usually could turn away even if every sense in his body was drawn to her. This time, he couldn't tear his eyes away even when his date returned. He stared so long that eventually their eyes met and he was forced to turn away. Even from across the large room he could see her dark eyes.

It took her a moment to look away, even after he'd turned away. He looked too handsome in his slim black suit with his black shirt underneath tieless and unbuttoned at the collar. She surreptitiously admired him and was so keen on him that she didn't even notice the brown-haired girl beside him. Now that she was paying attention she noticed how close they sat and that they were facing each other.

The hope she deluded herself into having for the night shattered like glass.

She swallowed the lump in her throat and turned around and continued to socialize with as much empty enthusiasm as she could. She didn't look in that direction again but eventually, Katherine did.

"What the hell?" she said, mostly to herself although it drew the attention of Syren and Lizzy. "I did not invite him here for him to bring a date?" Katherine fumed. "That piece of shit!" Katherine attempted to step away but Syren grabbed her before she could.

"It's okay," Syren said.

"No, it's not okay," she insisted.

"What are you gonna say to him? You can't date other people because my sister is pining over you?"

"No, I'm gonna kick them out. They could do whatever they want, just not in here," she said, undeterred.

"Please," Syren begged, the tears were threatening to spill over but she slowly blinked them back. "Just let it go."

Katherine relented. "Fine and stop crying!" She stomped away and disappeared into a crowd of guests.

"What happened to Kat?" Ruby asked.

"Nothing," Syren answered with a smile to soothe Ruby.

She continued to mingle. The crowd was a mixture of relatives from California, senior executives from Excellci Corp, socialites, models with whom Katherine had worked, some were from the tech world and some were entertainers and actors. The most excited group seemed to be the company executives who'd been thrust into a world of celebrity.

The mingling seemed unending but after an hour, she decided it was time to get away. "Gosh, I'm starving, will you excuse me, I need food," she said to the well-dressed guest before her.

Before the man could respond she stepped off with Ruby who hadn't left her side all night.

"Are you hungry?" she asked.

"Yeah, I'm so hungry," Ruby said as she rubbed her stomach.

"Why didn't you tell me?"

"You were talking."

'Yeah, and I wanted to escape," Syren said with a humorless chuckle.

After taking food for Ruby from the buffet she sat her at a table. "Rue, I need to go and get some air, are you gonna be okay?"

"I'll come with you," Ruby suggested.

"No, it's okay, just eat, Grandma will watch you," Syren assured. She found Katherine not far away, instead of May. "Can you keep an eye on Rubes, I need to get some air."

"Nope, stay and enjoy the party. I know you wanna go outside to get all maudlin and weepy, not tonight Syren, okay?"

"Kat."

"Syren," Katherine responded mocking her, then she felt regretful, "ten minutes, and then I'm getting you myself." She decided it would be a perfect time to con-front Alex.

"Okay."

Katherine handed her a plate of fruits and cakes she'd been eating. "Here, eat something."

Syren took the plate without fuss and headed for the large doors that led outside. Katherine immediately began scanning for Alex who was no longer in his usual spot. He was in the middle of the room, in a crowd of people but he kept aware of Syren's movements. He told himself this was the night he would do it. He already knew he was capable of traveling in and out the property unnoticed after trying earlier when he arrived. When he saw her heading for the door, he realized it might be his only opportunity and followed. Cleo was there to make sure he saw it through but now that it was time, he didn't need an audience.

"Go home, wait for me there," he said to Cleopatra, not waiting for a response.

Once Syren was out of the door, she walked up the marble stairs until she reached the balcony. There stood the most beautiful view of the city of Paris, with the Eiffel tower as clear as if it were daytime. She rested her plate on the stone balustrade and unstrapped the bows of her heels and kicked them off. She wiggled her toes once they were free from the confines of her heels and then stuffed a yellow gooseberry in her mouth. Finally, it was serene and she decided that she wouldn't go back to the party and as she made the decision she was preparing herself for a fight with Katherine.

It was a temperate night in December because though it was a frigid 45 degrees outside the barriers of High Palace, it was a temperature controlled 75 degrees inside.

Alex watched as she unstrapped her shoes and began snacking by the balcony. He walked slowly and couldn't stop the shaking of his hands. The sound of his heart beating drowned out the remixed 20s jazz music that escaped the ballroom.

"Alexander is approaching," Athena said to her.

Syren turned around to see Alex walking across the pavement. The sound of his shoes on the pavement became louder the closer he walked.

Alex, he was the last person she expected to see. He stopped beside her and reached out his hands to touch her and watch as she stared at him with confused black eyes.

Suddenly, he became terrified at the thought and pulled back and put his hands in his pockets.

"Black eyes on your birthday?" he said with a sigh. There was no point in dragging it out but that was what he was going to do until he found the resolve to do it.

"It's been that kind of night," Syren said as she faced forward.

"It seemed like you were having fun out there," it came out as a comment more than it did a question.

"Did it?" she asked rhetorically. "It seems like you were having more fun than me."

He shrugged off the snark in her comment, "with my sister?"

Even in the night, he could see the flush of heat on her cheeks. She was embarrassed and so he quickly changed the subject. "How are you feeling, after the attack?"

"Fine." was all she responded.

"You need more guards, you know that."

"No, I don't," she said sharply. "I wasn't hurt."

"You fell to the ground. Your nose was bleeding. How is that fine? You need better guards. They weren't able to protect you."

"They protected me as well as they could without killing anyone."

He made a gesture of disapproval that was somewhere between a scoff and a shrug.

Frustrated by all the mixed signals she felt he'd given from the beginning she decided to ask the question that truly perplexed her. "Why did you come here tonight Alex, it obviously wasn't for me? You've completed your internship, you didn't need to come."

"I didn't want to come, Katherine showed up to my house and told me I had to."

Syren rolled her eyes and stuffed another gooseberry in her mouth. "Of course she did."

"I read the letter you wrote for me."

"And?"

"Thank you," he said softly.

Syren softened at his gesture. "Thank you too, Katherine told me what you did for me when I was attacked. She told me you put a man in the hospital."

"I'm not proud of that but I didn't want you to get hurt.

"Still, thank you."

Alex sighed, "I know it's none of my business but whatever is going on with your father, that has you so sad, I'm sure it will pass."

She shook her head, "I'm mad at him right now because I think he probably chose the worst time to do what he did, but I know I can't stay mad at him for long...even if he is an inadequate father."

"What did he do?"

"He moved out of my apartment." She wiped her eyes as she said the words.

"Why?" Alex asked, knowing he was only being drawn in further.

"He said that it's too hard for him to look at me, that I'm too much like my mom so he's going to take some time away from me because I'm eighteen now and I can take care of myself. He took Ruby with him."

"Is that why he isn't here tonight? I didn't see him." Alex took solace in the fact that there was someone else who seemed to be as affected by her as he was, though he wasn't happy that what Teddy did made her so unhappy.

"He was going to come but then he saw me in this dress and it was my mom's dress and he kind of freaked out in the hall and said he couldn't do it anymore. By 'it' I guess he means me. I don't know."

"I'm sorry."

"It's fine, I sort of expected it, still, rejection isn't fun especially when you aren't used to it."

"You aren't used to it?" he asked, almost mocking.

"Do I look like someone who gets told no by anyone...well except for my father and you apparently…"

"What about me?" his voice was flat and sad.

She sighed, "please...you grow more repulsed by the day. I don't know if that says more about me or you...I will admit the boss who hits on the intern is kind of gross so I'm sorry about that. I let my affection for you ruin what could've been a really great four months-"

"-I love you," the words slid off his tongue before he could stop them but even so they were filled with sorrow.

"What?" was all she could respond, swearing she misheard. The words sounded so angry that she didn't think that was what he said.

"I love you," he said again, begrudgingly.

Syren was confused by his tone, it was regretful and even more confused by his admission."Then why have you been ignoring me?"

"I'm not good enough for you….not even close. " The tone of sadness was still thick on his voice.

"This is the most begrudging show of affection I have ever-"

"-Was it begrudging?"

"Very begrudging," Syren said with a smile.

They both broke into chortles. She fell into his arms and laughed on his chest.

"I was aiming for somewhere between sincere and begrudging," Alex mumbled through laughter.

Syren covered her mouth and laughed. "I think you fucked it up."

Alex forgot all about the reason he'd come out to the balcony now that he was lost in laughter with Syren.

Syren leaned up and sighed. "Say it again with no grudge this time."

Alex took a breath and he was grounded once again. "I love you," he said, softly, sincerely.

"See, now that one was perfect."

It was impossible now.

He took her hand in his and willed himself to disappear with her. It would only take a second to get to Egypt then he would never have to see her again. He closed his eyes and pressed her palm against his cheek and willed himself to do what he spent years preparing to do.

It was impossible now.

Instead, he pressed his forehead against hers, hoping she would show some resistance so he would have to stop. He wanted her to chase him away so he could never show his face again. To his chagrin, she melted into his embrace. Without her heels, she had to climb on the tips or her toes to be on his level.

"Do it. I want you to," she whispered breathlessly, pulling him closer by the lapels until there was no space at all between them.

He finally pressed his lips against hers and kissed her. Softly at first but with each moment as he reveled in the feel of her lips and the taste of her mouth, it grew more intense. Time passed. He only stopped when Syren broke the kiss to draw in a breath and then he immediately found his tongue between her sweet lips again.

The rush, the energy they both felt was intoxicating...to a fault since there seemed to be no room for breath.

Syren broke this kiss again, panting this time as she pressed her face against his chest. Alex found himself breathless as well and used the time away from her lips to even his breathing.

When he wrapped his arms tighter around her and stroked her hair. It felt like silk under his fingers, exactly the way he remembered it when he held her in the van as they traveled to the hospital. There was the faintest aroma of sweet vanilla and lavender that clung to her skin and hair, always.

He couldn't anticipate a future with her so he wanted to commit the moment to memory.

Syren pulled off her gloves and reached up and touched her lips where they'd kissed, she felt the strangest tingling sensation that made her smile and then she looked up at him.

"I love you too...I'm in love with you too," she said softly.

The deep purple hue in her eyes, visible because of the bright full moon over them had confirmed the words that sounded like a song to him.

"Terrible judgment on your part," his voice was serious.

She shook her head because of how utterly ridiculous he sounded."No. You're exactly perfect."

"You should go back to your party…" Alex began. He was beginning to feel uncomfortable.

"No."

She was still staring into his eyes. He felt like she could see into his soul but if that were the case, she wouldn't have been standing there with her arms wrapped around him, gleaming at him with so much love.

"Katherine got you a large cake…"

"No."

"Ruby is probably waiting for you…"

"Nope, not going to work."

He sighed.

"Kiss me again," she commanded.

Robotically, as if he were in a trance, he leaned down and cupped her cheeks and kissed her waiting lips. It seemed better than the first time even more intense, he didn't want to let her go. She felt a fire in her belly that she'd never felt before and found herself clutching her thighs together hoping to stifle her want.

It did not work.

Alex lifted Syren and sat her on the edge of the balcony. Their lips never parted from each other. Syren opened her legs and pulled him in between them.

"Syren?" Katherine had been calling them from the staircase over a hundred feet away. Now both Katherine and May were beside them.

"Syren stop," Athena said and had said repeatedly before, only to be ignored, "Grandma May is here."

They both broke this kiss and looked over to a grinning Katherine, standing beside May.

"We've been calling you," Katherine said.

"Oh," was all Syren could get out of her mouth while she was still catching her breath.

"You have to cut the cake," Katherine said.

"Cake. yeah," Syren said absently with a nod.

Katherine smiled and pulled her.

"Come on birthday girl," May said as they walked.

Syren looked to Alex hesitantly.

"You should go," he said with a small smile that didn't reach his eyes.

"Are you coming?" she asked.

"I'll be right behind you. I just need a moment," he said softly.

"I'm sure you do," May responded.

Syren's cheeks were flushed once again.. He collected her shoes from the floor and placed them in her arms then Katherine pulled her away. She looked back at him a few times and saw him at the same spot and felt the need to turn back. She stopped only to have Katherine pull her forward.

"Just cut the cake and then you'll have the rest of the evening to yourself," Katherine scolded.

She reached the marble stairs and when Alex was no longer visible May stopped, "Kat, give me a minute with my granddaughter"

Katherine raised her eyes and smiled, "I'll see you in a minute." She said suggestively then disappeared down the stairs. Syren pulled her arm length gloves back on.

"I'm sorry grandma," Syren said. She seldom apologized after May had scolded her more than once about offering nonsensical apologies for merely existing but now she felt it was necessary.

"That's nonsense, sorry for what? For kissing a boy? You should be thanking me because if you'd stayed there another two minutes, the way you two were going at it, you might've been pregnant." May joked then began to walk slowly and Syren followed. "Is that the black-haired beauty you've been lovesick about?"

Syren nodded, shyly.

"I expected as much when I saw him at the hospital. I'd hope only a man as pretty as that could make a fool of my granddaughter."

"Grandma," Syren whined.

"I'm old, but I'm not cold," May joked.

"Grandma!" Syren howled louder with a chortle.

"You're a sweet girl Syren, you're sweet and smart and tough. To survive in this world as a woman you need to be the last two but the first one, no- you don't have to be that. Not if you don't want to." May took Syren's hands in hers and gazed into her eyes. "I'm telling you this, today, on your eighteenth birthday because I want you to grab life and squeeze until you've fulfilled all your desires. I don't want anything holding you back. I want you to love yourself more than you love any man and I want you to be careful because you know what happens to women on your mother's side of the family when they have children."

Syren nodded.

"Are you going to have sex with that boy?" May asked.

Syren shrugged, too embarrassed by her grandmother's forwardness to respond with words.

"You'll need to be on birth control for that dear. Are you?"

"No."

"I can take you. If you'd like that."

Syren nodded.

May smiled and responded, "good. These are things I wish someone would've told me at your age, it would have saved me from a lot of unhappiness. I want you to take this to heart. okay?"

"Okay," Syren said with a smile.

"Good," May responded then they continued to walk down the stairs. "You're very good you know, that boy up there is wrapped around your fingers. He has been since I saw him at Thanksgiving, whether he knew it or not," May said with a chuckle.

"You should've told me, you would've saved me a lot of unhappiness if you did," Syren said.

"Never let a man make you unhappy. Besides, it wasn't my business to tell. It was between you two to figure it out."

"It's easier said than done," Syren countered.

"You're inexperienced now but you'll learn." May said, "Your eyes are the most beautiful I've ever seen by the way."

"What?"

"It's purple."

"Oh," said with a smile.

"So, you finally got what you wanted," May remarked.

"Yes, I'm so excited."

Syren hugged her grandmother as they walked down the hall. The music grew louder with every step.

"Grandma, how do you know I haven't done it before?"

"Because you're my granddaughter - my favorite one- I know you. I shouldn't say that but we all know it's true."

The suited doorman opened the door to the party and they both disappeared inside.

Alex had followed behind, staying far enough out of sight until he heard them enter the ballroom then entered as well. Cleo's rage emanated from her in waves he could feel when she saw Syren enter the room. She left soon after.

He didn't rush to find Cleo. Instead, he watched as Syren cut her large feather tiered cake. He listened as she was serenaded with the happy birthday song by some popular musician he didn't know. It might be his last moments seeing her, he decided to enjoy them.

At the end, he found her.

"There's something going on with my sister, I have to go."

"No," she said with a pout.

"I'm sorry," he took her hand and kissed it and found himself annoyed that her glove stood as a barrier between his lips and her skin. He hoped the gesture wouldn't attract too many eyes to them. He was already exposed just by being near her for so many months of endless media and paparazzi stalking them. He knew he'd have to disappear for decades to fall into anonymity again.

Syren was hesitant to accept his explanation for leaving but relented.

"I hope she's alright," she responded. "Let me walk you to your car."

"No, you don't have to."

"I want to," Syren insisted.

Alexander shook his head and kissed her hand again then he left with waiting for a response. He found the bathroom and once he was locked in, with thoughts of home on his mind, his body warped into a beam of violet light and he vanished.

Chapter 13: The Cabin

"So you made your choice?" Seth fumed.

"I did," Alex responded.

"I hope she's worth it because it won't last long. I'll make sure of it," Seth barked.

In an explosion of anger, Alexander grabbed his brother and they both vanished in the beam of light. Then they were falling over the ocean, kicking and punching until just before they fell in they both vanished then they were in Paris just outside the borders of High Palais.

"You're not gonna touch her," Alex barked, punching his brother's face while still struggling to focus on keeping them out of the palace. He was able to travel them to the Sahara desert, the most desolate place he could think of and they fell through the air until they hit the sand. Alex grabbed him by the neck, squeezing with a force that would kill a normal human instantly but wasn't enough to kill his brother though it did render his brother unconscious.

Once Seth was limp under him, Alex traveled them back to his house, in his bedroom, and locked the photon cuff around his arm.

The photon cuff was a thing of his creation and its purpose was to stop his kind from traveling through light.

As soon as he locked the cuff on Seth's arm Cleo appeared in the room. She'd been a bystander to their argument and though she didn't get a chance to speak, he was sure what she would say.

"After everything you're doing, I hope she's worth it."

"How very original. Seth said the same thing," Alex remarked humorlessly.

She leaned down to take Seth's unconscious body and Alex locked a cuff on her arm as well. Her eyes widened in shock. "What did you do?" She tried to travel but it was no use.

"I did what I had to because she is worth it."

She tried yanking the small metal cuff from her wrist but even with her inhuman strength, it was useless.

"It won't work," Alex said.

"Think about what you're doing?" Cleo said severely. "You can't take this back."

"I know." He sighed, "I tried to do it but I couldn't."

"Really? Because I don't think you ever planned on doing it," she barked.

Alex shrugged with an empty expression on his face.

'I will never forgive you for this," she barked.

"That's fine. We're not a family, we're a bunch of Set and Hhera's experiments pretending to be one. I'm done."

Cleopatra chuckled sardonically, "we were born. You were created. You're the only experiment here."

Alex ignored her jab at him, "I'm going get Isis, no matter the cost to me, just not to Syren." He sighed softly, "I've wasted enough time as it is."

"Taking away my ability to travel doesn't stop me from telling her what you planned to do to her. I don't see how you'll be together after that," she responded.

"We're not together and If I survive at the end of this I planned on telling her anyway so go ahead."

Cleopatra howled in laughter. "All of this and you're not even together?"

"I don't need to be with her to know that I'd rather not see her in Set's hands." Even saying the word in reference to Syren felt wrong on his lips and now the fact he was so close to committing the act disgusted him. "I want you and Seth gone by tomorrow. You can't stay here anymore."

Alex disappeared in the violet light before waiting for an answer.

~~~

Now, almost two days since he last saw Syren, he found himself on edge. It was harder than usual to be away from her this time, now that he knew exactly what he was missing. Never far from his thoughts were the feeling of her lips against his or how perfectly she seemed to melt into his arms. She always had the faintest aroma of lavender vanilla on her skin and citrus in her hair, true to her brand of existing in two opposing states, always.

He'd committed every facet of her face to memory and now when he closed his eyes, he saw her just as she existed.

It was a task keeping himself focused.

He was busy in the days that passed fortifying the proton shield around his cabin at the foot of the Andes mountain, in case he needed to go there with Isis or Syren. He knew Set would know by now what his decision was. How inconvenient it was that he had a futura vessel. According to Hhera, they were extremely rare even in Ahsylla. Set had one that Hhera created for him. She never revealed how many were in Ahsylla, wherever that was, it was protected so well that after almost two millennia they still couldn't find it.

After almost two days away, he landed on the outside porch. It was night but it seemed early as if the sun had just gone down. The lights were on which immediately annoyed him because he'd ordered his siblings away.

When he walked inside the scene that appeared before he left him frozen in place. Seth and Cleo, kneeling in front of a decayed body. Cleo was in a fit of hysterics.

"YOU-" Cleo screamed through her wails, "you did this!" Her entire body trembled. The utter rage she felt had her body breaking into convulsions. Cleo had never been keen on controlling her temper.

Alex was still frozen in place and then suddenly Seth was on top of him as he slammed into the wall. His fingers wrapped around Alex's throat, his teeth clenched together growling as he squeezed. Alex stood unmoving, allowing him to squeeze and it was only when his attempt to strangle him was futile that Seth defeatedly fell from him and dropped to the floor.

Alex was completely numb now as if his brother hadn't moments ago tried to suffocate him. He walked robotically to Isis' body and kneeled in front of her. When he reached out to touch her, Cleopatra shoved him away.

"Don't touch her! You did this! This is your fault- this is on you- don't you dare touch her. Look at what you did to my sister!"

Tears welled in his eyes now as the sting of her words rippled through him.

The sound of a car pulling up in front of the house became quite audible, breaking the silence. For a moment, it seemed like everyone was frozen in place and no one made a sound.

The doorbell chimed moments later.

Alex could feel the hairs on his neck standing stick straight. The bell chimed again. He looked to Cleopatra then to Seth wondering what they were going to do.

"Alexander?" Syren called impatiently.

In the blink of an eye, he'd flashed across the room in a blur and grabbed Syren's arm as he walked through the front door.

"He's coming for you, we have to go," was all he said as he walked with Syren.

Before Syren could respond Cleo called Alex from the porch behind him.

"Alex?"

He was already down the steps and in front of Syren's car. It was just his luck, he thought, that she brought no guards with her, the first and only time he'd ever seen her do that was the worst possible time to do it.

"He can kill us now Alex, don't you see- he's finally figured it out, you can't leave us here," Cleo yelled.

He turned around and now Seth was beside her. He didn't trust them knowing how angry they were but he couldn't leave them.

"What the hell is going on, Alex?" Syren asked, worried, and confused.

"Is everything alright?" Athena asked in her ear but Syren was too focused on Alex to answer.

Syren came to ask him why he was ignoring her calls. For days since he'd left the party, she couldn't reach him. He was so hot and cold, she couldn't figure him out but with everything she was hearing now, her reason for coming seemed to fall from concern.

"No matter what, don't let go of me," he whispered as he walked forward.

"Athena, send my guards, quickly," Syren said inwardly.

"I'll launch a team from Osiris, I already have the satellite in position. standby," Athena responded.

Seth and Cleo stepped down the porch and met him halfway too fast for her to see them. Alex pressed his finger on the bar of the cuffs and it opened at his touch. As soon as he took Cleo's cuff off, he heard the rustle of grass under boots and when he looked over, it was Set and four of his siblings.

"You know bastard, all of this could've been avoided if you'd just given the Ahsyllan over to me long ago." Set stepped forward with a smile, "of course now I can see why. She is a great beauty but unfortunately for you my dear, I've evolved past being affected by your charms, though my bastard clearly has not." He paused, "hand her over Alexander, I might leave your disappointing brother and sister alive if you do." Set revealed in his hand, a stainless syringe with a black chemical inside.

Syren found herself reeling. Alex told her his father was dead, who was the man in front of them and why was he asking him to hand her over?

"Athena. Now. Right now!" Syren barked, not caring who heard. She tried to pull away from Alex's hand but he held her tighter. He didn't move at all at her resistance, like he was a large slab of granite.

"T- three minutes, just hold on," Athena said in her ear.

"Let me go right now Alex," Syren barked.

The picture of his cabin flashed in his mind as clearly as if it were in front of him but he knew he couldn't go there, not at first. Set was in close enough range to catch him.

Time seemed to slow as he grabbed Syren closer to his body though she resisted. He could see everyone converging on them. Cleo grabbed his arm as their bodies warped into a beam of light and they disappeared. In light time, the medium through which traveled, along with Alex and Syren, were Cleo, Seth, Set, and his siblings; Adom, Horus, Odion, and Ra who followed Set. He could see through the stream of distorted vision Seth and Cleo were fighting off their other siblings.

Set clung to him, trying to pry Syren from his arm. He heard her scream but tried to focus on not letting her go and getting them out of light time. Until one person could focus enough to overpower the others and take them to a specific destination they would stay in light time, traveling around the earth in perpetuity. Alex focused and after what seemed like ages in light time but was really a few seconds they fell out of the medium into an ice plain in Antarctica. It was dark and windy and absolutely freezing. He knew he could keep Syren there for long, he had to get away.

Everyone was scattered from the fall except for Alex who'd never let go of Syren. He pressed her against his chest and Cleo was within arms reach of him grabbed his foot and with Seth attached to her, they were off again. When Alex realized they were alone in light time, he finally traveled to his cabin.

~~~

They landed on grassy green terrain right outside the photon shield over his cabin. He hadn't intended for Seth and Cleo to know about the cabin but now he had no choice.

It was just after sunset and the sky was a mixture of blue, violet, and strips of burnt orange.

When Seth and Cleo sat up, Syren didn't move from beside him. The nausea from the traveling had her curled over him on the grass. He lifted her quickly and walked up to the edge of the shield and with Syren scooped in his arms, he pressed his palm against the shield. Cleo and Seth held him and they were allowed to pass through.

The shield was dome-shaped. The night was lighter than it was in New York. It stretched out a few hundred feet from his log cabin. The cabin he'd built himself some centuries ago stood hundreds of miles from any settled area. Behind the cabin, was the view of the Andes mountain in the distance and a large lake that had the image of the snowy distant mountains reflected on the still waters.

The proton shield protected his property from light travelers.

He walked slowly to the porch of his two-floor cabin and sat her on the chaise lounge.

"Put your head between your knees," he said softly.

He remembered her screaming.

"Are you hurt?" he asked.

She offered no response as she bent her long legs and Alex helped her wedge her head between her knees. She sat there for a moment and she could feel contusions on her body where Set grabbed her as her adrenaline waned.

Every time she tried to think about what just happened, how she'd ended up from one part of the world to another in seconds, a new wave of nausea hit her.

She couldn't get words out of her head. Alex was supposed to give her over to his father. How was his father alive and why would he do that? She couldn't stop the scene from replaying in her mind until it made her sick enough to vomit. Syren jumped up quickly and with two long strides she off the porch, kneeling in the grass and regurgitating the orange chicken she'd eaten for her early dinner.

She could feel him beside her almost instantly, running his hands down her back, trying to soothe her.

"Can one of you get me a bottle of water?" Alex begged as he was still beside Syren rubbing her back. He pulled her hair from her face so she wouldn't soil it with vomit.

He hadn't paid much attention to his brother and sister, except to notice that Seth seemed frozen and barely moved from his position of staring at Syren and Cleo seemed to glower at him with disgust.

"Get it yourself," Cleo spat back.

Alex ignored her and turned to Seth. "Seth?" he called and was surprised when his brother nodded and walked off to find it in the cabin.

Once she'd thrown up, Syren was beginning to feel clear-headed again. The nausea waned quickly and when Alex handed her an opened water bottle, she took a sip and gargled it in her mouth to get the bitter taste of vomit out.

"It's a little cold out here, we should get inside?" she heard Alex say softly.

He held out his hand to help her up but she didn't take it. There were so many questions she needed answers to. She started with the most obvious one.

"How did we get here? How did you do that?"

"It's called light travel. Come inside with me, I can explain it all to you."

"What was that man talking about? He said he was your father- you told me your parents were dead. He said you were supposed to hand me over...is it true?"

The look of twisted agony on his face told what she needed to know. His severely sad eyes told her that there had to be more as well but she didn't care.

"Is it true?" Syren asked again.

"I'll tell you everything but we need to go inside-"

"-I'm not going anywhere with you. Answer the question." She peered into his eyes. As she stared she recognized the look. It was the look he'd had when they first met. The one she couldn't figure out. Now she knew what it meant.

"It's true," was all he responded in a low flat voice. He stared back into her dark eyes as he spoke.

"Athena, get me out of here," she said frantically as she stood quickly with eyes filled to the brim with hot tears. She began walking into the dark terrain, the direction whence they came.

Athena didn't respond and suddenly she realized Athena had been oddly silent.

"Athena?" she said frantically.

"Athena won't work in here," Alex said as softly as possible so she wouldn't feel threatened, "the shield stops everything. There's no communication to the outside."

He stepped closer and instinctively she took a step back.

"I would never..ever...hurt you Syren."

"We're way past that part Alex," she said angrily.

The words somehow cause his throat to burn, as if the next words that came out would be one gargled cry. He tried to respond but he couldn't get anything out of his throat and the burning was too severe.

She could see how it affected him and knew she had to get herself away from him, if she stayed there any longer, she might be the one consoling him.

"I want to leave," she said, not looking directly at him anymore.

"I won't force you to stay. If you want to leave," he said, the burning still raged in his throat, "then I will take you back but the moment I take you back Set will be there."

"I don't care, you're working with him, aren't you? Isn't that what you just said?"

"I'm not."

"You just said you were going to hand me over to him. What would you call it?" She retorted sharply.

"Set just dropped my dead sister's body in my living room because he didn't get what he wanted. I'm not working with him, I never was. I just wanted my sister back," he said softly as he stepped closer. This time Syren didn't step back from him. "I promise I'll tell you everything I know just-"

"How am I supposed to trust you?"

He shook his head, unsure of how to respond.

"-What do you want from me?" she asked, confused. "Is this about money or-"

"Money?" he said in disgust, "no I don't care about that- look, I can explain okay just give me a chance."

Out of the shield behind him, one of her guards dropped from the sky in the grass. Then another and another. Syren turned around to see scores of guards forming a barrier around the shield. It was getting dark but the glowing light from the cabin made it visible enough to see.

"It looks like Athena heard you," Alex said defeatedly.

Syren shook her head- "She just picked up my last location. "She looked to her guards then to Alex. "You said you would tell me everything...what does that mean?"

"It means I'll tell you what I am and everything I did. I'll tell you why Set wants you. I'll tell you about the Ahsyllans and anything else you need to know- well...as much as I know."

Syren realized the conundrum she faced because she wanted to stay. She wasn't sure if that was because he seemed so authentic as he stood before her with grief-stricken features or because she was madly in love with him and desperately want-ed to salvage something of their relationship. She wanted him to redeem himself fully so she could give herself an excuse to forgive him.

Syren reflected and after everything she'd just seen if he was able to fool her for so long then her judgment was askew.

"I'm sorry Alex but I don't trust you- I can't...too much has happened."

He seemed strained as he walked in the direction of the shield. Syren followed but was stopped by Seth.

"I'm sorry, I can't let you leave," he said matter of factly.

"What are you doing?" Alex asked.

"Isis is dead now, if Set gets her, whatever he had planned will make him more powerful and then he's coming for us- I can't let that happen. I'm not losing any more family."

"Seth, move out of her way," Alex commanded.

"Isis is dead because of you so you're the last person I care to hear anything from, brother."

In a quick movement, Alex was between Seth and Syren.

"I'm not fighting you, Seth, this has nothing to do with you, leave, now."

"I won't," Seth said as he took a few steps closer to Alex.

"Have you ever won a fight between us?" Alex asked as he walked and stopped inches away from Seth. "Think hard Seth because you have fun starting fights but you can never finish them," he said in a flat, low voice.

"Alex?" Syren called, snapping him from his fit of rage.

Alex turned around and faced her. He took a breath and calmed himself.

"Can I trust you?" she asked, desperate to avoid a quarrel between the brothers.

"You won't ever come to any harm at my hands."

She nodded as she ignored the thumping in her chest and the chance that she was possibly making a mistake. Even after everything that happened, she didn't fear him, not truly.

"What about your siblings?" she asked, looking at Seth.

"I won't let them hurt you."

"Okay, I'll stay...just until you tell me what's going on."

Alex nodded.

She passed his sister who was still on the porch. Cleo glared. Alex was behind her in a blur and reached the front door before her to open it.

When she walked into the cabin, the fireplace was lit. It was warm which was a drastic contrast to the outdoors and it was only in the warmth that she realized her finger tips were numb. Cleo and Seth walked in behind Alex.

"Are you hungry?" Alex asked her.

Syren shook her head as she looked around for somewhere to sit.

"We can sit on the couch?" he suggested.

She followed him over to the couch and unzipped her short Moncler jacket, pulled it off her arms and dropped it on the couch before she sat and folded her legs.

Alex sat in front of her on the coffee table.

"Give us a minute," he said to his brother and sister who were still standing just a few feet away behind the couch, with the same opposing stares.

"I want to hear you tell her," Cleo said angrily.

Syren turned around to look at his sister. She was rather plain, Syren judged, with clear olive skin and chocolate brown hair. She was nowhere near as unbelievably beautiful as Alexander, neither was his long-haired brother Seth.

"I'm not doing this right now Cleo," he said impatiently.

"No, I want to hear you tell her- tell her how you let your sister die because of her."

"Cleo, you chose to come here and I didn't ask you-'

"-If she can stand to look at you when you're done then you deserve each other."

"Flavia," he barked, calling her by her name given at birth. "Go then!"

Her breath hitched in her throat at the raw anger in his tone, she stood glaring at him for a few silent moments, and then she stormed out of the cabin and slammed the door behind her.

Alex sat on the coffee table trying to calm himself but the shaking in his hands wouldn't stop.

"I'm sorry- I need a minute-" he said as he disappeared from the door. Syren didn't see him, all she heard was the door towards the back porch close. While the front of the cabin was made of mostly logs, the back was almost entirely glass which afforded a perfect view of the lake and the dark mountains in the back.

She saw him pacing for a few moments before he sat down at the edge of the porch. As angry as she was at him, she couldn't bear the way his sister spoke to him. She slipped on her jacket and grabbed the throw blanket from the couch and headed towards the door.

Syren ignored the stares from Seth and opened the glass door and stepped out to the back porch. Alex didn't turn around. She stooped and wrapped the blanket over his shoulder then sat beside him with her legs folded.

"Thanks but I would've been back in a minute," he said, still looking forward.

"It's fine. It was getting quite stuffy in there actually."

He turned to look at her eyes. With the reflection from the porch light could see them. They were pitch black.

"You can ask any question you want," he said, "because I don't know where to start."

Syren thought for a few moments. "What happened to your sister?"

He shook his head and chuckled humorlessly as if that was a ridiculous question to ask. "That's the question you ask?"

"You said I could ask and you would answer,' Syren said matter-of-factly.

He sighed heavily and was silent for a few moments before answering.

"A few years ago, Set took my sister Isis, his condition on returning her was that I bring him the Ahsyllan Prime."

"And who is that supposed to be...me?"

He nodded.

"Ahsyllan prime?"

"You're the first Ahsyllan, the prime form, and the queen."

Syren chuckled and shook her head, "I'm not a queen and Ahsylla doesn't exist."

"It does."

"It's just a place my mom told me stupid stories about when I was younger."

He didn't know where to start."That wasn't your mother Syren, that was you...just in a previous form. Ahsylla does exist, I've never seen it before but that's because it's shielded with a shield like the one I have here only that shield is probably a thousand times stronger and more advanced"

"You can't shield an entire landmass, Alex-"

"Yes you can," he insisted, "especially if it was there before primitive explorers set out to make maps."

She tried to wrap her head around his explanation and it did make sense so she decided to press on."You said I was in a previous form?"

"Yeah. You're a-sexual, all the Ahysllans are." He paused, "it's homogenesis, you give birth to yourself, over and over again and that's how you've been able to live so long. It's a form of immortality called cyclical-immortality. That's why all your ancestors look exactly like you, it's not that they're your ancestors, it's you and that's why you die after reproducing. After you produce a new form of yourself the old one becomes weak and dies while the new gets stronger."

Syren began hyperventilating, this information was not something she was prepared for. He instinctively reached to her and held her cheeks gently, staring into her eyes.

"It's okay, I know it's a lot...just breathe."

She inhaled deeply and exhaled. They did this a few times together before her breathing returned to normal.

She had a million thoughts in her mind, each of them utterly insane to contemplate. There were so many things about herself she couldn't explain for so long. It felt overwhelming to get answers to questions she ignored for many years

"So my father isn't my father, he's just an ex-lover?"

Alex nodded.

Syren broke into loud cackles, so loud she had to cover her mouth. Soon, the cackles turned into sobs. Alex nestled her into his chest and for a while she allowed him to hold her as she cried but once she calmed she remembered she was supposed to be angry at him and turned from his embrace.

"Why don't I remember anything? Do I always forget?" she asked as she wiped her eyes.

"No, I wondered that too. I think the only reason you don't have access to your memories is that your past form didn't want you to. It should be in your head though, you just have to figure out how to access it."

"If I'm supposed to be the prime or the queen of...Ahsylla," she felt ridiculous even saying the words, "why aren't I there?"

Syren remembered the stories Isabeli told her.

He sighed."There was a war and a lot of your people died, this was some 3000 years ago. Some of your people had to scatter, including you, to hide or prepare for the fight which-"

"-Excuse me, did you just say I'm over 3000 years old?"

"Syren-" he paused, unsure of how to say it, "you have to be at least...millions of years old, if not a billion, at least."

This time her face was unreadable. "If this is true, what do you and your family want from me?"

He hated the way she phrased it because he didn't want anything from her...at least not anymore. "I don't know, I just know that he's hungry for power, always trying to get stronger, and he's become increasingly cruel in the ways he tries to do it. He's obsessed with you, your people, and your power so if he wanted you, it had something to do with your power."

"Why now?"

"This form was supposed to be the strongest but you're suppressed, I don't know if you did that on purpose or if it's something else. This form of you is what everyone's been waiting on. He knew he couldn't try it with previous versions of you. He thought this was his only chance."

She was silent for a while as she thought about everything that happened up until that point.

"So, you pretended to go to university for years to get an internship at my company because somehow you knew I'd be there before even I did and this was all to get close enough to kidnap me and give me to your dad. Why didn't you?"

Her eyes were solidly black as she stared at him.

"Isn't it obvious?"

"When were you gonna do it?"

"At your party," he said after a while. "I followed you when I saw you leave. I planned to just grab your hand and take you to him and get my sister in return but I just couldn't do it to you."

"There were many opportunities when you could've done it before the party. Why didn't you?"

"I kept finding excuses to put it off because like I said, I knew that it couldn't do it."

"What about your sister?" Syren asked. "He killed her because you didn't bring me to him?"

"I didn't know he was going to kill her," he said with sadness thick on his voice, "I didn't think he could. We are extremely hard to kill. I thought it was impossible until now but after almost 2600 years I guess he figured it out."

She was breathless for a moment. "You're 2600 years old? Are you Ahsyllan like me?"

"No, I'm a cheaply built, less sophisticated imitation...all of us are."

"What do you mean built?" she asked confused, hoping it didn't mean what she thought.

"I'm a vessel."

Chapter 14: Vessel

She felt a knot tighten in her stomach when she said the words. She stood from the porch.

"You're not even real!" she said angrily.

"I am real," he responded, now on his feet too. "Look, you said you wanted to know everything, at least let me tell you. I don't expect you to want to have anything to do with me after all of this is over but at least let me tell you."

Syren teetered nervously. She wasn't sure if she wanted to hear the rest. The man she loved was a robot, that seemed to bother her more than everything else he'd said. Was he programmed to make the choices he'd been making or did he have free will?

"Why should I believe anything you say?"

"Because it's true."

After a few breaths, she was able to stand still enough to listen. Alex began again.

"There are two types of vessels; bi-vessels and cy-vessels. Cy-vessels are robots or androids or whatever you want to call them. Bi-vessels are engineered humans. I was born."

"How?" she asked.

"Hhera, she was an Ahsyllan scientist. After the war, some of you scattered from Ahsylla. Some five hundred years later in Egypt, she met my father. They fell in love and she told him about her secret. He became obsessed with her power and convinced her to make him and his children stronger. The lifespan of humans was abysmally low, she agreed and at the time my father had nine children."

"How did she-"

"She had a serum. In Ahsylla you'd engineered all sorts of large species of animals so it wasn't far off for one of your scientists to be able to replicate that on a smaller scale. She refused to make any more after she realized he was going mad. When she refused he turned on her."

"Why didn't she just kill him?" Syren asked.

"Because he killed her first. As I said, you guys are a-sexual, when you reproduce one form gets stronger and the other weaker until the weaker one dies. That's the only time you'll have any luck killing an Ahsyllan. She made the mistake of telling him that and so when it was her time and she gave birth to her new form, he killed them both but that was after she created me.

"My sister Isis took me and hid with me. She was barely a teenager herself at the time, fourteen I think but she raised me, and then eventually Seth and Cleo found us and joined us.

"I don't think he ever forgave Isis for saving me from him which is exactly why he took her as soon as he figured he could kill her." He shook his head, "I am real Syren. If I'm not and someone created this life- this horrific, endless, miserable existence..." The thought angered him and he couldn't finish the words. "Hhera gave me immortality but I like to think that I created this hell for myself, by my-self."

He felt Syren's arms around his waist and immediately shimmied from her grasp, pulling her arms from around him.

"Don't- don't feel sorry for me...just don't." He shook his head and walked back to the edge of the porch where he'd left.

"Don't turn your back on me," she said softly.

He turned around, begrudgingly.

"What happened to your sister-" she was at a loss for words, "-I'm truly sorry. I should've said that sooner."

"There's nothing to be sorry about. I made my choice, now I have to deal with it."

"Yeah but the fact that it was even a choice for you...you could've given me over to him...but you didn't. She couldn't find the words to sufficiently describe her emotion. "I appreciate it." it felt woefully inadequate.

"I didn't do it because I wanted you to be grateful and if you appreciate me not kidnapping you and handing you over to a psychopath then you've set a very low bar."

Syren rolled her eyes and shook her head in response. "I don't understand you, Alex, I don't. What was the point of this? Why did you tell me?"

"Because you deserved to know."

"Okay so now that I know, don't expect me not to react." she began, "Just thinking about having to make the same choice between you and Ruby is enough to never give me a night of sleep again," she tried to sound light but his lips never moved from the tight pressed line that seemed to be his facial expression now.

She walked closer and wrapped her arms around his waist again.

"Syren, no," he said hesitantly.

"Don't push me away," she said firmly.

"Syren, when I made the decision that I did, I didn't expect there to be an 'us' after and now that my sister is...gone-" The words got stuck in his throat and he stopped.

Her hands dropped from his side immediately. Her irises became flame red.

"So that's it, you've made all the decisions. After months of lying, you decided you finally needed to come clean and you tell me all these things that have completely turned my life upside-down," she said with angry, hot tears, "I forgive you for everything. I'm telling you that I forgive you but you've decided that's not what you want. You've decided to drop this on me and then what? You're done?" She was fuming with anger, so much so that she hyperventilated as she spoke.

"Good, you should be angry." He said.

Syren shook her head as she inhaled deeply to even her breath. "You're right. There is no us. You and I are very different. You don't even know if your sentient. Everything you've ever thought could be a lie, planted in your head, by code. How do you know what's real? I was a fool to think that meant nothing."

"Syren, that's a little far," he said angrily.

"You're not human, Alex."

"Neither are you," he shot back. "Does that change how you feel, or how you act or how you think."

"Yes, it changes how I feel about you."

Alex didn't respond, there was no response he could form to the fact that Syren had reduced him to a mindless drone. Everything burned inside him and after a hard gulp, he took a breath. She was angry and rightfully so but he had to believe she didn't mean it.

He reached into his pocket and took one of the photon cuffs he'd stuffed inside."This is a photon cuff, it prevents you from traveling through light which is what we did earlier. I'm the only one who can open it. Do you want it? It will prevent Set from taking you."

"I don't want it," she responded.

"Syren, please."

"No Alex-"

"I know that I've caused you a lot of pain, with everything I've done and everything I've told you today. If there's anything you believe, just please believe that I love you, more than anything and I would never want anything to happen to you.

"I need you to know exactly what you're up against. I can try to help defend you against Set, I can try to help you to figure out why your powers haven't materialized, I can try to help you with your memory. Whatever you need."

"I need you to get me out of this shield so I can get the fuck out of here. That is what I need," Syren retorted sharply.

She couldn't look at him. The urge to throw herself into his arms was still there. With everything she knew about cy-vessels, and how they were created, how they function, she hoped Alex was nothing like them.

"Syren, I told you, it's not safe-"

"You said when I was ready to leave I could. I'm ready to leave," she said angrily.

"Sy-"

She turned and walked through the cabin quickly and came out through the front door. Alex was behind her in an instant. It was then that she realized there were so many questions she didn't ask but at the moment it didn't matter, she just wanted to leave.

He grabbed her hand as she stepped off the front porch.

"At least wait until the morning," Alex begged.

"Alex, all I need is for you to take me outside the barrier."

He sighed angrily. "Why are you doing this Syren? I know you're angry at me but you have to understand- my sister is dead because I chose you, because I wasted time. The guilt that I feel- I don't know when it'll go away. I can't just be with you and be happy with you while my sister's body is rotting. You're not leaving here tonight. I'm not taking that chance. When it gets light out, I'll take you wherever you want to go."

"Is this the kidnapping you told me earlier you couldn't bring yourself to commit?"

Alex stared at Syren for a moment. His ice-blue irises met her scarlet red and for a moment he was stuck in place. After his brief pause, he regained his senses and stormed back inside the cabin, not bothering to wait for her but he did keep a watchful eye until he saw her head back. Minutes later she walked in behind him and sat on the couch.

"Are you hungry?" he asked.

"Don't say a word to me, Alex," she said venomously.

"Are you tired?" he asked. Syren didn't respond but he figured she was. "I'll get the bed ready for you, in case you are," he said as he disappeared up the stairs.

She didn't bother waiting for him, instead, she removed her jacket and laid a cushion against the arm of the couch. Syren covered herself with one of the throw blankets then laid staring at the fire.

Fatigue weighed her down but too many thoughts plagued her mind for rest to come. Her family wasn't her family. Her life wasn't her life. Everything that she'd thought about herself and the world had been a lie. But somehow, the worst of all was once again, Alex's rejection, even if he believed it was justified.

Syren closed her eyes when she heard footsteps descend the stairs.

When Alex returned, he saw her laying on the couch with closed eyes and figured she was asleep. He slid off her boots and covered her feet with the blanket and then sat in front of the coffee table watching the glow from the fireplace dance across her features.

Hours passed when Seth walked from the kitchen with two empty glasses and a bottle of aged whiskey.

"We're toasting to Isis." Seth filled a glass with liquor and sat it beside Alex on the coffee table.

"You have all this great liquor in the cabin but you never drink it so I figured you can have one glass for her."

Seth sat on the armchair across the room, careful to give himself a line of vision to Syren. As he sat he shifted the chair, causing a screech across the stone floor.

Syren shuffled in her sleep then opened her eyes and saw Alex in front of her, staring down at her.

"It's okay. It was just a chair."

Her heavy lids slowly closed.

Seth raised his glass, "to Isis," he said.

"Don't wake her," Alex said quietly.

When Syren heard Alex speak she realized she couldn't go back to sleep, though she never opened her eyes.

"Truce?" Seth asked hesitantly.

Alex didn't raise his glass, or respond.

"Look, the timing of everything...I think he was gonna kill her regardless. I don't know if you noticed brother but he seemed all too excited to flash that vile at us in the yard."

"I noticed."

"Who do you think he'll kill first?" Seth asked.

"Me," Alex said.

"Yeah, he hates you the most," Seth agreed with a smile, "his bastard."

Alex shrugged.

"Back in the 1690s in Massachusetts, Isis fell in love with a christian preacher-"

"I'm not in the mood to reminisce, Seth. We had our toast, now leave." Alex took Syren's hand and pressed it against his cheek then closed his eyes and sighed.

"You didn't toast," Seth joked.

When Alex was still silent Seth decided to change the subject.

"You know, I didn't expect her to look like this- I thought Hhera was unreal, I thought Khmya was unreal and she was just a futura but her…I guess I understand why it was so hard for you."

"My affection for Syren has nothing to do with her appearance," Alex opened his eyes and snapped at his brother, only to remember Syren was sleeping.

"Of course not," Seth remarked sarcastically. "After 2600 years of being impervious to everyone, I'm sure a rather plain-looking Jane could've wrapped you around her fingers in the span of a few months."

"I don't expect you to understand my feelings for her and I don't care."

"Fine but answer this: if you could make the choice all over again, knowing you'd end up right here, would you?"

Alex groaned uncomfortably at the question before he even attempted to answer. "What does it matter? She hates me." Seth tilted his head to the side, eying his brother and urging him to answer the question. "If I knew he could've killed her I would've tried to get Isis the second he took her. Syren would have never been involved and everyone would've been the better for it."

"You know it wasn't that easy. You would've never gotten her out of there without Syren to exchange or we would've tried that."

Alex sighed, "I wanted her to be angry with me and now that she is, it feels," he stopped, "it's agonizing. The things she said about me being a vessel, I think she only said them because she was upset at me but I can't imagine she doesn't actually believe them."

"Did you expect anything else, she's an Ahsyllan. If they cared anything about us, they wouldn't have left us to fend for ourselves for thousands of years. Hhera didn't create you out of love, she created you as a weapon. How many vessels does she have serving her and catering to her every whim daily?"

"Those are cy-vessels. I thought she would know we were different. I thought she would understand."

"I never expected her to, which is why I was surprised you even let yourself fall in love with her at all."

"Do you think it was a choice?" Alex asked.

"I hope not," Seth answered, "I know you would never let that happen if you knew it would lead to Isis dying. All this planning, all this plotting for years it was all for nothing. We should've just taken her when her other form died this wouldn't have happened. She was eight years old. It would've been easy and this would've been over but you decided to wait till she was older and this is the result."

"When she was eight years old. I was supposed to kidnap an eight-year-old?"

"Well if you'd done that instead of spending years creating this fake life-" Seth paused and thought for a moment before he continued, "what does it matter. Set would've killed her either way."

He felt the sudden need for the burning in his throat and gulped his drink.

"Do you think she'll be ready? This Majikai guy is coming for her. Hhera said he murdered half their population…"

"I don't know what to think," Alex tucked a few strands of her golden hair from her face as he spoke. He observed her eyes moving under her lids and worried that she was awake. "I'm going to bed, Seth. We can talk tomorrow," Alex said. He let go of her hand and tucked it under the blanket.

"It has to be a reason she's not ready yet or maybe they got it wrong, maybe it's not this form," Seth continued, ignoring his brother.

"I'm going to bed," Alex said again.

Seth sighed."You know you can't let her leave right?" Seth said.

"It's not up to me. I want her to stay but I'm not keeping her hostage here. She doesn't want the photon cuff and she doesn't want anything to do with me."

"I heard your entire conversation. You made sure she was mad at you."

Alex didn't respond.

"So you're giving up?" Seth asked.

"What else can I do Seth? She's made her choice." Alex shook his head and stood.

"Convince her then."

"She won't listen to me."

"But you're not even going to try? If I hadn't stepped in earlier she would've been gone already."

"I remember very clearly what you did!"

"I was trying to help you."

"That's not how you do it."

"See that's your problem. You're too worried about whose feelings get hurt and who's mad, you tried to spare everybody's feelings and Isis is still dead and your Ahsyllan girlfriend hates you so now what. And Set is still out there. After she leaves then what...all of this was for nothing. Set gets her and we all die..." Seth wondered aloud.

"She already made clear that she doesn't want to. I'm not forcing her. I'm done. I'm not talking about this anymore."

"She loves you, if you ask her, truly ask her, she will stay-"

Alex shook his head, "You've known her for the space of one conversation...not even...a few sentences. I don't need advice from you."

"No, you don't. I don't know her but I know you," Seth said. "You won't make her stay and not for the reason you say. You won't because you know that if she's here with you, you won't be able to resist her and because Isis is dead, you'll feel guilty about being with her. Guess what, I know Isis and you know her even better than me. She spent centuries trying to convince you to find someone. Do you seriously think that she would be upset that you did, regardless of how it happened."

Alex didn't respond, "as I said. I'm going to bed. This conversation is over."

"Maybe you just feel guilty about hurting her."

Alex looked back at Syren. Her eyes were no longer moving under her lids.

"She'll get over it. She can have anyone she wants," he said then he took a seat on the coffee table once again.

"You can have anyone you want. Does that make you feel better?"

Alex sighed and shook his head, "at the end of this form, she'll get a new one and it'll be like none of this ever happened...well...for her at least. I hate that I've sprung all this on her but at least now she knows what she's up against."

"And you?" Seth asked.

"It's gonna be harder this time, I won't see her every day and I won't get to hear her voice or spend hours trying to decipher the feelings behind her eye colors when she's staring at me but it won't last long. Set is going to kill us. He seems very determined. I guess the only thing I can do now is figure out a way to take him with me. If I get the cuff on him then that will at least neutralize him. That's the one thing I can do to protect her right now so that's what I'll focus on. Then I have to figure out how to kill him. If the serum he made can kill us then it can kill him."

"There's a beautiful symmetry in that," Seth said with a chuckle.

"I won't let what happened to Isis happen to Syren."

"I'll be right there with you," Seth said matter-of-factly.

Alex furrowed his brows with shock and confusion."Where is all brotherly love coming from?"

"You're my little brother and you're a maudlin little asshole to an annoying degree but if we're gonna survive Set, we need to be together. If we had figured this out earlier instead of leaving you alone to get Isis back, maybe we wouldn't be here."

"I don't think Cleo will appreciate you making plans on her behalf," he remarked sadly.

"She lost her sister. Give her time, she'll come around. It can't only be your fault because the truth is anyone of us could've gone and tried to get her back. We didn't and now she's dead, we have to share that."

Seth stood and sighed."You can't let her leave tomorrow."

Alex took a small cuff from his pocket then he took Syren's arm from under the blanket and locked the cuff around her wrist. "Now no one can take her and I don't have to keep her against her will."

"Was that so hard?" Seth said."I'm going to bed."

Alex nodded and then watched as Seth disappeared up the stairs and then turned back to Syren. She had a pained look on her face as if she was having a nightmare so he leaned down and stroked her cheek lightly with the back of his index fingers until she seemed to relax.

"I love you Syren…" he breathed out.

She wanted to open her eyes badly to tell him she loved him too but she knew nothing she could say would change his mind.

~~~

Syren woke to the smell of eggs and bacon. When she sat up, the fire in the fire-place was out and it was extremely bright out.

Alex walked in moments later,with a platter of food and placed it on the coffee table in front of her. Then he lifted the large wooden table as if it were made of paper and placed it a few inches closer to the sofa, so she wouldn't have to stretch.

"I heard you wake and figured you were hungry and you did say you felt light-headed if you missed a meal so…"

He could see her eyes were still pitched black but he tried to sound cheerful, even if it was fake.

When she looked down one rectangular white plate, it was filled with eggs, bacon, waffles, and sausage. On a second plate, there was toast, jams, sliced tomatoes, and creamed cheese. There was also a small dish of whipped cream to the side. On the tray, there was orange juice, tea, and water.

She had no idea why he thought she could eat so much food and though she was hungry, she couldn't eat."I'm not hungry."

"Syren-please." He gave her a knowing look and hoped it would guilt her into eating.

She took a moment to look him up and down since he was in front of her. He'd changed his clothes, it looked obvious that he'd showered. Now he was wearing black sweatpants and a white long-sleeved tee. His face was beautiful, the way it usually was but his fake cheerfulness couldn't hide how tired he looked. She decided not to give him a hard time about the food and pinched a piece of the waffle and ate it.

A half-smile spread across his lips and she immediately looked away. She couldn't be angry at him while he smiled. The two things conflicted too fiercely to exist together in a moment.

She took a sip of the orange juice and then remembered he placed the band on her wrist. Now she had to pretend to be shocked

"What is this?" she asked.

Alex took a breath before speaking. "It's a cuff that prevents you from traveling through light. Please wear it Syren, it's the only thing I can do to protect you from my father."

Syren offered no response to him. After hearing his conversation during the night she decided not to quarrel about the band if it would give him peace of mind. Instead, she leaned down to put on her boots but Alex stopped her.

"It's okay, I've got it, just eat," Alex said, elated she didn't object to wearing the cuff.

He kneeled and lifted her leg gently. He could feel her skin under her sheer black tights. Her legs stuck out from under her leather mini skirt. Syren looked down at him when she felt his hand on her skin, the contact lit her nerves on fire. Alex could feel her staring and looked up only to see a severe pout on her face then she looked away. He turned away and slipped her feet into her boots. He could feel her staring again and looked up again. Their eyes met and then she turned away again. He finished strapping on her boots then stood.

"I'm ready to go," Syren said as she stood.

"You barely touched anything," he complained.

"I have food at my home, Alex. I'm ready to go."

"I don't think you should go, not until we've done something about Set. I just...I can't risk him hurting you."

Syren gazed into his eyes. After overhearing his conversation with Set during the early morning she had expected him to ask.

"I can take care of myself, Alex, don't worry about me."

As Alex attempted to respond, Seth walked downstairs, looking so unusually cheerful that even his brother took notice.

"Morning," he said with a smile as he walked over to Syren and stretched his hand for a shake, "I didn't get to introduce myself last night and sorry about yesterday, it just wasn't safe for you to leave."

Syren stared at his outstretched hand."I'm not really a hand shaker so - no thanks-and the next time you get in my way or try to force me to do anything against my will again, you'll be sorry," she said then turned back to Alex, "I'll be waiting out-side."

She walked outside and her scowl was quickly removed when she became awestruck by the scenery. Syren noticed it was drastically warmer during the day than it was at night.

Behind his cabin were lush green rolling hills with the view of the bright snowy Andes further back. She could see the beautiful still, glacial lake. The water was a beautiful cloudy turquoise blue. She stood in awe of the scene, time seemed to stop as she committed it to memory though it was slightly distorted by the shield which seemed like a clear film over the view.

She walked to the shield and curiously reached out to touch it only to observe that her finger could pass through. She pulled it back and saw that her hand was fine and that didn't need Alex to pass through. She walked right through the shield out to the other side. Her guards were still there, standing statuesque, almost two dozen of them, waiting for her. There also was a small Excellci Corp aircraft.

"Athena, I'm ready to go," she said, hoping that her time in the shield hadn't disrupted Athena's connection to her mind.

"Ah, I was worried about you, I almost went down to get you myself."

"Athena, I need you to get Osiris to scan a mile radius behind me, there's some sort of shield, I need you to figure out its structure and properties."

"Been scanning since last night," Athena responded. "It's a shield similar to the dome at High Palace though his one is much stronger."

"Can our shield be converted to something as powerful as this?"

"It's too soon to tell. There are components of this shield that are not familiar to me."

"Fine, just keep scanning."

The engine of the small silver aircraft smoothly ignited and she realized this when she heard the quiet whirling of the turbines. When she stepped towards her aircraft in a sudden beam of light, Set and almost half a dozen other vessels appeared in front of her.

"Hello," he said with a smile. "We meet again, Queen Ahnais, or what do you call yourself today, Syren? It doesn't have the same ring though does it? Ahnais meaning 'the first one', Syren meaning what exactly?"

"Syren meaning 'killer of men'," she retorted sharply.

Set shook his head and laughed.

"How did you find me?" she asked, curious.

"My son's proficiency in shields would be inconvenient if the futura hadn't anticipated it. Human technology is basic but impressive, a simple tracker in your jacket
pocket sufficed."

She reached into the pocket of her winter jacket and found a small beacon.

"That was smart."

Athena assembled her guards behind her. They became invisible to all as they
stood in two rows of twelve.

Set chuckled nervously.

"I can have you on the other side of the world in the blink of an eye- and if you do
as I say, maybe I'll let your family live. The sister Katherine and the child Ruby- is
it? There's a father too I'm sure but I admit I don't understand the logic of that."

Syren inspected him and the vessels who accompanied him, tilting her slightly as
she examined him. All the guards, she realized looked to be the same age as Alex,
Seth, and Cleo. They also had similar features and it was then that she realized that
they were his children. Alex said Hhera had turned nine children that Set had previously and he must've been the tenth.

Her eyes were burning red in fury. "You've had millennia to make your demands of my other forms but you've chosen this one. Why is that? Is it because you've been told I'm weak or I'm defenseless and so like the predator you are you decided that this was your shot?"

"A smart man knows how to find an opportune moment."

She shook her head. "It's truly a shame, if you'd left me alone, you might have lived another millennia or two," Syren said dryly.

"See but that's a lie, isn't it? When you become realized, you intend on turning all of us into soldiers for your war. Mindless drones to be slaughtered."

"What?" Syren asked, confused.

"That may be your plan for me but I have other plans for myself and my loyal children that don't include dying in someone else's war and losing sentience. I killed Hhera, your scientist and I can kill you too."

Alex finally finished speaking to his brother and stepped out of the cabin, only to have his hairs stand straight at the sight a few hundred feet away from him.

"Syren," He roared angrily. She had the photon cuff but even then, he couldn't take any chances.

Seth ran out of the cabin. Cleo, who'd barricaded herself in one of the second-floor rooms came sprinting outside as well.

Set immediately tried to lurch at Syren but only to find himself frozen in place. He couldn't move, none of them could, she'd taken control of his body and the body of his sons beside him. All of them, at once.

"Kneel," she barked, in a thousand voices, of a thousand forms all mashed into one.

They dropped the ground on their knees.

"You will do whatever I tell you to do. You will be whatever I tell you to be," she said softly. "And you will like it."

Alex was the first to reach her but he was frozen as he watched.

She closed her eyes and wished them on fire and when she opened them the men kneeling in front of her burst into blue flames that clung to her body like skin.

Cleo and Seth arrived

"Syren, let go," Athena said.

The screams of agony were deafening, she could hardly hear Athena's whispers in her ear.

"Let go," Athena said again. "Let go."

The pain to hold them was too much and she had to break the hold she had on them.

Set and his sons fell to the ground but they still burned, charring the green grass around them. She felt weak from the strain on her body and dropped to the ground as well. It was as if she'd lost control of herself and someone else was in charge but as the moments passed the feeling waned.

Syren looked at Alex and the look of bewilderment on his face distorted his features. She was well aware that she'd given him the impression that she had no abilities at all.

"Athena, get me out of here," she begged.

The guards became visible again and as she watched Alex's eyes he seemed even more astonished. Enguerrand, the tallest, walked over and lifted her from the ground and brought her back to the aircraft.

Alex never moved except to watch her plane ascend into the air until it was no longer visible.

Chapter 15: Guilt

The invisible aircraft landed on top of the helipad on her glass facade high rise.
She walked into her condo to find Katherine sitting by the large white leather sec-
tional, flipping through a magazine.

"Guess who's on the cover of Flair Magazine," she said excitedly, "and also I'm
guessing last night went well since your just getting back-"

She noticed the swollen eyes and pained look on Syren's face.

"Or maybe it didn't. Are you okay? I've been calling you…"

"No."

Katherine tossed her magazine on the couch seat and stood, annoyed.

"What did he do now? At this point, he's not worth it."

"It's not like that," Syren mumbled.

"Then what is it?" Katherine asked.

"I don't want to talk about it. I'm really tired and I just need to go to bed."

"Come on Sy, you can talk to me," Katherine said softly.

Syren relented and retold the story of her night and for seemingly the first time Katherine was speechless.

"Was that why Marcus ran all those experiments on you when your mom died?"

Syren recoiled horror even hearing the name. "I don't think he knows anything about that. If he did, why would he take you and all those other kids?"

"Yeah, you're right," Katherine said with a nod."I still can't get over Teddy being - like...your ex-husband...that's gross. I just can't wrap my head around this, it's a lot."

"I know, it's hard for me too."

"So you think if you take the chip out of your neck you'll have all this power they're talking about?"

"I don't know...my mom.." she remembered and corrected herself, "or I guess I put this chip in me for a reason. Marcus couldn't remove it no matter how hard he tried. I must not have wanted it to be removed." Syren sighed, "I'm so confused and then everything with Alex on top of that is just too much."

"But I mean, you can't be surprised can you, I'm not..I've seen you move things with your mind you must've know that meant something even if you didn't know what it was."

Syren chuckled humorlessly, "I knew something was wrong with me but a million year old- or billion year old, a-sexual Queen from a hidden land who apparently has some war that's impending, was not what I was expecting.

"Are you gonna tell Teddy?"

"No. He can't even handle the fact that I have powers now and I can barely do anything. I definitely can't tell him I'm his ex-wife who he's been pining after for a decade."

"Yeah but Sy, you made a man burst into flames with your mind, that's not nothing. The things you could do before have never been nothing."

"I can't control it, you know that. I think the only reason I was able to do that was because I was so angry and for a moment I lost myself. I felt like I wasn't in control."

"Well at least you killed his dad. He hates him so how can he be mad at that?"

"I don't know if his dad is dead. I think I can kind of feel him still burning. I can feel all of them still burning. It's like I'm still connected to them."

"How would he survive being on fire that long?"

"I don't know. They've been alive for over two thousand years. If burning them alive was all it took I'm sure his dad would've killed them long ago. His brother said something about a serum, I don't know. At the time I was upset that he threatened you so I burned him."

"Yeah but it's been hours if he's still on fire he may be praying for death."

Syren shrugged sadly and then she pressed her lips into a tight line to stop them from trembling and wiped the tears that began to roll down her cheek.

"Aww don't cry…" Katherine hushed.

She looked up, though at nothing in particular and let out a long breath. "It's always something. Nothing is ever simple with me. I can't just be a normal girl. My dad can't just be my dad. The guy I love couldn't just be a normal guy that loves me back. Everything has so much baggage and it always has for such a long time. It's exhausting."

"At least me and Ruby are outstandingly normal that's good I guess," Katherine smiled softly, "everyone else hates normal and your the first person I've met who pines for it. I guess now I understand why. You're not normal." Katherine groaned. "I'm sorry, I still can't get over Teddy. Do you think he feels any romantic feelings...yuck I can't even ask."

"No," Syren shouted. "Eww...no. Not ever."

"You should look into all your history. Your palace has been around for over five hundred years so I'm sure that's the best place to find information on all the old...what do you call it..your form?"

"Yeah. That's what Alex called it but I'm not looking into anything. If I was supposed to know and if this so-called war was so important then why didn't Isabeli tell me."

"Maybe there's a good reason. You can't just block all this out Syren, that's what you do. If you don't want to deal with something you pretend it doesn't exist, just like Teddy. You can't do that now."

Syren shrugged, "don't go there Kat."

"You're being willfully stupid."

Syren didn't respond.

Katherine sighed "Are you gonna call him?"

"No, he made it quite clear how he was feeling and I know he loves me but his sister just died and he's grieving." Syren took a breath and shook her head, "I said some things I wish I could take back but I can't and I can't change his mind so I accept what is. Also, I set his father and brothers on fire."

"That was the most complicated sentence I've ever heard but you know what I think?" Katherine asked the rhetorical question then answered. "I think he's probably hurting. I can't imagine how I would feel if I lost you or how you'd feel if you lost me. You said that was the sister he was closest to and on top of that he's being blamed for her death and he did all of that because he didn't want to betray you. I think you should reach out. If not now then maybe after a little while."

Syren shook her head and wiped her eyes again. "Alex made his decision. He doesn't want to be with me. I will not beg him for affection."

Katherine shook her head and hugged her, "It sucks being rejected doesn't it? The very first time you're rejected. This is what normal people have to go through," she slightly teased. "You wanted normal. This is normal. Heartbreak is normal. Rejection is normal."

"God, I hate it so much," Syren whined with a humorless chuckle and wiped her eyes.

~

Angel Falls, Venezuela, it was one of her favorite places in the world and it was Christmas day, her favorite holiday. Alex reflected on the memories of Isis jumping from the top of the falls, down the stream of water. He thought it was appropriate for her to do so one last time in death. Moments before they dropped her Alex stared at the decayed body that was once his sister. He'd tried cremating her but fire did nothing to her corpse. She didn't smell like death, she smelled like fire and chemicals. Her face was no longer recognizable in it's mummified appearance but he could still tell that it was her. He kissed her cheek one last time as tears gathered in his eyes then he let her fall from the top of the cliff.

Cleo still kept her distance from Alex, a fact he was keenly aware of.

Seth poured a gush of whiskey over the cliff and then continued sipping from the bottle.

"It still doesn't feel real...like she's gonna show up at any moment," he said as he sipped the amber liquor.

They were all silent for a moment.

"Do you think he's still burning?" Seth asked.

"I don't know," Alex responded.

"If he is I think he'd prefer death at this point."

"Death would be too kind," Alex spat bitterly. It was hard to be angry as he looked out to the sea of greenery but somehow he managed.

"What are you gonna do now?" Seth asked.

"I don't know."

Cleo turned to them both.

"Tell her thanks for me and when you see her again I hope she doesn't discriminate against which vessels she sets on fire."

Alex shook his head and chuckled humorlessly. "Goodbye Cleopatra."

"Where are you going?" Seth asked.

"Somewhere far from both of you." As she said the words she vanished into violet light.

"She'll come back. She always does," Seth mumbled. "What are you gonna do about Syren?"

"Why the interest in Syren? And why all the brotherly love?" he shook his head angrily, "You don't have to pretend anymore. Syren is gone and Set is no longer a problem. You can go, just like Cleo."

Seth chuckled sardonically and rolled his eyes. His signature condescending smile emerged on his features.

"You've got to get over this self-pitying, lachrymose, bullshit. I guess we can probably blame Set for that. He's had you fighting since you were born. You've never really had time to stop fighting or hating yourself and live but guess what Alex, we've all been fighting for our lives and while we tried to live the best of it you were just a walking reminder of all the worst parts of it. That's why me and Cleo can't stand to be around you. I care about Syren, because you care about her. I wanted us to change, to get closer but you'd rather self-loathe." Seth stepped forward."I know you have a lot on your plate right now so I'll leave you alone. I'll visit you in a few years to see how you're doing," he said as he jumped off the cliff and disappeared midway down.

Seth was right and he knew it. He'd endured a miserable existence and that was all he could reflect on sat at the edge of the cliff, staring into greenness until nightfall.

~~~

There were a few things he needed to do. The first was to fire his housekeeper and pay her severance. The second was to pack all of his personal effects and take them to his cabin. The third was to call his real estate agent to discuss selling his property. Real estate investments was how he'd acquired his wealth. He'd realized the value in real estate thousands of years ago and began purchasing land from his days in ancient Egypt and Rome Now, he owned more property than he could readily identify.

It was on his second day at Park Hill that he received an unexpected visitor. Katherine showed up on his front porch at almost 8pm in the dark, cold night.

She banged on the door ferociously until he opened the door and was standing in front of her.

"You don't answer your phone?" she asked.

Alex was a little shocked and slightly confused."What are you doing here?" he asked.

"I was calling you and if you answered your phone then you would know I was heading over."

"I didn't know that was you," he said.

Katherine pushed past him and let herself inside.

"Nice house," she complimented as she scanned the foyer and large family room.

She could see a few boxes around the room, as if he were packing items.

"Katherine-"

She turned around and gazed at him. He looked empty, as if there was nothing in him, no emotion, no warmth, no life. He had dark circles under his eyes as well, as if he hadn't slept in days.

"Are you leaving or something?" she asked.

"Why did you come here Katherine?" he asked.

"Can we talk?" she said as she walked to the sofa in the family room. The tone in her voice hadn't changed since he greeted her at the door. It was still airy.

Alex walked to the couch but never sat down. He stood across from the coffee table, facing her.

"Are you leaving?" she asked again.

"Yes," he responded.

"Why?"

"Because it's time to leave," he said simply.

"Where are you going?"

"Nowhere very interesting."

"How long will you be gone?"

"As long as possible."

"Ugh- why are you being so withholding in your answers," she whined.

"How did you know I was here?"

"Athena told me."

He was silent.

"So...are you gonna say goodbye to Syren or no?"

"I already told her goodbye."

Katherine rolled her eyes."I don't get you, I really don't- with age comes wisdom and if were counting your age then you should be the wisest of us all yet you're really fucking stupid."

He shrugged as he realized Syren must've told her everything.

"Look- I know your sister died and - I can't imagine what I'd do if Syren died, she's like the other half of my body-" she got frazzled which was unusual, "whatever- that's not the point, I just think that you shouldn't shut out Syren because your grieving. Syren is so amazing. I love her with all my heart. Everyone loves her which is kind of annoying but it makes sense."

"Why are you telling me this?"

"Because I know you love her too and well...Syren's been really sad for the past four days. When she's not sad, she sleeps but not because she's tired, she makes Athena put her to sleep to pass time. I don't see how you can love her and do this to her."

It was a low blow and Katherine knew that but she believed the end justified the means. She waited for a response but there was none from him, just the same empty look behind his eyes that bothered her.

"So?"

"What do you want me to do?" he asked softly.

"You need to go talk to her and make her feel better," Katherine suggested.

"There's nothing I can say to make her feel better."

"She won't hurt you. She told me maybe you were freaked out because of what happened with your father. She's really sorry about that."

"I don't care about my father."

Katherine stood and sighed, annoyed. "What are you expecting to happen Alex, what's the ideal situation for you?"

"Nothing about this is ideal Katherine-" he sighed in frustration, "I'm done talking about this."

"I'm not." she said angrily, "when you love someone, who don't hurt them even I fucking know that and I'm not a two thousand year old moron."

"Do you think I want to hurt her," Alex barked angrily.

It was the first time since she arrived that she saw any meaningful emotional response from him.

"Well that's all you've done since you met her. You made her fall for you and then you ignored her for two months and then you tell her you love her and then you ditch her again. Then you tell her how it all a lie becuase you were trying to get your sister back and because she's an idiot she forgave you and then you ditch her again, after dropping a fucking hydrogen bomb of information about past forms and Ahsylla and everything else." Katherine drew in a deep breath to ease the anger she felt and continued, she was now pacing. "She's left reeling because who fucking wouldn't be and your response is 'what do you want me to do?' Do I have that correct?"

"All the more reason she should be done with me," Alex said defeatedly.

Katherine stopped her light pacing and walked to him. She stopped inches from his face.

"Stay as far away from her as possible. Don't contact her and whenever you change your mind about whatever your feeling and think you can come around again, don't," she warned.

Katherine headed to the front door and the moment she opened it and stepped on the porch Alex was there, in front of her. She jumped back. Syren told her he was fast but even so she was shocked.

"Syren," when he said the word everything else seemed stuck in his throat and tears filled his eyes, "she's the love of my life and it kills me that she's hurting but my sister is dead because I chose her. What do you want me to do Katherine?" He pleaded, "Everytime my sister had to make a choice, she chose me and when it was my turn to choose her, I didn't and she died because of it. How would you get over that? Could you just pretend nothing happened and live happily ever after with the person you chose over your own blood?"

"I don't know," Katherine mumbled, flustered.

She hopped quickly down the stoop and hopped into the back seat. A guard who was standing beside the car got in the driver's seat and seconds later the engine purred as they sped down the driveway.

Alex was been disabled for the night after Katherine had flayed his mind so deeply.

Syren laid in bed, hugging on to her pillow as she stared at the wall blankly.

"Katherine is approaching," Athena said.

Seconds later Katherine opened the door and walked into her bedroom.

"It's new year's day. Izzy, Josie and Lizzy are coming over for brunch soon, you have to get up."

"I won't be joining you," Syren responded.

"You can't just lay in bed Syren, it's pathetic and beneath you and the old you would've never acted like this. The old you would have been disgusted."

"The old me?" Syren asked.

"You before you met that man," Katherine spat. She stopped saying Alex's name out loud, out of spite.

"If you won't leave me alone Katherine then I'll just go to Paris and I'm not crying, I'm fine, I just want to be alone."

"I'm worried about you. I'm going to call May."

"Please don't call her."

"Why? You're afraid she'll talk some sense into you or she'll be disappointed your behaving like this."

Syren was silent

"God! I hope you get bed sores," Katherine sniped as she stormed out of her bedroom.

Katherine walked out and Syren went back to staring at the wall.

That was how her days went. They were empty. Things she usually found joy in were now tedious. Food she usually enjoyed now tasted bland. She couldn't focus on anything for any meaningful period of time nor could she leave her building. The farthest she went was to her office occasionally for an important meeting but it hadn't been business as usual since her night at the cabin.

The days grew harder to endure but she persisted, hoping that time would heal her. It was futile and weeks later she found herself again, in the same spot on her bed, trying to fend off the urge to call him.

Early in the morning, she surrendered to her desire after weeks of holding her resolve.

"Athena-"

"I will," Athena responded.

Her heart thumped in her chest violently as she waited to hear his voice in her ear. She felt tears gathering in her eyes as the seconds ticked by then she heard his voice.

"Syren?" he said softly.

All the words she thought to say in response got stuck in her throat.

"Sy, are you alright?"

"No," she said as she finally found the word.

"What's wrong?" he entreated softly.

"You've broken me, that's what's wrong."

"Sy-"

"I was fine before I met you. I was whole and now- it's like everything is empty," she said through sobs. She could hear his jagged breaths in her ear but he didn't speak. "You never should've told me you loved me. You should've just left me alone."

"What do you need me to do," he asked, in a quiet voice.

"Tell me you never loved me, tell me I was stupid to believe that you ever did."

"What does that accomplish Syren," he mumbled, frustrated.

"I just need to hear it."

She waited a while for him to say it. The seconds seemed like eons as they ticked by.

"I've done enough lying Syren."

She shook her head and rolled her eyes as she wiped her wet cheeks."Do this for me," she begged.

There was a pause before he spoke. "Where are you? I'm coming to you."

"No-"

"Just for tonight...let me hold you."

"No. You're not doing this to me again."

"Sy-"

"What happens in the morning Alex. When you leave? What happens then." she said angrily, "tell me you never loved me. That's all I'm asking. Do this, so I can move on. That's all I need from you."

He was quiet for what seemed like eons then he spoke."I'm not saying that you Syren. Those words will never leave my throat. Now tell me where you are so I can come or I will travel into every place I think you might be until I find you."

Syren was silent for a moment, "I'm in my bedroom in New York." The line went dead and when Syren looked up, Alex was standing at the edge of her bed looking as handsome as she remembered him. He wore a white shirt and sweatpants. His hair was perfect as it always was.

She wiped her eyes and suddenly felt dramatic for sobbing the way she was. Now that he was standing only a few feet from her she felt calm.

The only light in the room was from the sconces on both sides of her bed.

Alex gazed at her for a moment. He had to adjust himself to her beauty. Her skin a shade of brown, her golden hair, her pouty lips and her beautiful feline eyes. She wore tiny pajama shorts that her long legs stuck out from.

He had to take it all in again.

Suddenly, he reached across the bed and grabbed her by the waist and pulled her to the edge of the bed. Syren gasped as she grabbed unto his arms. She felt his hands on her thighs when he parted her legs and moved between them. The contact made her breath quicken.

Alex held both her cheeks and pulled her to him until their lips met. He slid his tongue between her lips and kissed her hungrily. Syren wrapped her arms around his shoulders then felt Alex's arms lift her against him, pressing their bodies together as he devoured her mouth.

The kiss got hotter and hotter and hotter. Now she was writhing in want underneath him.

Suddenly, they were at the head of the bed against the mountain of silk pillows. Alex was on top of her. He moved her hands from around his shoulders and intertwined their fingers then pulled them above her head. Syren wrapped her legs tightly around his waist. She could feel his large erect bulge pressed between her legs behind the soft fabric of his pants. Syren curled her toes at the sensation driving her mad.

She had never wanted anything in life the way she wanted to feel him inside her.

Then, he broke the kiss, suddenly and devastatingly. He was breathless and when he stopped she watched his eyes. They were hooded with lust, and love, and need, and Syren knew he wanted her just as badly as she wanted him.

"Alex," she panted "please." As she said the words she saw the fight behind his eyes. He was trying to find the resolve to stop and after a few moments he did. The need and lust that clouded his eyes had disappeared. Now there was nothing, only resolve. The same resolve that was there the night he told her there was nothing left between them.

He leaned up and in a flash he was standing at the edge of the bed again with a large, distracting bulge in his pants.

Syren turned her face away from him as her eyes filled with hot tears.

"I'm so sorry, Syren. I should've never come here," she heard his smooth voice say just above a whisper.

From the corner of her eyes she saw a small flash of violet then she was alone.

~~

The next morning, Katherine was surprised to see Syren in the kitchen, dressed in fabulous business attire as she ate breakfast.

"What's going on?"

"I'm having breakfast?" Syren said.

Katherine noticed she still had an empty expression on her face but she appreciated the fact that she was dressed in something other than pajamas and had finally left her room.

"Where are you going?" Katherine asked.

"I still have a company to run - Athena can't do all my work for me," Syren responded.

"Great, so you're getting better. That's good!" she said with a smile, "you should come to my fashion show today."

"I can't katherine- I don't want to."

Katherine rolled her eyes and sat at the kitchen island on a stool beside Syren. She took a bite of the poached egg Gus had laid out for her.

"Wooh," she howled as she scarfed down the hot runny yolk. "Rue wanted to come over today. She's been calling you and you haven't been answering her calls. She's really upset," Katherine said after swallowing her eggs.

"I'll call her later and talk to her," Syren answered.

She stood from her stool. "I'll see you when you get home for school," she said as she left the kitchen.

"Did I do something to you? You've been really distant to me in the past few weeks, I know you're mad about that guy but you should be mad at him. I didn't do anything."

Syren turned around. "I'm not mad at you Katherine, I just wish you knew how to read a room."

"What?"

"Katherine, I obviously don't want to talk. You badgering me for the past few weeks hasn't made me feel any better."

"Fine, I won't talk to you. I'll leave you alone to cry about a guy who obviously doesn't want you and won't change his mind," Katherine retorted.

She saw the water gathering in Syren's eyes and immediately felt remorseful.

"I'm sorry, that was a low blow-"

"I can't believe you just said that," Syren said softly before she turned and left the room.

Katherine followed her. "I'm sorry. I shouldn't have said that. That was mean."

"Katherine, do not speak to me alright, you've said enough," Syren said angrily then she turned and walked through the front door, leaving Katherine standing in the foyer.

~~

It had been days since his encounter with Syren and Alex found himself doing any and everything to keep himself busy.

He returned to his cabin with blocks of wood after chopping the scattered trees a few kilometers away. As he walked, he saw a quick flash of violet light glare through the open front door.

He was immediately annoyed, expecting to see Seth or Cleo he walked quickly to the front porch with the intention of sending them away. He was to be utterly and completely alone, their presence would disturb that.

From the front door, he saw jet black hair and olive skin. Even without seeing her face he knew who it was and was in utter disbelief.

Isis turned around.

"Alexy," she called.

"No-" he said, shaking his head, "it can't be you, you're dead?" he mumbled, disoriented.

She ran over to him and hugged him but he was too stumped to return it.

"How are you alive- this is not possible?" He broke the hug and stepped back, inspecting her face that looked the same as the last time he saw it years earlier. "What happened?" he asked, his voice trembled as he spoke.

"Set forced me to drink something- I don't remember much after that honestly because I think I was asleep then I woke up I was in the middle of nowhere and so I came here hoping you'd be here," she said with a smile as she hugged him again. "I missed you baby Alex."

"I still don't believe this-" he said, ignoring her nickname for him.

She stepped back, "wait- you asked how was I alive. What do you mean?"

"Set brought us your dead body- I was so sure that was you-" he wondered aloud, still confused.

"Set can't kill us? You know that."

"I thought he figured it out. He was certainly acting like it."

"Did it look like me?"

"It was decayed- like a mummy-"

Alex scanned her face, her familiar green irises with grey flecks. She looked exactly the same as he remembered. Everything about her felt familiar and he began to ridicule himself forever believing she was gone. Set was a prevaricator and had always been so, he should've sought more proof before believing it so easily. The next thing that came to his mind was Syren and how he'd cause her so much pain all because he believed another one of Set's lies.

While Alex got lost in thought, Isis inspected him and his features. His sad eyes and dark under eye circles. She knew what those signs were indicative of.

"So you really believed I was dead?"

"We had a funeral for you," he answered.

"Where?"

"I took that thing Set left us to Angel falls. Seth and Cleo were there. I threw it down the fall."

"That would be a nice funeral, poetic, if that were me," she said with a chuckle. "God, I miss everyone, where's Cleo, where's Seth?"

"I don't know- I don't have Cleo's number but I do have Seth's, maybe he was hers."

He pulled his phone from his pocket. It was new with the same number and he kept it handy incase Syren called back. He quickly dialed Seth's number but only received a voicemail.

"Meet me at my cabin as soon as you can, it's an emergency. Bring Cleo if you can, I can't get in touch with her." Alex hung up after leaving the message.

"Are you okay? I just realized you've been thinking I was dead this whole time?"

"Thinking you've lost the person you're closest to does leave you feeling very shitty but I'm fine- now" he said with a half smile.

"Something else is wrong- why are you being so withholding. Spill it."

"It's a long story Isis-"

"Great, I'm back from the dead- that was a joke-" she said laughing at her quip, "and I have all the time in the world- after I make myself something to eat, I'm starving."

She walked to the kitchen quickly. She'd been at the cabin enough times to know the place as if it were her own. It hadn't changed in her years gone.

Alex followed behind her and watched as she rummaged through the fridge and gathered food to eat.

"What has Set been doing to you- during the time you were gone."

"Starving me- obviously," she said with a laugh, "and testing a whole bunch of chemicals on me, some of them made me burn for weeks."

"Ouch."

"Yeah, tell me about it. He's done worse though, at other times, he was too busy preparing for the Ahsyllan Prime. What happened with that?"

"When she found out what he wanted from her, she burned him."

"Life comes at you fast," Isis said glibly.

She had gathered leftover food from the fridge. It wasn't much.

"I can grab you something from a restaurant," Alex offered.

"No, this is fine." she said as she unwrapped the food to be heated. "So what happened to the Prime? Is she everything Hhera made her out to be?"

"Something like that."

"Did she hurt you?"

"No," he said with a humorless chuckle.

Isis turned around."What happened?"

"Too much to tell."

"I'm not going anywhere."

He told her everything, focusing on the last six months since he'd met Syren and the events thereafter. Seth received his message and travelled to the cabin with Cleo. After being reunited, all of the tension and dysfunction from the last few years seemed to be resolved in one night with Isis back as the glue between them.

After a sleepless night Alex was up early in the morning debating what he should do next. The words Katherine said to him played in a loop in his head. 'Don't change your mind and come back.' He wondered if Syren felt the same and after their emotionally charged encounter he had to believe she did.

Isis found him outside when it was barely the onset of dawn.

"What are you thinking?" she asked as she sat beside him on the edge of the porch.

Her voice brought him from his deep thought. "Nothing."

"If I ask you again will you tell me the truth?"

He shook his head. "I'm thinking."

"About the prime of course" she said with a smile, "I mean, you can just go tell her what happened. I'm sure she'll understand- well I don't know, she seems understanding."

"The only thing more pathetic that what I've put her through already is to go to her now and say it was all a misunderstanding."

Isis sighed, "you have to stop this Alex. you're always looking for reasons to be unhappy-"

"It's not about me Isis."

"Yes it is. It's about you punishing yourself-always and punishing others around you as an extension of that. You have to stop. If you don't go and tell her I'm alive, I will."

"You're not doing that," he said flatly.

"Oh yes I am. You finally found someone Alex, don't fight it."

"This is not a joke Isis," he said sharply.

"I'm not laughing, if you don't do it today, then I'll do it tomorrow. I'm gonna do it anyways honestly, I'd like to meet the woman who brought Set to his knees."

Isis stood."I'm making breakfast, I haven't cooked in ages," she said cheerfully.

Isis skipped to the kitchen and pulled ingredients from the fridge and pantry to make a large breakfast for her siblings. As she did this, she took Alex's laptop and googled as much information as she could find about Syren, namely, the address of her residence and office. She was pleased to see that they were in the same building, it would make finding her much easier.

"Breakfast is ready," she screamed in a hulking voice when she finished cooking.

Seth was behind her in a flash and then so was Cleo.

"This looks great," Cleo said with a smile.

She reached over the large setting of food on the table top only to have her hand swatted away by Isis.

"I'm waiting for Alex," she scolded.

"ALEX!" Cleo screamed.

They waited for a response but there was none.

"Go get him, Seth," Isis commanded.

"He's probably outside suffocating himself," Seth mumbled as he left the kitchen.

Cleo chuckled, "he's gotten worse since he met the prime."

Isis shrugged but said nothing in response.

Moments later Alex and Seth returned to the kitchen.

"Great, now we can eat as a family," Isis sang.

They dug into their morning meal. All but one. Alex sat at the table staring at nothing in particular and eating nothing. After breakfast Isis approached him again.

"Where are all my clothes? Are they at my apartment in Milan?"

"Yes. I locked the place up, I have your key, if you want it," Alex responded.

"Sure and can I have a credit card? I'm sure mine are cancelled and I need clothes- you don't expect me to wear old fashion, do you? Of course not- you're not a monster," she said with a smile.

"You're not going to see Syren, are you?" he asked as he reached into his pocket for his wallet.

"I said I'd give you one day and I meant it," she responded with an open palm, stretched towards him.

Alex placed one of his credit cards in her palm.."Isis I need you to leave Syren alone. She's had to deal with enough from me."

"I don't have to listen to you, baby Alex. If I were you I'd use this time to figure out what I'm gonna say."

Alex closed his eyes and shook his head."Isis-"

"-I'm going to shower and get ready," she said excitedly.

"You're not even a little traumatized by what Set did to you?"

"It was only a few years Alex, I'm over 2600 years old. I'm over it." She walked in the direction of the staircase and disappeared.

After her shower, she travelled to her home in Milan. There, she found everything as she'd left it and even after years gone, the apartment was sparkling clean and she immediately knew that Alex, in his neverending thoughtfulness must've had a cleaning service detail her apartment at regular intervals.

She searched for her cash before she changed into appropriate clothing then traveled to Syren's building.

In a flash, she was in the employee bathroom on the 10th floor. She walked out of the bathroom and took the elevator down to the fourth floor which was where she read that Syren's office was located.

~~~

"There's someone in the building that didn't enter through security at the entrance," Athena said to Syren from across the office.

"Someone?" Syren asked, "who?"

The picture of Isis' face popped up on the large, glass screen computer.

"Who is that?" Syren asked, she looked familiar

"Isis West," Athena said, "she appeared from the bathroom, camera scanned her face in the hallway."

"Isis West is supposed to be dead."

She examined the picture and noted how much she looked like Alex. She was closest in beauty to Alex. They had the same jet black hair and dimpled chin and cheeks. Where his face was sharper and longer, her face was round and child-like.

"Can you bring her to me?" Syren said, mystified because this couldn't have been another thing Alex lied about. Now she was terrified that he wasn't the person she thought at all.

"Sure, it seems like she's headed directly to you, I'll have fourth floor security let her through."

Syren nodded and waited, with her heart thumping in her chest.

A few minutes later, Isis walked in with a squad of guards surrounding her. She had a smile on her face as bright as the sun and her expression was kind. It immediately disarmed Syren's suspicions.

"Syren?" she asked softly.

Syren stood and waved to guards, signalling that they leave.

"Who are you and why are you here?" Syren asked, to be sure she hadn't misidentified the woman.

"I'm Isis, Alex's sister, I came here to talk to you," she said in a genteel tone.

"Alex told me his sister died, so you must see why I'm confused."

"It's such a long story, I needed to explain it to you, Alex didn't lie to you so you have no reason to mistrust him but maybe we can have an early lunch while we chat, my treat to you or go somewhere more comfortable."

Syren shook her head."I don't know you Isis-"

"Okay, we can talk here if you prefer," she said with a smile, "no problem."

Syren nodded and sat over on the white leather couch. Isis walked over and sat at the couch opposite Syren.

"You're really beautiful -if my brother weren't so in love with you I'd be trying to steal you for myself," she said with a chuckle.

Syren was befuddled and couldn't form a response.

"How are you alive? I thought Set killed you."

"He didn't, he injected me with a chemical and I passed out, it was only yesterday that I regained consciousness and was able to travel to Alex."

"Alex said he had your body?"

"That wasn't me but it's not the first time Set's gone out of his way to lie like that."

"Why are you telling me this? I don't know you. Why didn't Alex tell me this? Did he ask you to come here?"

"No, he actually specifically asked me not to come but I know my brother. He overthinks everything, his rationale is that he's put you through enough already so he doesn't think he has any right to come to you now and tell you this."

"He's right," Syren said after a while.

"What?" Isis asked, confused.

"I'm happy to know you're alright, I'm ecstatic actually because I know how hard it was for him when he thought you were gone but it doesn't really change anything between him and I."

"Why not? The whole issue was that he felt guilty about my death, now he doesn't because I'm alive," Isis said, matter-of-factly.

Syren sighed and shook her head dejectedly."The very fact that your here and not Alex, tells me that Alex has no interest in being with me. Whatever his reasons are, they're not going away anytime soon." Syren tucked a few strands of loose hair behind her ear. "I've just started to be able to function after weeks of crying and wallowing in sadness, I don't need this Isis," she said "I just need to forget about all of this and move on."

Isis shook her head, unmoved in her resolve. "I'm sorry but I'm not letting this go. I know Alex loves you because the way he talks about you, I've never seen him like that in the 2600 years I've known him as my brother. I've been begging him all this time to do something other than exist and brute and he's finally fallen in love - I can't let this go, sorry and you know what, I think once all this gets worked out you'll be thanking me because he's great, I raised him myself," Isis said with a smile.

Syren folded her arms, steadfast in her resolve. She refused to be softened.

"Fine, I'll go to him and tell him that you want to see him and that you're ready to jump back into things."

"No, you won't-"

Isis smiled, "you have to meet me halfway here."

"What do you want?"

"I'm glad you asked," Isis began, "I'm going to tell Alex about our meeting. After he tries to successfully kill me this time, I suspect he'll come to see you. All I'm asking is that you hear him out. I can see you love him too and you're probably just trying to protect your heart- I've been heartbroken too, I've been there and know how you feel but trust me but Alexander is different, annoyingly noble to a fault yes but different and I think that's the disconnect here. He's so busy over-thinking everything and trying not to hurt that maybe he is. We'll fix that." Isis stood, "I'm leaving now, I have to go shopping to refresh my wardrobe, this shirt is from like ten years ago, I must rectify this presently.."

Syren furrowed her brow confused at the stark difference between Isis' personality and Alex's.

Isis walked around the other side of the coffee table and hugged Syren.

"We're gonna be great friends- you and I, I can tell," she said with a smile and then she stepped back and disappeared.

Chapter 16: Flesh

When Syren walked into her apartment later in the evening, the first thing she noticed was Alex standing by the glass wall across the room.

Even though she had been preparing herself to see him for the better part of the day, she was still shocked. He was unpredictable, at least to her.

"I didn't mean to just drop in on you-" he began, awed again by her beauty even with the severe expression on her face.

She had red lips that were stark against her white-gold hair. She wore a monotone cream outfit and a matching waterfall wool coat.

"Why are you here," she asked as she dropped her taupe Hermes Birkin 25cm bag on the sofa and stepped closer to him, still conscious that she wanted to keep distance between them.

"I wanted to talk to you."

"We're talking right now," Syren responded.

"I know you're angry with me and I know I don't even deserve to be here asking you this but I would like you to have dinner with me tonight?"

She inspected his features as he spoke. He seemed vastly more cheerful even if it was measured as he waited for her response.

"What's the point, Alex? Really? What are you trying to accomplish here?"

"I just want to make it right between us."

Syren shook her head.

"Look, I understand if you can't. Trust me, I do especially after the other night," he said softly, "just tell me what you want. You decide."

"What I want- no, what I need is for you to promise me that if I come with you then I won't be disappointed at the end of the night."

"I'm that bad."

"Yes. You have a penchant for disappointing me and I'm giving you one more chance so promise me that you won't again."

He stepped closer and gazed into her dark eyes. Syren met his gaze.

Alex pressed his palm against her cheek and stroked it gently with his thumb. Syren closed her eyes and let out a soft breath as she laid her head in his palm. He kissed her softly on the lips and felt his insides come alive. He quickly parted from her lips and took a deep breath to calm himself.

"I promise," he said.

Syren sighed, dazed. "I have to change-"

"There won't be anyone around, just us. For where we're going, you won't need to," he said with a small smile.

Alex dropped his hands from her cheeks and took her hands. The second his skin made contact with hers she felt chills again.

"Are you okay to travel?" he asked.

She got anxious as she remembered the nausea that overcame her.

"Was that the first time you traveled through light?" he asked, picking up on her anxiety as he remembered her nausea as well.

"Yep."

"It's better the second time around, closing your eyes will help."

"Okay."

Alex wrapped his arms around her and in an instant, they disappeared and reappeared in his warm cabin.

"You can open your eyes," he said softly.

Syren opened her eyes and looked around, there was no nausea this time. A few white pillar candles were lit in the room, enough to keep the room dimly lit. In front of the fireplace where the warm orange fire's reflection danced across the room. The coffee table had been moved and instead, there were fluffy white blankets laid out on the floor with enough cushions to build a fort. She noticed the sofa had been pushed back as well.

"Is it too much?" he asked hesitantly

"No, it's perfect."

Alex smiled, "dinner's in the kitchen. I left it in the oven, so it would be warm when you got here."

He reached over her shoulders and pulled her coat down her arms.

"How did you know I would come?" she asked.

"I didn't, I just had hope that you would."

He hung her coat on the coat rack against the wall of the cabin by the door then slid his shoes off. "I'll be right back."

Syren slipped off her heels as she waited for Alex and placed them by the coat rack at the door.

A few minutes later, Alex appeared with two trays. Syren was now sitting on the blankets on the floor. He placed the trays on the floor. The food looked delightful and smelled even better.

"So it's grilled lobster glazed with herbs and creamy herbed pasta," he said as he sat.

"This looks great," she mused as she took her fork and swirled it in the pasta then took a bite. "Mm-oh god. This is so good." She took another bite. "Mm..this is good and a little spicy too."

Alex smiled his sideways smile as he watched her. After she swallowed a piece of her lobster and took a sip of water she stopped. "Aren't you gonna have some?"

"I'm not that hungry anymore," he said but still took a piece of his lobster with his fork and ate it.

"You don't like food, do you?" she asked as she took another bite of food.

"I like food but it's just that after so many years it's boring. There are only so many different ways I can eat chicken or cow or lamb. If there are any new animals I don't know about- that would be interesting?"

She laughed with her mouth full of pasta.

"Like a new, better-tasting species of chicken?"

"Yeah or rabbit or lamb…"

"You eat rabbit?"

"It's my favorite then duck, then lamb."

She chuckled softly, "I guess I'll have to try rabbit sometime then, maybe I've eaten it before in a past life and I just don't remember."

He decided to ask the question that had been troubling him."How do you feel about me?"

"I don't know what you mean?"

"Are you angry with me? Have you moved on from the other night?"

Syren took a moment to think before she responded."I'm angry with you. I'm really angry with you but I haven't moved on, if I did I wouldn't have come here tonight."

"Tell me what you're angry about?" He asked, needing to hear her say the words.

"I'm angry that you left me and I'm angry that you didn't come back, even when you knew I was having a really hard time- well, you did but you only made it worse. A part of me understands why you left but another part of me- maybe the selfish part- doesn't understand or care, honestly."

"When you called me I shouldn't have come," Alex responded.

"Yes, leaving me horny and crying didn't help at all," she said with a humorless chuckle.

"Can you forgive me?" he asked, softly.

"I don't know," she mumbled after a silent moment, "I just feel like you try to find every reason to be away from me, you're sister came back and you weren't the one to tell me."

"Yes, I'm a coward, I couldn't face you Syren, after everything that happened, what was I supposed to say to you that could even begin to make up for everything that happened?"

"You could tell me you love me," she said tearfully, "you could say you're sorry and that there is nothing you want more than to be with me. That would have sufficed."

He took her face in both his hands and pulled her so close they were inches apart and stared intensely into her dark violet eyes.

"I love you more than anything and anyone and I'm sorry I put my guilt about Isis above us. The one thing that the last month has shown me is that I'm an empty shell with you. I need you...I don't want to lose you. I can't."

She nodded slowly, with her wet cheeks wedged between his palms.

"I love you too and I need you too," she whispered.

Alex kissed her pouty lips softly but was careful not to lose himself in the kiss before he broke it reluctantly and let her go. Her stomach growled loudly as she blushed. Alex smiled in response. "You should finish eating," he said softly.

Syren twisted her fork around some of the pasta and stuck a piece of lobster at the end before stuffing it in her mouth. Syren aimed to eat as fast as possible so she could return to his lips.

Alex watched her eat with a smile on his face.

"Why didn't you tell me you had abilities? Is it because you don't trust me?" he asked after watching her for a while.

"Well, I trust you now but..." she began, "that part of myself is not something that I share with anyone. Kat knows, so does Teddy and a few others but Teddy just pretends it doesn't exist and I guess I do too. When you told me all those things about what I am and about what I should be able to do it was just too terrifying to contemplate especially when I never wanted any of this to begin with. I know I should've told you, I'm sorry."

He shook his head, "you shouldn't be sorry...it's just that I think I would've saved myself a lot of worrying about you if I knew you could take care of yourself but I guess that's what I get for assuming."

"I don't think you assumed wrong, I have no control over it and I can barely use it. What happened with your dad was just because I was so angry when I saw him, he chose the worst time to confront me and as angry as I was even then I was only able to do it for a few seconds."

"If that's what you can do in a few seconds then I'm impressed. Did he say anything to you?"

She shook her head as she recalled his threats, "he threatened Kat and Teddy and Ruby but it wasn't just about that, I mean..I thought he killed your sister and then in the night I heard you talking to Seth and you said you thought he was gonna kill you and I just couldn't let that happen. I was trying to kill him but I didn't know how I thought the fire would work but I guess not. He was burning for a while then it stopped but when he did burn I could feel it and he was in a lot of pain."

"You heard everything I said to Seth? I saw your eyes moving and I thought I was paranoid but you were awake."

"I love to eavesdrop," Syren said with a chuckle, "almost as much as I love watching soft porn and eating orange chicken."

Alex chortled and shook his head.

"I'm joking...kind of," Syren added.

"I know it's not the orange chicken. Is it the porn?"

"Kat and I surreptitiously watched it together when we were younger but not anymore Kat been having sex and a lot of it so she doesn't need it anymore."

"You?"

"What about me?"

Alex smiled boyishly, "are you having lots of sex?"

"With who Alex? A ghost? It hasn't been you because you left me."

Alex sighed slightly. "Let's talk about something else," he said, changing the subject. "You can see him, you said?" he'd been trying to process so much of what she said it was to keep up with what was important.

"Kind of- I don't know, I took over his body, all of their bodies and since then I kind of just know what's going on with him and the rest of them. It's slight, I couldn't tell at first, it's kind of just like a feeling, I knew he was in pain and he was exhausted," she paused. "You aren't upset, are you? About what I did to him?"

She intentionally left out what Set had said about the war.

"Seriously?" he asked with a furrowed brow.

"-The look on your face was kind of scary."

"I was stunned, that part is an understatement but upset at you, Syren, no. Never," he said as he gazed at her. "I just- I wonder if the fact that I'm a vessel is something that might be a problem for you."

"I'm sorry about what I said to you that night. I was terrified because I've always known vessels as one thing but with you, I realized that I was wrong. I'm okay with being wrong, I'm really glad I'm wrong actually. I just don't want you to ever want you to feel like I don't love you...all of you. I don't care if you're a vessel if you weren't you wouldn't be here so I'm more than okay with it."

Alex smiled but wasn't sure what to respond. All he could do was gaze at her.

She looked around the cabin, shying from his gaze, "where are your brother and sisters?"

"They left."

"Where did they go?"

"To Milan, I think, with Isis. I wasn't listening, I was too nervous about seeing you."

"What did she say? When she came back?"

"She called me a self-pitying, maudlin asshole."

"That's harsh...phrasing," she said with a smile.

"So you agree. I'm not shocked. It's true- but she also told me that I was going to lose you if I just kept being stuck in my head and that I would regret it forever which when you don't die is forever. After that, I just knew what I needed to do."

"Which was…"

A side smile pulled on the corners of his lips."I needed to see you. You had to make me say it didn't you."

She nodded and bit her lips that pulled apart into an eventual smile.

He stared into her violet eyes that had been growing more purple as the night played on."Everything I said earlier was true but being away from you is agonizing…I mean I miss you when you leave the room…I'm not sure how I thought I would survive being away from you completely but what's even worse than that is you love me too and I was hurting you with my selfishness. I guess a part of it was that I didn't think I deserved your love- I still don't but that doesn't mean that I can't work hard to be deserving of it. I have to unlearn a lot of bad ideas I've acquired in the last few millennia."

"Yes, particularly the one where you think you don't deserve love."

"I deserve love, just not from you."

She stared at him seriously for a while before smiling with blushing red cheeks particularly visible with the glow of the fire on her skin.

"Yeah your sister was right," she teased.

"I'm trying to change- just bear with me."

"So no more emotional whiplash from you," she teased with a smile this time.

"God, I'm sorry-"

"Stop apologizing Alex," she scolded.

"You have to give me some time, I have a lot to apologize for."

Syren leaned on top of him and kissed him softly, "request denied Alex."

"One week," he bargained.

"No weeks," Syren countered she said as she stroked his cheek gently.

"What- a few days," he bargained again.

"No days, no hours, no minutes," she said with a smile.

"Seconds?"

Syren shoved her tray with mostly empty plates to the side. Alex watched with a raised brow as she took his tray as well and shoved it to the side, off the blankets. Syren climbed on top of him then shoved him back against the pillows, all while unable to keep a smile from her lips.

"When you brought me here tonight you promised me that I wouldn't be disappointed at the end of the night," Syren began.

Alex pressed his palm on the small of her back and tipped her forward on him. He could feel the blood rush almost instantly.

She fell on top of him and they both broke out into a fit of soft chortles with their faces just inches away. Then his hands were cupping her cheeks as he pulled her forward and kissed her lips.

"I meant it. You can have anything you want, you need only ask."

Syren smiled winningly and found his lips again.

"What do you want?"

"I don't know," she said with a smile. "Everything. My grandmother said not to get my hopes up because guys your age don't know what to do with a vagina but that was when we thought you were twenty, not 2600."

Alex guffawed and shook his head, "you're not ready for everything Syren. Not in this eighteen-year-old body."

She blushed and covered her cheeks with closed fists, cheesing widely. "Now I'm kind of scared."

"Don't be..." he said as he kissed her lips softly.

What came next was dreamlike.

He slowly unbuttoned her silk shirt and began kissing slowly down her neck, over her stiffened nipples where he sucked until she yelped then he continued down her torso. He tasted every inch of flesh where the aroma of lavender vanilla lingered until he reached between her legs. His lips seemed to vibrate down there, throwing her body into a paroxysm that left liquid seeping into the blanket. She peaked with fists full of his jet black curls scrunched between her fingers.

She didn't remember if she undressed Alex or if he undressed himself but she remembered the exact indescribable feeling when he entered her, whispering a string of profanities in her ear. It was so slow and so sweet that she wept as she swallowed him inside her wet walls, inch by inch, and stretched to accommodate him.

She closed her eyes and committed it all to memory.

Indelible was the feeling of the hard muscles of his torso pressed against her back. One hand gripping her breast while the other pulled her lips to his. The hot wetness in between her legs and the sweet, torturous slowness with which his hips ground circles into her. The feel of his tip and the bulging veins that ran down his engorged shaft. It was like a bolt of lightning in her, electrocuting her senses to overdrive with every thrust.

She writhed and twisted and rode on him until she'd been floated to a world beyond pure physical pleasure, she'd entered the realm of the psychedelic.

When their peak came, it was together. What was still an intangible mystery, was the pulse of energy that radiated from her. It held them, wrapped in a cocoon of energy, stiff, while waves of pleasure swell through them. Time seemed to stop then. After that, her recollection of the night was a hazy dream.

When she woke the next afternoon the sweet aroma of the outdoors filled her nostrils. She opened her eyes and it was so bright that she had to shut them immediately. She flexed her muscles and to her chagrin, found no signs of her night in her limbs. It was a pity, a physical reminder would have been satisfying but her pesky accelerated healing that washed all evidence away. It only made her need to relive the night more urgent.

She didn't have a physical reminder but memories of their activities up to a point in the night came flashing back and she smiled and stuffed her face in the pillow.

She felt chills down to her toes as she relived the night then she popped her head up frantically.

"Alex?" she called, her voice slightly strained. He wasn't beside her and she didn't hear him in the cabin.

There was no response.

"Alexander?" she called again.

Still, only quiet.

Syren took a breath and then saw a small spark of violet light across the room. It was Alex, fully dressed as he carried two large paper bags.

"Hey Angel," he called from across the room as he kicked off his shoes. He walked over with a wide smile and kneeled beside her on the blanketed floor. Alex kissed her softly then smiled even wider.

As close as he was, the smell of breakfast food, emanating from the large bags, filled her nose.

"I was hoping to be back before you were up," he said. "I went to get you breakfast. I'd be a terrible partner if I were to let you starve."

Syren smiled, "partner?"

"What should we call it?" he asked. "I hate the word boyfriend, it's foolish for I am not a boy nor am I your friend, in the platonic sense."

Syren wondered inwardly, "I like partner, it feels...sufficient."

"I'll be right back, let me get this on a plate for you," he said before kissing her softly and rushing out the kitchen.

She laid her head back on the pillow, smiling. She was hungry, she realized as she laid her head down and the smell of the food only made her hungrier.

Moments later he came with one large tray of food. Much like the same spread he'd made for her on her last visit to his cabin. There were two servings now. He kneeled with the tray with a bright smile on his face.

"Hungry?"

She looked up and lost her line of thought examining his beautiful features.

"Sy?" he called, snapping her from her thoughts.

"What?" she asked, absently.

"I asked if you were hungry?" he said with a sweet boyish smile.

"I'm starving."

When she sat up, her blanket fell from her body, exposing her breasts. She pulled her golden hair back and twirled it around her fingers attempting to get it away from her face.

"It's not fair for you to be naked," Alex said, flushed from his quickening heart rate.

Syren smiled, "then strip."

Without pause, Alex stood and pulled off his sweater and pants. Now, he was bare-chested in only black boxer briefs. She examined his body. It was the first time she saw it in the daytime light. He had a hairless chest, smooth, with defined abs. His core muscle formed a vee and disappeared into his underpants where she saw his bulge. Syren smiled at the memory of it inside her.

"Good," she said.

Alex sat beside her once again and leaned over and slightly pinched her chocolate brown nipple. "So beautiful," he mumbled in awe.

Syren blushed and smiled, "I've never seen you this happy Alex."

"I've never been this happy," he said with a smile. "You almost bloody killed me last night but I've never been happier."

"I didn't know I could leak so many fluids," she said sheepishly.

"Some of which found its way to my nose. I choked a bit but it was one of the best things that have ever happened to me."

"You did not.." Syren defended with a wide smile, "maybe I did. I thought I peed a little-"

"That was not urine," he said with a raised eyebrow and smirk.

Her cheeks flushed."Stop talking about it!"

"Fine, can we talk about the fact we were amazing last night, you know that?

"What?"

"You were amazing," he said again with a smile.

"What?" Syren placed her hand by her ear and cocked it.

"You were amazing," he said again with a chuckle.

"Even for a first-timer?" Syren she said with a light chuckle, "I hate the idea of virginity and in my cause, it's even stupider because I've had sex before in my previous forms."

"It doesn't matter to me how many people you've slept with, in this life or others, you would have been gently laid regardless."

Syren chortles, "gently laid? What's the opposite of being gently laid?"

Alex nodded, "having your insides destroyed."

She fell over on the tray, laughing.

"Did you know that was gonna happen? That thing you did?" He asked as he sat and stuffed bacon into his mouth as his eyes roamed all over her body.

Syren shook her head, still fascinated by his cheerfulness.

"Well," he began, "that's never happened before, I've never felt anything like that it was…"

"Indescribable." she finished for him.

"Yeah," he said with a nod and a smile, "that's the word."

She laughed and rolled her eyes. "I'm covered in too much body fluids. I should go clean up."

"Why? You should eat first," he suggested.

"Okay," she agreed. She took a sip of her tea and found her eyes wandering over the edge of her cup to gaze at Alex.

"You know," Alex said as he stared back into her deep purple irises, "I hoped that if you knew about that thing you do, you'd have given me a warning because christ Syren, you could've killed me."

"Not that again. You are extremely dramatic," she teased. "But I did worry that something happened to you. You weren't breathing- I can barely remember" Syren said as her lips curved into a smile and she scrunched her nose at him, amused.

"I did die, I think, just for a moment, I went to heaven and when I came back I was still inside you, feeling like I'd transcended," he teased. "I didn't expect that, nothing close, not even from the Prime of Ahsylla. So tight, so wet...amazing," he said as his bulge stiffened at the memory.

Syren blushed heavily.

"You're uncomfortable talking about sex?" Alex asked.

"A little," she admitted. "You're not though, obviously. You're kind of crazy in bed. I didn't expect that."

He was intrigued and still eating. "What did you expect? Everyone thinks I'm a bore but I can be quite fun. I'll have you know, I was a very welcomed guest at plenty of roman orgies."

"Oh, gawd," Syren exclaimed with a chuckle. "I didn't need to think about that, Alex." She was silent for a moment, thinking before she continued. "I thought about it a lot …you in bed," she began,

"Really?"

"Yeah...haven't you?"

"Oh, I have. I could tell you all about the tribulations my penis has faced the past few months but I'm much more interested in what you have to say."

A laugh got caught in her throat and she choked on a piece of her waffle.

"Are you okay?" he asked.

She took a sip of water and then laughed.

"Yeah- what was what about the tribulations of your penis?"

"No, you have to go first," he insisted.

"No, tell me," she begged.

"Fine," he relented, "I was just gonna say that it wasn't easy, with you on my mind all the time. Right now, if I put my right hand even close to my penis, it'll flinch, not in excitement, but fear."

Syren howled in laughter. Tears came to her eyes and she wiped them.

"There was a lot of rubbing...maybe too much rubbing."

"You are disgusting...I love it."

"Okay, now you, what were you saying about how you thought I'd be in bed?"

She inhaled deeply to catch her breath."I was just saying that um...you're really quiet and I thought that meant you'd be...tame, I don't know if that's the word I'm looking for but you were the opposite. You're like possessive and sure and confident and a little dominating..a lot actually and it's kind of perfect. Last night was perfect."

He leaned over their tray and pressed her against the pillow as he caressed her cheek and kissed her tenderly. To his chagrin, he felt his appendage of flesh stiffen and broke the kiss and leaned up quickly.

"What?" she asked, confused and breathless.

"I have an erection," he said while his heart thumped like a beating drum in his chest. "I'd hate to bombard you with my penis. You just woke up."

She smiled a cheeky smile, "You'd love to do it."

He stood and as he attempted to remove his underpants Syren stopped him.

"Let me," she said, looking up at him through her lashes.

Syren removed his underpants. Then the peak of his erection stood inched from her face, she felt brave and leaned over and kissed his tip.

Alex smiled and lifted her without hesitation then wrapped her legs around his waist. Syren wrapped her arms around his neck and kissed his lips softly. Alex pressed her closer against his chest and felt the flesh of her breasts and hard nipples press against him.

"We should wash off first," she suggested, breathless from the kiss. "I'm filthy. Your semen is in inexplicable places...like my hair."

"I like you filthy," was all he responded before he kneeled to the ground then Syren was underneath him with legs open on both sides of his hips.

The movement was so fast that she didn't see at all when it happened. She just felt her back against the floor and the crown of his erection pressed against her orifice. Teasing her and feeling for wetness.

Her breath quickened with longing. It felt heavy in her lungs as she waited impatiently, running the soles of her feet against the cotton blanket. She had fistfuls of fabric in her palms as she braced herself.

Alex watched intently, as she writhed beneath him. He had a full view of every crevice of her front and it was too beautiful a sight to turn from. His beating heart in his chest accelerated exponentially with each passing moment, a sensation that was both intoxicating and exciting and something he would have to get used to with Syren.

He slowly ran his palm down her inner thigh, desperate to feel her soft skin under his. When he leaned down and ran his tongue up her inner thigh. He immediately heard the utterance of his name."Alex!"

Now she was hot with want. Too hot to patiently wait through his teasing.

"Alex, I can't wait…" she panted.

He couldn't refuse her then. Slowly, he slithered his way inside her, limp with pleasure as he was swallowed up by her walsl of flesh.

He grunted instinctively as he thrust slow circles into her wetness.

Syren had her back arched, at times she gasped with every thrust and at others, she forgot to breathe at all. Every nerve in her body opened a synapse and clamored at the sensations. She closed her eyes and bit her lips. Her face was distorted with utter pleasure.

She felt his lips against her and his tongue in her, swallowing every cry that came from her and she swallowed every cry that came from him.

When it was over she was a ball of spasms on the floor with Alex stiff beside her, much like last night. But still, she needed more. She wanted more. She had never imagined feeling as complete as she did when he was inside her. When he was gone, all she could feel was the absence of him and the gaping hole he left in his place.

Minutes passed. Her breathing had returned to normal, in sync with Alex's.

"Can we clean ourselves now?" she asked.

In a flash, he was at the top of the staircase, holding Syren around his waist as he carried her into the bathroom. He sat her on top of the bathroom vanity as he walked to the shower to gauge the water.

"I love this," she said, as she inspected the decor of the bathroom. It was very rustic, with stone floors and a wooden vanity with a carved stone sink top. The shower was made of stone walls with a glass screen. "Did you do this?" she asked.

"Yes," he said with a sideways smile and tousled hair.

"You're good at everything, aren't you?"

Alex walked back over to the sink and lifted her off. Syren turned around and looked into the wood-paneled mirror. She'd never seen her eyes that hue before. When she saw both their reflections in the mirror even she had to admit their beauty hitched her breath.

Her hair was untidy, matted. Her lips were swollen. Her mascara leaked around her eyes but still, she was beautiful.

She watched his hands roam up the flat planes of her stomach. His fingers barely touched her skin but still, he left a trace of tingles everywhere they roamed. Then his hands were over her supple breasts, squeezing the flesh that spilled through his large hands and pinching her sensitive nipples between his fingertips.

She let out a sharp gasp and then instinctively reached behind, grabbed into his curls with one hand, and kissed his lips hungrily. She could feel his hard flesh pressed against her back as he lifted her slightly so she was standing on his feet and bent one of her legs over the vanity countertop, to dissipate their difference in height.

He entered her, whispering a curse against her lips. She hadn't realized until last night that Alex even used that kind of language but given the context, it seemed fitting. In the midst of it, he seemed to grip the edge of the stone skin with enough force that the stone crumbled under his grasp. The shock was enough to give him pause.

"Are you okay?" he choked out with sharp breaths.

Without answering the question she was pulling him against her again. The now-familiar perpetual ravenousness for pleasure had set upon her again and now stopping seemed impossible until she reached her peak. She'd only first experienced it last night and was convinced it wasn't normal. There's no way it could be. Not even when Alex's tongue was between her legs was her peak comparable to when he was inside her, nor when she touched herself to climax did it compare.

They were both bent against the table and it had been so for some time now. She wasn't sure how long, it could've been a second or an hour, though she seriously doubted she couldn't survive that level of intense pleasure for any time exceeding a few minutes. Through half-opened eyes, she could see them reflected in the mirror and she knew it wasn't just the intense love for the man that stood bent behind her over the surface of the table that induced some sort of psychedelic experience. It was real and most probably an effect of her powers which at this point, seemed only to materialize when she experienced a level of heightened emotions.

She closed her eyes and breathed strained, sharp breaths. She willed her trembling legs to still and focused on reigning herself in until she found herself falling back on the stone floors with Alex behind her.

She drew in a deep squeaky breath and she heard Alex do the same.

The lactic acid build up in her muscles made her limbs flimsy and sore and she relished the feeling because it would soon disappear. They stayed on the floor for some time. She recovered quickly, and Alex even quicker. The sound of their slow breathing drowned out by the droplets of water that pelted the stone tiles in the shower.

Syren sat up. "Hey, we have to get up…" she said as she turned to him. His seed was sticky between her legs.

He was laying on the floor, staring at nothing in particular and when she spoke he sat up then stood.

They had a silent shower, standing under the showerhead, hugging with Syren's head pressed against his chest.

Downstairs, they finished eating their cold breakfast. She'd never seen Alex eat so hungrily as he did when he ate the entire tray of food in minutes. The competitor in her tried to catch up but she couldn't. After breakfast, Alex scooped all the blankets, some with small droplets of blood from Syren's first time, into a pile while Syren gathered all the empty plates and utensils on the tray.

"It's okay Angel, I'll take care of it when I'm done."

"Alex, you don't have to wait on me hand and foot. I can bring the trays to the kitchen while you clean up the sheets," she said matter-of-factly.

"Fine," he relented.

She smiled and brought the trays to the kitchen, which, similar to the rest of the cabin, was tastefully arranged with stone floors, rustic wooden furniture. She washed the dishes and tray, which was something so domestic and rare for her she felt strange completing the task.

In the living room, she found Alex standing by the fireplace.

"I washed the dishes," she said triumphantly," I haven't done that in forever and I truly mean forever. I've never done that."

"Do you wanna go for a walk?" he asked.

Syren looked at her clothing. She was wearing one of Alex's t-shirts now since hers was inexplicably torn but she had no underwear on.

She lifted her long shirt and flashed him her naked private.

"Oh-" Alex said with his heart rate significantly higher than it was moments ago, "you need underwear."

"I remember specifically you telling me I wouldn't need to change," she teased.

"Yeah, I did say that, didn't I," he said with a chuckle.

He pulled his sweater off and slipped it over her head then he pulled her into his embrace and squeezed the flesh of her bare ass in his hands.

"Oh-," she mumbled, dazed as she found his lips and kissed them hungrily.

He lifted her and sat her against the inside back of the sofa. She quickly pulled off the hoodie he just slipped over her head and threw it on the floor. Alex was leaning over her, his body inches above her as he kissed her fiercely.

In her excitement, she quickly pulled down his pants and underpants in one quick motion then grabbed his hard flesh and shoved it roughly into her wet fold. She regretted the action immediately when she felt pain between her legs.

She winced in response, something that Alex detected.

"Sy-" he began breathlessly.

"-I'm okay," she said through sharp breaths. She opened her legs wider, hoping it would help her to adjust to his girth faster.

Alex leaned down and kissed her again, slower and softer this time and when he felt her hands against his ass, guiding him into her, he began to thrust in slow and deep.

~~~

Isis walked into the cabin to see both Syren laying on top of Alexander with her head pressed against his chest. Partially nude.

"Oh - christ," Isis mewled, frozen. There was a strange energy in the room that made the hairs on his skin stand up.

Syren half-opened her eyes and saw the three spectators and gasped.

In a flash, the three disappeared in bursts of light.

"Your siblings saw us," Syren mumbled. Embarrassment came after they'd gone.

"What?" Alex asked as he sat up.

"Isis, Cleo and Seth, they saw us."

"What? When?" he asked, confused.

"They were just here, they opened the door and saw us. Didn't you hear?"

"No," he said. "I'm sorry, maybe they thought it was safe to come back..."

"Gosh, now it'll be awkward," she mumbled.

"No, it won't. I'll talk to them and tell them they need to be more careful about showing up."

Syren nodded.

"Let me get you some pants, I think Isis should have some upstairs, if not maybe you can wear one of mine, we'll just adjust the waist."

"I'll come with you, I have to clean myself up a bit," she offered.

There were no clothes for his sister so she had to wear a pair of Alex's sweatpants with the waist adjusted as tight as possible to prevent it from falling down her legs.

"It's not that cold out today, it's 74 degrees but still windy," he said as he slipped his grey hoodie over her head.

She pulled her almost dry hair out from inside the sweater as she followed him downstairs to the glass doors that lead to the back porch.

"Gosh, this is breathtaking," she mused at the view of the snowy Andes and the still watered lake.

She slipped on his black sandals, they were so large they flopped on her feet as she walked. They walked from the porch onto the green grass and passed the lake.

"When did you build this?" she asked.

"In the 1800s."

"Wow," she was stunned, it would take some time to casually work his age into conversation. " it looks so modern."

"Yeah, well I get bored a lot so I'm always trying to find something else I can add or switch." As he gazed at her while they walked, he was awed by the sunlight reflecting on her lustrous hair.

"So I have something for you..for your birthday," he began. "Granted, it's February now and your birthday was in December but I still needed to give it to you."

Syren smiled softly, "you told me you loved me that's all I needed for my birthday...of course what I didn't need was you vanishing for days after…"

He chuckled, thoroughly amused, "that wasn't a gift, that was just the truth that I needed to let you hear."

He took the small piece of jewelry from his pocket. It was a vivid pink diamond, emerald cut ring. It wasn't an engagement ring, but a promise ring. The diamond in the center of the ring size of a pebble.

"Woah, Alex-"

He took her hand before she could protest and placed the ring on the index finger, hoping it would fit and to his pleasant surprise, it did. He brought her fingers to his lips and kissed the back of them.

"Alex," she said tearfully, "It's too beautiful. I love it."

He smiled brightly, pleased she liked her ring."When I found it I thought it was the most beautiful thing I'd ever seen. Now it's bleh...well in comparison to you."

She stared at the ring, examining the work of the diamond. Syren was no stranger to fine jewelry and still, the ring was exquisite.

"You made this?"

"Yeah, I found the diamond. It was beautiful in its natural state. Shortly after I met you I started working on. I was inspired by you. I brought it to your birthday party."

"You make jewelry too," she teased lightly, "and why didn't you give it to me?"

"Well, that's kind of all I had for a long time. To pass the time I build things, learn things...doing what I could to not feel the time. I didn't give it to you because even though I made it for you I wanted to keep it because to me, it was probably the only thing I would have of you."

He took something else from his pocket. A matching necklace.

"This is the Christmas gift, I know I'm late but...I still want you to have it." He stepped behind her and clasped the necklace around her neck then he pulled her hair from under the silver.

Syren fiddled with the diamond under her fingertips.

"Can I get you something too?"

He chuckled and shook his head, "the relationship is lopsided as it is. You-loving me is already everything I need."

Alex was in front of her now.

"That's not fair, you can give me things and I can't give you anything," she whined.

He pulled her close and cupped her cheeks. "Life isn't fair," he said as he kissed her lips softly. "What you did to me last night and earlier also isn't fair," he said as he broke the kiss.

"I have a theory about that," she responded with blushing cheeks.

Alex kissed her again and again and then peppered kisses all over her face while she giggled before he stepped back.

"What is it?"

"So I've noticed, the only time my powers- I hate using that word but whatever- the only time my power surfaces is if I'm overwhelmed emotionally. If I'm really angry like I was when I saw Set then I'm able to do something but I've only ever been able to when I was angry or traumatized or something." She paused, "what if when I'm feeling intense love then that's what happens?"

Alex played with the idea in his head and smiled. "You think that's what it is?"

"It feels similar to other times I used my powers, I feel the same energy only it feels a thousand times better..."

"You're probably right, I just know that I've never felt anything...even comparable to that in the 2600 years I've existed."

"Thanks to me.," she said cheekily.

He kissed her lips again, "thanks to you," he agreed.

They continued walking towards the green rolling hills.

"So what now?" he asked, "Have you figured out anything since I told you?"

"No, I was otherwise consumed."

A wave of guilt washed over him and Syren noticed and stopped him right away.

"No, no guilt, just pretend I didn't say that."

Alex nodded just to comfort her though it wasn't that easy to wash his shame from his mind.

"I don't know if I want to know any more."

"Why not? I think it's important for you to know."

"I just think if it was important for me to know, they wouldn't have made it so hard for me."

"All I've heard about for almost three millennia is how important this is. I think you should look into it," Alex insisted.

Syren nodded and responded, "alright. I trust you. If you think it's important to know then I'll go to High Palace. It's been there for half a millennia, I'm sure I can find a ton of information on my past forms. There was a lot my mom- I mean I- told myself that I never followed up on with Ahsyllan culture and all."

"Oh and what about your abilities?"

She stopped and took his hand then ran his fingers on the lump at the back of her neck.

"What's that?" he asked.

"It's a chip. My mom put it in me."

"Why?" he asked, confused.

"I don't know. I just know that it's the thing that prevents my power from getting out of control. Every once in awhile I'll feel pain...like that night at Coney Island and Excellci plaza."

The memory of her writhing in pain flashed in his brain and it made him shudder.

"Why haven't you taken it out?" he wondered.

"Someone tried, it almost killed me every time they did."

"I don't understand- why would you put it in and why can't you take it out?"

"I don't know either but maybe I'll find some answers in High palace."

He nodded."When did you want to go?" he asked hesitantly, dreading the end of their retreat.

"Whenever we're done here...although I'm not sure I want this to end."

He smiled as he pulled her close and kissed her temple. They began walking again.

"I was dreading the end as well but-"

"-No buts. Let's not end it, not right now at least. We can go back to my condo and hide from Kat and grab some more clothes and underwear then we can stay here as long as we need - wait, you aren't going back to MIT are you- ever?"

"No," he said with a chortle.

"Okay. I'm ready when you are."

She wrapped her arms tightly around his waist and closed her eyes. Alex kissed her forehead and closed his eyes. In a moment, they vanished in a beam of violet light.

Chapter 17: History

"Where were you born," she asked him as they sat at the edge of the porch, facing the still watered lake.

"Sais, Egypt, around 542 bc," he said with a smile. "

"You're Egyptian, I didn't see that coming…I mean the names were kind of a give away but-"

"-Well, I'm not Egyptian. I was born there but Set was from the old Roman Republic. My mother was a scandinavian slave girl, Set's slave, her name was Cassia and she was pretty young, according to Isis, probably fourteen or fifteen when she gave birth to me."

"Gosh, that's really young."

He nodded. "If I'd been born to her in republic, I would've been a slave too."

"It's good that you weren't."

Alex shrugged.

"So you're Italian and what...Swedish? Do you know?"

"Not sure, maybe Swedish or Danish, Finnish, Norwegian. It could be any scandanavian country."

"How were you conceived...like this?"

"Hhera artificially inseminated my mother with some concoction of the serum she made and Set's sperm. I was the only one born this way. Isis, Cleo and Seth were already born when they were injected with the Serum. They continued to grow until they were fully matured, I did as well. If you were like Set who was already an adult the serum just preserved you."

"So you're eighteen and not twenty?"

"I'm neither."

.

"I just mean physically, you stopped developing when a human would... around eighteen right?"

He nodded.

"Do you know why your mom died?"

"Isis tried to help her deliver but she was just a kid herself. She said there was a lot of blood and I came out feet first so it's probable she hemorrhaged pretty badly."

"What was Set doing in Egypt?"

"He was very wealthy in Rome, one of the wealthiest Romans. His family made a lot of money through trade and real estate but that wasn't what he was interested in. He went to Egypt because he'd heard of new advances in technology there and he made the trip to see for himself. He met Hhera there. He changed his name and the name of all my siblings."

"What was his real name?" Syren asked, utterly amused.

"Marcus Augustus Marius. Cleo's name was Flavia, Isis' name was Julia. Seth's name was Cato. they were raised in a massive villa in Rome surrounded by slaves and servants."

"Do you know your other siblings well?"

"Not particularly no, I know their names but every encounter we've had has been hostile."

"So what was it like back then?"

"Grim. I spent the first few years of my life barely surviving with Isis. We were very poor."

"What about your powers, didn't that help?" Syren asked.

"Not much, it took us decades to become proficient in using them and the world was so small back then. We didn't know anywhere outside of the scope of Roman Peninsula, Greece, some of Europe and Northern Africa and the Middle East."

"Really?" she asked, fascinated, "what are your powers? What can you do?"

He began vibrating so fast that he became a blur then he stopped and she could see him. "You know about travelling though light. The speed, the strength."

"Wow, so that's what you did to me- I swore you were vibrating-"

"The first time we made love- yeah, I got carried away licking you-."

"-I came immediately," she joked with blushing cheeks.

Alex chortled and gave her a peck on the lips.

"So how does your ability work? Light travel?" she asked, trying to find out as much as possible before she succumbed to her desire to drag him back into the cabin.

"To best and most accurately travel, I have to be able to visualize myself relative to my position on the globe or I have to be able to visualize where I'm going relative to its position on the globe. Like I said, the world was so small back then, our abilities didn't help much until we got a better sense of the world around us but we were still able to use them."

"You don't have to have seen where you're going, do you because you came to my room when you'd never been there before?"

"I don't have to have seen it before, I actually got lost a few times that way when as a child."

She laughed, "seriously?"

"Yes"

She caressed his cheek and gazed into his eyes. His cheeks were smooth as glass as she ran her thumb against his skin.

"I love you," she whispered as she kissed his lips softly,

"I love you too," Alex returned.

They shared a chuckle.

"Okay, have you met any historical figures?" she asked.

"I was Alexander the great," he said.

"No."

"Fine, I wasn't but I knew him," he said with a smile. "I spent a lot of time in ancient Greece and Egypt and ancient China. I've always been interested in medicine because I was curious about my body. I couldn't exactly have a regular doctor check me so I became my own. When you're alive as long as I have been, you see a lot of injustice, mostly against women, slaves. My mother died giving birth to me after she was impregnated against her will by Hhera, and my father did much worse to her and his other slaves. I didn't want to see that happen anywhere else. I can't stop all women and girls from being raped and beaten and subjugated but I could offer medical aid. I mostly was an ob/gyn. I helped during labor, pregnancies, abortions, miscarriages, infections, everything."

"Wow, when did you start practicing?"

"I think I began studying in 520 BC. I surrounded myself with a lot of philosophers and scientists, plenty of the times I inspired their work, I did that until it was no longer prudent to do so."

"You still aren't naming names Alex?" Syren teased.

"Plato, Aristotle, Socrates, Pythagorus, René Descartes, Muhammad ibn Musa al-Khwarizmi, Copernicus, Galilei. Hippocrates - to name a few."

"You never came across me before?"

"Set knew about you long before we did. I found out about you in the late 80's. When you started dating Teddy publicly, I remember first seeing your face on a tv screen, it was the news. At that time an entire new segment of the world was introduced to your beauty and your face was plastered everywhere. I thought, like everyone else that you were just an extraordinarily beautiful human. It wasn't until Set took Isis that I really looked into you and realized you were the Ahsyllan everyone was talking about."

"Wasn't the white gold hair a giveaway?"

"Not particularly for me. I've never seen Hhera, my siblings have. I couldn't have known it was the same."

Syren shrugged. "What were you doing before you met me?" she asked.

"Sleeping. I went to sleep in the early 90's and woke up in the mid 2000's when Isis was taken."

"What?" she said, perplexed.

"Oh- I can sleep for really long periods of time."

"How?"

"If I abstain from food long enough my body will stop functioning and I'll sleep."

"For decades?"

"Yeah well for a decade or two then I'll be flung out of the coma ravenous and if I can abstain I'll shut down again but if I eat then I'm back functioning normally."

"Why would you do that to yourself?" she asked, annoyed.

"2600 years is a very long time to exist, Syren. I think you have the right formula. You live a life filled with growth and progress, you have a new identity each cycle, you can achieve things and get to experience having a family and then you die and it starts over. That at least sounds bearable. I'm stuck, I never changed, I can't stay in one place for too long.

None of my achievements or discoveries have my names attached to them. I can't form meaningful relationships because people die and I don't. I can't have children because I'll outlive them. It's a recipe for madness so when I feel I can't stand it anymore, I sleep for a few decades- the longest I've gone down for is a century and a half. When I wake I have a new world to discover."

She was silent for a moment.

"Where were you going to go to sleep when you thought Isis died?"

"I wanted to- it was very selfish of me I admit but I couldn't just leave you."

"Um..you said you can't have children because you'll outlive them does that mean you can...if you wanted to?"

"In theory I can, I've never tried."

"I never thought about that- I never thought that was possible, why didn't you tell me before..."

"Before we had sex?"

She nodded.

"Because it didn't matter. I can't get you pregnant."

"So I can only give birth to myself, no one else."

"According to Hhera, yes."

"How does that happen?"

"I couldn't tell you honestly," Alex responded.

"Have any of your siblings had children?" she asked, trying to change the topic.

"Cleo has had many children, I delivered them all. She's ecstatic at first but they all die then she grieves for decades after and then she does it again to fill the sadness. Her last child died in 1998, she was a 108. Seth had one back in the first century AD but it was an accident. That's how we found out we could reproduce. Isis doesn't particularly care for children."

"Has she had any? I imagine 2600 years is a long time to skirt pregnancy, you as well, how were you able to avoid having children when your having sex with women."

Alex sighed and began to answer the loaded question, unsure of where to begin."Well, Isis mostly loves women though there have been some men so her chances were significantly reduced even still there was a baby girl named Juliet, she lived a full life and died well into her nineties. I found a quite effective way to avoid the responsibility of fatherhood."

"How?" Syren asked.

"I just slept with older women. Women who are menopausal, they're better in bed anyways."

Syren slapped his arm and chuckled."Are they?"

"Oh yes, well not better than you of course not, you almost killed me, if I'm with a human, I almost kill them. It's a nice flip, I like to be the one sexually over-whelmed."

Syren smiled widely, "I'm very impressed with myself I must admit."

Alex chuckled and shook his head, "very modest."

"Modesty is boring."

"Are you the same person who spent the night on the beach trying to convince me you were ugly?"

"No. I'm not but back to you; you've only ever had sex with older women?"

"No, primarily but not always and not at all for the few hundred years I existed where I didn't know I could impregnate anyone. If it's someone younger then it can't be a spur of the moment thing. It's not worth the threat of pregnancy. I loved the invention of the condom, though in the grand scheme of things it hasn't been around that long, not for me anyways. I can't tell you how many times I've tried to render myself sterile. Never worked."

"So does that mean the rest of your family has descendants?"

"No- that's another thing- our children can't reproduce."

"Like a mule?" she wondered.

Alex nodded, "they don't have special abilities but they are rather healthy. They live long for humans, always ninety to over a hundred. Cleo's children anyways."

"How many has she had?"

"Thirty five, she's had twins sometimes, triplets at others, sometimes she had multiple children she raises at once."

Day had turned to night around them and it wasn't until there was a break in the conversation that Syren noticed.

"Why don't we go inside..." she said.

She didn't see him move but in a flash he was standing in front of her and helping her off the porch.

"What should we have for dinner?" he asked.

"I'm craving spicy sushi," she said as she stood and stretched her muscles and rubbed the back of her legs where the edge of the wood of the porch pressed against her flesh

"I can go to Japan and pick some up, I have a place."

She nodded excitedly.

"Okay but you should change, February in Japan is pretty cold."

"Okay," Syren responded.

Inside the cabin, she slipped on the cream waterfall coat she'd left on the coat rack by the front door. When Alex was dressed in something warmer he wrapped his arms around her and then disappeared.

~~~

Every day was a new adventure, filled with stories of Alex's past that she listened to as eagerly as a child listen to their bedtime story. Every morning and night, they made love ravenously and so it continued.

After two weeks in Alex's Cabin, they travelled to Syren's condo. When they stepped in from the balcony Katherine, Ruby and Teddy were sitting on the couch.

"SYREN," Ruby screamed as she ran to her from across the room.

"Hi Ruby," Syren said as she returned Ruby's hug.

"When did you get outside?" Ruby asked.

"We've been there for a while," Syren lied.

"I've been calling you Sy, you don't answer," Ruby complained softly.

"I'm sorry Ruby, I was just really busy but I'm here now."

Syren looked to Teddy and Katherine. "Teddy, this is Alex, I think you may remember him from his time interning for me."

Teddy walked across the room and stretched his hand to shake Alex's. "It's nice to see you again Alex. We were going to have breakfast together. It would be great if you could join us."

"No," Syren interjected, "we're leaving."

"Honey, I'm sure you can stop to eat. I've hardly seen you since your birthday party."

"The birthday party you didn't attend," Syren questioned.

Teddy smiled nervously, "I think we should talk about this."

"There's nothing to talk about Teddy. I'm not angry at you, I understand. Regardless, we can't stay."

Katherine rolled her eyes and shook her head from across the room. "Let her go Teddy, she doesn't want to stay."

"No, Sy, please stay, I miss you," Ruby said.

"Rubes, I'm sorry but I can't." Syren kissed her cheek. "I'll see you later okay. When I get back, we'll have a fun sleepover or something."

Syren said the words and rushed up the stairs. Alex was left standing awkwardly.

"It was nice to see you again Mr. Prinsloo, Ruby, Katherine. Excuse me," Alex said then walked up the stairs. Katherine rushed across the room and followed behind Alex. She reached him as he entered Syren's closet.

"Where have you guys been?" Syren asked.

"Katherine, I'm not in the mood," Syren responded as she skimmed through her wardrobe of clothes, trying to find options to bring back to Alex's cabin.

"It's just a question. It's been more than two weeks since I've seen you. You barely answer texts or respond to calls. Athena is running everything. You haven't showed up at work-"

"Aren't you the one who's chastised me for not having fun, not being a teenager. I'm doing that now and Athena keeps me aware of everything. What's the problem?"

"I'm your sister. It's kind of shitty for you to just avoid me. I didn't do anything to you. I know you and him are apparently fine now but that doesn't mean you get to just leave and not say anything to anyone."

"Katherine, I'll call you more often and I'll respond to your texts alright?"

Katherine rolled her eyes and responded, "you're the worst kind of girl, The kind that ditches everyone the second they find a guy they like enough."

"That is not true," Syren fired back.

"Isn't it? Ruby, who you supposedly love so much has been trying to see you for weeks and you've been ignoring her. What's worse is that you know everytime she calls because Athena tells you. Tell me it's not true?" Katherine waited but Syren didn't respond. "That's right, you can't say it's not true."

"Alex, can you get me out of here, "Syren said angrily. She didn't bother grabbing clothes.

Alex took a few steps forward and took her hand then in a flash they disappeared leaving Katherine standing alone.

~~~

They arrived in High Palace on the balcony overlooking the city of Paris, which is the place Alexander most vividly remembered about the palace and the place easiest for him to travel back to.

It was a winter afternoon in Paris but at High palace it was a temperate 75 degree day due to the dome shaped proton shield Syren had over the estate. It was a shield over the palace that had been there for decades before. The proton shield was flawed in only one sense; it couldn't prevent light travellers from entering, only the photon shield could.

"Are you okay, that was heavy?" Alex said.

"I'm fine, I'm used to Katherine. She's right of course but still, it is annoying being lectured by her. I need a break from my family and I'm taking it," Syren said with a shrug.

They walked up the grand staircase and through the gilded halls filled with portraits of what she used to think were her ancestors but now were really previous forms. The high ceilings above them were painting with angels in the clouds, gods at war, all manor of ancient greek, egptian, nordic and roman mythology depending on what wing of the palace you roamed.

"Is it odd to you that I have so many pictures of myself here?" she asked as they walked in the decorated marble floors.

The halls were teeming with workers, all fulfilling their daily tasks.

"Bonjour madame Excellci," she heard from several workers as she walked.

"Bonjour," she would greet occasionally. Sometimes it was just a nod and smile. She felt gross as she watched the halls buzzing with vessels now that she knew Alex was one too.

"No, it's not weird," Alex responded, "not when you have a face like yours."

"Shut up," she responded shyly. Then they arrived at the main court, Athena had already instructed one of the vessels to prepare two of Syren's horses for a ride. They waited for her by the Isabeli fountain in the main court.

"This is Peony, my favorite horse," Syren introduced, "and this is Primrose, I call her Prim," she said of the other horse.

She stepped into the stirrup and climbed on the saddle.

"Come on, get on," she encouraged.

Alex climbed on, "she's gentle," he said lightly as he pet Prim.

"Race you to the lake," she yelled quickly as she took off on her horse, leaving Alex behind her.

He slapped the mare's ass lightly and galloped behind her. As he chased her all he would see was her golden hair flowing in the wind, it became distracting after a while and he found himself not truly participating in the race but rather gazing at her.

He watched as the strands of white and gold danced in the wind. When he reached the lake, shortly after her, she'd already dismounted her horse and was waiting by the stone bridge.

Alex dismounted his horse and walked over to Syren. He was awed by the scenery before him, which was unusual.

"This is great," he mused at the scenic view before him. Sapphire lake with the royal blue waters and the colorful garden behind it.

He could no longer use the word beautiful to describe anyone or thing but Syren. There had to be some standard set for the word if it was to be apt in describing her so he decided to set that standard.

"I want to show you something across the bridge."

She mounted her horse and headed to the bridge, Alex mounted Prim and followed beside her.

When he looked down in the water, it was so clear he could see to the bottom. There were all manner of fish and aquatic life swimming in the water.

Across the lake was High garden. They rode through on the horses until they reached the Excellci memorial.

Syren dismounted her horse first and Alex followed. He looked around at the marble sculptures, all of them looked exactly like Syren. It was alarming to see.

"I used to come here once a month and cry my eyes out because I knew there was a spot here waiting for me," she said. "There was always a connection there and now it's gone."

"Because you know now?" he asked as he stared into violet eyes.

"I guess so- thinking I'm destined to die after childbirth and fall in line as an Excellci was very grim but knowing there's some inevitable war coming that I need to be prepared for but have no answers to help me prepare is even more grim," she said dejectedly.

"I'll help you," Alex said softly.

"I don't know where to start. I mean, I still can't figure out why aren't they here to help me?"

"I don't know. Whatever Hhera told us was three thousand years ago but Syren, I truly believe you should try to find out what you can. Find another way to use your powers that don't involve you being angry or hurt. You should be able to use it when you need it, without any trauma."

"You don't understand Alex," Syren responded tearfully, "I physically can't. It feels impossible, as if I were actually human. I can't count on being angry because there have been times when I was angry and still couldn't access it."

"When we have sex it happens, it may not be harmful but it's still your power."

Syren chuckled, "It's different, that's just an extension of my love and ecstasy. I can't control it anymore than I can control an orgasm. It happens to me, same as it happens to you."

Alex felt a wave of heat flash over his body. "Okay, no more talks of orgasms unless you want us to desecrate this memorial."

Syren smiled, "okay, okay, no more talk of the orga-"

Alex raised an eyebrow.

"Fine," she said with a smile.

They spent over an hour in the garden and then rode back to the main court for lunch. She gave him an abbreviated tour of the residence and then she brought him down to the underground lab.

After a tour of the lab she took him another level down.

"Where are we going?" he asked.

"There's a vault down there. When I was a child, Isabeli told me to open it when it was time. I never knew what she meant or what that time was so I never went. Now seems appropriate."

The door to the vault was a plain silver metal. There was no knob or keypad, nothing to allow access.

"I never knew how to get in," Syren said then pressed her palm against the metal door. It slid open at her touch."Oh, I suppose that's how."

She walked into the room with Alex in tow.

It was a large, rectangular room with three metal walls and one glass mirror wall. The first thing in her line of vision was a silver metal mannequin in the form of a woman. The mannequin was clad in a streamline golden armor. There was a head piece that covered the hairline and protected the front of the head. The face remained uncovered. On the body, there was a full suit that covered from the neck to the feet. The metal of the suit seemed both hard and soft. It wasn't like typical armor, the fit of it reminded her of a scuba suit only it was made of hard metal. Over the suit was an overpiece, a cloak with a hood pulled back, made from an almost sheer fabric that had a pattern of small lines and curves that seemed to move so quickly it vibrated.

Syren turned and looked behind the armor, there were two broadswords, pinned against the metal wall. The hilt of the sword was gold with black jewels scattered into the carvings. The metal blade was an icy white silver. She turned around in the room against the wall and there were several items. A very old book that looked like a diary; a thin, square pad; a string less bow with no arrow.

On another mannequin further back in the room was a long red gown. It was simple. The fabric seemed like silk sheer doubled until it was no longer opaque. Covering the head of the mannequin was a sheer red veil that covered the entire dress down the ground. It was a simple, modest dress. There were no frills or designs and it covered up the clavicle of the neck.

"What exactly is this supposed to be," Syren asked, confused.

She walked over to the armor and reached out to touch the metal. The moments her finger made contact with the metal, it crawled up her skin like moving liquid until she was fully suited in the outfit.

Syren didn't see this. The image of the armor up close brought flashes of memories through her mind:

She saw other golden armored women running. Everyone had hair like hers, long down their backs that was sparkling white-gold like hers. She saw a range of brown, black and cream skin. She couldn't make out faces, they were too fuzzy. She saw a green terrain with the ocean ahead, almost as if she were standing on a cliff. She heard explosions. They were loud, menacing roars around her but she couldn't see where they were coming from. She heard footsteps headed to her. "Praesaedia, protect our queen!" a voice yelled.

"Syren?" Alex called, taking her from her memories and into the present.

"Woah," she said in wonderment.

"Where did you go?" he asked.

"I think I had a memory-" she looked down and saw that she was clad in gold, "what?"

"It crawled up your skin when you touched it...what did you see?"

She turned and looked in the mirror. When she moved the cloak of the armor, it became invisible. She moved it again and it was visible. It was so light it felt like she wore nothing at all.

"I saw a bunch of other women who look like me and were dressed like this. There was some kind of fight but a massive fight like a...battle. I heard roars as if there were some large animals and explosions. I was there, standing in the middle of it..."

"Maybe you left this here for yourself, to jog your memory…"

He reached out and touched the metal of her armor. It burned him like hot lava.

"OW!" He groaned.

"Alex, are you okay?" Syren turned around quickly to him.

He was holding his fingers. It burns all five of his distal phalanges on his right hand.

"It burned me."

He looked down at his fingers. It began to blister.

"This has never happened before-"

"What?"

"I've never been scarred from a burn…"

Syren sucked her teeth angrily, "How do I get this thing off." Frustrated, she touched the mannequin and the armor crawled back unto the mannequin.

"Let me look at your finger," she said softly.

"It's okay, I'm fine."

"Let me see," she insisted as she took his hand and inspected his fingers.

"You said this never happened before?"

"Yeah, I can't even be sure if my blood is red, I've never been cut or burned. My skin has never broken. The only reason I know our blood is red is because Isis and Cleopatra bled during childbirth."

"I thought you said you did feel pain?"

"I do. I could be on fire for days and be in agony but my skin wouldn't be penetrated."

"But Set burned…"

"Because it was your fire, same as this burned me."

"Will it be alright?"

"Yeah, it'll be fine."

She took his fingers and kissed them.

"You looked unreal in the armor," he said softly.

"I hated it," she said as she walked closer to the wall and inspected the items. She took the book and flipped through it, it was like a diary.

The black tablet turned on at her touch and a video of Isabeli played automatically.

"Syren, if your watching this it means that you've come searching for answers. I can't tell you what's going to happen. I've disconnected you from our memories for a reason. They wouldn't help you. There are a few things you need to know.

"First, Majikai is coming. The last time he was on Earth, he killed half of the Ahsyllan population with a few men. That cannot happen again and everything we've done and will do is to ensure that outcome."

"Second, once you've fully realized your powers the Ahsyllans will come for you. It's very hard to keep the timeline in tack but if my calculations are right, we won't have much time after that.

"Third, and this is the hardest part, everything that happens from this point on, will be for a reason, no matter how hard, no matter how painful. There's a lot I had to do to us and there's a lot I let happen to you but it was inevitable and necessary for the good of Ashylla and all Ahsyllans. I left notes that you may read, you won't like what you find. Since you've seen this message, your only job now is to let things play out and react exact how we've groomed you to react...and Syren...Hhera's vessel, will only make you soft, you must abandon him, if you're to reach perfection."

The video ended.

Syren turned to Alex but could barely see his face through the haze that covered her eyes and the thumping in her chest drowned out his voice.

"Sy, what's going through your head," Alex asked softly. He was also confused by the video and even more confused that Syren's former self knew of him but that fell behind to his concern for her.

She stood silent, all the pain and emotional trauma inflicted on her through her adolescence now seemed manufactured by her former self to break her. It was too much.

"I need a minute-"

"Hey, let's go back to the cabin,"

Syren nodded, still panting lighty.

"Do you want to take the book?" he asked. "She said we won't like what we find but it's better to know than be ignorant."

She nodded absently. Alex grabbed the book and it burned him.

"Ah," he said lightly, "I'm guessing she doesn't want me touching anything in here."

Syren grabbed the book and hugged Alex's chest, careful to keep it from his skin. He tried to travel but he couldn't.

"I can't travel from here, there has to be a shield built in…"

He walked with her to the door and it slid open automatically. He tried again in the lab and was still unable to. They travelled back down the long white hallway, up the metal elevators until they reached ground level. Once they stepped out, they vanished.

Chapter 18: Trauma

In the cabin, Syren was still shaken. Alex sat her on the couch. In a second he was back from the kitchen with a bottle of water. He sat beside her and opened the bottle for her.

"Here, take a sip," he offered.

Syren drank a few gulps of the water then closed the bottle and fell into his chest. She laid there a while and didn't move from her comfortable position nestled in Alex's embrace.

"Are you hungry, Angel?" Alex asked.

"No."

He checked the clock on the wall, "it's late, please just let me make you something okay?"

She nodded reluctantly to appease him.

Alex gladly went to the kitchen to prepare something for Syren. He made vegetarian pasta, the easiest and quickest thing he could find that would be filling for her.

She shoved the pasta around her plate with her fork for a few minutes before she excused herself to take a bath. Her violet irises were now obsidian black and he needed to figure out a way to fix it. What was said in the message that triggered her so? There was so much, it was hard to know.

He left her food covered in the kitchen figuring she might eat some later and then he went to the second bathroom to shower as well.

Syren was sitting on the bed, wearing his white towel robe. It was dark in the room and the only source of light came from the hallway. He didn't realize she was crying until he heard a soft sniffle.

"Sy?" he called as he walked over to her and pulled her up by both hands from the bed. "You're crying," he began but before he could finish, Syren pulled from him.

"I'm tired Alex…"

"Why are you crying?"

"I want to go home," Syren said. "Take me home."

"No. If you want to go in the morning I'll take you but tonight you're staying with me."

She shook her, "No. I want to go."

Alex held both her cheeks and peered into her eyes. "You're staying with me." He pulled her into his arms and held her. For a moment Syren let him until she broke the hug and pushed him down on the bed then she climbed on top of him and untied her robe.

~~~

Later, Alex laid in bed staring at the ceiling. Syren was directly on his chest, soundly asleep and every so often her stomach would growl. Eventually, hunger was enough to wake her. She sat up, naked, holding her stomach.

"You're hungry?" Alex asked, knowingly.

"Starving," she answered with a nod.

Alex stood and wrapped his towel around his hips. Syren stood as well. Alex opened the large towel robe and she quickly slipped her arms in the sleeves then tied the belt around her waist.

They went down to the kitchen. Syren sat at the wooden island and devoured her cold pasta. In the light, Alex could see her eyes had relaxed back into dark violet.

"Are you ready to talk about it?" he began once she finished her food.

She averted her eyes to the ground, "not really…"

He sighed, "at least tell me what bothered you so much? Was it because she said I'd make you soft?"

Syren groaned, "I didn't know what that meant until I begged you to have sex with me while sobbing on top of you." She rolled her eyes, at herself, "that's not a problem. If that's soft then I don't care."

"Why did you need that tonight?"

"We have sex every night," she answered simply, "the only difference tonight was that you made me beg you for it."

"You've never cried before, during, or after sex. That was the difference tonight."

Syren shrugged but offered no response.

"Are you gonna tell me what's going on?" he asked, frustrated.

She answered, "...just give me tonight."

Alex agreed reluctantly.

"Aren't you hungry...you expended yourself a lot tonight..."

"No, I'm fine," he said, his voice was flat and clipped. He stood.

Syren didn't know what that meant.

"Let's go back to bed."

Syren nodded and followed him back to the bedroom.

In the morning, Syren was up before Alex. She was determined to change their morning routine, if only for one morning. Alex was usually up before her with breakfast prepared when she woke. This morning, she decided it would be her turn to prepare breakfast. She could count how many times she'd cooked in her life but, she thought, it was just food, how hard could it be to prepare when you followed a recipe.

She made pancakes, eggs, and sausage with fruit and tea. Alex's kitchen was filled with groceries and he'd restock every few days since she'd begun her stay with him. She set the food on the tray and brought enough back to the bedroom. He was still sleeping when she sat on the bed beside him with the tray in her lap.

"Wake up, Alex," she called.

He didn't budge.

"Alex?" she called a little louder.

His eyes fluttered open and he smiled as boyish sideways smile at the sight of her.

"You're up before me, Angel," he said as he sat up.

"Yes and I made you breakfast," she said with a smile. His mood seemed vastly different and she was glad.

Alex looked down at the tray.

"I didn't know you could cook."

"Any asshole can follow a recipe. The pancakes are a little burnt but..."

He smiled and took the fork, broke a piece of the pancake, and put it in his mouth. He cleared his throat as he chewed and Syren noticed his facial expression was off.

"What?"

He leaned over the plate and spat it out.

"How much salt did you use?"

"I used sugar to make it sweet- oh wait- was that salt? God," she said with a sigh, "I'm the asshole who can't follow a recipe."

He shook his head and smiled then kissed her lips.

"It's okay, I appreciate it but you know I have no problem feeding you? I like it."

"I know. I wanted to do it for you..for once. The sausages should be edible...try it?"

He took a piece of the sausage and chewed.

"It's good."

Syren smiled widely and took a piece as well, "see, I can cook, you just needed to label the spices in your kitchen."

Alex chuckled, "so now it's my fault."

"Yes."

They ate breakfast then after, they went down to the kitchen to drop off the tray and wash the dishes. Alex sat at the island watching her from behind after Syren insisted on completing the task.

"So, what's the real reason you made breakfast?" he asked.

She sighed and turned around, the water from the faucet still streamed on the dishes as she faced him.

"Can't I make you breakfast, innocently with no ulterior motives?" She said with the words so quickly they all seemed to join together.

He shook his head.

"Okay well...I guess after our conversation this morning I couldn't help but feel you were a little upset at what we did last night."

"I wasn't upset...I just didn't want you doing it for the wrong reasons."

"What reason would've been wrong?" she questioned.

"Doing it because you were upset and wanted to hurt. I'm not gonna have sex with you to hurt you Syren."

"You didn't hurt me."

"If I'd listened to you, I would have. You have to remember until you are fully realized in your powers, you are still vulnerable and I am strong, I might not break everything I touch because I'm exercised in controlling myself but if I get too excited and reckless, I can hurt you. You heal quickly but I still don't want that."

She sighed, "You're right, okay, maybe I wasn't doing it for the right reasons, I was angry, watching that video yesterday brought up a lot of things that I wasn't prepared for."

"I figured," he walked to her by the sink and wrapped his arms around her waist, and kissed the blade of her shoulder.

"So you hated it then?" she asked.

"No, not at all. It was amazing except for the fact you kept demanding, 'harder, harder, harder-"

"-Sshh," she whined, covering his mouth with her palm as her face flushed hot.

"You'll find it exceedingly hard to hatefuck someone you love so intensely, Syren."

"Okay, I get it. Now I feel terrible," she whined.

"Don't." He wiggled out of her grasp and kissed her lips then slowly traced kisses down her neck. She closed her eyes and bit her lips at the sensation so sweet it left her breathless. He traced the lines of her clavicle with his finger and continued kissing down, opening her robe as he went down her torso.

Syren held the edge of the sink and closed her eyes but couldn't manage to keep her eyes from him for long.

He roamed lower, staring into her purple irises as he feasted in between her thighs. Licking, kissing, sucking and driving her mad.

"Oh Alex..." The moan came from her lips like a soft song.

They switched positions and then it was Syren on her knees, staring into his sapphire eyes with his flesh so far in her mouth that it touched the back of her throat.

He lifted her to the couch where Syren bent over with her face pressed against the cushions and welcomed his thrusts from behind. In the bath together they embraced in hot water pelting their bodies.

Later in the afternoon, they laid on a blanket on the far banks of the lake.

"I'll never get over how beautiful it is here?" she mused.

She had Isabeli's small leather book resting on the blanket beside her.

Alex kissed her knee then laid his head back on her lap.

"You're stalling…"

She chuckled, "alright, alright."

She took the small book and opened it to the first page and read aloud:

"In the case that an Ahsyallan dies, it is so rare an event that we hold seven days of mourning. In Ahsylla, the exanimate form is marched across The Narrow Way by the Cold Cliffs where they are burned on a pyre in The Horizon. The exanimate forms must be shroud in our color.

Syren skipped forward.

"The broadsword found in the vault has been in our hands for eons, first forged by Ahnais, an ancient form. It is made of a rare metal called Anthium, found in the mines of Planet Kahlar.

The Ahsyllan armor, called amora, was last worn in the battle of the Viridescent Front. It fell woefully short and succumbed to our enemy's weapons.

The bow of Ahnais-"

Syren stopped and sighed, "there's nothing very important in here other than her telling me about funerals and armor."

"In the video, she said something about you not liking what you'd find in the book?"

"Because it's boring probably."

"Syren, you need to take this seriously," Alex insisted.

"I know," she said with a sigh.

Alex smiled softly, "I don't mean to be so severe."

"It's alright, you're not. You're the least severe person I've ever met Alex. You're incredibly sweet and gentle and caring and perfect."

"I wouldn't say that about myself but I'm alright with you saying it," he said with a sideways smile.

Syren shoved him playfully and smiled, "ask something else, you know you want to?"

"Everything you had to go through...what did she mean?"

"I guess I have to start from the beginning."

"I've got no plans for later..." he said softly.

She carefully placed the book on the grass far away from Alexander so it wouldn't burn him. She eased his head up from her lap and laid beside him so their faces were only inches apart.

"Isabeli got sick immediately after she gave birth to me. For a while, it was just weakness. As I got older, she would go to sleep for long periods, months at a time sort of like a coma. During that same time, I began to experience a lot of pain. It was a very unique pain, almost as if I needed to burst out of myself, like every cell in my body needed to burst free and I couldn't contain it like I would explode. I honestly don't know when she put the chip in, it must've been while I slept but I don't know exactly when or how long it took to start affecting me.

"Around the time the pain was getting worse, Teddy found a doctor who was supposed to help me. His name was Marcus. He was supposed to be some great doctor and Teddy gave him a lot of money to help me."

"Marcus, the same name as my father. Do you think it's a coincidence?" he asked.

"I wondered that when you told me but now I'm not so sure. If Isabeli knew you'd be in that room with me and she died a decade ago I'm not sure what they know or what's connected."

Alex sighed, unease. "I'm guessing then that he didn't help."

"No, but out of the experience, I met Kat. She was there too."

"Where?"

"A clinic in Switzerland. I was there, along with a bunch of other kids Marcus thought had special gifts. Katherine is really smart, she was an orphan in Vietnam, in school, they quickly found she was brilliant, a quantitative savant."

As Syren said the word she wondered if there was any possibility Katherine could've been like Alex. A vessel. It was too much to contemplate so she quickly dashed the thought from her mind.

"Kat?" he said with a chuckle.

"Yeah. she doesn't show it now. I think it's because all the trauma and torture made her shut that part of herself away, just like I did. She's much happier dumbing herself down but-"

"Wait- torture?" he asked, the words burned his throat.

"Yes. They used quite cruel methods in an attempt to push abilities forward…" she gulped hard, "he became obsessed with trying to get my powers to manifest, and once he realized that the right trigger could evince my powers, he kept trying to find the trigger. Nothing worked twice of course and I was very unpredictable so it was a process."

"Isabeli let this happen?"

"Based on what she said, I'm guessing she planned it. At the time I was only seven and shortly after I went there, even then as young as I was I threatened to tell what was going on and he threatened my mother. She died a little while later so at the time I just guessed he did it or had something to do with it. After that there was no way I could tell, I just felt like he'd do the same to Teddy, my grandmother, the family."

"You're telling me Teddy never knew any of this was happening?"

"He may have but he was mostly busy grieving Isabeli so he didn't have time for me, he took it very hard, maybe she planned that too and whatever Marcus did to me, would heal, very quickly. So it's not like I came home bandaged or anything."

"How long were you there?"

"A few years. Marcus became reckless and he was arrested on other charges separate from his business at the clinic. It was shut down but most of the horror that went on never got out. He's in a high-security prison in Switzerland right now. He almost escaped back in September, a day before you arrived for your internship."

"If he gets out now you could easily disarm, right?"

"Maybe...but I don't plan on ever seeing him again. He did a lot to me. That ruined me for a time and I don't know how I'd react if I saw him. He's dangerous because he has a lot of people who follow him, who believe in him. His whole premise of having the clinic was that there were special, superhuman people on earth and he needed to find them...of course every kid there was just a normal kid...maybe they were smart or had some gift but they weren't superhuman. I was the only one that was different."

"He reminds me of Set after Hhera died, he had this idea in his head that he needed to find Ahsyllans and kill the queen because they planned to turn him into drones or something - what does that even mean?" he asked, puzzled. "He had this irrational drive that never faltered, not in 2600 years."

They were both quiet for a moment as a million thoughts formed between them.

"If Isabeli knew that Hhera created us, maybe it wasn't an accident, maybe they let her or they told her to do it. I mean, it never made sense to me that Set was able to kill her or she even let it get that far that he could kill her." Alex stopped, "now I'm wondering if he even did. In the journal Isabeli said it was really rare for an Ahsyllan to die, didn't she?"

"You think she...or I..planned Hhera creating you and all the other vessels? Why?"

"I don't know, it's just a thought...I think what Isabeli said just kind of stuck with me. Why would this random human take such an interest in things he shouldn't know anything about and then he just pops up into your life, Isabeli dies after, Teddy is consumed with grief so he's unavailable then you're just left to this monster."

Syren was silent for a moment as she reflected.

"You think that she sent Marcus to traumatize me hoping it would trigger my powers? I thought that too."

He groaned at the thought but he had something slightly different in mind.

"Yes, but I was going to say I think Marcus might be a vessel..."

Syren didn't respond, she'd had the thought too but she dare not say it aloud.

"Think about it, it's just too...manufactured," He said.

She sat up, anxious, and jittery.

"It doesn't make sense...it's too many pieces. They can't possibly know all of these things and plan for events thousands of years in advance. I mean I have free will..for all of this to work I'd need to make very specific preordained choices. If she thought Marcus would trigger me then why would Isabeli make the video, she had to have known it wouldn't have worked before she did. I don't understand."

"Have you heard of Futuras?"

"Yeah, Set said it once to me," she replied.

"Did I ever tell you how I was able to know exactly how I would get to you, you know, before?"

She shook her head, "that was always a mystery to me."

"Well, when Set took Isis and made his demands, he had a futura and she told me exactly what to do when to do it…"

"What do you mean?"

"They told me when I had the best chance of getting to you. She told me when I would meet you, where, and they knew that years before it happened."

Syren was puzzled.

"So what are futuras?"

"They're vessels. They don't see the future per se…but they calculate various actions and reactions and choices and possibilities until they find the best path to the outcome they want. Set has one of them. I was told there were few in existence but that never made sense to me and also why would Hhera make Set a futura unless she wanted him to use it."

Syren began to hyperventilate. Hearing Alex talk about how he manufactured their meeting brought up insecurities about the relationship she wasn't prepared to face.

"Syren…hey," he held her face and looked into her eyes. They'd grown darker but were still violet.

"I can't talk about this anymore…" she said, devoid of expression.

"Syren, you can't just shut this out-"

"Alex, I can't okay, this is too much," she said tearfully.

"Okay," he agreed outwardly though he didn't think that was best."let's talk about something else."

Syren took a few deep breaths and waited.

"I have something planned for us tonight."

"What do you have planned?" she asked, trying hard to think about everything but their prior conversation.

"A date."

"Where?"

"To the capital, Buenos Aires."

"I thought we agreed it would be hard to go somewhere public.

"It is but so what...at least for tonight...I want us to go somewhere there's music and life and normal people. It'll be night time so you'll be able to blend better. I can't play my guitar for you every night and then watch episodes of curb until we fall asleep."

"But curb is my favorite show and I love it when you serenade me with your guitar, although I don't know why you won't sing."

Alex smiled, "maybe I'll sing tonight."

She nodded with a smile, all the while new strengthened doubt filled her mind. Was he too perfect? The question replayed in her mind, incessantly.

Now as she stared at him, she questioned why everything about him seemed perfectly suited to her. He had all the features she found attractive on one face. Even his slightly dimpled chin, so small a detail, seemed to make him complete.

His disposition attracted her even more. He had the perfect temperament that could co-exist with hers.

His sexual prowess was something else entirely. He anticipated her needs before she spoke to them. He knew where to touch, where to kiss, and where to hold. As she thought about it now she wasn't sure any human man or any other man could compare to him. She blushed at the thought and then realized there was another question she needed to ask. The only question more important than whether or not his affection was real or manufactured was if she cared.

Knowing it could be manufactured, that he was a vessel probably sent to her as part of some plot that she didn't understand, that was thousands of years in the making was terrifying but it didn't change anything for her. Not yet.

She looked up at his beautiful eyes and stroked his cheek.

"What are you thinking about?" he asked.

"Just how much I love you," she said with a smile.

~~~

Later, she dressed in a red cotton mini dress and her black converse sneakers. Alex wore black chinos and a white t-shirt with black vans old skool, the outfit he seemed to have infinite variations of and wore almost everywhere`.

"Alex, your entire closet is white t-shirts, chinos, isn't it?" she teased as she slipped on her diamond knobs.

"Don't forget the old skools?"

"How could I," she joked. "For someone so proper you dress quite comfortably."

Alex walked closer and pulled her by the waist against his body.

"Don't start, I'm going to get all tingly and then we'll have to stop and have sex and then we'll be here all night," Syren said with a smile.

He kissed her neck and stepped back."Okay, best behavior."

"And then worst behavior later, right?"

"Katherine's calling again," Athena said.

"Tell her I'll call her back."

"Sure."

Moments later Alex's cell phone chimed from across the room.

"What's wrong?" Alex asked.

"It's just Kat, calling me."

"She knows you're here with me…" he said, mostly to himself. "Should I answer?"

"I don't know."

Alex took his phone and declined the call.

Syren pulled her hair into a high ponytail.

"She's been calling more frequently for a few days now, you sure you don't want to answer."

She shook her head, "I think Katherine is just making a point."

Alex chuckled.

"Um.. has Calabar called you wondering why you aren't back at school?" she asked in an attempt to change the subject.

"I'm sure they called. I just haven't answered my landline since I'm not home in New York," he said with a chuckle.

"He'll think I'm horrible, especially if he sees us out together - I mean I guess he's already seen us. We've been spotted together a few times already."

"Do you care?" she asked.

"Not particularly, no," Alex said with a chuckle.

Syren walked to the mirror across the room and slid clear lip gloss on her lips with the flat wand lip of her gloss then slid it into her tiny velvet pink Chanel handbag.

"I'm ready now."

Alex walked to her and wrapped his arms around her waist.

"You look beautiful," he said before they disappeared.

They reappeared in a dark alley between buildings of a busy street in Buenos Aires.

"Are you okay?" He asked, "Any nausea?"

"No," she whined, "I'm used to it now."

"Okay."

They stepped out into the busy street and blended into the pedestrian traffic.

"Where are we going?" she asked.

"You'll see," he sang.

They walked down the street with lively traffic filled with casually dressed locals. The architecture of the city seemed to be a mix of the centuries-old structures and the newer. She could feel the smooth, uneven cobblestone of the pavement under feet as they slid through crowds of people.

After a short block, she saw a fluorescent sign that read "la canción y la danza" outside of a color-blocked building perched at the edge of the intersection. There was a small seating area outside with small, round metal tables and chairs. They were rickety and painted red. The outside walls of the small building were color-block painted red, sky blue, aqua green, sunny yellow, burnt orange. It was teeming with lights and life.

They crossed the street filled with pedestrians and she could hear music from the bar. It seemed like a live band. Up a set on small concrete steps, they were greeted by a man at the entrance.

"Alex?" the man greeted him with a half hug. "Long time, no see."

"Good to see you too Ronaldo," Alex said with his charming smile.

The tall, heavyset man with a friendly face turned to Syren and smiled.

"Muy linda mujer…" he said as he turned back to Alex, awed.

"That's an understatement," Alex responded with a sideways smile as he kissed her hand.

"Encantada de conocerte," he said to Syren.

"Yo también," Syren responded.

They passed through into the lively bar. The live music had stopped and now it sounded like karaoke. In the middle of the large, packed, teal colored room was a dance floor. To the front was a wooden, well-built stage with a live band. A mic stand and a small screen were protruding from the ceiling with what Syren expected was a karaoke machine.

In the middle of the dance floor, Alex spun her around and pulled her close. She took a look around and she was surrounded by normal. There were old faces and young faces. Fat bodies and slim bodies. There was beautiful and there was less than beautiful. Around her, a sea of colorful clothing danced, spun, and rocked. Long hair, short hair bopped up and down, back and forth. The normal was warmer than the 85-degree night. The normal was perfect.

"Are you hungry?" Alex whispered in her ear.

Syren nodded.

"Our table should be ready soon," he whispered again.

As he spoke a small, unnaturally blonde woman dressed in black slacks and a button-down shirt walked over to them through the sea of people. She nudged Alex and whispered something in his ear and in response he nodded.

Syren felt a pang of jealousy at the close contact but she quickly realized it was a waitress letting him know the table was ready.

Feeling ridiculous, she followed Alex and the small woman over to the metal table for two by the open wooden windows.

Once they were seated she handed them two paper menus.

"Alguna bebida?" she asked Alex.

Though she seemed to be giving all her attention to Alex, she couldn't help but steal envious glances at Syren.

"Aqua," he answered and turned to Syren, "Sy?"

"Water," Syren responded.

The woman nodded, glancing at them both again before leaving.

"I plan to order the asado," he whispered in her ear.

"What is it?" she asked.

"A lot of meat," he said with a chuckle, "barbequed."

"I love meat. Let's do it."

He flashed her a smile, seemingly pulling a double meaning from her response. Syren winked at him, glad her response had its intended effect.

The small woman returned moments later with two glasses of water and placed them on the table.

"Usual? Alex?" she asked.

He nodded and placed two fingers up to her, shooting her a quick look of acknowledgment before he turned back to Syren. She took the menus and left.

Syren slipped her quilted leather bag from her shoulder and pulled the double strap into a single lined long strap then placed it over her head, across her body.

After she did this Alex took her hand and kissed it. She leaned into him, "this is perfect."

From the corner of her eyes, she saw a camera light flash. She turned and looked only to see several people taking pictures of her and Alex, some openly, others surreptitiously.

Alex rolled his eyes and took her hand and pulled her up before she could get annoyed at the voyeurs.

They walked to the front of the wooden stage and he motioned for the members of the band to come to him. The guitarist walked over with a friendly smile. She wondered how many times he'd been to the bar to get such a friendly welcome from the staff.

She couldn't hear what Alex said but after speaking for almost a minute, the man handed him the mic from the mic stand and then motioned to the band members something she didn't understand. A few moments later the music changed.

She heard the thumping of the bass so loud the floor vibrated under her feet.

The two female background singers on the stage began humming "ahhs" and "oohs" into the mic as the band played the set.

Alex took her by the hand with the mic in his hand and spun her as he began to sing.

"Keep your old and wasted word…" he began. A lyric from one of her favorite songs by the band Bombay Bicycle Club.

She wished she could say his voice was a surprise but it wasn't. He held her by the waist as he serenaded her with music to the cheers of the crowd. She fed off his energy, following as he moved, stepping as he stepped. Somewhere in the song, she forgot about the people around her and only saw him. The music pulled her in and Alex swallowed her up. He sang and danced lightly but the evenness of his voice never faltered. When she couldn't take it anymore, the raw places his voice was taking her, so sweet and so beautiful, she pulled him in and kissed him, breaking him from the song.

There were cheers but she didn't hear them.

She broke the kiss only when she was sure she would pass out. When she looked up at Alex a smile peered down at her. She wiped the lip gloss that traveled to his lips and smiled.

He handed the mic back to the guitarist and moments later they were performing live music again.

She found herself magnetically kissing him again, on and off as they swayed to the music that seemed too lively for their movement.

The waitress walked over and tapped Alex's arm and pointed to the food on their table.

They sat and Alex watched anxiously with a smile as Syren tasted the asado, chewed, and swallowed with an unreadable expression.

"How was it?" he asked loud enough for Syren to hear.

She kept her face straight for as long as she could then she broke into a smile. "It's delicious."

He chuckled and shook his head.

They ate then quickly found a corner of the room where they could sway to the music away from the dance floor.

The music was perfect, changing from the lively indie music to soft hums from the singers while the band played Spanish ballads.

Swaying turned to kiss and when kissing seemed inadequate she decided it was time to go but before she could say the words, Alex guessed them.

"You're ready to go?" he whispered.

Syren nodded.

He took her by the hand and walked back to their table. He dropped cash on the table and then they left.

~~~

In the early morning, they laid cuddled in bed. Articles of their clothing scattered around them, on the bed, and the floor. Syren traced lines along with the curves of his chest lazily, waiting for the sleep to take her. It was hard, her body was well weary but her mind buzzed with thoughts, calmed by Alex's singing.

He sang softly in her ear. He was a fan of old soul music, as was she; The Four Tops, The Chi-Lites, The Spinners. He would play their records on his record player during the days she'd been there.

Alex stroked her arm softly as he sang, waiting for her to sleep so he could too.

"Tonight was perfect," she said after the song ended.

"I'm glad you liked it."

"Why didn't you tell me you could sing?"

"I can't."

She leaned up and scolded him with a stare.

"Okay...a little."

She smiled."How often do you go there?"

"I found it a couple of years ago. I go there every few months. I like the band."

"The music was perfect…"

The memory of the night flashed through her mind and sourly, she remembered the waitress.

"The waitress who wouldn't stop staring at you, do you know her well?"

"We had sex once, it wasn't that great."

She leaned her head up and glared."I'm kidding Sy," he said with a smile.

"Don't do that to me," she said with a chuckle and rested her head again.

"You know I'm not a virgin right?"

"Don't remind me. I don't even want to think about you with anyone else." She realized then that she didn't know anything about his past loves, not specifically. "How did you do it...your first time?"

"It was with a woman named Sepia, she was Roman. She was about twice my age and she had a husband."

"You home-wrecker," she accused lightly. "Did you enjoy it?"

"I did, I absolutely did."

She chuckled."Have you ever been in love? You said you haven't but come on 2600 years, you have to have been?" She asked.

"Once."

"Tell me about it?"

"I think it was instant. I tried to fight it but I don't know...I was all sorts of helpless. She had this beautiful smile that made you smile, it would break your heart and then mend it in the same breath. She loved fiercely but she had to think you were deserving of that love. Her eyes were so beautiful, so big and expressive that it was the first place she would pull you in. She affected everyone around her, like some airborne drug. People trip over their feet just to catch a glimpse of her. She had this beautiful white gold hair that just-"

She leaned up and smiled.

"Okay, I get it."

Alex chuckled and sighed. "Dolores was her name. I didn't love her but I had a great deal of affection for her and I cared for her. I was always careful about love because I knew it wouldn't end well. I'm imperishable, humans are not. Isis would fall in love with a different man or woman every decade, I don't know how she did it but she was happy."

"Is that why you think you loved me because you knew at least if I die I'd come back."

"When I fell in love with you I don't know that I was thinking that. It didn't real-ize how fast I'd moved from the realm of infatuation to deep love until it was too late. I didn't have time to stop myself although I'm not sure what one does to stop themself from falling for you. I realized I loved you when I saw how much the little things you did would disproportionately affect me. I mean...if you seemed sad then inexplicably I'd be sad. If you were happy then I'd be happy. Ultimately I knew for sure when choosing between you and my sister was an impossible choice. I couldn't deny it then."

"Is this real?" she asked softly, hoping the question wouldn't hurt him.

He stopped stroking her hand and for the moment all she could feel was the ab-sence of his touch until he began again."I was worried you'd think that after our conversation earlier."

Of course, he knew what she was thinking, she thought.

"I made the choice. Futuras can tell you what path is best, they can even help oth-ers manipulate you into making a choice but they can't force you to do anything."

"Isabeli knew fifteen years ago that we were going to end up in that room together. It's too precise."

"Do you doubt me?" he asked. "After everything that's happened, that's under-standable."

"I don't doubt that you love me Alex. I could never doubt that." She raised her head so she gazed at him as she spoke, "and I love you...I love you so much but...sometimes it just feels like you are too perfect for me like it can't be real. You just popped into my life and I've changed.

"I did things that I never thought I'd do over any man. After Coney Island, when you told me you wanted our relationship to be strictly professional, I was devastated and that's not me. What I felt wasn't proportional to reality. I'd only known you for two months at that point. Then when you decided we should be apart again, I cried for weeks. That's not me. That's never been me."

Alex swallowed hard at the reminder of his failing.

"Have you ever considered that you think I'm perfect because you love me...That I'm not actually perfect."

"Interesting idea...but no," she said with a chuckle. "It never even occurred to me that you're not perfect." she sighed sadly, "it just feels like something is coming and I don't know what and it's terrifying."

"I know what you mean but Syren, you have to admit that you're doing the opposite."

"You're right," Syren replied. She thought for a moment before responding. "I don't know that it will work but we can try to provoke my powers tomorrow? If you think that will help. That's what they want right?"

Alex shrugged, "I don't know but it's better than doing nothing. I think it's more important for you to read the journal Isabelli left you."

"I know. I will."

When Syren woke in the morning, Alex was gone from the bed. She walked downstairs in her white robe and saw Isis, Cleo and Seth gathered in the family room.

Her cheeks flushed immediately as she saw all their eyes on her. It was her first time seeing them since the incident - which is what she called it- had happened. Seth's lingering eyes felt different now, she was always aware of his ogle at her but this time it felt more intense and inquisitive.

"Hi Sy," Isis said with a smile. She walked over and hugged her tightly, "how are you?" she asked.

"Fine," Syren said shyly.

Cleo walked over next. "Hi, I'm Cleo," She began. "And I realized I've never actually introduced myself, nor have I been the most welcoming. I'm sorry. It's been a rough few years." She stretched her hands for a shake which Syren returned.

"I thought you said you didn't shake hands," Seth said.

"I made an exception," she said with a smile directed at Cleo.

Alex walked shirtless from the kitchen, straight to Syren, and kissed her lips softly, and smiled.

"Good morning," he said softly.

She blushed and turned away from his stare.

"Are you hungry?" he asked.

Syren nodded.

"Great, we can all have breakfast together, seeing that you haven't seen me since my second day back," Isis said.

"Sy, what do you think?" Alex asked.

"Sure. I do need to take a bath though."

"Should I pick something up or make it?" he asked her.

"Whatever is easier," she said as she rushed up the stairs.

"You look very...bright," Isis quipped.

Alex didn't respond as he walked over to the couch and grabbed a sweater that hung over the arm and slipped it on."Any volunteers?" he asked.

"I'll come with you," Cleo offered.

"Me too," Isis said.

"Seth?" Alex asked.

"I'll stay here," he said as he took a seat on the sofa.

"Fine," Isis said.

Both Isis and Cleo grabbed his arms and in a flash, they were in Paris. They were back in just over twenty minutes. Seth never moved from his spot.

Isis and Cleo laid the spread of decadent Parisian breakfast food on the counter of the kitchen island. Alex went upstairs to Syren. He found her in his bedroom getting dressed.

"Hey, the food's downstairs," he said softly.

"One sec," she pulled on her yoga pants. "I'll be right there."

Alex waited as she finished getting dressed and then they both walked down to the kitchen together. It was a silent breakfast, awkwardly so. Isis grew tired of the tension and decided to speak.

"We saw you after you had sex, it's not a big deal- don't be embarrassed, we were just coming to check on Alex because he wasn't answering our calls. We won't show up unannounced again and Alex had already told us to give you guys some time alone so..." Isis declared.

Syren closed her eyes and shook her head.

"Can we just forget it," Syren mumbled with a mouth full of fruit.

"Yes. I thought we'd all agreed on not talking about it," Alex agreed.

"Well I just wanted to clear the air, Syren is mortified although- you know what you're doing. My brother was dead to the world. I've never seen that" Isis teased.

"Oh my god-" Syren said, mortified.

"I'm just kidding Sy, you're practically a part of our family now, I'm allowed to make fun of you. I have participated in countless orgies-"

Syren gasped.

"-As has Alex. As had Cleo. As has Seth." Isis pointed to each sibling as she called their names.

Syren looked to Alex and chuckled.

"I already told her, Isis," Alex said. "I don't have any secrets. Syren knows every-thing about me."

"Even that time…" Isis began, waiting for Alex to stop her but when he didn't she continued. "Fine. I have nothing. You really are boring."

Alex chuckled and shook his head and continued eating.

"What are you two doing today?" Cleo asked.

Alex looked to Syren and when she nodded he spoke. "We are going to try to prac-tice Syren's abilities today."

"I'd love to stay and watch," Isis said. "I'll even help."

"Me too," Cleo added quickly.

Alex was hesitant, "I don't think-"

"Come on Syren," Isis implored, "it will be fun."

"Fine," Syren said.

~~~

Outside the cabin, a few hundred feet from the lake they stood, scattered.

"I don't know what to do," Syren said.

"Well don't set him on fire," Isis said.

Alex chuckled. "Why don't you take control of me, like you did Set."

Syren nodded. She closed her eyes and tried to focus solely on Alex. She tried to access something, anything, that felt more than herself. There was nothing and immediately she knew any attempt would be futile.

"I can't."

"What do you mean you can't?" Isis said.

"I mean, there's nothing. It won't work. I don't feel anything."

"You were able to do it to Set?" Cleo said.

"Yes," Syren said with an eye roll. "After a night of emotional turmoil, I was able to do it for a few seconds after he threatened my family."

"Fake family," Seth interjected.

Syren glared at Seth.

"What if I suffocate Alex. Would you be able to do it then?" Seth asked with a chuckle.

"I might," Syren answered, "but I don't think you'll like what I'd do to you then."

Seth walked to Alex, "sorry mate." Alex smirked slightly when he realized what would come next.

In an instant, Seth broke Alex's neck with one quick motion. There was a loud crack and then Alex fell to the floor.

Syren gasped, shocked and grabbed her stomach but then she saw Alex sit up.

"Son of a bitch," he cursed as he held his neck. "Owwwwww!"

Syren chuckled at Alex's reaction.

"Let's try again and this time brother I really need you to sell it."

The smile disappeared from Syren's lips. "Don't play with me."

"Okay," Seth said with a nervous chuckle, "I think that's my cue to go." He stepped away from the group and In an instant, he vanished.

~~`

Syren settled on the couch shortly after the trio left. Alex joined her moments later and laid his head in her lap.

"That was a disaster," she whined.

"It's alright, we can try again."

"Alright, tomorrow."

Alex nodded and then a thought crossed his mind. "We should get Set here so you can use him as your target practice," he said with a chuckle.

With the mention of Set's name, Syren realized something she'd forgotten to tell Alex. "I don't feel him anymore," she said. "I don't feel his consciousness, none of them, as if they don't exist."

Alex was perplexed. "Is that a bad thing?"

"I don't know," she answered. "Maybe the connection is just broken."

"Maybe…" Alex responded.

The day went on and turned to night. They'd just made love by the glow and warmth of the fire and now Alex had indulged himself in much-deserved sleep. Syren couldn't indulge the same, as tired as she was.

Now in a familiar space, her mind was ragged again. After tousling for some time she left their bed on the floor with worries of waking Alex. In the kitchen, she took a glass of orange juice to her lips and was unable to finish. Then she was on the cold, leather couch, wrapped in a throw blanket hoping again to indulge sleep but it would not come. In the absence of sleep, she wandered the cabin until she found Isabeli's diary. Where she'd previously stopped, she began again.

"The bow of Circii is a very useful tool in the hands of any Ashyllan. It is also true that it is only in the hands of an Ahsyllan that the bow may be of use."

Syren sighed and covered her mouth when a yawn came. She skipped down further and continued reading.

"Vessels are a useful tool in fulfilling the will of any Ashyllan, though the action of creating a vessel must be done with great care and prudence. 'Tis an intricate pur-

suit to manufacture such controlled chaos. Cy-vessels, once proposed as useful servants, have proven even more useful as cannon fodder capable of providing a great pause in battle, albeit they are the least of us."

"Bi-vessels a later and in many ways more useful and subtle creations have been spectacular agents of expanding the influence of Ahsylla for many centuries past. When created pre-genesis a bi-vessel may be boundlessly engineered, Post-genesis this option is limited in materialization but unlimited in the rest. Bi-vessels may indeed be accorded sentience or they may not, whichever option is most conducive to the path they must travel."

"The Serum, created by Ahsyllan Hhera, acted through an invasion of the victim's nervous system, it further placed an inccursio on the cognitive complex of the victim, relenting dominance of all facilities to Athena to be controlled, stored, replicated as such."

Syren gulped, hard, and continued reading.

"The first insentient bi-vessel and all that followed were created by direct order of My (forma prior) Ahnais. Marcus Augustus Marius (622 bc), (ISBV-001) scouted through Athena, was a human of extraordinary intellect relative to his kind. Besides, nine offspring, who shared in that intellect were also approved for post-genesis creation."

"Alexander Marius, (582 bc), first sentient bi-vessel (SBV-001) was a unique and at times problematic creation."

Syren's heart thumped in her chest as she read Alex's name.

"Experiences psychological terror associated with prolonged non-cyclical exis-

tence - organically enhanced to hone (melancholic-phlegmatic) temperament, most

suitable for companionship with my (postea forma) Syren."

Alexander Marius SBV-001 Compendium - Nov 1, 1999

Designation: Timeline agent

Bulk Intelligence: *Bulk Per-*

sonality:

Emotional intelligence quotient: 95%   *Openness:*

93%

Perceptive intelligence: 91%

Conscientiousness: 97%

Logical/Analytical Intelligence: 96%

Extraversion: 45%

Creativity: 91%   *Agree-*

ableness: 73%

Neuroticism: 22%

Bulk Capabilities:

Bulk Attributes:

Combat: 94%

Courage: 96%

Speed: 98%

Humor: 85%

Strength: 95%

Aggression: 39%

Light Travel: 90%

Loyalty: 98%

Sexual prowess: 95%

Sadism: 13%

Agility: 90%

Empathy: 98%

Memory: 90%

Self-Control: 98%

Flight: 0%

Attributes determined most successful for future pairing satisfied.

1. *Predetermined meet date (fixed) - 3 September 2019 - 4:54pm - 79% probability*

Location: Fourth-floor office, Excellci Tower.

Facilitated: Athena

1. *Predetermined meet date - 3 September 2019 - 8:54am - 21% probability*

Location: Locke School, room 103.

Syren closed the book with tears in her eyes, overwhelmed at her previously written admissions but moments later, she began again.

Chapter 19 - Trigger

When Alex woke and stretched across the makeshift bed, Syren was gone from her place beside him. He sat up and gazed around the perimeter of the room for his love, gone.

It was too quiet, he was almost sure he was the only one in the cabin.

"Sy?" he called.

To his dismay, there was no response to his holler. He stood and through the glass wall at the rear of the room, he could see she wasn't outdoors. He thought she might have left their floor bed in search of a more comfortable resting place. In his bedroom, this bed hadn't been touched.

He noticed her small pink Chanel purse was gone from where he'd last seen it on the wooden night stand. Quickly, he ran down to the kitchen where he'd left his phone and called her. After waiting for what seemed like eons, his call was left unanswered. This was an odd thing, since he knew that Athena had a direct line to her mind and could tell her he was calling. If she ignored it, he worried that something was wrong.

The clothes he'd removed from her body and thrown on the floor in the heat of their passion was gone. All left was his sweater and pants, which he quickly slipped into and then travelled to her condo in New York.

She was nowhere to be found and when he called Athena, she did not answer. He traveled to High Palace and searched the grounds himself. The banks of Sapphire lake and the paths in High Garden; she was nowhere. The vessels that roamed the gilded halls were gone.

She had many properties across the world, most he didn't know about. Feeling frustrated, he called the one person that might have been able to answer his question.

"Why are you calling me?"

"Is Syren with you, I can't find her," he asked.

In her pause, he could feel the eye roll through the phone. "Syren's not with me and hasn't been with me for weeks, thanks to you."

Katherine hung up in his ear.

He stood in the main court, absent options and trying vigorously to wrap his brain around where Syren could have gone that made him unable to find her. After extended thought, only one place came to mind.

~~~

In the vault, Syren stared at the broadwards in her hands. The hilt felt exactly made to the specifications of her palm. She turned them in her hands, inspecting the iridescent blade and the gilded, jeweled pommel.

She wondered how the blade was stored for a fight and as the thought crossed her mind she watched the blade melt up her palm as if it were liquid gold and settled into a small gold cuff around her wrist with the black diamond stone from the hilt at the forefront of the cuff bracelet.

Awed by the action, she grabbed the second systyr sword from the wall and watched as it melted metal formed around her wrist.

She turned to the iridescent armor and ran her finger across the metal that seemed to be both the hardest and softest things she ever touched. The two contrasting elements exist perfectly together.

She commanded the armor on it and smoothly slid up her skin like the melted gold it resembled and then there she stood, hoping the image of herself reflected back at her would trigger a memory.

She spent hours in the vault. Her resolve crumbled and then removed the armor and walked to the exit. When the metal door slid horizontally open, she was greeted by familiar eyes.

She quickly looked away. Even with the brief glance, she was aware that his beauty no longer had the same effect on her senses - or maybe she just wished it so hard that she believed it. He now looked like the perfectly manufactured being he was. His eyes were now too blue, his lips were too full, his jaw was too angular, he was too beautiful, he wasn't real. She knew it before but now, she believed it.

"Leaving a note would have saved me from a lot of worry," he said with a small chuckle.

"My apologies," she said simply when headed to the hall.

The metal door behind her closed as she stepped from the access.

"Syren, what's going on?"

"Return to Argentina, Alex. I'm going home," she said, still walking.

Alex caught up to her easily and stopped in front of her.

"What were you doing in the vault?" he asked, "it upsets you to go there. Why would you go back?"

"I don't want to talk about it," she said, flatly, devoid of emotion.

Alex pulled her face towards him.

"Why aren't you looking at me," he asked as gazed in her eyes.

She shook from his grasp with wet eyes. They were black.

"Don't."

"Sy-"

"No, give me some space Alex-fuck!" She barked.

"Give you space? You weren't asking for space last night," he said, coolly.

"It's not funny-"

"No, Syren- what's not funny is this whiplash you're giving me. We were perfect last night and then weeks before that. Somehow between last night after I fell asleep and now something has happened. Whatever is it, you can tell me or not but I'm not letting you push me away."

"You did it for weeks-" she said as she tried to push past him and continued walking.

"Yes and we both suffered for it and agreed I was wrong. How does that justify what you're trying to do now," he asked, frantic and puzzled at the thought of Syren leaving him.

She watched the panic crescent upon his features.

"This feeling, the panic you're feeling right now- it's not real," she said.

He shook his head, even more confused. "Are you doubting my feelings for you?"

"I don't doubt them. I know they don't exist...not in reality. Everything you are feeling, everything you are, it's not real."

His face twisted in agony as he shook his head. "It's because I'm a vessel…" he responded knowingly.

She pulled Isabeli's diary from the pocket of her jacket and began to read.

"SBV- 001 or in other words: sentient-biological-vessel one, Alexander Marius - experiences psychological terror associated with prolonged non-cyclical sentience - organically enhanced to hone (melancholic-phlegmatic) temperament, most suitable for companionship with my (postea forma) Syren or my post form but you speak Latin Alex so you must understand."

"Syren-"

She flipped a few pages back and read.

"I ordered you to be created.," Syren said. "The Serum, created by Ahsyllan Hhera, acted through invasion of the victim's nervous system, it further placed an inccursio on the cognitive complex of the victim, relenting control of all facilities to Athena to be controlled, stored, replicated as such-"

"-Stop- I get it," he insisted.

"Bulk Attributes: Courage: 96%, Humor: 65% , Aggression: 39% - everything about you, even the way you fuck has been manufactured exactly the way it is to pair you with me. It's all in here, I wrote this twenty years ago. You couldn't give me to Set because you are incapable of it. You couldn't betray your sister either. Your empathy is 98%, your loyalty is much of the same. Instead you did nothing which is exactly what they wanted you to do-"

"-That's enough Syren!" he barked furiously. He couldn't hear anymore.

She locked the book and stumbled back to the wall until she felt the hard surface against her back then her eyes filled with water.

"I'm so sorry I've forced you to endure 2600 years of agony just to satiate some sick game I've created for myself."

"I've always known my life wasn't my own," he said mostly to himself, "when I tried to take my own life but couldn't- I realized it wasn't mine to take."

Syren didn't respond.

"It was over two thousand years ago and knowing everything I know now, I would have lived my life a hundred times over if it meant I got to know you."

"That's not how you feel."

"Yes it is," he insisted.

"No you don't- you've never had a choice. They call you a timeline agent, your job is to go out into the world and ensure the desired outcome for Ahsylla. You, being with me, is just your job to ensure whatever plan they have is effectuated."

He shook his head tearfully. "I love you. That's the only truth I know. You don't have to leave me. You don't even know if what she's written is true."

"It is. She knew twenty years ago the exact date, down to the minute we would meet. There is no truth here. There's only the plan. Whatever it is, I don't want you to be a part of it."

"What do you need?" he asked softly.

"I need you to leave."

"I can't do that," Alex said as he stepped closer to her with outstretched hands.

"Cease all sentient capabilities," Syren commanded.

Alex dropped his hands and froze where he stood, just as Isabeli had noted in the dairy.

"Alex-" she called.

He didn't respond or move. She stepped closer to him and inspected his features. His painful expression from moments ago was now replaced with a vacant look. She stepped back to her position in front of him.

"Resume," she said.

Alex continued stepping towards Syren, unaware of the interruption. The display was all she needed to confirm what she knew was true about Alex.

"I'm very sorry." Apologies were not something Syren offered often but now more than ever she felt they were needed, even inadequate, to express to Alex her lament.

"If you're sorry then you won't do this."

"I have to. For you."

"This is not for me Syren, don't pretend it is."

Syren offered no response and so he turned and walked the hall until he was able to travel back to his cabin with his heart shattered asunder.

~~~

"Athena," Syren called softly after some time on the cold floor.

There was no response.

"Athena?"

She waited then she remembered that it might be the photon shield around the vault interfering with Athena's connection to her.

Syren wiped her eyes and pushed herself off the ground. On the ground floor of the palace she tried again and there was no response.

"Athena?" she said frantically. Athena always responded. She was always there. Only inside of Alex shields had she been absent and if Alex was able to leave the palace, Athena should be able to connect, she thought.

Syren went down to the lower levels of the palace to her lab. She tried to open her lab door with the usual biometric scan. It wouldn't open. She went to her bedroom frantic, something was happening and she didn't know what. Athena was programmed into the palace, there must be some form of her that was responsive. In her bedroom, she called Athena, no violet light appeared, no voice answered. She checked her nightstand for a phone or any device she could use to call.

With no phone, she wandered down the halls searching for a vessel. The hallways, usually teeming with workers; both vessels and humans, were empty. She went to the vessel quarters, it was barren. She took Peony from the stables and rode to the open airplane hanger a mile across the greenscape from the open court.

The first silver aircraft she came upon, ignited at her command but then she found herself wondering why it did so. It must be what they want, she thought, to get her in the jet. She didn't know the reason but in defiance, she refused to take the jet. She couldn't trust her own technology, not after Athena had disappeared on her.

Her dependence on Athena had left her crippled. She knew no telephone numbers to contact anyone. Nor did she know how to transport herself to New York without an army of bodyguards and servants at her side. Athena had transported her to Paris just hours earlier, what could have happened between her time in the vault and now.

She remembered that she'd left her purse in the vault, with her driver's license and cash she could use for a flight. She ran down as quickly as she was able to the lower level of the palace. At the access of the vault, she tried to complete her biometric scan with her palm against the door but this time it wouldn't go. She was unable to enter.

"FUCK!" she screamed as she banged hopelessly against the metal wall. "What do you want from me!"

If she hadn't sent Alex away he could have travelled her to New York in mere seconds but now he was gone.

Something was happening. Something was happening. Something was happening. The thought frolicked through her mind on a loop.

She took a few breaths and decided to try something else. She figured she might be able to get herself through an airport with no identification. Everyone in Paris knew her name and her family's name and had so for centuries. She hoped that could get her through the airport and on to a plane. After that, she hoped to improvise her way through John F. Kennedy airport. People tended to have different standards for celebrities and the wealthy, usually she was annoyed at that fact, today, she was counting on it.

Syren found cash in her wardrobe room. She changed to something she felt wouldn't attract many eyes to her; leggings and sweater and a trench coat for the cold Parisian spring. She slid a black beanie hat on her head and threw as much cash as she could fit in her purse and went to her garage for a car.

As she stood in the garage, she felt utterly ridiculous and wondered if she was do-ing exactly what they'd wanted. She didn't know what to do or if every action she took had been predetermined. She didn't know if she had free will or was just a figment of her past forms.

She decided to stick to her original plan and take her personal aircraft to New York. A usual eight hour flight from Paris to New York had been reduced to just over an hour when she travelled at mach five speed.

She landed on the helipad on the apex of the building. She quickly took the eleva-tor down to the penthouse.

There weren't guards outside her entrance of the penthouse as usual.

"Katherine?" she called loudly. It was Sunday evening."Kat?" she screamed as she ran up the stairs. She didn't find her in her bedroom. Syren ran to her bedroom.

"Athena? Gus? Fleur? Tumas? Anyone?" she called.. There was no response. She rumbled through her room until she found the cellphone she carried occasionally when she couldn't speak to Athena freely. She tried to turn it on but it wouldn't work.

"You have to be fucking kidding me," she cursed.

With Athena programmed through her house, she had no need for a television or a phone or laptop or anything of the sort for Athena had functioned as all of them. She went to extreme heights to ensure Athena was invulnerable to a power outage, cyber attack and anything else she could think of so she was baffled that her pro-gram had disappeared.

She ran back down to the living room, she figured that she could find something, anything that could be useful down the headquarter of her company. As she ran towards the door, Katherine, Teddy and Ruby walked in, escorted by guards. They weren't their usual guards, they were new and she didn't recognize them.

Syren jumped on Katherine and hugged her tightly and inhaled her scent. As she hugged Katherine she felt Teddy hugging her as well, tightly as he wailed.

When she stepped back and saw their faces, Teddy's eyes were filled with tears. Both Ruby and Katherine looked devastated, though less so than Teddy.

"What happened? What's going on?" she asked frantically.

"Sy," Katherine began.

"What?" she asked again.

"Um-"

"What-" she asked, impatiently.

"-Grandma May is dead, so is grandpa Thomas," Teddy said as he stepped forward, the grief in his heart surpassed his flesh and contorted his features.

"Grandma?" Syren responded absently, as if the words hadn't registered. It was a different kind of guilt she felt, knowing she'd ignored May for weeks while she locked herself away from the world with Alex.

"Aunt Diana, Uncle Lenny, Aunt Tiana, all your aunts and uncles, their children, all our family- gone," Teddy said, in tears. He swayed, as if he were about to fall, two guards quickly grabbed him and brought him over to the couch.

"Get him some water please," Katherine said to one of the guards as she rushed over to him quickly and tried to console him. Syren was still frozen by the door. Rue stood watching, with tears in her brown, doe eyes.

"Oh Ruby," Syren mumbled through sobs as she grabbed her and held her but Ruby pulled away.

"Ruby?" Syren said tearfully.

"Where were you Sy?" Ruby asked through sobs.

Ruby's cries were an unusual sound, so soft and melancholic that they made her unravel at the seams and no matter how she tried to hold herself together, she couldn't. May wasn't her biological grandmother but she was a good as. Never far from Syren's ear was May's sage advice on life and womanhood. With the auspicious timing, Syren believed the Ahsyllan's were responsible though she didn't know how.

"Where were you?"

Syren didn't respond, she couldn't form words or even a thought to counter her so she was just left standing. Ruby walked over to the couch where Teddy was lying curled up in a ball against the arm of the sofa. Syren followed her and this time when she sat beside her and held her, Ruby didn't pull away.

Teddy was calm enough to sleep a while later after taking sleeping pills. After Syren put Ruby down to bed, she found Katherine out on the balcony, staring out to the city on the cold spring night.

"What happened?" Syren asked shakily.

"I don't know. Alex called asking for you then all of our guards just disappeared. Athena stopped working, everything stopped working. Then we saw on the news what they did."

"What?"

"They slaughtered them. I saw them drag your grandmother from the backseat of her car and they cut her throat," Katherine said with tears in her eyes. "They all came here because May wanted to talk to you. You hadn't been returning her calls and she was worried about you. We were going to have an intervention for you."

"How did you see?" Syren asked with fresh tears.

"Paparazzi recorded everything- it played on the news, it was awful. Teddy saw it, he fainted. Ruby saw it too. They wanted you to see this."

"Who?" Syren asked.

"I don't know," Katherine said sharply, "maybe if you'd been here instead of with Alex then you could answer the question!"

Syren shook her head ashamed. The burning in her throat intensified as she swallowed."I was wrong to leave with Alex, I know that now."

"You should've known then- it's one thing to fall in love and that's fine, it's another thing to fall in love and then disappear for weeks and not answer your phone at fucking all- do you know how worried we were when all this is happening and no one can reach you."

"I'm sorry," Syren said tearfully.

"What happened?"

"I was a fool."

"What do you mean?"

"I don't know what's happening Katherine. I can't be the one doing all of this- I'm not this person."

"What-" Katherine turned around, confused, "is this about your past forms- what does that have to do with anything?"

Syren shook her head and pressed her lips together in a pout. "I don't know," she answered softly.

"What about him?" Katherine asked.

"I-I can't talk about it."

Katherine rolled her eyes, annoyed. "Syren!?

She shook her head, "I just know they wanted us to be together or maybe they don't want us to be together. I don't know but I let him go."

"Who is 'they'?"

"Them. Me. They. The Ahsyllans. I don't know," Syren said defeatedly.

Katherine decided not to press further. "Are you okay? I know how much you loved your grandma?"

"I'm not okay," she said, "it's my fault this is happening."

"What are you talking about?"

"I don't know. I just know that all of this has something to do with my powers."

"How? Why would that have anything to do with this?"

Syren shook her head in disagreement. "I ordered Alex to be created, Kat. I made him live, knowing he was unhappy, for 2600 years for some sick reality I wanted to create for myself. I don't know what I'm capable of and that terrifies me."

Katherine tried to wrap her head around Syren's words. "It's not you. It's them," was all she could say.

"What does it matter when our family is dying Kat?"

Katherine shook her head. "It matters. This isn't you."

Syren was silent for a moment before she continued. "Promise me you won't leave the apartment- not until we figure out what's going on?" Syren begged.

"I won't. I promise." Katherine stepped back so she could gaze at Syren. She was ruinous inside, it was painful to witness.

Syren crumbled under Katherine's gaze."I love him- I love him- and he's not even real," she sobbed violently as she hid her face in Katherine's embrace.

~~~

In the morning, sunlight seemed to radiate everywhere except inside the grieving house.

Syren spent the night and morning on her balcony, curled around her legs, agonizing over the actions of her past self. She found herself with the unique conundrum of having to contemplate the extent of what she was capable of while having no control of her past actions.

She was trying to trigger herself, that part was obvious but how far was she willing to go to do it? Who would she hurt to do it? Teddy, was the first, when she pretended to die and left him to grieve. Then it was Alex, who she'd sentenced to a miserable existence. Who was next?

She wasn't capable of hurting any of her family, she kept trying to reason with herself, it had been someone else. She couldn't reconcile that action, not on her worst day, not in her worst form could she hurt her grandmother, sweet May, or anyone else in her family. It had to be someone else. She couldn't survive if it was her.

In the mid morning, guards provided them with working phones and laptops which allowed them to communicate outside. Syren found herself trying and failing to keep her family at home. Crippled by Athena's disappearance, there was no one she trusted to perform any task for her, not even Teddy's guards.

The fallout from the shutdown of all Excellci products awaited her outside although she wasn't sure how bad it would be. Her headquarters stood twenty floors below her, empty, since Teddy's security and police had blocked the building.

Katherine mentioned protests, information she received from the guards but Syren paid it no mind,

"Teddy, you can't leave," she begged, "it's not safe out there."

"Syren I have bodies to claim at the morgue and one very large funeral to plan and the detectives need to speak to me," Teddy countered softly. His eyes were still swollen from his intermittent sobbing. "I can't stay locked up in here, I have guards."

"Teddy, they're all gone. Whoever it is hunted them down and murdered them. How do you know they aren't outside waiting right now?"

"I don't-look, I'm terrified," he said with sodden features, "but I can't leave them at the morgue- I have to go see my mother- I have to."

"What if I come with you? I can protect you…"

"Sweetheart, I'm supposed to protect you- and with all the protest outside I don't know if it's best for you to face that right now."

"I'm coming with you," she insisted, "It's grandma May- I have to be there for her."

Teddy nodded and caressed her cheek, "oh sweetie look at your eyes," he said softly. "I always hated this color."

"Dad," she said with averted eyes. It was the first time she'd called him that since Alex revealed her true heritage."Stop."

Syren had resolved that it was safer to have Katherine and Ruby accompany her. She wasn't familiar with Teddy's new hired protection and didn't trust them.

At the anterior of her building, was a swarm of rambunctious protestors. The guards decided to exit through the garage. As they drove out in the back of the black SUV, the crowd became enraged.

"WHERE'S MY MONEY, YOU BLONDE BIMBO," one man yelled as he banged against the bulletproof window. "I PAID $1400 FOR THIS PHONE THAT'S NOT WORKING!"

The police worked on clearing protesters from the congested street.

"EAT THE RICH!" a woman yelled with a placard that read the same.

"COME OUT AND FACE US YOU BITCH!"

"THIEF! - I SPENT MY LAST ON ONE OF YOUR DAMN EXBOOK LAP-TOPS," the man spat on the glass of the window.

"I WANT A REFUND! I'M SUING YOUR ASS YOU BARBIE DOLL BITCH!"

Teddy grabbed her and hugged her, "it's okay sweetheart, just block them out."

"They're right," she mumbled, "even if their insults aren't very original." Syren sighed. "I want to give them back everything but with Athena gone- I don't have access to any of the money. I'm locked out."

"What do you mean? What about your accountants or asset managers? Syren, your mother left trillions."

"Athena did it all.."

"What about your bank?"

"I don't have access to my bank, not with Athena gone."

The SUV began to shake laterally, with protestors on both sides.

"Stay calm," the driver said.

"Don't tell us to stay calm, get my daughters out of here," Teddy yelled angrily. "Ruby it's okay sweetie."

"Why are they so upset?" Ruby asked angrily. She sat with Katherine in the seat behind Teddy and Syren. "Leave me sister alone," Ruby screamed as she banged against the tinted glass.

Katherine ignored the calamity around.

The police and protestors clash outside the confines of the SUV. The slurs grew louder and more derogatory.

Every slur felt like a lash against her skin. A lifetime of being pampered and lauded with praises of her heavenly beauty, allure and intellect hadn't prepared her for this.

"BITCH." one lash.

"STUPID SLUT," two lashes.

"YOU'RE A FRAUD!" three lashes.

It became too much and finally she broke into sobs in the car and curled into the comfort of Teddy who consoled her and covered her ears. Ruby climbed over the seat and sat beside Syren, consoling her as she cried.

"Don't believe them, they're just angry sweetheart- shut it out," Teddy said.

Everyone who seemed to have a quarrel with her had shown up to the plaza.

"YOU HAVE BLOOD ON YOUR HANDS. STOP SELLING WEAPONS TO THE GOVERNMENT!"

Even as he comforted her, she craved the comfort of her father and not her ex-lover. She wished for ignorance. She wished Alex had left her in the dark because now his touch and his comfort reminded her of the agony she's allowed him to endure in believing she'd died as Isabeli. She felt disgusted and pulled back from his embrace.

"I'm fine," she said through sniffles. She didn't deserve his comfort. "I'm fine." Syren wrapped her arm around Ruby and was content with the contact.

Time seemed unmoving as they waited helplessly in the back of the van but before long the police cleared the path and they were allowed to pass.

~~~

When they returned to Syren's building, after visiting the morgue, the visage of her building had been tarnished, with spray painted slurs and littered trash. The protesters tried breaking through the glass facade of the ground floor but were futile against the impenetrable material.

They were gone now, chased away by the police and the anterior of her building had been barricaded off. They entered through the garage and were escorted back to the penthouse.

Teddy was able to coordinate a number of celebrants to plan the mass funeral. He'd asked Syren if he could carry out the ceremony at High Palace. He wanted to burn their bodies on the Sapphire Lake similar to the ceremony Isabeli instructed him to perform after her death. So, they travelled back to High Palace, the place that haunted her. Many bodies were wrapped in red cloth, garnished with flowers and placed on wooden rafts on the blue water. The poetry wasn't lost on her. The funeral rites written in the diary were now taking place.

There weren't many in attendance, along with Syren, Teddy, Katherine and Ruby, there were a few of Teddy's in-laws and that had been spared from the assault. There were some of her cousins' romantic partners and their families who were in attendance as well. There were very few who were invited who were of no relation.

High palace stood barren. Usually teeming with vessels, the halls and grounds were now empty. After the ceremony they were quick to leave back to New York under the security of Excellci Tower.

~~~

It was dusk as she looked out to the city that despised her so. She could see the blackness of Central Park from her view, it seemed the only respite in a constant flutter of light surrounding her.

"You know you can't keep us cooped up on here forever," Katherine said as she walked out to Syren on the balcony. "You also can't pretend you're not in deep shit. Athena isn't working; you need to figure out why or you need to build a new one. You need to pay these people back for the Excellci products that aren't working or you need to figure out how to make them work. The self-loathing won't help."

"Why do you need to go outside?" Syren asked.

"School? I graduate in two months and I've almost missed two weeks already."

"High school Katherine? Do you think I give a fuck about your high school diploma?" Syren barked angrily.

"Not all of us have our own personal bank created by our family to store trillions of dollars, Syren. Wake up! If you get mad at me tomorrow and kick me out then guess what: I'll have to make a living and I'll at least need a high school diploma to start. I'm going back to school on Monday?"

"They pulled May out of her car and slaughtered her in the middle of the street. She had guards, Katherine. Guards I thought I could trust because they were vessels but obviously I'm not the one controlling them. Guards will not protect you."

"I know that but I also know that unless you plan on creating a new Athena or fixing this, it won't change."

"How can I fix it when I don't know the cause of all this?" she cried. "I don't know if I'm doing this or-"

"You're not doing this Syren, get that out of your head right now. You're not evil, no matter what form or life or whatever you're in."

"You keep saying that. Look at what I did to Alex..and Teddy," she countered.

"Well I hate Alex after what he did to you and Teddy can be kind of annoying so I can understand wanting to get out of a marriage with him. No harm done. You're welcome."

"It's not funny," Syren mumbled angrily.

Katherine sighed. "I know it's been intense but you can't just do nothing."

"In the book Isabelli left me it says that Athena controlled vessels as far back as Alex. That was 2600 years ago so there's now way I can break into Athena and fix her. She wasn't mine to control," Syren responded, "Nothing I build will be able to compete with Athena."

"So you're going to do nothing?"

"This is what they wanted. Isabeli made sure I would be just shy of useless."

"Great," Katherine said, "be useless then. I'll go figure out a way to not get us all murdered."

Syren sighed and shook her head. "Kat-"

"-She can't help you Katherine." The voice Syren could recognize anywhere.

Both Syren and Katherine turn to see Marcus standing in the family room. The only barrier between them was the clear glass wall. Marcus had Teddy in front of him with a large serrated edged knife pressed against his throat.

"NO-" she screamed then she felt pain radiating through her body.

Katherine stood frozen at the sight before her. Marcus, after everything he'd done to her during her childhood, was not someone she was prepared to face again. Marcus stood in a dark suit. He hadn't aged a day from when last they saw him.

Syren lurched towards him only to fall to the floor in agony, clawing at her skin, needing to rip free from it. "Athena-" she barked before realizing Athena was no longer there to soothe her.

"Help your father-" Marcus began, "oh wait. Have you told him?" Marcus asked. "I think you should tell him." He waited and when he got no response he urged her further, "go on, tell him."

Syren writhed on the floor, unable to coordinate controlled movement or or form intelligible speech.

"Okay, I'll tell him," Marcus said as she shoved Teddy to the floor.

Teddy with hesitation ran over to Syren, through the open glass doors and began consoling her.

"It's okay sweetheart, don't worry about me," he cried.

"That's not your daughter Theodore, that's your wife,"Marcus said. He was a tall, slender man with greased down brown hair and sadistic grin never far from his lips.

Teddy turned to look at him as if he believed it but for only a moment, then he turned back to Syren.

"You don't want to believe it, I wouldn't either, the deception is too much but you must've known right...look at her. There is not one chromosome of your DNA inside of her."

"Shut up- you evil soul," Teddy barked.

Marcus chuckled sardonically.

"Come on, the exact same physical characteristics and temperament as your wife and you never once thought she was just reborn?"

"Stop," Teddy barked, shaking now. "That's not true, right Sy," he said mostly to himself as he tried to console her on the floor.

"She must've been so tired of you," Marcus said, " a problem I'll rectify presently."

"Leave him alone," Katherine said, defrosted and suddenly in discovery of her voice. She pulled a small handgun from the small of her back and aimed it at Marcus. It was an Excellci gun easily procured by Athena over a year ago at Katherine's request. She'd been travelling with it since May was attacked in the street.

"I'll shoot you, I swear to god I will."

Marcus stepped forward with a menacing smile and in response Katherine growled and shot him. The bullet ricocheted from his skin and lodged in the wall across the room. Katherine's mouth fell open in horror at the sight.

Marcus took another step forward, Katherine shot him again and the result was the same. Teddy Marcus easily grabbed Teddy by his twisted hair and pulled him from Syren who still laid, crippled by pain, unable to move.

When he had Teddy on his knees before him, he pressed the knife against his throat and without pause tore the edges of the serrated blade into his skin. Scarlet liquid spumed from his flesh and the sound of the edges of the blade abrading his cartilage and bones was almost loud enough to overtake his Teddy's final suffocating gargles of breath.

Katherine screeched in terror at the site but once again she was frozen in place.

He didn't stop cutting until Teddy's head dissociated from his body. Syren's face was red with splatters of Teddy's blood. She witnessed it all through a haze of pain and horror. Now it was over and she felt black inside.

Marcus kneeled in the pool of Teddy's blood and lifted Syren's face and stared into her wet, empty eyes.

"You're not ready yet, that's okay, we have a little time, I'll be back." He leaned closer to her ear and whispered, "For the good of all Ahsyllans.".

Marcus warped into a spark of violet light and vanished and the pain finally stopped and everything went black.

Katherine fell to the floor, shaking with sobs as she tried to wake Syren.

~~~

In the morning Syren opened her eyes she was immediately overwhelmed by the sound of sobbing. It was soft and emanating from Ruby.

Everything came back to her and even with all her grief, with the sounds of Teddy's last plea looped in her ears, she was despondent.

She wasn't on the floor which was where she remembered being. She was on the couch. The blood from her face and clothes had soiled the white leather. At the other end of the sofa, Katherine consoled Ruby. Syren was slow to comfort her, she didn't know what to do or what to say to the grieving ten year old.

"Ruby?" she called softly.

Ruby looked up and ran over to Syren and buried her face in Syren's chest. A glimpse at Katherine's swollen eyes did nothing to calm her.

"Daddy dead Sy," Ruby wailed. "He's dead."

"Shhh...it's okay," Syren said softly.

"No. it's not okay. It's not okay," Ruby screamed.

Syren could form no response to Ruby and instead held her as sobbed until she fell asleep in Syren's arms.

"Where is my father?" Syren asked once Ruby began to snore lightly.

"In the pantry fridge," Katherine responded. "Unfortunately I wasn't able to bring him there before Ruby heard gunshots and came down here and saw his head separated from his body."

"She saw?"

"Yes and she's been up all night trying to wake you but you wouldn't wake," Katherine said angrily.

"We have to get out of here?" Syren said.

"We can't leave- the guards that Teddy got apparently work with Marcus, they won't let us leave and after Marcus left last night they came and took everything, phones, laptops. So I can't even call the police- not that they could help us."

"It's oka-"

"Don't tell me anything is going to be okay. I already know what's going on. They're going to kill me and Ruby. You know it too. I heard what Marcus said last night. It's all to trigger your powers isn't it?"

"No- I'm not going to let that happen-" Syren began.

"-You can't stop it, you know that too," Katherine said with tears in her eyes.

"I'll jump off that balcony if that's what I have to do."

"How can you be sure that will stop this?" Katherine asked sarcastically.

"I can't be sure about anything Katherine- I feel like every move I make is only leading us further towards their end so maybe I should just end it."

"We need to get to Alex, he could take us out of here and bring us under the shield thing that you told me about. That could give us some time and we'd be safe."

"We can't trust Alex. He's a vessel just like Marcus. We need to stay away from him."

"Alex is different."

"He's not," she said with fresh tears and then attempted quickly to change the subject. "What are we going to do about Teddy's body?"

"I can't get the image out of my head- everytime I blink I see it and I just hate that Ruby saw it too. She's too young..." Katherine said with more tears falling down her cheeks.

Syren was silent for a moment as she ran through options in her mind. Then, she spoke.

"Can you take the chip from my neck?" she asked.

"What?"

"That's what this is all about-"

"You'll die."

"It's between me or you and Ruby, I'd rather it be me. Marcus can come back any minute- we have to try something," Syren responded, "they can't take anymore- I can't lose anymore," she cried. "We can't lose anymore."

"You're not understanding Syren, if you're dead he'll still be here- it solves nothing."

"I was useless last night alive, Katherine. They are trying to do this because they want my powers to manifest, if I do it myself then there's no reason for him to kill anyone. If I keep it in, it's how they control me, last night they paralyzed me and made me watch. That can't happen again."

"How are you sure?"

"I'm not totally sure- he's doing this because of me- everything I've read, everything Alex's said- I can't trust any of it but still I think it's what they want."

"You said your previous forms want this- if you're doing this-"

"It can't be me- I would never allow any of this to happen. I'd never do that to Teddy or you or Ruby or grandma May or anyone. It can't be me."

"It wouldn't be you exactly- a previous form…" Katherine said through sniffles.

"There is no version of me that's capable of this Kat, not even the darkest parts."

"So who's doing it then because Marcus is obviously a vessel thing so someone is making him do this-and if Isabeli allowed him to torutre you in the past why wouldn't she do it again? She doesn't know me nor did she know Ruby before she died, if she planned all of this like you say, what would stop her from killing us. She didn't love us like you love us."

"But she loved Teddy-"

"Did she Syren? Are you sure about that?"

"Her eyes were purple with him. She loved him, I know she did because I loved him too," Syren shot back.

Katherine shook her head. "What if she could control the color of her eyes? Maybe all you need is practice."

Syren groaned annoyed.

"You have to consider the fact that you could be doing all of this Syren."

"You don't think I know that Katherine!" She barked, "and that's what I'm afraid of. How do I fight myself? Everything that I could have possibly done or even thought-" she paused and broke into sobs. "I'm crippled, I had no chance once they took Athena away from me and they know- or I know. I don't know anymore. If I did this- if I agreed to brutally murder my entire family just to gain more power then I deserve to die. I need you to take it out if this works and I can control my power then I can protect us."

Katherine wiped her wet cheeks.

"Okay," she said with a nod, "I'll do it."

While Katherine walked to the kitchen for a knife, Syren kissed Ruby's temple and eased her from her lap then laid her on a section of the sofa not marred with blood. She wiped her eyes and prepared herself by pulling her hair into a high ponytail on the top of her head. She wrapped the loose hair around her scrunchie so it was away from her neck.

When Katherine returned she had a sharp boning knife and a towel from the kitchen. Syren kneeled on the ground before her.

Katherine handed her a small towel, "bite on this," she said, "so Ruby won't wake up and see."

Syren took the towel and stuffed as much fabric as she could hold in her mouth.

"Bite hard," Katherine said.

Syren nodded.

Moments later, she felt a sharp pain in the base of her neck. She bit down as hard she could and closed her eyes that sprung water. Her fingers gripped like talons around her knees but she didn't move, her resolve was unshakeable.

Breaking into her skin seemed almost painless compared to Katherine's attempt to remove what she believed was a chip. Without an x-ray device, she could only feel for the chip under Syren flesh with her finger and a knife and it took minutes for her to find it under the scarred flesh.

"Power is a parasite. Power is a parasite. Rip it out. Rip it out," she chanted inwardly as the pain rose higher.

It was a task to pull it from her flesh. After so many years it felt like a body part, not a foreign object inserted there. She felt pain that engulfed her every sense and every thought. Even when her world turned black there was still that pain.

When she fell unconscious, Katherine dropped the knife and kneeled beside her.

"Syren, wake up," she called as she shook her. There was still blood coming from her wound so Katherine quickly took the cloth from Syren's mouth and pressed it against the wound.

Syren was still and after a while Katherine realized that she was too still. Her chest didn't rise and fall with her breath. Syren wasn't breathing.

In a panic, she felt her carotid artery. She didn't feel the lively thumping as proof Syren's blood still circulated her body. There was nothing.

~~~

When Syren woke, she heard screaming before she opened her eyes. The sound pulled her from the darkness and when she opened her eyes Marcus was standing over her, staring down at her. The pain was still there, the most intense that she'd ever felt. She was in a pool of sweat. Her body felt as if it was stretching. Her bones, her joints, her flesh, her skin all felt like they were stretching.

"Sy," Katherine screamed. She was locked in the grasp of an unknown man and she'd been waiting for Syren to wake when Marcus came. Katherine had thought her dead until minutes after her succession of breath she began showing signs of life again.

"Syren-" Ruby screamed from across the room. "Help me!"

Marcus stooped and stared into her eyes.

"You're still not ready."

"No- please," Syren begged, she fought through pain to form each word. "Help me-just help me, I'm trying, please don't kill them."

"It's the only way- you know that."

Katherine screamed in response to her impending doom, an agonizing, ear-piercing scream as she clutched her stomach and fell to her knees.

"I'll kill you- " Syren barked angrily, shakily. "I'll kill you all and then I'll kill myself and all this will be for nothing." Then Syren remembered. "Cease all sentient capabilities," she yelled.

He walked away, ignoring her, but as quickly as she could manage while stunted by pain, she commanded her swords to form from the cuffs on her wrists. It was a thought she was unable to construct only a night earlier. They wouldn't. She was impeded in every way she could imagine.

She dropped her head back on the floor, writhing in pain and sweat and tears.

"Watch," Marcus commanded.

He walked to Ruby who was held by another vessel across the room. He took her hand gently, all while she wailed in horror but was too terrified to protest, and walked her back a few steps in front of Syren.

"Who should go first?" Marcus asked but then answered himself, "what am I saying, I know who should go first because you've already chosen."

"Syren?" Ruby bawled out desperately. "Please don't let him hurt me. Please. Help me Sy please-"

Marcus' serrated edge knife surfaced once again at Ruby's trachea.

Syren closed her eyes. She wished for the strength that had surfaced when she faced Set. She wished for any ounce of power or any defense she could mount to protect her sister. There was nothing, only pain and incapacity. She could feel it in her head but it was still out of reach, as if it were locked away she had no key. With the chip removed from her back she thought her powers would come but she was wrong.

"Open your eyes," Marcus commanded.

She could still hear Ruby's wailing.

"It'll be longer and more painful," Marcus warned, "and you'll still have to watch it."

Syren opened her eyes.

He pulled the knife's edge across Ruby's thin neck. The blade tore through flesh and bone until her head was severed then Marcus dropped it to the floor beside her body then without pause he turned his attention to Katherine who was shrieking manically at the sight of Ruby. Again, Syren was splattered with blood and again she found herself in a pool of it as Ruby's blood drained from her body.

He yanked Katherine by her hair and brought her to the same spot Ruby's lifeless body lied.

"It's all a lie," Katherine barked. "There is no chip. I Couldn't find-"

Marcus cut into her neck then. Katherine's screams filled the room and it was only the blade, hot with Ruby's blood, entering her throat that the screams turned to gargles that turned to silence as her lifeless body laid separated from her head.

Chapter 20: Perfect

Syren looked out from the balcony of the condo with purple bags under her eyes and tear drenched cheeks. She drew in a deep breath.

Her irises were the same shade as the blood on her cheek and in her hair and soaked down her arms and legs. She hadn't showered in days, nor had she taken a meal. Ruby and Katherine's body began to turn and in the walls of the house, they produced a heavy scent of rotten death.

From her peripheral she saw a twinkle of violet light reflect against the mirror. She didn't turn around. It could have been Marcus, or any other enemy of hers. It didn't matter, she would kill them all the same.

The pain was still there, under her skin. Clawing at her from the inside as if she wanted to escape herself. Every atom, every molecule, every cell in her body was too excited to be contained in her. She felt energy, growing in her with every moment, like a balloon being filled to bursting. Some parts of her felt both stretched while others were constricted.

The fact that she was able to stand and to walk through the pain she felt was a testament to her growing powers. Even with those powers she knew it wasn't enough to face Marcus, not yet, she wasn't ready.

When Alex travelled to the room the first thing he witnessed was Ruby and Katherine severed heads and bodies in a pool of blood on the floor. He was frozen at the horrific sight then he smelled them. The smell was grotesque even to his nose that was no stranger to the smell of dead bodies.

Through the clear glass windows and open glass doors he saw Syren, standing at the rail of the balcony, still as deep waters.

"Sy- w-what happened here?" he choked out.

His voice, she thought, his soft, perfect, manufactured voice, how she loathed in it now.

"How very convenient of you to show up now," she said coolly, "after they've died."

"I didn't know this was going on, I went to the cabin- I put the shield up- I had no idea Syren- I came because I found out what happened to your grandmother. If I'd known-"

"-Of course you didn't. They didn't want you to know so why would you," she responded.

"Who did this?"

"I did," she responded flatly.

"What?"

"Well- some form of me did it. It doesn't matter, it is not a particularly relevant distinction."

"Syren - you're grieving," he walked to her slowly, avoiding the blood as he stepped out to the balcony. "I'm really sorry-" Alex hesitated, unsure of how to continue. Twenty six hundred years on earth hadn't prepared him for the words to utter to console the woman he loved after such a loss. "Just let me be here for you. Don't push me away…" he begged.

"Leave!" she screamed and turned around. The anger she felt boiled over. "You're just another robot here to play your part but guess what Alex- I'm not playing anymore. I've lost. Everything. So please spare me empathy and your consolation because I don't want it. I don't need it. I don't deserve it."

"I'm not leaving you alone like this-"

"Oh but you will. You will leave Alex. You won't have a choice," she said in a tone of calm anger that was disturbing to see.

She closed her eyes and when she felt his arms around her, she turned around and softly pressed her fist against his chest. With his sensitive nose he could smell her. She smelled of old sweat and blood.

"I love you Syren, don't push me away-"

She commanded her sword to form and in a moment the hot, iridescent metal pierced through his chest.

She could see the shock in his eyes when he felt the sword in him. She could hear his flesh searing over the hot metal and there was the smallest whiff of burnt flesh rising from his center.

"I'm sorry. I know this is not your fault," she whispered with tears in her eyes. "But I told you to leave me alone, you should have listened."

When she pulled her sword from his chest, it was thick with his blood but it fell away as it melted back into a golden cuff around her wrist. There was a hole in his chest where the sword was and where his heart should have been. It was empty...burned away. Blood drained from his lips and the look of shock and hor-ror never left his eyes but the life behind them did.

She stepped back from him and he fell to the ground, a few feet away from Ruby and Katherine.

It was what they wanted, she thought, another thing making her weak and distracted. Isabeli was right when she said he would make her soft. All she wanted was to drop to the floor and scream for him but she couldn't because that was what they wanted. She could see his eyes, the shock and horror of his last moments permanently etched in them now. Even when she turned back to the balcony, she saw his eyes. When she looked out to the city, she saw his eyes. There was nothing but his eyes, staring back at her.

After a moment, it became too much. The weight of what she'd done pulled her down to the floor. The agony once again consumed her.

Now she was alone. There was not one person left in the world for her. This was her surrender.

She inhaled and exhaled again and again and again. Quiet breaths turned into loud, painful heaves.

After she gained strength she pulled herself up the railing and flung her body over the balcony from the penthouse, with a fall of seventy four flights down.

Either of two things awaited her on the ground, she knew.. First, there was death and though she was prepared to welcome death with open arms she knew she wasn't lucky enough to have it all end so soon for her. Not with her past forms calling the shots. The second thing that waited for her was a fight, a fight she'd never felt more prepared for.

The winds blew through her unkempt hair as she fell. Her velocity slowed as she landed on the ground with a soft thud of her bare feet on the pavement. All she wore on the chilly spring day were black leggings and fitted black long sleeve shirt. The same things she'd worn for days now.

The second she landed a crowd of armed men appeared around her with their guns pointed to her. They were waiting for her, as if killing Alex and jumping from the balcony was something they'd been prepared for. At the curb of her building, were protesters blocked off by police. None of her guards were in sight. The cacophony of their protest was loud but the chaos in her head was much louder and their sound could not break the barrier. She didn't know or care if they saw her fall.

The cuffs on her arms collapsed into small liquid particles. It moved down her hand until it formed into the systyr broadswords.

When she lifted her arm there was a barrage of gunfire aimed at her. She felt the sting of each one but none penetrated her skin. They bounced from her skin the way a ball bounced from a wall. The force of the bullets pushed her back when it made contact.

Angered, Syren swung her systyr swords around and was surrounded by severed heads. It cut through the men like a knife cut through soft butter. The golden forged blade was now red with blood.

She took a breath and felt exhilarated. Teeming with energy and anger and dreams of retribution she marched to the now silent crowd. They'd witnessed the encounter and now began to scatter.

As she marched she saw his eyes again and stopped abruptly, as if she'd hit a wall.

"LEAVE ME ALONE ALEX!" she screamed.

She saw twinkles of violet light around her and she was surrounded by more vessels. This time it was more than hand full. It had to have been at least threescore men. They were armed, but now it was as if the bullets were solely to irritate her.

The physical pain she felt waned with every moment, even as she was bombarded by the sting of bullets on her skin from the police officers who stood by the barricade. The inner anguish she felt never flattered, it grew more intense, directly inverse to her physical pain.

She found herself cutting through men. Slicing, chopping and maiming. With every kill she found herself teeming with more energy, more power, more force.

When she was done with the men behind her, she began walking towards the crowd again. Now the few left were police who formed a front made of riot shields and guns pointed at her.

She saw Alex's eyes again. Staring into her, blue and broken. She stopped.

"Put her hands up! Drop the swords," one of the officers said. She guessed they must've been shouting it for a while though she did not hear it. In the officers eyes, though he was at least fifty feet away, she could see Alex's as clear as if he were in front of her.

She stood again and looked down at her blood stained words. There were people scattered in the street, recording the event, so was the media who'd been covering the protests.

She commanded her swords to break and the metal melted back up to her wrists. She continued walking but she wasn't sure why, all the rage she felt towards them moments earlier had dissipated into sadness.

As she continued walking, they shouted more orders until she was just paces away then they began shooting. When she felt the hot metal pellets against her skin, tearing through the fabric of her clothes, her anger returned. With a command from her mind, she parted scores of people, flinging them from her path with a gust of wind. It felt easier this time, there was no pain to make the command nor was there pain to hold it.

In the middle of the street, Marcus appeared.

"You're almost there, aren't you" he said with a teasing smile.

Before she could react, he disappeared.

With an angry growl, she flung the police vans from her path and trudged down the street. Civilians around her scattered in horror, all while trying to record her and capture pictures and videos.

Vessels began appearing around her. Too many to count. Each attacking, pulling, shoving, shooting her- all pushing her to her break. When they became too much, she pushed herself off the ground and was surprised when she floated into the air, twenty feet above the crowd of men and was able to stay there. With force, she dropped herself back into the crowd and the impact of her fall flung them back. The asphalt where she dropped was broken and crumbled like a crater.

She felt stronger.

They came again this time when she commanded them on fire, scores of vessels around her were ablaze.

She saw Alex's eyes again.

"STOP!" she barked.

She floated into the air, trying to flee from the city but moments later she felt someone kick her down to the ground. She crashed into asphalt and then she looked up from the rubble that had formed around her, it was Marcus, floated tens of feet above her.

Syren realized now what Alex's matrix had listed his flight capability at 0%. She hadn't made the connection that it meant other vessels might have been capable of flight.

"Not so fast," he scolded with a smile and a wag of his finger.

She flew up to him but when she reached his spot, he was gone in a moment then he reappeared behind her and kicked to the ground again.

She growled angrily and went after him again but he was gone. Furious, she covered her face and screamed into her hands. The sound of her voice echoed around her broken walls of glass on both sides of the street. The splinters fell all around her like a blanket but she did not feel them.

It took her a moment to calm down. She'd forgotten that she'd surrendered. Why was she fighting, it was futile.

Syren dropped herself to the ground and kneeled in the middle of the street.

Marcus reappeared with Alex's body and flung it at her feet.

"Alexander suffered all those years because of you. Everything about him was organic, never changed. He never took orders and he never followed code. You killed him- for nothing- well, you kill him for Ahsylla. Thinking of giving up- you can't, you're so close."

He disappeared again.

More vessels came charging at her.

Alexander's wide, lifeless eyes stared at her now. The expression of horror was still frozen on his face.

The vessels converged on her and pellet her body with sharp blows but she didn't move, nor did she break her eyes away from Alex's. She stared, and stared, falling deeper into anguish. Tortured by the loss of her lover and friend. She lost herself in the grief and for a moment the world stopped around her. She screamed at the pain, and howled and screamed and shrieked. She was at her limit. Inside, she stretched and constricted to the point of no return.

She began to shake violently until shaking turned to vibrating- so fast she felt light as air and left multiple mirror images of herself around her.

Then, she burst.

A cocoon on white energy surrounded her. It flowed like flames through every atom, through every molecule, through every cell.

The pain fell away. The anguish fell away. The torment fell away.

The men around her froze mid-movement as if they were statutes. So did the civilians in the crosshairs and police hundred of feet back who were regrouping from her assault.

She closed her eyes and relished in her new state of painless existence. The power she felt, the exhilaration. It was intoxicating. It was *perfect*.

She stood from Alex's lifeless body.

She turned around and looked at the men frozen around her. Marcus reappeared then, with his same deriding smile.

"You're ready," he said.

"Cease all sentient capabilities." Marcus froze in place, in the midst of motion.

She watched his eyes, there was no emotion, it was blank, devoid of feeling or expression. It was not like Alex's.

Alex, she remembered then her entire world went black.

~~~

Cirche, Hhella, Achylles, Ananke and Sytyanna, all members of the Queen's council, appeared at the scene in a warp of violet light. The civilians and police were now thawed and moved around in a panic. They were of a lesser concern because it was as planned to reveal their existence to humans. The most pressing was the state of their queen.

Vessels appeared as well, this time, they were tasked with cleaning the mass of bodies left behind. No humans had died but some were injured, they would take care of that.

Achylles was the premier of the praesadia, the army of Ahsyllan warriors. Her concern was the protection of Ahsylla and all Ahsyllans. She was nine years into her form and stood at only 4 feet 10 inches with the body of a prepubescent girl. She had golden white curly coils and she was a lighter shade of brown. She kneeled beside her Prime and gently pulled her tousled hair from her face. "It's finally done. You did it."

She placed her hand over her Queen's body and it pulled in the air under her palm, levitating under her control.

"Let's take her home," Hhella said.

Chapter 21: The War To Come

Everything was bright, so bright she almost didn't want to open her eyes.

"She's awake," she heard a woman's voice announce.

Syren opened her eyes, awakened as Ahnais, The Queen Prime of Ahsylla.

She remembered now, her infinite life. She remembered her previous forms and their consciousness.

She saw five beautiful familiar faces staring down at her.

"Queen Ahnais," one voice said. The woman attached to it was breathtakingly beautiful. She had skin like obsidian, just as shiny just as dark. Her hair was the same golden white shade as Ahnais'. Her irises were sky blue and she had full pouty lips.

"Give her air," the voice said lightly.

Ahnais sat up and took in her surroundings. The room was just as High Palace. It was the same extravagant opulence with a futuristic edge.

She looked around at the women and she remembered them, completely, from lives before her current one. Their lives from she'd known them an eon ago.

Ahanis sat up with wet eyes. She felt different, exponentially stronger, as if she had energy bursting from every cell in her body, but not the way that hurt her when she was Syren. It was intoxicating and there was no pain and she felt like nothing was holding her back. Everything felt possible, she felt like she could reach into the sky and lift the moon from it.

She ran her hands over her face and wiped her cheeks, closed her eyes. The power she hid and hated. The power that tortured and antagonized her now wrapped around her like a blanket of love and energy.

She remembered everything she overcame to get access to it. The thousands of years of plotting every choice, every path, every thought just to get that outcome.

She opened her eyes. They were blood red as she took in the beautiful faces around her. They looked overjoyed.

Alex. She remembered him before her present form. She'd been watching him for centuries while his gentle soul roamed the earth lost and tortured but still his heart remained pure.

Presently, Majikai didn't matter. The war didn't matter. There was only Alex. As the thought crossed her mind, she saw him through her eyes. He was lifeless, laying in the vesselage bay with Isis, Seth and Cleo frozen on beds beside him.

She could see everywhere and anywhere. That was another facet of her power. She needed only to think of a place or a person to see them.

She stood quickly, feeling so light on her feet she momentarily floated into the air and when she realized she dropped her feet to the ground.

"My Prime, where are you going?" Achylles asked.

"Alexander," was all Ahnais said.

She disappeared then reappeared in the vesselage room where Alex's healed body lay on the pod. Isis, Seth and Cleo were on the other three beds adjacent to his. In the room, the walls were a grey metallic material as were the floors and ceiling.

Ahnais walked to Alex's bed.

"Come back to me," she commanded softly.

Alex opened his eyes and began panting frantically. He felt his chest where he remembered burning and pain but it was gone.

"It's okay Alexander, you're alright," Ahnais held him and tried to console him but Alex pushed her away. Her voice was different. It was deeper and her cadence was different as well, robotic and regal. She looked different as well, dressed in large draped red robes that stretched a few feet behind her.

"Don't touch me," he barked. "Where am I?" He sat up, looked around and saw his siblings. "What's going on. Why are they here?" Alex felt his chest again. "You killed me, Sy- you killed me."

"I had to. It was the only way. You're in Ahsylla and you're safe. I can explain it all to you."

"How am I alive?"

"We healed you." she answered. "You're siblings are alright. They are just...asleep."

He took a deep breath but didn't speak. She could read the thoughts as they crossed his mind. He was scared and confused.

"Come with me," Ahnais said with an outstretched hand. "I'll explain it all then you can decide."

Reluctantly, Alex took her hand and in an instant, they were standing in a sea of green grass.

In front of him, was Ahsylla.

It was breathtaking and for a moment all he could do was stare.

He turned slowly and consumed his surroundings. Behind them was the sea. The water was a glowing royal blue. A mile from the edge of the cliff was a barrier of ice shelves, rising from the water in large spikes that blocked the view further. He turned again and saw a large magnificent palace in the distance. The outside walls look like they were made from mirrors. Beside it were two large buildings that looked like citadels.

"That's The Forge, our factory for building the things we need, and The Six, where our premiers tend the Ahsyllans needs. The six premiers are the prasaedia or the military; The futura, the vessel, the superfluity and the build." Ahnais said, "In between those is my home, the Palace Prime. Where we stand is the viridescent front. Behind us, is the Glowing sea."

"Where are we?"

"Ahsylla."

"Where is Ahsylla?"

"At the bottom of the earth. The ice shelves you see around us is what the humans call Antarctica. We artificially control the temperature and protect ourselves with a photon shield."

Alex sighed, "why am I here?"

"You're angry with me. That's understandable."

"Angry? You killed me and your entire family for this," he said with raised arms to the palace.

"They weren't my family. My family is here, in Ahsylla. A thousand people and twenty Ahysllans that I have to protect."

Alex shook his head, "there are no vessels in that count, I'm sure but it doesn't matter what I feel, it doesn't matter what I think. I don't matter. I was just a part of the plan. I'm not real."

"That's not true. That's never been true," Ahnais said softly, "Syren loved you, because I loved you. I've watched you for thousands of years. Every choice you made was your own. I made sure no one altered your matrix."

Alex chuckled humorlessly, "yes, free will that you allowed me to have. Free will that you could've taken at any moment if it didn't fit your plan. It's not really free will is it?"

"I'm sorry you found existence so miserable but it was for Ahsylla. If I didn't get my powers, we wouldn't stand a chance against Majikai-"

"Why should I care what happens to Ahsylla? Why should I be grateful that I sacrificed my entire existence to a country that doesn't give a damn about me," Alex barked. "You killed an entire group of people who did nothing but love you. You used that love as a reason for them to die."

"There were vessels," Ahnais said. "Teddy, Katherine, Ruby, all of them."

"So am I." Alex closed her eyes and took a breath. "How many vessels are there?"

"In Ahsylla? Thousands. In the world? Billions."

Alex was aghast his mouth fell open and for a moment he was speechless. "How have you managed to make billions of vessels?"

"Six hundred years after you were born we dispersed the serum and made it so it would be passed genetically from parents to children then we waited until it consumed the entire population. Most humans who carry the serum aren't activated so we rarely consider them true vessels until they are."

Alex shook his head confused, "why do you need so many vessels?"

"Because a war is coming and we need soldiers."

"They're just cannon fodder."

"We need soldiers," Ahnais repeated. "I'm sorry I'm not the benevolent, tenderhearted ruler you want me to be. I used to be and because of that half my citizens were murdered at this very spot. I won't ever be that again. I would let this entire world burn, if it meant saving my Ahsylla. Humans are many. We are few."

Alex swallowed hard. "What now? Do I get repurposed? Do you put me aside until I need to fight? Do you just shut me off since I'm not agreeable? What happens to the man who is just a vessel?"

"I won't do anything to you Alex. You have to choose what you want now that you know."

"There is no choice, Syren-"

"-That is not my name, Alex. My name is Ahnais," she interjected softly then she let out a breath. "You may call me Syren if that makes me feel more familiar to you."

"Well Ahnais, there is no choice that I can make that means anything. As long as my life and the lives of everyone like me mean nothing to you then I'd rather you end it."

She read his thoughts and knew his meaning. "End it? I won't," she shot back sharply.

"You won't even give me that."

Ahnais sighed. "I'm willing to rethink our use of vessels and the way we treat them. I'm willing to rethink a lot of things if it means I get to be with you Alex. If it means you'll feel loved and valued and a part of Ahsylla I will rethink it all but not until after the war."

Behind Ahnais, five Ahsyllans appeared. Three looked like older women. One looked like a teenager, like Ahnais. The last one was a child, looking no more than ten years old.

Alex noticed them all. With the same golden-white hair and striking beauty as Ahnais. Their skin ranged from shades obsidian to ivory. They were all dressed in white draped gowns, similar to Ahnais.

They were all premiers and ruled on the Queen's council under the authority of the Queen Prime Ahnais.

Ahnais turned to them.

"The second marker picked up a reading from a craft similar to the signature of Majikai's," Sytyanna, the Queen's shadow announced. She was the right hand to the queen and ruled in the absence of the queen.

"He's traveling faster than expected. He shouldn't be this close," Hhella added. Hhella was the premier of the race. Her duty was to the Ahsyllan race. She stood as a conduit between the needs of the people and their queen.

"It doesn't read at the signature we expected, it's smaller than what we prepared for. I hypothesize he's sent a scouting ship ahead," Achylles responded. She was the premier of the praesadia, the Ashyllan warriors. Her concern was the protection of Ahsylla and all Ahsyllans. She appeared to be the fiercest of all the women and stood at only 4 feet and 11 inches in a prepubescent form.

Ahnais took a deep breath then she turned back to look at Alex.

In her mind, the hive mind, she could communicate with all the Ahsyllans. It was a learned skill, mastered for hundreds of thousands of years. She called them all to meet at The Horizon. It was their meeting place when it came to matters of the most grave concern.

One at a time, all five women disappeared from sight in sparks of violet light after receiving the message telepathically.

Alex watched as her distant eyes changed from dark purple hue to a fierce red. Ahnais turned to him.

"I've gathered the Ahysllans at The Horizon. As you heard. Majikai just passed our second markers and whether it's his entire army or an isolated craft they're traveling faster than expected." Ahanais stepped closer to him and caressed his cheeks.

"You can take your family from the vesselage bay where you woke. If you decide to leave no one will harm you or your family if you do." She stared deeper into his blue eyes. Hers were now wet with tears for more reasons than Alex's possible departure. The bright red shade now darkened to black. "I know I hurt you," she said softly, "I know you feel scared and betrayed because I can feel what you feel. I love you and I always will even if you feel my actions betray that. But you have to decide Alex, now, if you're with us or against us."

She vanished into a beam of light leaving Alex standing on the front, contemplating the two choices before him.

Asia Gouldbourne

Made in the USA
Monee, IL
27 November 2020